MW01254817

GALACTIC BREACH

BOOK 2 IN THE RUINS OF THE GALAXY SERIES

J.N. CHANEY

CHRISTOPHER HOPPER

JOIN THE RUINS TRIBE

Visit **ruinsofthegalaxy.com** today and join the tribe.
Once there, you can sign up for our reader group, join our Facebook community, and find us on Twitter and Instagram.

If you'd like to email us with comments or questions, we respond to all emails sent to ruinsofthegalaxy@gmail.com, and love to hear from our readers.

See you in the Ruins!

STAY UP TO DATE

J.N. Chaney posts updates, official art, previews, and other awesome stuff on his website. You can also follow him on **Instagram**, **Facebook**, and **Twitter**.

He also created a special **Facebook group** called "JN Chaney's Renegade Readers" specifically for readers to come together and share their lives and interests, discuss the series, and speak directly to me. Please check it out and join whenever you get the chance!

For updates about new releases, as well as exclusive promotions, visit his website, jnchaney.com and sign up for the VIP mailing list. Head there now to receive a free copy of *The Other Side of Nowhere*.

CONTENTS

1

ADMIRAL KANE WAS SURPRISED at how well the Bull Wraith's captain handled being flushed from an airlock. Captain Pace stood at ease, hands behind her back, chin up, as Kane went through the list of her failures. Failure to confine the prisoners to their ship. Failure to prevent the prisoners from escaping. Failure to track the prisoners. Failure to recapture the prisoners. It was too much for Kane to overlook, as much as he hated to punish an otherwise worthy officer.

But if you don't, Kane, you'll be just as guilty as them, the familiar voice said. *Inconsistent, soft, weak.* Those kinds of failings were why the Republic was crumbling, a shadow of its former self. He knew the voice was right.

Immediately upon returning from the metaverse

and the odd events that had transpired there, Kane learned of Captain Pace's actions to capture Senator Stone and his family. It seemed that the captain had also taken on board a small contingent of Marines and navy personnel who, no doubt, assisted the Stones in killing several troopers and fleeing the Bull Wraith in the escape pods. Kane's instructions not to harm the senator's family had been explicit. Still, the captain had ordered her Marines to open fire on the escapees. At least she hadn't targeted the escape pods, though Kane assumed that was more a stroke of coding luck than any wise decision on Captain Pace's part.

Still, even if the senator's family had survived the descent to Oorajee, the planet's inhabitants would have seen to their demise by now. Kane felt a strange taste in his mouth as he thought of his past dealings with the hyena-like beasts. "Savages," he noted to himself as he stared at Captain Pace behind the airlock glass.

Like you.

"Not like me," Kane replied. "I am not ruthless."

"But, sir," Captain Pace protested. "I have served you faithfully for fifteen years without failure. If you would only—"

"I am not ruthless!"

The voice in his head laughed at that. He would have argued with it, but the voice was always right. It was cunning. It even had a name now, but Kane dared not say it.

Kane's rage boiled over as he thought of the Jujari slaying his daughter and devouring her flesh. More pain gripped his chest as he imagined what they would do to the granddaughter he'd never met.

Then Kane wondered what *she* would think of all this.

Why does that matter?

"Because she's the reason."

"She, Admiral?" Pace did nothing to hide the confusion on her face. "The reason for what? Are you speaking about me, sir?"

"She's the one who forced this to happen."

She is?

"*Yes*," Kane hissed. "If she had stayed with me, if she had resisted the Republic with me, none of this would be happening."

But I thought we went over this, Kane. You told me that you chose.

"I *did* choose. I chose to move forward when she could not."

Then what she thinks about their deaths does not matter, does it?

Kane thought for a moment, licking his lips. He looked out at Captain Pace. The woman looked so resolute—so confident—as she met her end.

"Admiral Kane, if you are not ruthless, then you are at least mad."

That's exactly what she said about you, too, isn't it? Ignore her.

"And I... I have nothing left to say, sir." Pace straightened her uniform and raised her chin.

Precisely how she *will look in the end. When she defies you unto death.*

"Perhaps." Kane looked down. "No, I... I can't do it." He gripped his head. The stabs of pain between his temples were coming more frequently. "I can't." He looked back up. In place of Captain Pace's face was another face—*her* face. "I won't."

Then I will.

His fist swung up and pounded the blinking "Open" button beside the airlock's frame. Captain Pace screamed as her body was yanked into the void, but no one heard her.

"I DON'T CARE about his infernal dark arts," Admiral Kane roared at the man in the holo-vid. He sat alone in his quarters, lights dimmed, his teeth bared, fists clenched on his desk.

"Perhaps you should," the man said. "Never underestimate your enemy, Kane."

Kane had grown tired of the implicit insults and blatant condescension. This senator—who was he, anyway? He wasn't much older than Kane. He'd never seen combat, never led men and women into battle, never escorted them to the gates of hades and left them to rot.

Not like you have, Kane, the voice said. *His power is so shallow. So political. Yours, however, is real power, the power to hold someone's life over the edge of eternity—something he's never known aside from ordering back-door executions. Why do you still tolerate him?*

"I don't know," Kane replied.

"Don't know? You should have ended him while you had the chance, Admiral. You're getting sloppy."

"Terminating the Luma emissary was of greater importance," Kane replied, still seething. He wanted to strangle the senator and watch his eyes bulge beneath his manicured gray hair. The picture of doing it gave him a strange satisfaction. "She obviously knew the location of the quantum tunnel, as did her crew. We couldn't allow them to live."

"Be that as it may, you must now dispose of the

Luma master. Since you don't know what's in the book he took from the temple, he's a liability. If you hadn't been busy tying up irrelevant loose ends, we wouldn't even be having this conversation right now."

Are you going to let him order you around like this? When are you going to put a stop to it?

"When the time is right," Kane muttered.

"What was that?"

He is, after all, a part of the system that stole them from you—that stole all of it from you—isn't he?

Kane's eyes snapped back to the senator. "I said, I will strike when the time is right, Senator."

The gray-haired man sat back and stroked his chin, considering Kane. "You forget your place, Admiral. You belong to *us*. Everything you have is because of us—because of *me*."

"Everything you have?" Kane, you cannot let him demean all of your work, all of your sacrifice. You belong to no one. Let me talk to him. I will make things right.

"No, no," Kane said with a wave of his hand.

"What was that?" The man leaned forward, his face filling the holo-vid.

"I mean, no, you're right. I forget my place."

Do not betray yourself, Kane!

"Very well. Consider yourself reminded." The senator relaxed a little. "I want So-Elku dead and the book he took recovered." The senator tented his fingers and sat back. "Now, what else have you brought us from beyond the void?"

Kane cleared his throat as the other voice tried to punch through his will. *Don't tell him, Kane! Don't you dare.*

"I found no ships worth salvaging."

"No ships," the senator repeated, unimpressed.

"Our scans indicated thousands of vessels docked throughout the city, but all of them were in severe disrepair."

"Disrepair? Did, did, did you at least explore them?" the senator stammered. "Did you—did you glean from their technology as discussed?"

You see how he second-guesses you at every point? He doesn't trust you—he doesn't want what's best for you. Let me speak, Kane. Please let me speak.

"No!" Kane said far more forcefully than he intended to. "I mean, yes, we explored them. But what we found was…"

"Yes? What did you find, Kane? *Get on with it already.*"

Don't say anything, Kane.

"It was old. So old." He could feel himself trail off into the memories of that other world lost to time. "Consumed by the jungle and swallowed by age."

The senator waited for more. He stroked his chin again. "And?"

Kane's eyes snapped back up. "We were thorough, but there was simply nothing to obtain. It's not what we had hoped for."

"'Not what we had hoped for?' I see." The senator picked up a data pad and flicked through a few screens. "You couldn't have explored for very long, then. The log says here that you were only gone for... this can't be right." He glared at Kane. "Less than four hours?"

Don't you say a word, Kane. He doesn't need to know—doesn't deserve to know. Lie.

"That's incorrect, Senator. That should read less than four days."

"You're saying the navigation computers are wrong?"

"I'm saying I need to have a talk with my XO. It will be taken care of."

"Human error, then," the senator stated, unconvinced. "We have redundancy for this sort of thing. Why are you leaving AI calculations to humans?"

"It will be taken care of."

"Even still, three and a half days, Kane? We press the Jujari into a corner, spend countless lives, years, and resources to do so, and all you give me is four days?"

I told you he doesn't trust you! Why do you put up with this?

"It's just a matter of time," Kane said.

"I don't follow," the senator replied.

"Time. However long ago—thousands of years maybe?—the Jujari received that stardrive, and the civilization withered to nothing. It would be like searching the ruins of Goroboro for blaster technology. It's just not there to be found anymore."

"I don't believe you," the senator said.

He confesses! You see? Let me put him in his place, Kane. Just once.

"I will forward you the data files we captured," Kane said.

"That's not enough. I want you to go back."

"Back?"

"Yes. Now. Leave So-Elku to me. You *cannot* come back empty-handed like this."

"But, Senator—"

"There are no buts, Admiral. I order you—"

"The quantum tunnel is closed," Kane said.

The senator's face froze. It was several moments before he even blinked. "What did you say?"

"When we returned from the metaverse, the tunnel was nowhere to be found."

"Impossible."

"There were no guarantees that it was going—"

"That's impossible," the senator said, raising his voice and leaning into the screen.

"I'm only reporting what happened."

"Like reporting your missing three and a half days?"

"I will forward the sensor scans, sir," Kane said. "It's gone. There's no going back."

The senator wiped his face with a hand and sat all the way back. Kane heard the chair's leather squeak beneath the man.

Very good, Kane. Very, very good.

"I will take care of So-Elku," Kane said. "Then we move forward with our plans without the Novia tech. We have enough without it."

"Do we?"

"Yes, sir. We do."

"I'm not so sure anymore," the senator said, his voice lowered. "Await my orders, Kane. I must confer with the others on this. You are clearly unstable."

The fool. This is why he can never be a part of the future. He lacks imagination. Let the dead awaken, Kane. And let the living go down to die. It's time to set things right. It's time that you release me.

"As you wish," Kane said, looking at his clenched fists. "*As you wish.*" He opened his hands.

THE ADMIRAL STOOD in his quarters, pacing with short steps and quick turns. He caught glimpses of his bald head and puckered flesh in the mirror. Then he stopped and stared at his eyes. His pink eye grew dark like the other. Then both began to enlarge until new black irises pushed the white sclera to the edges.

The space felt cramped. He never understood why the most important person on a ship this size was relegated to such a small room. He would need to change that. He would need to change a lot of things.

The air felt stale, and his head ached. There was a growing throb in his forehead, and his nose felt dry. He needed to get out. Kane waved the doors open, stepped into the corridor, and turned toward the main elevator at the end of the hall. His boots clipped along the glossy black floors as he pulled his uniform taut.

Crew members saluted Kane as they passed. He nodded. They seemed more afraid of him than usual.

As some of them looked away in disgust, he felt something running out of his nose.

Kane touched his black-gloved fingers to his nose and brought them away. Blood covered the tips. He pulled a white handkerchief from his pocket and dabbed at his nostrils. By the time the bleeding stopped, crimson blood soaked the fabric. Kane folded the damp cloth and pushed it into his pocket.

The elevator gave a soft chime as the doors parted. Two crew members emerged and looked away from the admiral's face as soon as they'd saluted. That often happened when people first saw his one pink eye and one dark brown eye. But Kane also imagined that his nose and lips were not up to cleanliness standards. At that moment, however, he didn't care.

"Rear observation deck," he said.

"Rear observation deck, confirmed. Thank you, Admiral Kane," the synthesized voice said.

Kane felt the elevator slide backward and then ascend toward the aft of the Goliath-class Corvette —*his* Corvette, the Black Labyrinth, did not belong to the Republic, as much as someone like Senator Blackman might insist that it did. In fact, none of the ships in his fleet did. Weren't Blackman and his ilk the very ones to make him disavow the Republic? Wasn't the entire charade contingent upon severing allegiances?

Only when it suited them, apparently. If anyone were to be caught, there would be no record of backroom agreements with senators, just a rogue admiral gone mad. How convenient.

In the end, it was always about convenience. Anything could be categorized under that heading. His marriage, for example, could have been forged or terminated using convenience as a catalyst. Forgoing a relationship with his daughter had been predicated upon convenience. His life was always a matter of someone else's convenience.

But no more. From now on, he would do what was convenient for him and no one else. His wife was gone—she'd chosen *them* over him. His daughter was gone too—as was his love for the Republic. All of it was lost.

Something warm flowed from his nose again. More blood, he supposed. The pain in his head told him so. The handkerchief was already saturated, so he decided not to bother wiping.

"Arrived, rear observation deck. Thank you, Admiral Kane."

The elevator doors swooshed open with a chime. He stepped into an immense room the size of a small cargo bay. The entire ceiling was an intricate lattice-work of windows and girders, while the far wall boasted a spectacular view of a desert planet. The only better view of the Jujari's home world of Oorajee would be in a void suit. This was as good as any ship could provide.

Several crew were scattered throughout the popular space, enjoying their breaks or an off-duty picnic with friends. One at a time, conversations turned to hushed whispers as the crew noticed the admiral. Several covered their mouths while others put their food down.

One brave soul approached the commander. "Admiral Kane, do you need assistance?"

Kane ignored him. There was no time for this. "Everyone out," he seethed, noting that his voice sounded different.

The room began to empty, people rushing as one toward the elevator without a word. Once Kane was alone, he stepped closer to the wide window on the far side. The view was truly spectacular, the planet's curvature taking up the entire breadth of the window. Other ships in the fleet—*his* fleet—shot short bursts of light to the planet. Puffs of sand-colored smoke erupted hundreds of kilometers below. Everything looked so small from up here.

He turned and looked at the ceiling filled with stars and ships. Small bursts of light exploded against defense shields as the Jujari and Republic fleets sparred. These were just small slaps, but the real fighting would begin soon enough.

He activated the holo-screen on his wrist computer and opened a private channel. "Captain Nos Kil."

"Yes, Admiral."

"I want you in the rear observation deck."

"Right away, Admiral."

Kane closed the connection and turned back to the wide window to wait. Everything had gone according to plan. Well, mostly. The discovery that the Novia's ships were, in fact, derelicts was not fortuitous. But he knew there was more. The hidden halls of that forgotten place held more than any of them could imagine. The place called to him to wake it from its long slumber. And he would do just that.

After all this time, it was finally his turn to choose —his turn to tell the *traitors* what to do. He was not their lapdog or their errand boy. And they would not be able to steal power from him. Of course, he would not be inconsistent like them either. He would keep power free of the stains of compromise. He would not dilute the goals of the Republic with the whims of manipulators.

No, he must not call it *the Republic* anymore. It was too far gone. Its day was done. Instead, there would be a new name, a new dawn. The long slumber would be over soon, and the essence of perfect power, the paragon of rule, would take its place.

He heard the soft patter of blood smacking the black floor.

The Republic had taken enough. They'd taken his wife, his daughter, and now his granddaughter. They'd taken his career. He'd sacrificed his body in the temple of their bloodlust. And then they tried to play it all off as "the price of devotion." Isn't that what they called it? What a terrible price it had been. But no more. Now it was *they* who would pay a dear price.

"Admiral, sir," a voice said from across the room. Kane raised a hand to summon the captain, and footsteps followed as Nos Kil's armored boots thumped across the floor. "You summoned me, Admiral?"

"I'm not that anymore," Kane replied.

There was a pause. Kane knew the captain might need a minute.

"Pardon me, Admiral?"

"I'm not that—*Admiral*. Stop calling me that."

"Yes—sir." The captain paused. "How would you like me to address you, then?"

The blood had started to ebb, and the pain was beginning to subside. The voice—the other voice—had stopped talking to him as well. It didn't need to. It felt good to finally be a single soul.

He turned and faced his captain. The trooper stood, helmet under his arm, blaster maglocked to his thigh, clad in his black armor, three white lines on his chest and shoulder. Eyes wide, the Marine took a step back.

"I need you to do something very special for me, Captain Nos Kil."

Nos Kil pointed. "Sir, your—"

"Did you not hear me?"

The captain cleared his throat and lowered his hand. "What are your orders?"

"I need you to go back."

"Back, sir?" Nos Kil asked.

"To Ithnor Ithelia."

The captain hesitated, staring to the side rather than at Kane's mouth—bloodstained surely—and black eyes. "As you command. You don't wish me here, then?"

"I will not be staying long over Oorajee. I will

give the fleet its orders. I have other business to attend to—with the Luma."

"Yes, Ad—"

"The admiral, he is no more."

"Sir, your eyes and your voice are—"

Yes, his eyes and voice had changed. *For the better.* "From now on, you will address me as…"

Could he really say it out loud? Saying it out loud would make it real—something he could never take back. But it was true. He *had* changed. Something inside him had changed, and he would never go back.

So he could say it.

He *had to* say it.

"You will address me as *Moldark*."

2

Awen's strength returned after four more days of recovery, each marked by oddly placed sunrises and sunsets. She had remained confined to her makeshift bed in the large office, watching the alien world through the large floor-to-ceiling windows along two walls. When she did sleep, however, it was anything but restful. Her mind was filled with images of Kane and that *thing* that resided inside of him. She thought of her parents and their safety. And she wondered—with more interest than she cared to admit—how Magnus had fared in finding his men. As her strength returned, she was eager to leave her restless dreams and help her new friends find a way to return to the protoverse.

Ezo and TO-96 returned at regular intervals to

report on their findings, and Awen was happy to see them. They were like the old pioneers on planets in the Meridian Outskirts, playing out the stories her parents had read to her when she was a child. Ezo and his faithful bot would set out on an expedition to map some new part of the city, only to return to camp, eager to share their findings with everyone else —in this case, just her and Sootriman.

On her first morning of feeling fully recovered, Awen sat with Sootriman in the far side of the makeshift recovery room, treating the meeting nook like a small headquarters. It provided a good view of the city, safety from whatever beasts roamed the forest, and quick access to street level. The building's top floor had a better 360-degree view of the entire city, but none of them wanted to climb a hundred flights of stairs to get there. Ezo had done it once and said it wasn't worth it until they could find some way to recondition the elevators.

Awen sat with her elbows on her knees. Soot-riman had washed her old clothes, and Ezo had provided a new set from the Indomitable's holds. Like Sootriman, Awen wore green cargo pants, and tore the sleeves of her black shirt too. It was too hot for long sleeves. She also chose to keep her old boots since they were already breaking in—no sense starting over. She'd rebraided her hair and still wore her Luma medallion.

"You and Ezo seem to have worked things out," Awen said. They had some time to kill before Ezo and TO-96 arrived.

Sootriman blushed. "You know, being stranded on an alien planet in another universe has a way of forcing you to talk things through. That, or make you kill each other."

"Didn't you want to, though? Kill him, I mean."

"What makes you think I still don't?" Sootriman winked.

Just then, Ezo and TO-96 entered the room and glanced at the two women. "What?" Ezo asked, looking as though he'd missed the punch line to a good joke. "What'd Ezo miss? What were you talking about?"

"Oh, nothing," Sootriman said. "Just catching up."

"That's not true. According to my long-range audio sensors, you just said that you'd like to—"

"Shut it, Tee-Oh," Sootriman ordered, shaking her head. "You always were a lurker around the den."

"A 'lurker'?" TO-96 asked Ezo. "But you said I was—"

"Never mind what I said, Tee-Oh! That was years ago."

"Everyone is insisting I stop speaking," TO-96 said to no one in particular. "I was simply trying to help."

Awen laughed. She'd grown to love this bot.

TO-96 sat down in the headquarters while Ezo walked to the windows. Over the preceding days, the pair had brought reports of the city's infrastructure and how the planet's ecosystem had reclaimed it. The foundations and innermost sections of each building, however, had held up surprisingly well, a fact that they told with ample enthusiasm. Apparently, the Novia Minoosh had been a vibrant and dynamic culture right up until its inhabitants all disappeared.

"So, still no ideas why they're gone?" Awen asked TO-96.

"I am sorry, Awen, no. Not at this time." The bot's glowing round eyes stared at her through his clear face shield, almost managing to convey remorse. "We still have too little evidence to formulate any substantial hypothesis, let alone generate reliable conclusions. To put it in laypeople's terms, we are coming up short. We are unable to secure a suitable dance partner even though the band has begun playing. We are at the head of an inland waterway without a hand-propulsion tool."

"We've got it, Ninety-Six," Awen said with a laugh. "I think you need to work on your metaphors."

The bot tilted his head. "You don't find them applicable?"

"No, I do. But the wording is… you know what? Never mind. They're perfect."

"Very well. Furthermore, as far as we can tell, there are no signs of war or mass pestilence—a biological pandemic, for example. For either of those, we would have found bodily remains. And in the instance of war, we would have seen the structural damage and disarray emblematic of said activities."

"And you haven't found those," Awen concluded.

"No."

"It's almost like they vanished," Ezo said, stepping toward the angled floor-to-ceiling window. "Then there's the outstanding question of why it seems like no one else has been here."

"So, we're the first?" Awen asked.

"At least as far as we can tell."

"If other species have explored this place," the bot said, "then they covered their tracks well. There are no traces of vandalism, and all Novia belongings —personal or corporate—seem meticulously stored.

As far as we can tell, these beings were bipedal verte-brates, taller than the known humanoids of our race and significantly stronger, at least by my calculations."

The thought of seeing what these beings looked like and finding their possessions delighted Awen, but that would probably need to wait for later trips. "Seems there will be much to discover when we can return," she said, still lamenting the fact that they'd never actually meet the Novia Minoosh. She rubbed her hands together. "So, where do you suggest we scout today?"

She was eager to lend her efforts to the cause of finding transportation home. Also, she'd been bedridden during her recovery—following Doctor TO-96's orders—and she was sick of it. Sootriman had chosen to remain behind and care for Awen, further decreasing the team's effectiveness. The way Awen saw it, she and Sootriman had a lot of catching up to do.

TO-96 looked at the large coffee table in the middle of their oversized seats and projected a holo-map of the city as seen from their initial scans while in orbit days earlier. The metropolis pressed against a purplish-blue ocean to the south and a deep-green mountain ridge to the north. The larger peninsula was connected to a landmass farther north, one that stretched out of view. TO-96 zoomed in to Itheliana and changed the satellite view to one presented in white with gray lines for buildings, borders, and roads. He zoomed in even farther until a green dot blinked inside a square tower surrounded by several other buildings.

"This is where we are now," the bot said, indicating the dot. "We're in some sort of administrative building, as far as I can tell. Since we know nothing of their system of governance or enterprise, it is hard to know what type of administering they were doing here."

"We get it, Ninety-Six," Ezo said, returning from his long gaze out the window. "There's going to be more questions than answers for several—"

Ezo stopped abruptly, and Awen wondered what he was going to say. Months? Years?

"We're not going to have a lot of details filled in, so just stick to big picture stuff," Ezo said. "Got it?"

"Very good, sir. As I was saying, this is us, here." Then the bot zoomed out a little. "Over the last nine days, Captain Ezo and I have been able to chart the sections you see here, overlaid in blue." Colored patches emerged, indicating each day's scouting. They primarily emanated from the region immediately surrounding the admin building, with some small sections toward the eastern border.

"Is that where the *Indomitable* is?" Awen asked, pointing to the east side.

"Was," Ezo corrected with no attempt to hide his anger. "They tossed grenades into engineering and the bridge. It's a mess."

"To quote Captain Ezo from earlier," TO-96 added, "'If you thought she was a pretty piece of splick before, she's an ass-ugly piece of splick now.'"

"Thanks for that reminder, 'Six." Ezo rolled his eyes.

"My pleasure, sir."

"Have you explored the temple more?" Awen asked.

All three of them looked at her. "The temple, Star Queen?" Ezo asked.

"Yes. You know, the library in the plaza, 'the temple of all we've gained and the cost of all we've left behind,'" she said, reciting the inscription over the building's entrance.

"We remember," Ezo said, running a hand over his face. "It's just that—well, no one feels like going back there."

"I was fine with going back there," TO-96 interjected.

"And I wasn't with you," Sootriman added.

"Okay, okay," Ezo said, hands up in protest. "So Ezo didn't feel like going back there. Okay?"

"It's okay, baby," Sootriman said, reaching up and placing a hand on his forearm. Ezo didn't acknowledge the hand, but he didn't pull away either. "I almost died in there. I get it. No reason to go back."

Ezo stepped away and moved to the window. "No, *Ezo* almost died in there. Holy mystics, you always think everything is about *you*, Sootriman."

Sootriman winked at Awen. "That's because it is," she mouthed.

Awen smiled. "Well, if anyone would like to join me, I'd like to explore the temple," she said. "If I were the Novia Minoosh, I'd seek wisdom there. And I suspect it will be a very different experience now that we're not being chased by a madman intent on blowing us up."

"Sounds good to me," Sootriman said.

"Count me in, Awen," TO-96 said.

The three of them looked to Ezo.

"Fine," he said. "But Ezo doubts we'll find anything that's survived the trinitex."

THE ENTRANCE to the temple building looked different from the way it had during the firefight. The lighting was different perhaps. Or am I just more relaxed this time? Maybe a little of both, Awen thought. The inscription spanned the archway as before, and the blown-out doors invited them inside. This place felt familiar—perhaps because she'd been here once already. But it was more than that. Something piqued her interest. The feeling was deeper than she could articulate, like something on the edge of her vision that she knew was there but couldn't focus on.

Awen wanted to enter into the Unity, but she hadn't attempted it since leaving the temple nearly eleven days before. For the first time since she'd been a teenager at the academy, she was afraid to do so. The events surrounding Sootriman's rescue plagued her. Or worse—maybe they'd broken her. Still, with each step down the main hall, Awen knew she was getting closer to stepping across the Unity's threshold in order to see the temple from its truest angle. But could she? Would she?

As before, columns lined each side of the main hallway and supported an arched ceiling nearly thirty meters above. The late-morning light filtered down from high windows, revealing lavender beams cutting through air thick with dust particles. Awen had visited many religious monuments and cathedrals in her day, and this space reminded her of those if nothing more than for the echo her footfalls made in the long chamber.

The farther they walked, the less vegetation clung to the floor and walls. Before long, the jungle had lost its grip, and the air began to change.

"Look," Sootriman said, pointing to the right side of the hall. Rubble poured from the collapsed wall like a cold lava flow, black and scabbed. Two of the pillars lay toppled, and sections of the windows had blown out. "That was the doorway to the ramp."

Awen felt a shiver go up her spine. They'd almost died down there in the rotunda. Even after surviving the explosions, it had almost been their tomb. Were it not for TO-96 digging a way out of the rotunda and into an adjacent building, they would have been trapped forever.

The seven doors, which Awen remembered seeing before, had led to dead ends. TO-96 said they terminated in small foyers. The rooms boasted massive doors, but each set was sealed even beyond Ninety-Six's ability to punch through. His sensors could not read past them either. Whatever knowledge the Novia had stored behind those doors, they wanted it locked there forever.

"Let's just keep going." Awen suppressed a desire to run, and instead, she led the team to the left, picking her way through the debris. Once past the largest fragments left over from the explosion, she noticed a set of doors at the end of the hall. "Look, up ahead," she said, pointing.

The four explorers arrived at a large set of doors nearly ten meters tall. Splotchy ghosts of their former selves, they were made from silver that had tarnished over the centuries. As with the building's entrance, another inscription was carved, this time toward the top of the doors themselves.

"'Ninety-Six?'"

"At your service, Awen," the bot said, projecting the translated text onto the surface.

Awen read it allowed: "When we are one, we are whole. At the center, we find the fish." She winced. "Fish?"

"Oh, I am sorry," TO-96 said, the holo-display flickering. "My apologies. I am still learning their language. There."

"We find the beginning."

"That's better," Sootriman said.

"Ezo could go for some fish right about now," Ezo replied.

"Would you do the honors?" Awen asked TO-96, indicating the doors.

"My pleasure, Awen." The bot strode forward, examined the doors, and pushed. At first, the doors resisted the bot, protesting with a groan. TO-96's servos whined a bit louder. All at once, the sound of a latch coming undone gave way to a sliver of space appearing between the silver doors. The bot took a step forward and spread the doors farther.

Awen followed the bot as he stepped onto a balcony that looked over a room so wide and so deep that the ends of it faded into blackness. Light poured down from a vast array of inverted pyramids built from some sort of glowing glass, their windowed shapes stacked upon one another, moving higher and higher toward the room's many-storied apex.

Awen thought of the expression, "It takes your breath away." This sight truly did just that. For as far as she could see, tall double-sided shelves spread from the room's center, each made of dark wood and translucent windowplex, and trimmed with gold. The effect was dizzying as her intellect tried to rationalize just how many shelves there were. They emanated away from the room's center, much as a star radiated rays of light away from its core. More and more shelves filled in the ever-expanding space between the rays as the lines moved on.

As far as she could tell, the center of the room was open. The floor contained a beautiful golden shape against a black background. It looked like a ring whose outside edges danced with floral patterns like flares on the surface of a sun. And within the ring stood a lone pedestal of black marble.

"There," Awen said, pointing to it. "Let's go."

The four of them descended either side of the wide double staircases then turned up the aisles, which acted like rays leading from the pedestal. Awen figured each massive shelving case was at least three meters high and contained a myriad of things. The most common item looked to Awen like a data drive, its slender body edged in some sort of gray composite with walls that glowed light blue like the stardrive. Alien text etched in gold ran along each drive's spine. Occasionally, however, the hundreds of editions on each shelf case were interrupted by a windowed box containing something far more archaic: books and scrolls. She'd only ever read about such items, which dated to antiquity—long before the quantum age. Perhaps she would have time to open one of these boxes and touch the artifacts for herself.

The explorers passed rows and rows of cases, their footfalls on the black marble floor lost in the cavernous room. On and on the shelves went, stretching down either side of their path, broken only by gaps that allowed perusers to access cases farther in. The distance to the next radial lessened as Awen and the others neared the epicenter. Finally, they all arrived at the open space.

Awen realized it was much wider than it had looked from the balcony, and the ceiling with the glowing pyramids was even higher. She moved to the edge of the ring, where the floral designs touched her boots. Then she looked up at the pedestal and hesitated.

"What are you waiting for?" Ezo asked.

"I'm not sure," Awen replied. "I just feel like this is sacred space somehow."

"My sensors are not—"

"You're not going to pick it up with sensors," Sootriman said. "It's something she feels."

"Ah, very well," the bot replied.

"You want to do your Unity thing?" Ezo asked Awen.

Awen shook her head. "No. Not yet." Surely, there was much to see. The whole city, as she recalled, had been *alive* somehow. Of course, that could have been the jungle life clinging to it. But she suspected it was actually energy pulsing through the buildings themselves. And if any buildings were to have energy flowing through them, wouldn't these be the most likely? Seeing it in the Unity would no doubt yield innumerable discoveries.

However, the truth remained that she was afraid. She was afraid of it not working, afraid she might get stuck in the cosmos. *Oh, who are you kidding? You're just afraid of seeing... him.* The image of the ghost within Kane was a nightmare that floated at the edges of her mind between sleep and wakefulness. She saw him hanging on the rope in the shaft, glaring at her, then leaping to devour her.

Awen took a deep breath and turned to the others. "Remain outside the ring." They nodded, then she stepped through the floral patterns and over the edge of the ring. Something shuddered in her soul, a ripple that raced up from her feet and fluttered in her chest. She felt dizzy but not enough that she feared vertigo. She'd crossed some sort of meridian, some sort of line. She knew she should step into the Unity but still felt afraid of what she'd find—if she could enter at all.

"Your heart rate and blood pressure have increased by thirty-one and twenty-six percent, respectively, Awen," the bot said. "Are you all right?"

"I'm fine," she replied without turning around. "Just a little nervous, that's all."

TO-96 turned to Sootriman and then Ezo. "Sir, I don't see any reason for Awen to be nervous."

"Something she *feels*, 'Six. We already told you that."

"Something she feels. Logged, sir."

Awen moved one foot in front of the next, moving closer and closer to the pedestal. TO-96 was right, she realized—her pulse was increasing. She took short, quick breaths. Pressure mounted in her chest and her head. It wasn't painful as much as it was powerful. Each step made the sensations more apparent. This was more than just excitement—this was *otherworldly*.

Awen willed herself to slow down her breathing. The pedestal was less than a meter away and held a rectangular black box made of intricately carved marble. The shapes were floral again. *No, not floral. More like flickering flames or water in a spout.*

Whatever the design, it was beautifully constructed. It was about the size of... well, large enough to hold one of the countless books along the shelves. She reached a hand toward the box, and her fingertips instantly tingled like she was immersing her arm into a bath of warm water. But this bath was deep, the water pressure bearing down on her from hundreds of meters above.

She noticed the box had a lid. On its surface was the same ring that was on the floor, inlaid with gold, its edges radiating with undulating wisps. When Awen's fingers connected with its edge, a shock went down her arm. She yelped.

"Awen!" Ezo cried and stepped into the ring. "Whoa." One hand grabbed his stomach, and the other went over his mouth.

"Stay back," Awen scolded him.

Ezo wasted no time in retreating to Sootriman and TO-96's waiting hands. He staggered but eventually regained his balance. "What was that?"

"I'm not sure," Awen replied. She'd never encountered such a strong manifestation of what she could only guess was the Unity's physical dimension. The veil between paradigms was thin here. "I don't think it will hurt you, Ezo. But you won't function well inside of it."

"Just be careful," he called.

"I will." Awen returned her attention to the box and touched the lid again. The sudden power surge didn't startle her this time. She placed her thumb under the lip and lifted. The cover was heavy but moved easily. Awen opened it wide enough for the light far above her to shine into the black space.

"What's in it?" Ezo called.

"What do you see?" Sootriman asked.

"It's—" Awen swallowed, unsure of what to make of everything that had just happened. "It's empty."

3

MAJOR NOS KIL, his promotion insignia still fresh on his chest armor, stood beside the Valkyrie's captain, helmet hanging on the end of his fist. It sounded like Commander Forsyth was finishing some sort of preflight systems check with his executive officer. Nos Kil waited, having nothing to add to the conversation. Instead, he stared out the bridge window for what would most likely be his last look at the fleet for a very long time.

Outside, the remainder of Third Fleet sat atop Oorajee like children's toys, so minuscule in comparison to the enormous desert planet. Farther out, he saw Second Fleet and, past that, the newly arrived First Fleet, all engaged in intermittent volleys with

Jujari fleets. The blaster exchange was not meant to inflict damage. Rather, it was standard chest puffing as each side let the other know where it stood. Everything was going according to plan. Never before had so much lethal firepower gathered over one system, at least not in Nos Kil's day. He was sorry to leave it. But he had a job to do, and he would not let Admiral Kane down—or rather, he wouldn't let *Moldark* down.

Nos Kil's thoughts turned toward the admiral's transformation—his dilated black eyes, his altered voice. It was otherworldly but, in a strange way, not completely unexpected. Sure, the physical manifestations of whatever was happening were more than odd —they were startling. But rumors that the admiral had been talking to himself had been growing for a while now. Nos Kil had even overheard the man on several occasions. Still, the leader's command decisions were decisive, his timing impeccable, and he continued to emit the confidence that had drawn people to him in the first place. That, and everyone was terrified of him and in awe of his power. Moldark was the leader people longed to follow and feared to leave.

Nos Kil blinked and refocused on the ship that extended from beneath his feet and into the void. This particular Raider-class destroyer, the Valkyrie, had been a gift. It was Moldark's way of thanking Nos Kil for stepping into the shadows with him. In truth, Nos Kil didn't know what to do with a ship. He was a Marine after all—a *former Republic* Marine but a Marine nonetheless. Ships were only good at getting the warriors to the battle, but Marines brought the fight. Secondly, he knew nothing about running a navy ship. He supposed that was precisely why Moldark had assigned Commander Forsyth to the Valkyrie. Even though the commander outranked him, Nos Kil was still "in charge," though that didn't make giving orders any easier.

"How soon until departure, Commander Forsyth?" Nos Kil asked when the XO stepped away.

"Fifteen minutes, Major. The supplies are almost done being loaded, and the science team is on board. They're being shown their quarters as we speak."

"Very good."

Forsyth looked at Nos Kil as if something else remained to be said. The pause made Nos Kil uncomfortable. He noted for at least the second time in ten minutes how much he'd rather be on the ground with the enemy, outnumbered ten to one, than have to learn the rules and regulations of a navy ship.

This Raider-class destroyer had plenty of power

and lots of fight, despite its many moving parts. If he got this ship close enough to planetary emplacements, she'd put on one hell of a pyrotechnic display. He'd seen it before. It was nothing like commanding troops on the ground, however, and that was where he longed to be. The sooner they left, the sooner he could be planet-side again and leave the ship tending to Forsyth.

Forsyth raised a fist to his mouth and coughed. "Major Nos Kil, would you like me to double-check our destination coordinates with navigation?"

"Yes, very good."

"After that, I'll just check on engineering to make sure the modulators and drive cores are stable."

"Absolutely," Nos Kil replied. He sensed the commander was just as uncomfortable as he was. But neither of them complained, just as neither of them offered to approach Moldark about it.

"Estimated time to the quantum tunnel?" Nos Kil asked.

"Three days, sixteen hours," Forsyth replied, double-checking a data pad.

"Very well. Carry on."

Forsyth stepped away, and Nos Kil moved toward a holo-display of the ship above the bridge's center console. He'd always thought the Raider-class destroyers looked like blunt-tipped arrowheads. Their command bridges were in the bow and, as luck would have it, functioned according to the Marines motto: First in, last out. But were the ships ever to collide with an enemy target, they would be first in, never out, Nos Kil noted.

The aft of the ship bore twin stabilizers on the topside and belly, just in front of the main thrusters. These, along with the independently vectored thrust engines to port and starboard, made the ships incredibly maneuverable. The vectored engines had additional cowlings that made them look like concealed talons when not in use.

He'd paid a high price to stand here on this bridge. He'd severed family ties and friendships. He'd even terminated his career—at least, his public one. Of course, no one knew it yet—not his family or the Corps—but soon enough, they all would.

Nos Kil's family had been guaranteed safety, as had his fiancée. The senators had given him assurances. He doubted he'd ever marry Klara, but at least she'd be safe in whatever future she chose for herself. He'd also tried to convince his closest friends in the Corps to come with him, knowing they'd be safer following him. Five had agreed. But for every Marine he spoke to, there was an inherent risk—not for him but for them.

Nos Kil shuddered when he thought of the two Marines who hadn't agreed. The mere fact that he'd broached the subject with them in private meant he'd signed their death warrants. After hearing him out, they'd refused the invitation, saying he was psychotic and delusional. He'd tried to convince them to reconsider, but they'd made up their minds. So Nos Kil had done what needed doing. After that, he told the admiral he had no more friends to headhunt. He'd lied. But he'd rather they died defending what they believed was right than at the end of his MZ25.

Nos Kil looked over the Valkyrie from stem to stern again, the holo-projection spinning slowly over a rendering of Oorajee. The destination icon displayed coordinates on the outer reaches of the Troja system, where the quantum tunnel awaited. He was going back because, as he'd decided a long time ago, he'd follow the admiral anywhere. Even to hell.

The admiral had seen what Nos Kil was capable of. Whereas the Republic had placed limitations on the Marine, especially after everything that had happened on Caledonia, the admiral—Moldark— had not. Nos Kil had hit the windowplex ceiling years before. He'd grown tired of being told what to do with his gifts by COs who were less qualified than he was. It had worn on him and diminished his faith in what the Republic could do. Where the Republic had betrayed him—when his own brothers in arms had turned him in—Moldark had been faithful. The magnanimous leader had come to set him free and give him a place in the new order of the galaxy. Sure, Moldark seemed crazy, but weren't all leaders—at least a little? Wasn't he himself a bit mad? To make things right in the galaxy, one had to be willing to do wrong. The trick was to find safe people to do wrong with together.

Moldark would do in the shadows what the Republic could not do in the light. Nos Kil was even told that Moldark's activities had been sanctioned by elite senators. This wasn't some rogue mission—this was the will of those who cared most about the Republic's enduring legacy. This wasn't about agenda. This was about survival. And he and Moldark would be the hammer that beat out the impurities of the Republic. The metal would be heated, and they—the Paragon—would deliver cleansing blows. Where others had been weak, Moldark was strong. That meant that only the strongest warriors would follow him, and Nos Kil would be chief among them.

There was only one way forward. Nos Kil had made his decision. The only thing left was to do what he was best at—to do what the Republic would not let him—and he would continue with it until he died on the battlefield with an MX40 locked in his hand. The admiral would have his revolution, and Nos Kil would deliver it to him in blood.

MOLDARK ENJOYED BEING BACK aboard the Peregrine again. He liked the Stiletto-class warship far more than the superdreadnoughts. If the latter was more like a floating metroplex, the former was like a dune skiff without a governor—fast and maneuverable. It let him feel the void and, for the briefest of moments, set him free of his responsibilities as fleet admiral. He'd even take the conn from time to time and give the captain a break. Of course, he wasn't really free of anything with this particular plan. His presence on the Peregrine was just for show. And what a good show it would be.

Flight time to Worru would be just under six hours. After making the jump to light speed, Moldark surrendered the helm to his captain and made his way to his quarters. He'd ordered his crew not to disturb him until they arrived above Worru.

The door closed, and Moldark removed his uniform to take a shower. He caught sight of himself in the mirror just before the hot water began to steam up the glass. The puckered flesh around his torso spoke to memories that plagued him like Sorlium leeches on a druther snout fish. He could still feel the flames, still hear the screams of his men, still hear his own screams. Then he caught the glint of his pinky ring. Its gold band and red stone reflected the clear cabin light like a beacon, guiding his attention back to port. He'd suffered greatly, but then he'd been given a second chance that would let him right the wrongs and rebuild the future.

He stepped into the shower and let the water beat against his skin hotter and hotter. He pushed the temperature icon far beyond its routine setting; he'd ordered a coder to remove the maximum-temperature limit to allow boiling water through the shower-head. Try as he might, Moldark could not sense the heat or feel his skin burning atop his bones. The medics would scold him, the bots would treat him, and the same old story would repeat itself. Still, he wanted to feel again. He wanted to remember what it was like.

He thought he heard a scream in the distance—someone shrieking in agony—but he couldn't pick it out amidst the sound of water streaming over his head and splashing at his feet. That person, whoever it was, felt pain. In fact, everyone he knew complained about physical pain. Labored with it. Mourned it. Spent small fortunes to alleviate it. Moldark would have given anything to feel physical pain again. Its ghost haunted him and compelled him to do strange things in the hopes that it would return one day. But no matter how he mutilated himself, no matter how he tortured his aging body, the results were always the same: nothing. He felt nothing.

He turned off the water and reached for a towel. He already knew from the smell what he'd done. He dried himself, but the towel grew damp and sticky. He took a second towel and a third. Blood and pus matted the fabric to an unusable state. He reached for a fourth towel before pulling on his uniform again.

Moldark would visit sick bay. They would treat his burns. But they could not treat the pain *inside* his chest—the one that burned like a hot coal. He'd tried to douse it, but still, it raged—not the bright burn of new flames but the steady glow of old embers, the ones still hot even at dawn. That pain drove him now—not as Admiral Wendell Kane but as Moldark. The embers would carry him through the day, and he would fan them into flames again as the night drew near.

AN ENTOURAGE of no fewer than thirty Luma escorted Moldark and his large security detail to Elder's Hall inside the Grand Arielina. He noted, once again, how beautiful Plumeria was. Like the fragrant flower it was named after, the city radiated life. Learning, knowledge, youth—it was the intersection of the best of galactic cultures and included none of the bad. At least, not in the parts of the city he'd been shown. But he knew the bad was on the planet somewhere. It was always lurking, waiting for those who knew where to look.

The entourage surrounded him as the hall's large wooden doors opened to reveal So-Elku, master of the Order of the Luma, decked in ornate green-and-black robes. His tall physique, baldpate, narrow eyes, and meticulously trimmed wraparound beard gave him an air of sophistication.

"Admiral Kane," So-Elku said. "We've been expecting you."

Moldark spread his hands at his waist, palms up,

parting the cape that closed around his hips. He twitched at the mention of the old name. The Luma master would learn of his new one in time.

"Come." So-Elku motioned for them to enter.

Moldark noticed the man staring at his head, avoiding his hollow black eyes. *Kane* would have offered an explanation. The fool. Moldark said nothing. *Kane* would probably have said something about letting the Luma master live back on Ithnor Ithelia. There'd been a momentary battle between him and So-Elku, until Moldark realized that killing Awen and the others was a more pressing prize than dispatching the Luma master. Moldark convinced Kane to cease fire and give chase into the temple. Moldark had figured he might need the Luma master at a future time, which—as luck would have it—he did, as So-Elku would soon learn.

The pair walked to the center of Elder's Hall, followed by their joint retinue. "Can I offer you something to drink?" So-Elku asked. "Plumeria nectar? Or... perhaps something stronger? Svoltin single malt?"

"No, thank you," Moldark said.

So-Elku looked away from Moldark's head then back again. "Begging your pardon, but your voice—I don't know—has it changed somehow, Admiral?"

"It is my voice, as it's always been." Moldark tilted his head. "Has yours changed?"

So-Elku touched his throat. "No. But the wraps around your head, Admiral. Were you—were you injured?"

Moldark straightened his back, raised his chin, and took a deep breath through wheezy nostrils. "The medics say I will recover in time. It's what they always say."

So-Elku's eyes narrowed. Moldark could tell the man wanted to ask more questions. That was good. Having the advantage in every exchange, no matter how trivial, was important. He liked to keep victims off balance, always guessing. That was how wars were won—not through mass casualties, as historians liked to purport, but through attrition, winning one exchange after another until your opponent begged you to stop.

"If you'd like a more private space, your security may wait outside," So-Elku said.

"And leave me to your otherworldly whims?" Moldark shook his head. "They will stay."

"Admiral, you misunderstand me. When we were last together, I was merely disappointed that you broke our agreement."

"You still received access to your temple library."

"Thankfully, yes. Had I not discovered the location by tracking my student's mind, however, who knows how your troopers would have ravaged it."

Moldark snorted. He disliked this *Unity*. It was something he could not control, and anything he could not control was a threat. "They have no time for your incantations, nor do I."

"And still you killed my student."

"I told you that discretion was costly, and the price was more than you could afford."

"Yet I owe you nothing, since I delivered both Awen and the stardrive to you."

Moldark blew a blast of air from his nostrils. "But you did walk away with something, So-Elku."

"I'm not sure I follow."

"From the library."

"Ah. A small trinket, I suppose. Nothing more."

"But a trinket nonetheless."

"Something for my library, that's all," So-Elku said. "A *book*, as they were known in antiquity."

"And books contain ideas. Powerful ones."

"I suppose, though these only concern our pesky *incantations*, as you call them."

"So you owe me, then," Moldark said, licking his lips.

"Owe you? I believe we're even, Admiral. And if I were you, I'd—"

"If you were me?" Moldark took a step toward the Luma master. "You can't even begin to imagine what it's like to be me, Luma. If you were me, perhaps you'd wonder why I haven't killed you already."

"Are you threatening me in *my* house?" So-Elku asked, looking to his fellow Lumanarias.

"As a matter of fact, I am." Moldark swished the fingers on his right hand, and thirty-two MX40 rifles wielded by thirty-two black-clad Marines were brought to bear on So-Elku and his escorts.

So-Elku looked around the room, examined the blasters, and regarded Moldark. "That's it?" He chortled. "The leader of the rogue Third Fleet comes to threaten the Luma and their master, and you expect us to grovel at your feet with"—So-Elku counted with his index finger—"thirty-two blaster-bolt slingers?" He laughed again.

If So-Elku was looking for even the slightest hesitation, he wouldn't find it. Instead, what he would find, if he had the stomach to keep looking in Moldark's eyes, would make him scared. The Luma master was powerful, yes. But fear haunted the powerful and the weak alike.

One of So-Elku's elders threw off his outer robe and clenched his fists. "Enough of this!" the man cried. He closed his eyes.

"Elder Fossman, wait!" So-Elku yelled. But it was too late.

Moldark felt the elder's presence—this *Fossman*. The man's soul was close, examining Moldark, probing from within that cursed Unity. The elder seemed eager, which suited the dark lord just fine—he was hungry for a soul that day, so he would feast.

"What are you doing?" Fossman asked, his voice suddenly tight with panic. He looked as though he was trying to wrest himself from some invisible strongman's grip. "Stop it!" His eyes were still shut, head twisting from side to side. "Let me go! No!"

But Moldark wouldn't let him go. His spirit lunged, partaking of the Luma's life energy. He sucked as one might drain a piece of fruit of its juice before consuming the flesh.

Fossman shrieked, writhing in utter agony until he collapsed on the floor. So-Elku refused to watch the man's demise, choosing instead to stare at Moldark—which was fine but a waste nonetheless. The spectacle was so grim, so satisfying, that Moldark wondered why anyone would want to miss it. Fossman's body shriveled to that of a man twice his age in less than a few seconds. And moments later, his corpse became a leathery sack of sinew and wiry hair.

Moldark let out a deep sigh, exulting in pleasure. "Now, wasn't that delightful." Renewed power coursed through his veins, invigorating his spirit and tingling his body. The glossy leather squeaked as he stretched his body.

"Is that supposed to scare us?" So-Elku spat, but his eyes betrayed the slightest glint of anxiety. "I could disarm all your troopers and stop their hearts before they blink. Shall I give you a demonstration?"

"You could," Moldark replied. "Yes, you could. But I've left orders with my ship to destroy this… whatever this place is," he said, gesturing with a flitting hand, "if any of our vitals change in the slightest."

"Your ship?" So-Elku choked out, curbing another laugh. "The one in the docking bay?" He stepped toward Moldark. "Look around you, Admiral. This isn't the Republic Navy. This isn't even Republic land or a Republic planet. You're alone, and that ship isn't going anywhere unless I say it is."

Moldark smirked.

The Luma master raised an eyebrow. "What?" he asked, needy eyes darting between Moldark and his Marines.

"I'm afraid I misspoke," Moldark said. "I apologize."

"You see." So-Elku clapped his hands, his mood lightening. "There you go. It's nothing I can't forgive —in time, anyway."

"I said *ship*, didn't I? How inaccurate of me."

So-Elku squinted. "I—I'm not sure I follow."

"What I meant to say was *ships*. My *ships* have orders to level this place if any of us are harmed. In fact, they'll level the entire city."

So-Elku's smile faded. He looked to his other elders for assurance. They merely shrugged at him.

In a sudden burst of sound, So-Elku cackled like a wild animal, his head thrown back. "I'm sorry, Admiral," he bellowed, wiping tears from his eyes, "but I'm afraid you've caught me on a day that I'm quite"—his laugh vanished, and he bared his teeth at Moldark —"*impatient.* I'm calling your bluff."

"Very well." Moldark turned and regarded the nearest trooper clad in black armor, whose helmet was shaped like a racing visor. The trooper dipped his head, paused, and returned Moldark's stare.

The Luma master furrowed his brow and studied Moldark then looked at the ceiling. "Where is it, Admiral? Where's the threat, the blast, the explosion? Where are all the reinforcements?"

So-Elku took another step forward, but Moldark didn't budge. Instead, he interlaced his fingers and waited, watching So-Elku's face intently.

"You're a coward and a liar," So-Elku hissed. "I've had enough of—"

A concussion from outside the Grand Arielina cut the Luma's words short. The shock wave shook the walls and sent everyone but the Marines scrambling for cover. Ears rang as yells and screams went up from the elders, some of them tripping, others shielding their heads as debris fell from the newly repaired dome.

A moment later, emergency klaxons sounded outside the hall. Then the din of thousands of people shrieking in horror blew in on the wind of the orbital strike. The flood of noises filled the now dust-filled Elder's Hall as people dove for cover.

"What have you done?" So-Elku cried, his face twisted in disgust and covered in gray dust.

"I believe that was one of your second-year student dorms," Moldark said above the mayhem. "You'll want to double-check, though. Sometimes my battleships need a practice run before they get the targeting right."

"Are you insane?" So-Elku seethed, spittle flinging from his lips.

"Quite possibly. But the question you should be asking, Luma Master, is whether or not I'm *serious*. And let me assure you, I am very serious. Now"— Moldark began pulling on the fingers of his gloves —"I'd like to have that Svoltin single malt. I need you to do something for me."

4

MAGNUS'S new eyes were getting clearer every minute. By the time he'd dried off from his shower and dressed, he was able to focus on things about three meters ahead. His new eyes were starting to feel less like giant rocks in his skull and more like—well, more like nothing. More natural, though they would always be anything but natural.

The news of his operation under Valerie's super-vision had certainly disturbed him. His new bioteknia eyes meant the end of his career in the Corps. But, at the end of the day, he could see again, and he owed Valerie a debt for that.

One of Abimbola's Marauders escorted Magnus from the shower facility across the compound to a makeshift armory. Magnus didn't know where on

Oorajee they were yet, but this new hideout was nothing like Abimbola's headquarters in the Dregs. That place had been immense and secure, secluded from the outside world like a tomb. Here, a patchwork of canvas tarps and corrugated metal kept the sun at bay, while stacked shipping crates created rooms and vehicle bays throughout the thrown-together warehouse. Suddenly, Magnus wondered about the cleanliness of the operating room where his procedure had taken place. *Never mind.* He shook his head, realizing his blurry vision was probably for the best. *I don't even want to know.*

The guard left Magnus in the armory and told him where to find Abimbola when he was kitted up. Magnus nodded and heard the door close behind him with a whine. The space was constructed of two massive shipping containers, hollowed out and welded together, with bright light pads attached to the corrugated ceiling. He shielded his eyes and gave them a second to adjust then walked to three tables in the center of the room. On them sat his armor, or what was left of it. Abimbola's Marauders had cleaned it and laid it out, along with a selection of supplementary pieces.

Magnus sighed. He stood before the first and largest table, dressed in a standard black military hauberk tunic, fingers touching the blast marks in what remained of his Mark VII suit. The plates were riddled with charred holes and rough furrows left by blasted sand. If this was the best of it, he wondered what the worst looked like. Gone were the shoulder plates, left bicep, right bicep, and forearm enclosures. The left thigh enclosure, kneecap, and right shin guard were also gone. Both original gauntlets were missing as well as his mag boots. A few pieces were replaced with old Mark IV armor; he'd have recognized the mottled-green coloring from the Caledonian Wars anywhere. The other missing elements had been filled by components he'd never seen before —alien, he was pretty sure. Some were iridescent magenta while others were matted blue. They appeared to be trimmed to size, which made him wonder how big their former owners had been.

His original helmet would have been a sight for sore eyes had it been functional. The visor was punched out and the battery compartments and AI module gutted. The slits he'd cut for air vents, back when their escape pods landed, now looked like burnt-out gashes from mizlasaur teeth. He wondered if it wouldn't be better to just wear a bandana and some eye protection. Maybe the helmet belonged on Abimbola's wall after all.

Magnus moved to the next table and, to his surprise, found his MAR30 blaster, MZ25 pistol, and duradex combat knife, all intact. "Remind me to thank his gods." He picked up the larger weapon, and his hands ran across it instinctively, searching for anything out of place. Aside from a few dents and blackened streaks, the weapon remained a beautiful specimen of Republic engineering. He had to give them credit—they'd built this platform to last.

Magnus flicked on the primary-status holo-display and noticed that a fresh energy magazine had been installed. The weapon whined as it sprang to life, humming against his skin in his ungloved grip. It felt reassuring. All three firing systems displayed green indicators. Magnus racked a charge, pulled the blaster to his shoulder, and activated the HSD—holo-sight display. The series of mesmerizingly beautiful information-rich targeting reticles, vector indicators, and systems-status symbols glowed down the rails of the weapon. Magnus aimed at a utility shelf across the room, knowing one trigger squeeze would make quick work of it—as well as anything in the next room. He flicked off the safety and hovered his index finger over the trigger. The HSD read Missing for his helmet lock.

"That's not happening anytime soon," he

remarked as he looked over his carved-up Mark VII helmet.

Magnus flicked the safety on, powered down, and set the MAR30 on the table. He reached for the MZ25. The pistol had been cleaned but showed more damage than the MAR30. A finger-sized chunk of the handle had been gouged out, replaced with a hastily sanded weld. The top of the barrel also had a gouge repaired with a weld.

Magnus racked a round and noticed the Z had a fresh energy mag as well. He gripped the pistol with both hands and punched out so the barrel was pointed at the same shelf across the room. Valerie was the last person to have fired this weapon. He remembered her handling it with practiced ease. In hindsight, he found that startlingly attractive. He added the mystery of how the Z had taken so much damage and Valerie had not to his growing list of questions. He powered down and set the weapon beside the MAR30.

After checking the blade's sharpness—something he did out of ritual and not necessity, since the weapon was nearly indestructible—Magnus examined several fragmentation grenades that Abimbola had laid out. Missing were any of his unit's VODs— variable-output detonators—though he wasn't surprised. Those were Republic issued and hard to come by even within the Corps. However, Magnus did find three quantum detonators in a custom-lined munitions case.

Treating it like an unstable core element, Magnus removed one of the fabled devices and examined it. The truth was, he'd never seen one up close. QDs were dangerous and expensive—one of the few munitions the Recon had *not* sprung for. Also, they were illegal. "These might come in handy," Magnus said with a smirk.

On the third and final table, he found a black backpack, a first aid kit with laser sutures, a few days' worth of field meals, a flashlight, and a fire starter. There were several extra energy magazines for his primary and secondary weapons, a locator beacon, a field-grade holo-pad, and an over-the-ear comms device. The latter was a far cry from what he was used to with an integrated helmet AI, but it was better than nothing.

Magnus looked across the tables and ran a hand over his short beard. "Time to get suited up. Time to OTF." But the phrase sent a pang through his chest. Can I say it now that I'm no longer a Marine?

Stow it, Magnus. Once a Marine, always a...

He couldn't finish the statement. If he survived

what they were headed into, and if he could make contact with command—whoever endured the coming conflict—he knew he'd never be an active-duty Marine again. So he came up with something else—something that seemed fitting for subduing an enemy and rescuing whoever survived in his unit.

"Dominate," he whispered, staring at his MAR30. He tried to think of something else to complement it. Maybe another few words to craft a memorable acronym.

Just then, he remembered Awen, bound somewhere near this very compound, making fun of the Marines and of him. "All you military guys *love* your acronyms," she'd said. He smiled as he remembered the note she'd handed him with the letters NMB written on it. *Naked monkey butt.* He almost thought of using that as a mantra but decided against it. NMB was personal.

"Dominate," he said again, lifting his MAR30 and squeezing the stock and handle. The word wasn't exactly poetic, and it certainly didn't feel complete. But it did represent what he wanted to do to anyone threatening those he loved or had sworn to protect. Domination of the enemy—it was appropriate.

But what would Awen say? he asked himself then wondered why that even mattered. Try as he might, he couldn't get her out of his mind—Awen and her infernal peace-loving methods of trying to save the galaxy. The question plagued him: *What would she say about those in need of rescue?*

Then he had it. "Dominate," he repeated, bringing the weapon to his shoulder and activating the holo-sight. "Liberate."

"WELL, LOOK WHO WE HAVE HERE," Abimbola said, standing behind a holo-projection in the middle of the darkened room.

Several more control stations lined the room's perimeter, but Magnus couldn't make them out beyond blurry glowing lights. He looked down at his mélange of armor and wiggled in it. It didn't quite feel right, but it would do.

"I suppose I should thank you," Magnus replied, "but I'm still not sure."

Abimbola dismissed the comment with a wave. "You look like a Marauder now."

"Like I said, not sure I should thank you for that."

Abimbola laughed then motioned for Magnus to join him. Magnus's eyes were still adjusting, but he could make out Valerie on a stool and Piper beside her. The nine-year-old girl clutched the tattered remains of her stuffed animal. Talisman, she'd called it. By the look of the thing, it was about time she outgrew it, or there'd be nothing left to cuddle. A few more figures stood beside Valerie, and even more filled the room behind Abimbola.

"Good to see you, LT," came a familiar voice. Magnus blinked as a diminutive woman with short hair strode into view. She wore a hodgepodge of armor like Magnus.

"Corporal Dutch," he said, shaking her hand. Three more forms emerged, all in mismatched armor. "Private First Class Haney. Gilder." Magnus felt his heart swell with every name he listed, and he shook their hands too. "Chief Warrant Officer Nolan. It's good to see you."

"Good to see you too, LT," Dutch replied. The others nodded.

Then Magnus got a lump in his throat. "Dutch," he said, hesitating. "I'm not exactly sure how… I mean, as you probably know, my eyes…"

"Hey, LT, you're not out yet," she replied with a wide grin. "When that time comes, then I'll call you something else. Until then, orders haven't changed. Copy?"

"Copy," Magnus said. Valerie must have slipped

him some heavy meds, because he was feeling pretty emotional. He cleared his throat. "You're all ready to roll?"

"We are, sir," Dutch replied, pounding her chest plate with a fist. Magnus felt a wave of gratitude. No one was forcing them to go on this mission, and there certainly wasn't any Republic backing for it.

"Thank you, Dutch. Everyone."

"Eh, not to worry. Abimbola's given us armor and some new toys…" Dutch paused then lowered her voice. "Though his constant jokes against the Corps are getting a little old."

"I heard that," Abimbola said.

"Well," Magnus said, looking the Marines and the sailor over, "seems you don't have to worry about being mistaken for anything but Marauders now."

Abimbola thumped his chest with a fist. "And are they not blessed to be counted as such?"

"Not exactly the word I had in mind. But anyone who gives me an M101 blaster cannon is all right in my book." Dutch raised the bulky double-barreled weapon and tapped the upper receiver. Then she leaned in and whispered to Magnus, "Where did he get this? It's brand new."

"Best not to ask," Magnus replied with a wink. "What about the rest of the Stones' crew?"

Dutch paused and looked toward Valerie. Magnus tried to read their facial expressions, though the corporal's hesitation said more than enough.

"Abimbola says they'll keep monitoring all band-widths for communications," Dutch replied. "But as of right now, we've had no contact."

"Let us get started," Abimbola said, then cleared his throat.

Magnus placed a hand on Dutch's shoulder then looked at Abimbola. "Let's do it." He stepped toward the center table. As he got closer, he noticed several more bodies in the room.

"A few of my Marauders seem to be interested in hearing what you want to do," Abimbola said. "Mind if they stay?"

"Be my guest," Magnus replied. "Anyone who's willing to help rescue Marines is—"

"Not rescuing Marines." Abimbola cut him off. "Killing Selskrit Jujari. They are different."

"Selskrit Jujari?"

"Western packs. Pledge fealty to their own mwadim."

Magnus felt himself being scrutinized.

"You know, Selskrit, Dingfang, Clawnip," Abim-bola continued. "No?"

Magnus shook his head.

"For the love of the gods, you really do not know anything about your enemies, do you," Abimbola stated with no attempt to hide his disgust. "The Jujari you were meeting with were Tawnhack. Largest and most powerful of the packs. Most reasonable too."

"Reasonable?" Magnus said involuntarily.

"Yes. Reasonable. We have negotiated with them for years. But the Selskrit, they're something different. Not right in the head, you know?"

But Magnus didn't know. As far as he was concerned, all Jujari were *not right in the head*, and the fact that Abimbola saw differences between them made him *not right in the head* too.

"The Selskrit raided the mwadim's palace after the explosions, then the Clawnip took what was left. Fighting broke out between the packs. It seems the Selskrit took some survivors, probably to exchange for credits or ships or whatever they can barter from the Republic."

"And you think they have my Marines? Where'd you get your intel?"

"Is he always this slow?" Abimbola asked Valerie, and she shrugged. "I see." The warlord looked back at Magnus. "As I said, we have been trade partners with the Tawnhack for years. My sources thought we might like to know, and they passed the information on."

"So they just hand you information like this? Must've been a heavy price."

"More than you know," Abimbola said, straightening. Magnus waited for the man to say more, but he didn't, and Magnus didn't feel he should push it.

"So, do we have a location? Expected resistance? Estimated number of survivors?"

"One thing at a time." Abimbola turned to the holo-projection hovering over the table.

Magnus moved closer and felt everyone else press in too. A topographical map clarified, and Magnus recognized it from his own briefing on the Jujari's capital city of Oosafar. Abimbola manipulated the map with his hands, zooming in on a section of the city to the west.

"We believe the survivors are being held in the Western Heights. Selskrit territory." Abimbola zoomed in to a few city blocks. "This building here"—he pointed to a large house with an open-air square courtyard in the center, a sizable yard surrounding the building, and a walled perimeter at the street—"is our target. Three stories of sandstone and metal, most likely heavily fortified." Abimbola zoomed in farther then snapped the image with his wrists and flipped the camera view to street level. A three-meter-high wall ran around the perimeter of the compound with two guard towers at the front corners. "It is twenty meters from this wall to the building on all sides. We have reason to believe they have posted sentries in the towers, more on top of the building, and"—Abimbola flipped to the overhead view again—"snipers in the surrounding buildings here, here, and here."

"How old is your intel?" Magnus asked.

"Old enough for it to be wrong."

"How much of it?"

Abimbola eyed him cautiously. "All of it."

Magnus didn't like that answer and shook his head.

"Listen, buckethead, the Jujari are unpredictable and can move fast. Even if we had a live feed on this whole twenty-block section, which we do not because of the jammed airspace, there is no way we could keep up with their unit movements."

"No need to get testy. I was just asking," Magnus said, stepping forward. "So, two in the towers, say, three more on the roof—"

"Five more on the roof," Abimbola interjected.

Magnus glanced at him. "*Five* more on the roof, another five inside," Magnus said, and the warlord nodded. "And three snipers in the buildings. Brings our count to fifteen."

"Say, twenty to be safe."

"Twenty," Magnus echoed with a slight shake of his head. He knew this would be a fraction of the resistance they'd encounter once they were in the Western Heights. No doubt, they'd be overwhelmed without careful planning. He examined the home more closely, trying to gauge its size. "Hostages?"

"I was told fewer than ten."

Magnus swallowed. If that number was to be believed, it wasn't good. His platoon had numbered sixteen, as had that of Captain Wainright—the CO for Alpha Platoon and operation commander for the security detail. Ten or fewer hostages, assuming those were all Marines who'd survived due to their Mark VII armor, was less than a third of the unit's original strength. *A third.* And who knew how many of those were injured and might not endure the raid.

Magnus ground his teeth as he thought about the stupidity of the original mission. They never should have been here, at least not with anything less than an entire task force—one that was in a secure location. The mission had been a joke from the start. He knew it, his Marines knew it, and Captain Wainright knew it, though the man never said a thing. In the end, he'd realized that the point of the whole thing had been politics. Magnus pictured himself walking into some senator's office in Capriana and burning the place to the ground.

"How far's this from Tawnhack-controlled space?" Magnus asked.

Abimbola zoomed out. "This is the current territorial mark." A dotted red line appeared over a street that ran in a north–south direction. "It changes daily but not by much. Depends on who pisses where and who shoots whoever is pissing."

"Really?"

"Really."

"So, what's that distance, then?" Magnus asked, pointing to the area between the border and the compound. "Ten blocks maybe?"

Abimbola nodded. "About a kilometer."

Dutch whistled, and Magnus heard the others shift on their feet. He took a deep breath, which only made people shift more. "And how many of your Marauders have signed up for this?"

"None."

"What?" Magnus asked. Is this some sort of joke? Didn't Abimbola just say we want to sit in on the briefing and kill Jujari? He had the distinct feeling that he'd been duped, betrayed by his own assumptions. If he was going on a suicide mission without the Marauders, he'd be on his own; there was simply no way he was going to put Dutch and the others' lives in jeopardy again.

"At least, not yet," Abimbola said. "You have to ask them first."

Magnus blinked. "Ask them?"

"You think we are all going to risk our lives to help some buckethead rescue his unit's survivors just because you order us to? Or maybe because of your good looks?" Pockets of laughter went up from the Marauders behind Abimbola. "Have you even *seen* yourself lately?" More laughter followed.

Abimbola had a point. These warriors—whoever they were—were not Republic Marines. They could not be ordered around, told to lay their lives down for the greater good—at least, not by him.

"Abimbola," Magnus said, straightening. "Warrior to warrior, would you help me—" Magnus caught himself and considered the best way to parse this. "Would you help me kill some Selskrit Jujari for a day?"

"What do you say, Marauders?" Abimbola asked without taking his eyes off Magnus. An instantaneous cheer went up behind the warlord. The man gave a wide smile. "Seems we will."

"Thank you, Abimbola."

"You can count on, let's see…" Abimbola produced a poker chip and flipped it. He caught it and slapped it on the back of his hand. "Thirty of us joining you, including me—and I count for three."

"I'd say so," Dutch said, and Magnus and Abimbola looked at her. "What? He does."

The two men chuckled. "Thirty is more than I could ask for," Magnus said. Even with thirty Marauders and four of his own warriors, they were going to need a greater presence of force. Urban warfare was slow-moving and brutal. They'd need something to even the odds and make getting to and from the target manageable. "What about transport? Do we have armor? Personnel skiffs? Some mortars would be great too."

Abimbola winked then flipped the poker chip at Magnus, who caught it and opened his hand.

"Which side is up, buckethead?"

Magnus looked down. "The house."

"Then the gods say you have come to the right place."

5

AWEN STARED inside the empty box for several seconds before closing the lid. With so much power emanating from the circle, she was sure that whatever the box contained must have been the source. She closed the lid and examined the pedestal, wondering if maybe she'd missed something.

"What do you mean it's empty?" Ezo asked.

"I mean, there's nothing in it, Ezo!"

"Nothing, at all?"

"That does constitute the term 'empty,' I believe, sir," TO-96 said. Ezo glared at him.

"Why don't you just come back, love," Sootriman said to her, gesturing with her hand.

Awen nodded, a sense of defeat hitting her with each step she took toward her... *What are they to you, anyway?* she asked herself. The word friends came to mind, but she didn't know Ezo and the others *that* well yet. Did she?

"You all right?" Sootriman asked as Awen stepped out of the circle.

"I guess."

"What do you mean, you guess?" Ezo asked.

"I don't know. I just felt like there was going to be something in there. Something important." Awen paused, considering the circle, the pedestal, and the box.

"You're disappointed, then," TO-96 said.

"Yes. There are places in the galaxy where the Unity intersects the physical realm in ways that make any separation between them feel *thin*. That's the best way to describe it. And this place is the strongest I've ever felt that sort of anomaly. I just thought there'd be something in that box that—"

"That explained it," Sootriman said.

"Exactly," Awen said with a nod. She looked down in thought. "Something was in there—I know it. There was a dust outline in the shape of a rectangle."

"One of those books perhaps?" Sootriman asked.

"Maybe. Hard to say. I don't know why a book would produce such *thinness*."

"Logic suggests that it didn't," TO-96 said. "Even if someone had enchanted the book, as some of the mystics were purported to do to volumes, that effect is no longer present. By virtue of its absence, what you felt should likewise be nonexistent. Therefore, I propose that the *thinness* is the result of another factor, Awen."

She nodded, appreciative of the bot's assessment. His reasoning did make sense, and she felt hopeful that whatever had been in the box maybe wasn't as important as she'd made it out to be. Still, she couldn't shake the feeling of defeat.

"It's almost like someone beat us to it," Awen said.

"Kane?" Sootriman asked.

"Maybe," Awen replied. "He doesn't exactly strike me as the intellectual type, though."

"So-Elku," TO-96 suggested.

The others turned to him.

"Possibly," Awen replied. "If he survived the episode with Kane, which seems doubtful, maybe he made it in here and took whatever was in the box."

"Feels like something a Luma would be interested in," Ezo said. "After all, *you* are, so why wouldn't he?"

Awen nodded, pinching the bridge of her nose in irritation.

"Well, there is a bright side to all this," TO-96 said merrily.

"What's that?" Ezo asked.

"If we are stuck here indefinitely, at least we have what could be the metaverse's largest library to keep us occupied. We could, as you say, read ourselves to death."

"Not funny, 'Six. Not funny."

"Oh."

THE FOUR OF them had spread out and begun searching for anything of interest in the library. As promising as the supposed data drives were, without the proprietary hardware to access them, they remained worthless. TO-96 had already examined several of them, hoping to find a common connection port or frequency. However, the devices were devoid of all known interface types and went back onto their shelves.

The books and scrolls, while fascinating in and of themselves, lacked anything distinguishable to TO-96. Even though the data dump from the stardrive gave him a wealth of knowledge, at least to get them this far, it lacked whatever language was written on the old parchment. S

familiar to Awe:

another life, as if

however, the boo

shelves beside the (

Ezo had alrea(

Unity. She'd refuse(

that was true, at le

sound like a health

on fear. Sootriman ..... to her rescue and told Ezo to leave her alone then proposed the idea of having everyone spread out. Awen was grateful for the reprieve. She would enter the Unity, maybe even soon. But she needed to breathe, to think.

She wandered down one of the radials that stemmed from the room's center, her fingers gently brushing along the spines of data drives. There was so much here—more than she could learn in a thousand lifetimes. And all of it had just been sitting dormant for centuries. She hated to let it go to waste, hated that it might sit here for more centuries before someone figured it out—though, if So-Elku was the one with whatever had been in the box, maybe he'd figure it out.

Maybe he'll be back. The thought filled her with a sense of dread that crept along her skin like a newly lapod. *Of course, if he did survive the ne wouldn't have had much time to linger and stolen what he could, intending to return when it e convenient.*

That book, or whatever had been in the box, was the key to this library, and she cursed herself for letting him have it. But it wasn't her fault. It just felt like it was. Maybe if she'd gotten everyone here sooner. Maybe if she'd stopped Kane. Maybe if she'd hurt So-Elku back on Worru. Maybe if she had... she shuddered with where her thoughts led. No, she wasn't a murderer. Not like the Republic. Not like the Marines. Like Magnus?

The search went late into the afternoon until TO-96 warned everyone that the light was fading. They dared not stay in the open after dark, so they retreated from the library, exited the temple, and made their way back to their headquarters.

It was Sootriman's turn to prepare a meal, and she did her best to create something palatable out of the Indomitable's remaining foodstuffs, which were running out. She succeeded at not making anyone vomit, and that was saying something. Ezo's dish the night before had caused both women to run to the nearest bathroom.

"At least the Novia believed in really big toilets,"

Sootriman said, "or else you would have been wearing this, my dear."

––––––––––––

THE DAYS TURNED to weeks as Ezo, Sootriman, and TO-96 continued to map the city while Awen returned to the library to search for clues. She was beginning to feel at home in the temple, despite learning nothing more about the marvelous inhabitants of this once-vibrant planet. Each night around dinner, Ezo asked if Awen had entered the Unity yet, and each time, Awen gave him the same forlorn look.

No matter how much she wanted to view this world through her *other sight*, she couldn't bring herself to do it. And worse, her fear of doing it only grew with each day that passed, further distancing her from the explosion in the rotunda. At some point, however, she knew she'd have to enter the Unity, at least to satisfy the growing rift her fear was creating in the team, though she wasn't sure what it would solve. Even with all the knowledge in the cosmos, the only way they were ever getting back was if they could build a ship or if a ship came to rescue them.

The four sat around the table they'd placed in their makeshift dining room. TO-96 and Ezo had rewired some of the Novia's strange lights and hung them over the table. TO-96 had also figured out a way to resuscitate sections of the building's solar arrays, which he directed to power the portions of the building the team lived in.

The discovery of power had come none too soon. After the Indomitable's stores ran dry, finding food compatible with humanoid physiology was a matter of life and death, as was the even more important job of finding potable water. But TO-96 had proven himself yet again by salvaging the Indomitable's sole surviving water-reclamation unit and protein synthesizer. While neither was meant to sustain life, they would allow the team to get by until something better could be figured out.

TO-96 had already discovered several edible varieties of flora, some of which didn't taste half bad. Additionally, he'd managed to kill, skin, and cook a dozen small birds, which he'd given "a gastrointestinal acceptability rating of ninety-three percent." The GAR, as they'd come to know it, became the source of more than a few jokes whenever the cuisine wasn't up to the patrons' standards—mostly on the nights that TO-96 cooked.

"It may have a GAR of eighty-seven percent," Sootriman said and spit the green mash back onto her plate, "but it has a Sootriman palatability-and-tolerance rank of zero." Thus, the GAR-SPAT index was born and helped the team manage more than one dark night.

However, there was no amount of levity that would lift the depression that began to plague the team as weeks turned to months. Awen was fairly sure that the others wondered how life was going for everyone else back home, just as she was—not that she imagined Ezo and Sootriman having family, per se. They didn't seem like homebodies. Still, life as they'd all known it had changed, possibly forever.

For her part, Awen wondered how her parents were doing. She wondered if news of her mission had reached them yet and what explanation had been offered. If it was up to So-Elku, she imagined he would have lied, concocting some horrible story about the traitorous dau Lothlinium Luma. Would her parents believe the lie and be even more disappointed in her than they were already? No, she doubted that the Master even cared to attend to such things. Instead, if Willowood were still alive, perhaps she had sent them a holo-transmission or even made contact in person. That was the kind of woman she was. Awen hoped she was still among the living.

As each new day turned up fewer and fewer

discoveries, the pressure on Awen to enter the Unity mounted. Whatever tech, whatever ships, whatever new *toys* were discovered, the team found an equal amount of disrepair. Ships had been swallowed whole by the jungle, drive cores long drained, systems rusted out. Even if Ezo and TO-96 *could* make something void-worthy, no amount of solar power would charge a core, at least not without sending it to the sun's surface. Each day that passed was a reminder of how stuck they really were and how much Awen's giftedness was their only remaining hope.

It had been three months since their first excursion to the temple together. Ezo sat at the dinner table, pleading with her. "But you might see something inside the Unity to help us," he argued.

How many times had they been through this? Ezo was mad. He'd probably blow at any second. And he had every right to. The truth was, all of this was because of her. Sure, the longer days had something to with it, as did the stress of being trapped in an alien universe. But in the end, his frustration was Awen's fault, and she couldn't let that go.

Awen swallowed her bite of food and stared out the window as twilight fell, a deep-purple hue summoning the black of night. Sootriman had prepared the evening meal, but Awen had suddenly lost her appetite. "I know, *I know.*"

"Don't think you do, Star Queen. Frankly, Ezo's tired of being patient."

"Ezo, please," Sootriman soothed, taking his hand.

He yanked it away. "Ezo's pissed Splick, more than pissed."

"That's enough, Ezo."

"No," he said, glaring at Sootriman. "*She* has the power to see things we're missing. It's been… it feels like it's been *years.*"

"Actually, it's been sixty-three days, two hours, and—"

"*I don't care,*" Ezo said, his lips drawn tight over his bared teeth. "*It's time.* Whatever it is you're waiting for, whatever it is that's holding you back, it's time to get over it."

"That's it, Ezo!" Sootriman said, standing. "I've had enough of this!"

"Well, so has Ezo!" Ezo yelled.

"Me too!" TO-96 said. He bumped the table hard as he stood. The others glared at the bot. "It felt like the right thing to say."

"Sit down!" Ezo ordered the bot then turned to

tell Sootriman the same. She tilted her head at him, and he thought better of it.

"Don't you even think about telling me what to do, Idris," she said, cool as Antaran ice—voice low, words measured.

"It's not like you'd listen anyway," Ezo mumbled.

"What was that?"

"Nothing."

"He insists you don't listen," TO-96 said.

"Not now, 'Six."

"No, I'd like to hear him out, Idris."

TO-96's voice suddenly changed to a near-exact mimic of Ezo's and Sootriman's, saying, *"You know how she can be 'Six. She's always, like, 'Don't tell me what to do, Idris' and 'I know better than you, Idris' and 'You're just going to get caught, Idris.'"*

"Would you just shut up already?" Ezo yelled.

"But I was only trying to—"

"No!"

"As you wish, sir," the bot said.

"He's right," Awen said softly. Time seemed to stand still as everyone looked at her. "Ezo's right. I probably will find something that we're missing. I'm just… I'm afraid, that's all."

"Well, it's about time that—"

Sootriman gave Ezo a look that said she would tear out his lungs with her pupils.

"It's time that we listen to your fears," Ezo said, taking his seat once again. Sootriman sat down, too, followed by the bot.

"Back there, in the rotunda, I got scared. I mean, really scared."

"We were all scared, Awen," Ezo said.

"Let her talk," Sootriman said.

"I saw something." She took a deep breath. They'd think she was crazy. Unstable. Would they even believe her? "It was Kane."

"*What* was Kane?" Ezo asked. Sootriman raised her palms at him and gestured for him to slow down. "Go on."

"There was something about him, something very wrong. Do you remember how he seemed like he was talking to someone else?" Awen asked, and everyone nodded. "Well, he was talking to someone but not in the physical realm."

"You're saying he was possessed or something?" Sootriman asked.

"Something like that. I've never seen it before. Never read about it. It was as if another being was living inside him."

"Like a parasite," Ezo offered.

"Maybe. All I know is that it scared me, and I…" Awen's words hung in the air while the others waited. This was the heart of it, right here. She was face-to-face with what she'd been avoiding. "I don't want to go back in the Unity," she finally said. Tears welled in her eyes.

The truth was, the image of Kane's *other* self had shaken her more than she'd realized. To say that it had unnerved her would be an understatement.

"The image of his face—it haunts me. And I'm just afraid that as soon as I go back in, he's going to come for me." She could feel the tears running along her nose and down the sides of her face. She mashed them against her skin. "And make me do terrible things."

"What terrible things?" Sootriman asked.

Awen was weeping now. She wiped snot from her nose as Sootriman came around the table and put her arms around her.

"I had thoughts," she said with a gasp. "Thoughts of killing Kane. Of doing things to his body and causing him pain in ways I'd never thought of before." She let out a deep breath, her lungs shuddering, lips fluttering. "It's like it *wanted* me to kill him. It asked me to break my vows as a Luma."

"There, there, love."

"No, it's worse." Awen buried her face in her hands, embarrassed. Shame filled her heart like an ocean wave surging into an underwater cave. "I... I wanted to slaughter him. To do what the images in my mind said to. I want revenge because it's the only thing that will heal the pain."

She sobbed, and Sootriman held her, rocking in time with Awen's labored grief, like a mother with her child. All of the pain Awen had carried from the mwadim's palace, from Abimbola's prison, from the Elder's Hall, from the Novia's temple, and even from Sootriman's den pooled in her heart and poured from her mouth. She saw the bodies of her friends scattered in the skyscraper on Oorajee. She recounted her master's betrayal on Worru. And she felt her vulnerability under Kane's destructive gaze here in Itheliana.

Sootriman's arms cradled her as Willowood's had outside the Grand Arielina. Awen remembered confiding in Willowood that she'd wanted to give up, to just be done with everything. She'd told Magnus the same thing. And neither of them had resisted her, neither had told her that she *couldn't*. But they *had* told her to consider other factors before making her decision. And in the end, she chose to keep going, to keep pursuing what she felt was right.

But what is "right" on Itheliana, so far away from everything I ever knew? She was, after all, in a completely different universe from the one she'd been born to. She wished Willowood were here—Magnus too—to help her decide what to do.

"Listen," Sootriman said after Awen felt herself calm down. Awen sniffed, wiping her nose with her sleeve. She was being so unladylike, but she didn't care. "I don't know how the Unity works, so I won't pretend to. You're the expert there. But I do know that you saved my life with it—with *your* power. Kane tried to kill me, but *you* overcame him. *You* won. And since it's my life we're talking about, I get to tell you that you're stronger. You're stronger than Kane and whatever that other *thing* is. You hear me? You're *stronger*."

Awen nodded her head, her face hot and wet.

"And *you* escaped from So-Elku," Ezo said, picking up Sootriman's lead. "Twice. You resisted his attempts to get you to open the stardrive too. *You* did that, Star Queen."

"If it is my turn now," TO-96 said, "I'd like to add something."

Awen smiled and let out a small laugh. "It is."

"I reviewed footage taken in the mwadim's palace that I found on Republic servers. It is better not to ask how I obtained this, mind you. But the fact that you stood up to the Republic ambassador and held your own with the mwadim, much less survived the explosions, is exemplary. There is even footage of you saving a Marine in the street from a falling block of concrete. It would have killed you both. But you saved both him and yourself. I do not think I am using hyperbole when I assert that you are an amazing woman, one who…" The bot hesitated, perhaps processing more holo-footage. "One I am proud to call a *friend*."

"Thank you, TO-96," she said, trying to compose herself. "Thank you, all of you."

As Awen sat upright, she felt Sootriman kneel down beside her. "I need you to listen to me carefully," the woman said, her deep-brown eyes pleading with Awen. For the first time since meeting her, Awen noticed pain behind Sootriman's eyes. "What that voice said to you, that thing about revenge, it's not true. I've been there. I've walked that road. Revenge never heals you. It only masks your wounds and then makes them worse. You understand? It *never* heals you."

Awen nodded, letting the truth of Sootriman's experience confront the lie in her mind. And it was working. "Thank you. I understand." Awen took a deep breath, feeling as if the weight of the world had been lifted from her shoulders. It was the best she'd felt in a long time. She felt ready, reminded of who she was. While her *friends'* encouragement hadn't eliminated the sense of risk she felt in the pit of her stomach, she at least knew what she had to do next.

"Tomorrow," she said with her chin raised. "Tomorrow, I will go back to the temple and enter the Unity of all things. But only if you come with me."

6

THE FOUR-DAY JOURNEY from Worru to Capriana Prime had worn out So-Elku. No, that wasn't it. The pressure of living under Kane's threats had worn him out. The constant head games, the manipulation, the condescension. On top of it, the Luma master was quite sure the admiral had gone completely mad. Or worse.

So-Elku dried his face with a towel as an incoming communiqué chirped in his quarters. He swiped open the notification hovering a few centimeters off the mirror's surface. "What is it?" he said, dabbing his cheeks.

"Master So-Elku, we've received permission to enter atmosphere."

"Very good. I'll be up momentarily." He closed

out the channel, set his towel down, and reached for his robes.

His mind turned toward the admiral. So-Elku had seen madness before, at least in part. For example, Luma who'd lost themselves in the Unity could go out of their minds if pulled from it prematurely. But what ailed the admiral was something different. Kane's eyes had changed into black orbs, into something preternatural, as if he was possessed.

So-Elku slid his arms into his green-and-black robes and pulled the fabric over his shoulders. Their weight felt good, familiar, as did the power that came with them. He would need all the power he could summon when standing toe-to-toe with Kane. The admiral was dark and unexpected, and So-Elku had realized he wasn't dealing with a reasonable man anymore.

Before, the prospect of getting to see what no one from this universe had ever seen—the lost temple library of the fabled Novia Minoosh—was a prize worth doing almost anything for, including giving up one of his students. But the admiral had agreed not to hurt Awen—a promise he'd broken without an afterthought.

Then there was the attack on the dormitory, which had been an act of pure evil. Kane had called in an orbital strike on peaceful planet, and the response team was still sorting through the wreckage, still finding remains. Despite So-Elku's doubts about the Republic, not even they would sanction such a merciless attack in broad daylight—which meant only one thing: the Republic had lost control.

And then there was Kane himself. A man—no, *a monster*—who had consumed a Luma elder's life force. *And enjoyed it.* The episode disturbed So-Elku as much as the loss of the dormitory. Perhaps even more.

So-Elku looked down, drawing his robes closed with the loops and toggles. He took a deep breath and smoothed the fabric over his chest. An idea was forming.

The discovery of the Novia manuscript had opened certain possibilities, ones he'd never considered. No one had. But even with the little that he and his elders had deciphered so far, the potential—no, the *power*—seemed limitless. He wished to taste of it again.

So-Elku closed his eyes, entered the Unity, and sank through the ether as far as he could. Below all he knew and all he'd ever explored lay what the Novia Minoosh's codex had told him was there: the Foundation of all things. Here was the Unity's base, the ultimate beginning point. It was immovable.

Impenetrable. It was the bedrock upon which every-thing else in the cosmos rested.

It's been under our feet all along, So-Elku mused. The way forward—he'd recognized upon translating the first several pages of the manuscript—was not above them. It was below.

The Luma master gathered himself and pressed his ethereal body against the floor. The surface was cold and massive as if his body lay across a glacier. He spread himself over it, stretching out as if face-down in a large bed.

In the physical realm, children learned to walk by standing up—by pushing against the ground beneath their feet. But the ground was an assumption, its composition a construct, one that was only as real as anyone believed it to be. So So-Elku stopped believ-ing, stopped fighting against what he thought was the Unity's lowest level.

His will relinquished, the Luma master offered himself to the resistance, pulled into it by gravity—and passed through. At once, the cosmos inverted itself. He was right side up in a whole new landscape, one alive with power. Vibrant magenta swirled around him, the waves of energy sensing his sudden arrival in their sanctuary. So-Elku stretched and welcomed the energy into his soul.

Whatever the Unity had shown him before—a perspective of all things interconnected and emergent —it now showed him as power. Pure, unbridled power. That power was behind all the essential questions: How can something be alive? How can a sentient being have a soul? Where did the galaxy's energy come from before all things began? The answers to the greatest questions of the cosmos were here, in what lay below—or perhaps above—the Foundation of all things.

So-Elku let his soul linger in this convergent place —this new place the codex called the Nexus—and risked opening his eyes in the natural realm. The task required an exorbitant amount of concentration and discipline. But the reward was sensational: a surge of power that shamed anything he'd ever experienced before. He looked down at his hands, both glowing in the strange magenta halo he'd discovered with the elders. He felt euphoric. With this new resource, he felt invincible. He would complete the mission forming in his mind. He refused to let the malevolent admiral win, refused to let him jeopardize the cause of true galactic peace—a peace So-Elku would broker. And with his newfound power, he would never let it be compromised. Not by anyone.

So-Elku began to visualize Kane's face. In the

natural realm, Kane was repulsive—pockmarked skin, orbed black eyes, twisted sneer. Instead of that face, So-Elku thought of the one he'd seen when visiting the man in the Unity. The *other* face.

It took immense concentration to achieve such a distance with the ever-sight—to see the admiral on the bridge of his ship. But So-Elku wasn't the grand master for nothing. Lurking beneath Kane's face was another visage that was darker than any he'd ever seen in the cosmos.

At that moment, So-Elku felt *it*—the soul-sucking vacuum that tugged on his life's energy. That ethereal *thing* inside Kane knew the Luma master was there somehow. It was aware of his presence. And it was hungry, reaching out to devour So-Elku's strength.

So-Elku's body jerked as his life force left the Nexus, ripped through the Foundation, and stepped from the Unity. He grabbed the towel and wiped the cold sweat from his forehead and the back of his neck. He saw Moldark's face behind Kane's. That other personality. That ego. *That otherworldly being.*

"Moldark," So-Elku said with a sneer.

So-Elku ran a hand over his face then looked himself over in the mirror. He turned his chin from side to side, examining the thin beard that ran along his jawline like a wire, and noticed that he'd nicked himself shaving. He grabbed the towel again and dabbed the cut on his cheek.

"I'll find a way to stop you, Moldark," So-Elku said. "I'll *make* a way. I swear it."

CAPRIANA WASN'T the Republic's capital for nothing. If there was ever to be a gallery piece that conveyed the supposed merits and majesty of galactic harmony, this was it. It was, by all counts, the convergence of paradise and engineering, a city built from the sea, a jewel on top of a watery world.

So-Elku caught his breath on the ship's bridge as they descended toward the capital. Hundreds of islands of varying sizes made up the enormous crescent-shaped atoll. Sleek skyscrapers rose from the islands, their heights corresponding to each island's position. Those buildings nearest the crescent's tips were shortest whereas those toward the interior were tallest, such that the entire city was arrayed like the ridges of a jeweled crown. The large C shape seemed fitting, given the city's name as if their engineers had planned it that way. *They have enough power and money. Anything's possible.*

Within the city's cradle, massive pleasure cruisers

dotted the sea like glittering gems. Outside of the geometric enclave, smaller floating cities perched on giant stilts like flamingos on spindly legs. The entire picture was as stunning as it was obscene, and So-Elku would have turned away if it hadn't been so mesmerizingly beautiful.

So-Elku's ship approached the city's northern curve, heading for a series of docking platforms. The buildings towered in the evening light like spires made of costly pearl, gleaming surfaces boasting more square kilometers of iridescent windowplex than he'd ever seen. Translucent tubes linked one building to the next, even across islands. Composite gantries extended high above the water to support bubble-like pods that appeared to defy gravity.

Despite his animosity toward the bloated under-belly of organized bureaucracy, So-Elku admitted that it knew how to build a megalopolis. Knowing the construction had been funded with the blood of a hundred sentient species, however, kept him grounded, just like the ship as it touched down with a slight jostle. He would not be shaken by their charms, not dissuaded by offers of power. Their power really belonged to him, anyway. *They'd* ruled for too long and at the end of a blaster muzzle. The galaxy deserved something else, something new. It deserved peace, and those who resisted it deserved exile.

"If you're ready, Master," the flight steward said from the bridge entrance. So-Elku turned. The young man gestured toward the exit, inclining his head.

"I am ready. Let's proceed."

So-Elku walked with twelve Luma elders in his entourage, each committed to his cause. They strode through the great hallways and corridors of the Forum Republica, making their way to Proconsul Tower where *they'd* be meeting.

His elders' robes swept over the white marble floors like undulating ocean waves rippling in the twilight. Each step his retinue took was methodical— soft shoes silent in the cavernous spaces, clasped hands hidden beneath long sleeves, heads lowered beneath hoods, eyes forward. Senate staff stepped aside as the Luma passed, evoking hushed conversations and pointing. The Senate was no longer in session at this hour, but the work of running the Republic never ceased.

So-Elku's entourage passed the Senate chamber, White Gardens Court, and Representative Hall until they reached the Proconsul Tower's elevators. The ride up provided a panoramic view of the city's seaside cradle, the setting sun filling the bowl with pink light. So-Elku's thoughts turned toward the Nexus, the warm hue reminding him of the energy that flowed beneath the Foundation. He could sense it. It called to him—longed for him. And he would use it. He would learn to master it, and he would usher in a new era of ultimate peace.

The elevator doors opened, and So-Elku turned, his retinue emerging from the pod into an atrium. Even from here, So-Elku could see the larger dome of Proconsul Chamber rising outside the clear ceiling.

He looked down to see a woman behind a grand shell-like desk, the chamber doors sealed shut behind her. Her hair was pulled tight in a bun, and she wore the white dress coat of the Senate staff, trimmed in light blue.

"May I help you?" She sounded inconvenienced, as if she'd just been interrupted while reading a particularly engrossing novel or holo-vid.

One of So-Elku's elders stepped forward. "Master Luma So-Elku of Plumeria, Worru, to see *the members*," the man replied, his voice echoing off the walls.

The woman looked down and scanned their

group. Then, as if she'd no more than read some disappointing headline on a news feed, she said, "It seems they're not expecting you."

"No," So-Elku agreed, stepping forward, "they most certainly are not."

The woman looked confused. "Then I don't see what you expect to—"

"We will see them now." He walked around her desk, followed by the elders, and headed toward the doors.

The woman leapt to her feet, attempting to impede their progress. "Excuse me," she said, hands on her hips, "but what do you think you're doing?"

"I thought I made myself clear."

The woman suddenly froze in place, suspended as if in a wide-eyed trance. He'd release her when they left.

Satisfied, So-Elku returned to the doors and caused them to open. A darkened room—the windowplex adjusted to block the light—was illuminated by soft lights spaced around its circular perimeter. Nine figures sat at a circular table, all of them turning to see who'd interrupted their meeting. Each held up a hand to block the glare from the anteroom.

So-Elku smiled.

"What's the meaning of this?" a man asked.

"You're supposed to use the intercom," another said, apparently assuming the secretary had walked in.

So-Elku spread his arms, and his twelve elders spread out to surround the table. The senators rose in surprise as their room was flooded with guests.

"What's going on?" a third man asked. So-Elku sensed the man's unease. The question was followed by several more of the same kind, each demanding an explanation. Their voices were still authoritarian, confident, and proud. But that would change.

Without turning, So-Elku shut the doors. With the glare gone, the senators lowered their hands, their faces emerging in the soft light.

"Sit, sit," So-Elku said, beginning to circle the table. "Please, gentlemen."

"What is the meaning of this interruption, So-Elku?" asked a stocky man with thick shoulders. It was Senator Blackman.

"A marvelous question," So-Elku said with a chuckle.

Blackman let out an exasperated breath and leaned over to the comm panel on the table. "I'm calling security."

"I said *sit*."

With a sudden *wump*, all the senators fell into their

padded chairs, hands clamped to their armrests. The men glanced at each other, eyes wide.

So-Elku steepled his fingers and looked around the room at the others. "So this is the Circle of Nine. How exciting! I've heard *so much* about you."

The senators looked among one another.

"Oh, don't worry," So-Elku continued. "Your secret meetings aren't public knowledge. You're safe." He let out a laugh. "Relatively speaking, of course."

"What do you want?" Blackman asked.

"What do *I* want?" So-Elku raised his eyebrows, though he doubted the gesture would be noticed. "Well, now, that's an interesting question. My assumption was that these meetings were all about what *you* wanted."

Blackman glared at him but kept his mouth shut.

"And what is it that you want?" So-Elku asked, tapping a finger to his chin. "Oh, that's right. You wanted me *executed*."

Recognition dawned on the faces around the table. Eyes darted away from So-Elku and stared at each other.

"Yes, that's right. Your pet project Admiral Kane, is it?—was sent to kill me, by order of the Circle of Nine."

"We don't know what you're—"

"Please, Senator… what is it, Senator Miller? I see your thoughts like a holo-vid. You do know what I'm talking about. In fact…" So-Elku paused to examine a loose thread in the Unity. "I believe *you* were the first to affirm the motion."

The man blanched and jerked back in his chair.

"And you, Senator Long—you gave Kane complete latitude to take my life *by any means necessary*, isn't that right?" The senator refused to look at the Luma master, his eyes remaining fixed straight ahead. "That decision cost hundreds of lives—all students in the dormitory."

At this piece of information, the senators looked frantically at one another for verification.

"So the news hasn't reached you yet? Well," So-Elku said, shrugging, "it seems we can't be as all-knowing as we'd like, now, can we. In any event, I assume it's clear that Kane *did not* kill me, and you should be wondering why."

"You killed him?" Blackman asked.

"For all the mystics!" So-Elku spat. "Why is everything always about killing, killing, killing with you people? You do realize events can change *without* having to kill someone, right?" He waited for an answer. "*Right?*"

No one moved.

"No, I did not kill him," So-Elku continued. "We struck a deal."

"A deal?" Blackman asked. "What kind of a deal?"

"What kind of a deal, yes! What a marvelous question. Isn't that a marvelous question, senators?" So-Elku began moving around the table, brushing the top of each chair back with his hand. "It would seem, *senators*, that your puppet has gone rogue."

"Rogue? What do you mean?" Blackman asked.

"As in, he's no longer yours, he's no longer following orders, and he's no longer interested in doing your bidding! That kind of *rogue*."

"And how would you know this?"

"Because he sent me here to assassinate *you*."

Gasps filled the room as So-Elku moved behind Blackman's chair. The senators squirmed, still unable to move their arms.

"Fabrication!" one senator cried.

"Yes," echoed others. "Here, here!"

So-Elku marveled at how easily political power fought to preserve itself in the face of certain death. At least their Republic Marines knew how to face defeat with honor. Instead, these snakes would look for every other way out *but* honor.

"*Fabrication*," So-Elku repeated softly. "I wouldn't be so sure about that."

He snapped his fingers, and one of his elders sent a holo-pad sliding to the middle of the polished table. An image burst to life over the black-stained wood, glowing in the dimly lit room. In it, Admiral Kane could be seen surrounded by two dozen black-clad troopers. They faced So-Elku and his elders, discussing something.

"Listen," So-Elku said, "this is my favorite part."

"They have betrayed me, betrayed their own," the admiral in the vid said.

So-Elku watched the senators' faces as they tried to connect the strange voice to Kane's face. It was an exercise in futility.

"They deserve to die. All of them. And you will do this for me. You will execute the Circle of Nine one by one by one."

The holo-vid stopped and faded to black. No one moved. So-Elku let the tension hang in silence. Finally, he asked, "So, what now? What's the Luma master going to do?" He placed his hands on Blackman's shoulders, and the senator sucked in a startled breath. "Don't worry, Senator Blackman. I'm not going to kill you."

"Why not?"

"Why not? Why, isn't it obvious?" Again, So-Elku waited for someone to reply, but no one spoke. "Because I've been given a *gift*. You see," he said, moving to kneel beside Blackman, "I hate that monster. Maybe more than you, maybe less—who knows? But I hate him. He's already disobeyed your orders more than once, and you can't afford to let him off his leash. I can't afford to live in a galaxy where he roams free, so we both want the same thing."

"That's your gift?" Senator Miller asked.

"No, Senator. That's the context. The *gift* is that your admiral doesn't know I'm going to let you survive."

"And do what with us?"

So-Elku smiled, glaring into Senator Blackman's eyes. "Whatever I want, Senator. Whatever I want."

7

Magnus sat beside Abimbola in the front seat of a skiff that resembled a welder's psychotic break more than it did a reliable transport vehicle. The monstrosity was three times the size of a dune skiff and sported rusting plate armor on all sides. An angled cowling with slats covered the cockpit, while a spiked battering ram protruded from the front. The skiff's sides and rear were clad in reinforced metal with razor wire welded to the surface.

Above and behind them, a Marauder in a shielded turret rested against an M109 twin-barrel blaster, a lit roll of snash hanging from the corner of his mouth. Another man sat inside the skiff at a holo-station with targeting screens. The images came from four different rocket bays around the skiff—two forward, two in back. Six more Marauders lay in wait in the rear cargo bay, their weapons at the ready.

Magnus listened to the skiff's engine growl against the sand and the wind. Like everything else on the contraption, the power plant was heavily modified, boasting nearly five times the energy of a normal skiff's. As a result, not only could Abimbola's ride carry the crew and armament with ease, but it also soared six meters above the ground. That meant less driving around debris and much more driving over it —or, as Magnus noted, through it. *Hell's Basket Case*, as Abimbola had dubbed her—the moniker stenciled on the tail in red and yellow paint—was made for one thing: doling out death with extreme prejudice.

Magnus looked to his right at the line of similarly constructed vehicles that angled toward the horizon, the dust cloud blotting out the sky behind them. Some of them were smaller, sporting missile silos that left little room for a driver. Others were monstrous troop carriers, their front ends donning hydraulic wedge plows used for tearing into and separating solid walls for entry. Still others had second levels for added weapons arrays and observation lookouts. To an enemy, this was a ferocious sight.

"So, you sure about this plan?" Magnus shouted over his ear comm. He wore a black bandana, sunglasses, and the armor Abimbola had provided. His MAR30 rested on his lap, the Z and several grenades in his chest armor.

The giant beside him wore the same cut-off shirt and green pants as before. The skiff's controls seemed so small in the shadow of his hulking body. Sweat beaded on the man's smooth black skin, and the old scar that ran from head to collarbone was swollen in the heat. Against his seat, Abimbola rested some sort of enlarged blaster that Magnus had never seen before, presumably a piece from his home world of Limbia Centrella. Its main barrel, twice the diameter of any hand weapon Magnus had ever fired, was housed in a boxy vented stock with two assault grips.

"You like it?" Abimbola asked as Magnus regarded the weapon.

"She looks like a handful."

"Ha, she is. She really is." Abimbola patted the weapon. "A BFT6, known as the Tigress where I come from."

"Yeah, well, that's known as a wrist breaker where I come from. Better you than me."

Abimbola smiled and flicked the pair of dice that hung from his rearview mirror. "So, you asked if I am sure about the plan. Yes, I am sure about the plan, buckethead. We will enter the city from the east then meet up with the mwadim for permission. He will provide us with the intel from his sources."

"The Tawnhack sources?"

Abimbola nodded.

Magnus didn't like the idea of using Jujari as HUMIT—human intelligence. SAVIT was more like it—savage intelligence. He also didn't like meeting the new mwadim, whoever he was. Still, if working with these hyenas meant rescuing any of his unit, then it was worth it. He'd just have to suck it up and play nice with the puppies.

"You should not worry," Abimbola said, seeming to sense Magnus's apprehension. "They want those hostages alive too. Means a bargaining chip in their pocket for Republic negotiations if you play it right. You will know what to do."

"Copy that," Magnus said, suddenly wondering if the Tawnhack could be trusted when this was all over. "Who's to say they don't double-cross us and keep the hostages for themselves once we rescue them?"

"You mean, double-cross *you*."

"What?"

"You said *we*, but I have nothing to worry about. No double-crossing here. Just you."

"Perfect." Magnus looked ahead at the city growing on the horizon. The city's towers brought back all the memories from the ambush. His chest tightened. He'd almost died in those streets. So had Awen.

Awen. He missed her. For the hundredth time, he wondered how she was. But to keep his heart from overextending itself, he reminded himself that Awen had been just a mission. One he'd carried out faithfully. Now he had a new mission—one he'd be just as dedicated to.

"Stick to the plan," Abimbola said again with his hand on the wheel and a wide smile spreading across his face. "Just stick to the plan."

───────────────

"I'D COME WITH YOU, you know," the senator's widow told Magnus, clasping his hands. "I'd fight alongside you, as before."

They stood alone under a canvas awning, shielded from the morning sun. He'd just finished the briefing with Abimbola and was preparing to leave, filling his canteens from the well, when Valerie had found him. She'd snuck up on him—startled him really. But he tried to play it off. Magnus turned around and caught his breath yet again when he saw her. How could beauty be intimidating? He didn't know, but hers was.

"But Piper needs me more. I hope you understand."

"I do." Magnus nodded.

"You rescue your unit, you hear me? But then I need you back here. I need you to get Piper to safety —off this planet, away from here. Do you understand?"

"I'll do my best, Mrs. Stone."

"*Valerie*, please. Just Valerie," she said, looking down. Her amber hair glistened in the light, threatening to blend in with the sand surrounding them. When her eyes returned to his, they were wet with tears. "I fear that family name has died in me. But we've had enough death for a long time. So no dying out there, understand?"

What is this? Genuine concern? Or something else? Something... deeper? His heart pounded, the feeling of her hands in his sending an unexpected burst of dopamine through his system.

Magnus blinked some sand from his eyes and cursed himself for thinking of this woman in any other way than as a traumatized victim of a war-torn galaxy. This wasn't the time for... any of *that*. This woman needed help, needed to get her daughter to safety. And she only lost her husband… how many days ago? Call it a week. She's mourning, bereaved. This is no romantic come-on by some tavern skirt. *Get your head in gear, Magnus!*

"I'll be back before you know it, and then we'll have you and Piper on a Republic ship and on your way to Capriana."

"Not Capriana, no." She squeezed his hands harder.

"Not Capriana?" Magnus asked slowly.

Valerie shook her head. "Somewhere else. Somewhere safe."

Since when is Capriana not safe? What is this woman caught up in?

"Just come back to me, Magnus. Promise?"

The feelings returned. *Damn those feelings!* But before he could protest further, before he could even utter an answer, Valerie pulled herself up to his face and kissed him on the cheek. Her lips were warm, her face fragrant. Then she let go, turned, and evaporated into the warehouse.

Magnus reached for his canteens, but he'd knocked all three into the well.

———

OOSAFAR WAS close enough that Magnus thought he smelled it maybe ten klicks out. He trusted Abimbola's knowledge of this place, but that didn't make entering a hostile territory any easier. The other vehicles fell in line behind Abimbola's as the convoy prepared to enter the city's outskirts. If there was going to be any initial resistance, this was it. He'd laid siege to enough cities to know that plenty of fighting could take place before you ever set foot on the enduracrete.

Magnus always got amped just before a firefight. He figured they still had a way to go before they made contact with any Selskrit in the Western Heights, but to him, one Jujari was just as dangerous as the next. He removed his Z from his chest holster, double-checked it, then stowed it. Out of pure habit, he powered up the holo-sights on his MAR30 and cycled through its three firing systems.

There was plenty to worry about on this mission. There were many variables in play, not the least of which was a dramatically stronger enemy and unreliable intel. But more than anything, Magnus was worried about going in with an inexperienced unit. He was worried about jeopardizing Dutch and the others again.

He didn't doubt the Marauders could fight.

Abimbola had surely seen to that. Whatever Abimbola's past was on Limbia Centrella, it had made him one badass son of a bitch. But Abimbola's Marauders were not Recon. Not by a long shot. They had violence of force, maybe, but no unit cohesion, movement orchestration, or tactical precision. Not even Dutch and the others had that sort of training.

Disobeyed orders meant lives lost. Faulty steps meant lives lost. Dirty gear, jammed weapons, and missed commands—all of that meant lives they couldn't afford to lose, lives Magnus didn't *want* to lose. He was leading a ragtag bunch of miscreants, Marines, and a navy warrant officer on a suicide mission to rescue hostages he wasn't even sure were still alive. And he'd promised a beautiful woman he'd get her and her daughter off the planet once he got back. *Go for broke, Magnus. Go for broke.*

He reached for one of the canteens in his backpack behind the seat, undid the top, and took a swig. The water was hot. It was not even late morning, and already the sun was baking everything in the skiff— even with the constant headwind. He was going to be glad to get off this dust ball again.

Just ahead, Magnus noticed a checkpoint. A tall sandstone gate swept down to each side of the road, forming a low wall that stretched out in either direction. The gate was elegant if nothing else. The Jujari had a strange contradiction about them—their penchant for beauty, in things like architecture, stood against their brutal barbarian behavior. He wondered how such a violent species could endure so long and amass—much less utilize—so much technology. They were truly an enigma. *Perhaps that's why Awen likes them so much*, he thought then realized that statement might be taken as a slight rather than a compliment. *Well, she's an enigma too.*

Four Jujari emerged from two small gatehouses on either side of the thoroughfare, keeltari swords drawn and at the ready.

"Let me do the talking," Abimbola said.

"Be my guest."

The drive core whined as it worked to slow the skiff's momentum. The vehicle shuddered and sank to a half meter above the ground, a shower of sand and dust blasting in all directions. The Jujari sentries turned their heads only slightly as the wind matted their fur against their bodies. Magnus was aware of the rest of the vehicles clunking to a stop behind them and wondered if they'd be rammed. To their credit, Abimbola's men eased the entire line of vehicles to a halt without a single bump.

Abimbola unlatched several metal clasps and

forced the slatted armor window away on its hinge. He gestured for Magnus to do the same. The sentries approached, two at each door. Despite how high Abimbola and Magnus sat, the Jujari still managed to meet them at eye level.

"What business are you having done here?" snarled the lead sentry, the common speech garbled between his fangs.

Abimbola dipped his head and tilted it away from the Jujari, baring his neck. "Me and the boys," he said, thumbing behind him as he returned the Jujari's glare, "thought we would do some Selskrit hunting."

The lead sentry chomped the air at the mention of the rival tribe's name. The other three growled, their hackles standing up.

"I do not suppose you want to join us?" Abimbola asked.

"We would," the sentry said, "if we had not already had our fill earlier in this day."

"Did you leave any for us, then?"

"Perhaps." The sentry looked at Magnus. "Who is this him?"

"This him? Just another of my crew."

"He smells different." The big Jujari sniffed the air some more. "Smells like Repub."

"This guy? Repub? Nah. You probably just smell

the new armor he got. Picked it up off some dead soldiers not more than a few days ago."

The sentry eyed him. "Where?"

"Where what?"

"Where did you find the soldiers?"

"Out past Kellax Ridge. Some escape pods. You probably saw them go down, right?"

The sentry paused, looking between the two men. Magnus felt his grip on his MAR30 tightening. He couldn't think of a single thing that he liked about these beasts. "Very all right," the pooch said, mixing his vernacular to sound far more affirmative than he probably meant. "Who are you going to meet?"

"Rohoar," Abimbola said.

Apparently, this name meant something to the sentries. At once, they dipped their heads and bared their necks. Magnus raised his eyebrows and looked at Abimbola, but the warlord waved him off with a curt shake of his head.

The sentries looked up and stepped away, waving Abimbola through. "You may proceed. And find happy hunting of our bastard kin."

"Thank you." Abimbola flipped them each a poker chip. Magnus had no idea if the Jujari gambled, at least as humanoids did, but the beasts seemed appreciative of the currency. The warlord pressed on the accelerator, and the drive core jolted to life, the skiff lurching forward.

"I guess Rohoar is a good friend to have," Magnus said once they were through.

"Friend, no. But we respect one another, and sometimes that is better than friendship."

"So, he's one of the bosses around here, then?"

"He is the new mwadim."

"The new mwadim?" Magnus stroked his beard. "The old one didn't do so well in that blast."

"No, he did not. They are still mourning him and will for the next year."

"So, in the meantime, they picked a new one?"

"No picking. Fighting. Whoever wants to be mwadim kills all challengers until no one challenges him or he dies. If he dies, combat resumes for the victor in the same way."

Magnus whistled. "Pays to have a good campaign manager, then."

"A good what?"

"Campaign managers. Pay off your competition, put hits on…" He glanced at the giant's blank face. "You know what? Never mind."

Abimbola glanced at Magnus then looked back at the road. "You are strange, buckethead. One minute,

I think I like you. The next, I don't think I like you. So you are like a dog to me."

"I'm… like a dog…"

"Yes. If I like you, I keep feeding you. If I do not, I kick you. We will see how the day ends."

"Fair enough," Magnus said, looking up at the buildings. "Fair eee-nough."

THE CONVOY DROVE through the main thoroughfare of Oosafar, weapons at the ready. Abimbola gave short instructions over comms to keep everyone focused. "No sudden movements, keep it smooth, and don't look any Jujari in the eye."

Unlike the first time Magnus had been here, the city was alive with activity. Everywhere he looked, Jujari were barking, selling, wrestling, howling, trading, and eating. Pups kept close to their mothers. Adolescent males huddled in small packs. Older hyenas lounged in wide chairs with soft cushions on balconies that overlooked the street.

The city was much fairer than Magnus remembered it. Parks stood like oases amongst the towering skyscrapers. Palms waved, and water gardens filled the air with the sounds and smells of waterfalls. It was cleaner, too, though the smell still threatened to over-take him. The first time in Oosafar, he'd had his helmet on to filter the air, at least at the beginning. Now the pungent scent of dog permeated the air.

High overhead, Magnus made out the white curtains in every window on every level of every building. He saw the subtle blue glow of the force fields that kept out the elements. The wind played with the fabric, making it move like ghosts. *What did Awen call them again? Inook shrouds?*

The haunting movement took him back to the mwadim's tower. A chill ran up his spine. Throughout the city, Magnus felt thousands and thousands of eyes studying the convoy. The thought of another ambush made him ready his MAR30 out of pure instinct.

"Easy, buckethead."

Magnus looked at Abimbola. The giant reached over and placed a hand on top of his MAR30. "No need for that just yet. We do not want to start any wars we cannot finish."

Magnus lowered his weapon and looked out the right side of the skiff. "You don't worry about an ambush?"

"Sure. But those who ambush us are more worried about the mwadim."

"So you're *not* worried about an ambush."

"Right."

Magnus chuckled. "Fair enough."

The convoy moved farther and farther until Magnus felt like they were in the city's center. Something about the buildings felt familiar. And then he saw it—the ruins of the mwadim's tower. The entire structure was a heap of sandstone and metal girders. The air was sharp, filled with stale smoke and burned hair. The buildings around it were black with soot, many of them bearing shrapnel pockmarks.

"Look familiar?" Abimbola asked.

Magnus nodded. "The mwadim's tower."

"*Former* mwadim's tower."

"Right." Magnus strained to find the building he'd rappelled down with Awen in his arms. He picked it out because the grappling hook was still embedded in the sandstone, a gossamer-thin nanocable trailing in the wind. The more Magnus thought about it, the more he realized their escape had been a complete miracle. They'd been this deep in the city, yet not more than three Jujari had tried to prevent their escape. It was almost as if—

He shook the thought from his head. No, the Jujari wouldn't let anyone go free, not after what happened.

"The new mwadim's tower is there, at least until

his real one can be constructed." Abimbola pointed to a rather large skyscraper one block to the west. It rivaled what Magnus remembered of the other tower but definitely seemed shorter.

"You just gotta be taller than everyone else's towers, don't you?" Magnus said to the sky.

Abimbola faced Magnus. "I cannot help what the gods blessed me with, buckethead."

Magnus glanced at him, unsure what to make of the comment. But when Abimbola smiled and let out a laugh, Magnus realized the man had a sense of humor after all. He laughed with him, and the skiff pressed on toward the *new* mwadim's temporary home—all forty-some-odd stories of it.

MAGNUS AND ABIMBOLA were escorted into a waiting room while the rest of their fighting force remained in the vehicles. The room was covered in wall-to-wall white fabric with a bowl of fruit and a central column of fabric in the middle.

"Fladder," Magnus said. "The fruit of welcome, I know."

"*Fladaria*," Abimbola corrected as he took one of the succulent red orbs and bit into it. Magnus did the same and let the maroon trickle run down his lip. "So, you *have* studied a little of your enemy, then. Very good."

"It's more of a hobby really," Magnus said, thinking of Awen's scolding the last time they'd been in this situation.

"Listen, no matter what happens up there," Abimbola said, taking another bite and wiping his mouth, "do not back down."

"What do you mean?"

"Well, if you had studied more in your hobby, maybe with the dau Lothlinium woman, you would know the Jujari move aggressively toward any sign of weakness. So no matter what, when we speak to the mwadim, stand your ground."

"Is there something you're not telling me?"

"What?" Abimbola scowled at him. "No, not at all. Just standard procedure. Stand your ground. Do not show weakness."

"Copy that." Magnus had a bad feeling about this.

Once they'd finished the fruit, a sentry appeared, his shoulders matted with blood. At first, Magnus thought it was Chief, the blood wolf who'd greeted him last time, but he soon realized it couldn't be. Magnus was no expert in distinguishing one Jujari from the next, but that Jujari had been blasted to bits in the explosion. The carnage on that building top had been gruesome.

"The mwadim wishes to make intercourse with you," the sentry said.

"Intercourse?" Magnus asked under his breath.

"As in discourse," Abimbola whispered. "Dip your head and tilt. Dip and tilt."

Magnus did as he was told, and the sentry sniffed the air in acceptance.

"We are humbled by the meeting," Abimbola said, pressing a poker chip into the Jujari's paw. "Lead the way, and we will follow."

The sentry turned and passed through the thick white fabric. Unlike the last time, when the entourage of Luma and Marines had ascended a long and winding ramp, this time Magnus strode into an elevator that seemed to be centered in the building's layout. The doors closed with the three warriors inside, each startlingly different from the next. Magnus tried not to wince at the Jujari's odor; the beast smelled as if he hadn't bathed in weeks. Magnus wondered if his own scent was equally repulsive.

Heavy breathing and the elevator's hum were the only sounds as the floor counter changed shape in Jujari script. Eventually, the lift slowed, and the doors opened onto a beautiful terrace. Wide swaths of fabric billowed overhead, shielding the platform from the sun, while fountains and their streams fed patches of greenery and planters of desert flowers. Female Jujari moved about the scene, their long sinewy limbs making them markedly different from the males. Some sat with male counterparts, while others served trays of meat and jars of... whatever beverage the Jujari elite favored.

The sentry walked forward toward a raised dais, but unlike the last one, which had been decorated in exotic red-and-gold fabrics and secluded behind a massive curtain, this platform was simple and exposed on all sides. Atop it was a low table with several cushions, each occupied by a Jujari. Altogether, there were two males and two females. They appeared to be lounging on the mwadim's throne mount. The scene was totally different from the one he'd encountered before—far more casual.

The sentry yipped something in their mother tongue and bowed. Abimbola bowed deeply, and Magnus followed suit, trying not to stare at the four Jujari on the dais. Then the tallest one bade the men approach. There was something familiar about him

—the color of his fur, the shape of his head, the size of his shoulders.

"Abimbola," the mwadim said, now distinguishing himself from the others by moving down the dais. "Rohoar sees his Miblimbian warlord. How are you?" The mwadim spoke with surprising dexterity in Galactic common despite still garbling the words a little. Magnus knew that voice.

"It is good to see you again, Great Mwadim. We have come to seek your permission to hunt Selskrit, as previously discussed."

"It is a good day for hunting. But tell Rohoar— who is this?" The mwadim gestured at Magnus.

Magnus removed his sunglasses and stepped forward. "My name is Adonis Olin Magnus, and I am a Marauder." While he had yet to be honorably discharged, this statement was truer than he cared to recognize. He would never be a Marine again, at least not active duty.

The mwadim eyed him and paused. His gaze was uncomfortable. Magnus glanced at Abimbola, but the warlord jerked his head back toward the mwadim.

"Rohoar does not think so."

"And how's that?"

"Rohoar knows you."

"You know me?" Magnus asked.

"And you are not a Marauder. You smell"—the mwadim sniffed the air—"like Republic. And you've been here before."

Magnus swallowed, having felt bad for attempting to conceal his identity. Moreover, he wondered where this line of questioning would go. His weapons were back in the skiff, and he doubted they'd survive a melee for more than a few seconds.

A melee in the mwadim's tower... Suddenly, Magnus saw this mwadim's face again. They *had* met. But how did he survive? That would have been impossible!

"Chief?" he asked.

"What?" The Mwadim's ears bent back.

"What?" Abimbola echoed.

Magnus felt like an idiot for even saying it aloud. *Chief* was what he'd called this Jujari, but it wasn't his real name. "You're right, Great Mwadim," Magnus said. "We *have* met before. When the Luma were—"

"You are a *Marine!*" the mwadim growled, stepping forward.

This wasn't good. *Stand your ground, Magnus.* "Yes, but I was here to—"

"And you fired at Jujari in the mwadim's temple."

Aw, splick. There it is.

Time froze for Magnus as he considered his

options: lie and risk being caught in it or tell the truth and risk being filleted alive. Either way, he was dead.

Screw it. "Yes, I killed Jujari in an effort to complete my mission."

The mwadim was one stride away now, teeth bared in a sneer so cold it made Magnus's blood chill. He wanted to find cover, find a weapon, find some tactical advantage. But he had nowhere to go and no weapons to employ besides his fists—and those were no match for Jujari physiology.

"And was it worth it?" the mwadim asked.

Magnus hesitated. What a strange question. "Do you mean, was my mission worth killing for?"

The mwadim gave his version of a nod. "Worth killing Rohoar's kinsmen."

Magnus thought about it. Seeing as how he was about to meet an untimely end, he wanted to answer truthfully. He pictured Awen lying beside the mwadim, covered in blood and gore. He pictured her in his arms as they rappelled down the building. Then she saved them—twice. He saw her showered and in new clothes on Ezo's ship. She was, in his imagination, the picture of hope, struggling to find virtue in the rest of the galaxy, no matter how misguided that was. Where he was a cynic, she was an optimist. Where he believed in the sword, she contended for dialogue. It frustrated him to no end. *She* frustrated him. But was she worth killing for?

Magnus looked up at the mwadim and squared his shoulders. "Yes, she was worth it. And I would have slain a thousand more if it meant preserving her life."

8

"You still haven't told me where Daddy is," Piper said.

Valerie sat with her daughter beneath a canvas tarp on a third-story balcony overlooking the dunes. The sun had yet to reach midday, but already, the air was stifling. Still, anything was better than being cooped up inside Abimbola's makeshift headquarters. It consisted of nothing more than dozens of metal ovens connected by underground tunnels. The coolest room had been sick bay, and that was because it was underground. Valerie had already spent enough time down there—and enough time in triage lines—to last a lifetime. Still, she wondered if this conversation was any safer than a battlefield.

Valerie studied Piper, her beautiful daughter. The

little girl's face was freckled and dirt smudged. Valerie pushed wisps of loose blond hair behind Piper's ears then marveled at her wonderfully blue eyes and petite features.

You still haven't told me where Daddy is. The issue was not whether Piper should be told the truth—Valerie would never lie to her. She'd come from too many lies to ever wish that childhood on someone else, let alone her own flesh and blood. The real question was, how much truth should she tell the girl? How much could she handle?

Valerie was having a hard time handling the truth herself. There was no easy way to tell a child she'd inadvertently committed patricide. It would ruin her. Forever. But Piper also needed to know about her gift and her history. *If only my mother were here.* If her mother was still alive, she had to get Piper to her somehow.

"Listen, baby," Valerie said, aware of the tears sliding down her cheeks. "Daddy is dead. Daddy's not coming back."

"Why?" Piper's lower lip had stiffened.

Valerie knew her daughter was trying to be tough, and it broke her heart. No child should have to be that strong. *Why? Because evil men wanted your father to give you up,* she wanted to say. *Politics and power claim to regard life, but in the end, they only seek to preserve themselves. Why? Because in any other time in the galaxy, you would have been celebrated, Piper. But today, you are hunted. And instead of being nurtured in the ways of the Unity, you are left to stumble through the wreckage of actions beyond your control.*

But Valerie couldn't say that to her daughter. She wouldn't. She would not rob the little girl of even more of her childhood just so she herself could have a clear conscience and feel morally clean. Valerie would hold on to the truth for a little while longer and preserve the beauty of her daughter's innocence. Mystics knew it wouldn't last much longer.

"The escape pods," Valerie said. "He didn't survive the trip."

"Oh," Piper said in a voice so small Valerie thought the girl would vanish.

"It was dangerous, and he knew that. But he wanted us to be safe, and it was worth the risk."

"Mr. Lieutenant Magnus buried him, then? In the desert?"

"Yes, my heart," Valerie said, choking back more tears. "Yes, he did, so we didn't have to."

"Okay."

Valerie reached forward and pulled the girl to her chest, then wrapped her in her arms. She kissed the top of her head long and hard, more tears rolling into the child's golden hair. Piper whimpered against Valerie's chest but did not let go fully. She was restrained even in grief.

"I was so worried," Piper said, mouth muffled under Valerie's grip.

"Worried?" Valerie sat Piper up on her lap and looked in her face. "Worried about what, baby?"

"I was worried"—Piper sniffed, smudging tears and grime in streaks across her cheeks— "that maybe I had hurt Daddy. That my power had, had... that maybe *I* killed him."

"Piper, no!" Valerie said. She lied for all she was worth without even given it a second thought. All morals, all ethics, all arguments died in her mad rush to keep her daughter from leaping off the precipice that summoned anyone who dared get too close. "Don't think such things! Your daddy died in the escape pod. You had nothing to do with it. You hear me?" Valerie snapped Piper to her chest again as the little girl started sobbing. "Your gift only gives life, Piper."

She'd repeated this phrase a hundred times before, but at bedtimes and on long walks. She never imagined she'd be saying it at a time like this. "You only give life. You hear me? You only give life."

"Yes, Mama," Piper said, trembling in grief.

Valerie and Piper wept together under the canvas tarp in the makeshift chairs on the hot planet. They rocked for several minutes, Piper grieving over her father, Valerie grieving over her daughter.

The truth was, Valerie missed Darin. She'd loved him. But the marriage had been... the result of two careers that were supposed to collide to make a strong legacy within the Republic. He was the next Stone in a long line of respected senators; she was a decorated veteran and a budding doctor. Together, they'd been given more praise and political power than any young couple their age. They hadn't been creating a legacy —they'd been forging a dynasty. But it was never meant to last.

Valerie looked westward at the horizon. Magnus was out there, fighting for his Marines, fighting to bring them back alive. She admired that—no, she *loved* that. It was in her blood too. She'd done the same things. Those days felt like a lifetime ago, before Capriana, Senate dinners, and the commemorative galas. Even while she was dancing, she'd felt an MC90 in her hands.

Valerie fought off flashbacks of firefights and screams for a medic. She'd lived and died a thousand times in her dreams and wished she could go back to kill more of the enemy and save more Marines. So fighting outside the village beside Magnus just before the orbital strike, or escaping from the Bull Wraith and being blindly flung into the void in an escape pod —those had been the most exciting moments of her life, at least in a long, long time.

Magnus had made those moments happen. He'd called her back from the dead—back from a life of silverware and sycophants. He'd rescued her in more ways than one. When she was with him, she felt alive.

"I saved you, right, Mama?" Piper said from beneath her arms.

"What's that?" Valerie pulled the girl up to look in her face.

"I saved you. When the starship shot us. I protected you, didn't I? You always say my gift gives life. So I protected life."

"Yes. Yes, you did, my love. You saved me and everyone else."

"But not Mr. Lieutenant Magnus's eyes. You did that."

Valerie smiled. "I tried. I gave him new ones. But trust me, your gift is far better than mine."

"I felt it coming, Mama."

"Felt what?"

"The starship's big blaster bolt."

Valerie stared at Piper. "You... felt it coming?"

"Uh-huh. I heard them talking. Someone told someone else to fire. Then I saw the big gun. It was aimed at the village. So I reached out and pulled everyone close. Like when you hold me. So they wouldn't feel afraid."

Several moments passed while Valerie tried to make sense of her daughter's words.

"Mama?"

The little girl was a telepath, but more so than Valerie had ever been. More than even Valerie's mother had been. Is it even possible to hear orders on a starship or see an orbital strike before it's fired?

"Mama, are you okay?"

"I'm fine, baby." Valerie reached out and wiped one of Piper's tears away with her thumb. "You are a marvel and a wonder, you know that?"

"You tell me all the time, Mama."

"I know." Valerie sighed. "I know." Then she reached out and hugged her daughter again, but this time, it was to conceal her fear.

9

AWEN STOOD in the middle of the circle with the pedestal and the empty black box beside her. If she was to enter the Unity anywhere in the city, this was the place.

"You okay, love?" Sootriman said from outside the golden floral designs on the floor, her voice swallowed in the cavernous room.

Awen nodded. "I'm okay."

"You've got this," Ezo said.

"Give them hell," TO-96 added.

Ezo shoved the bot sideways. "No, 'Six. Wrong context."

"My apologies."

"It's all right, Ninety-Six. You always help me." Awen lifted her chin and closed her eyes. This was it.

Perspiration moistened her clothes and hair. Awen focused on taking long, steady breaths. She could feel her heart rate begin to slow. In the darkness of her mind, she was alone. All was quiet. Perhaps this wouldn't be so difficult after all.

But that conclusion had been premature. Like a rogue wave crashing onto an unsuspecting beach, the image of Sootriman and Kane hanging from the rappelling line appeared before her. Her heart rate quickened. She tried to tell herself it wasn't real anymore, that it was in the past. But the mind had a funny way of believing what it wanted to. She tried to push the memory aside, tried to rush past it and charge into the space beyond, but it followed her like the painted eyes of an old portrait. If she was going to enter the Unity, she had to walk through this memory.

Sootriman's calls pleaded with her, as did Kane's taunting. She trembled, not sure if she could stand to see *his* face again. She knew how this ended, of course: Sootriman survived, Awen moved the rubble from the doorway, and they sought refuge in one of the seven tunnels beyond the rotunda.

So why is this so terrifying?

Because of *him*.

No, it wasn't a him; it was an *it*. It was not of this

world—not of any world, at least not one she wanted to visit. Inside Kane lurked a monster, the likes of which she had never read about, either in children's books or Luma books. She'd seen it once, and that was enough. To face this again was… well, it was the whole reason she'd waited so long to return to her second sight.

Awen had promised her friends that she'd return. She'd promised herself. And now was the time to make good on that promise. There was no going back, only forward.

"Are you in yet?" Ezo asked.

"Idris! For all the mystics, would you leave her alone?"

"My sensors show her heart rate has increased significantly."

Awen turned her head toward her friends without opening her eyes. "Give me another moment. Please," she said softly. "Just another moment."

She heard TO-96's servos and gyros whine as he recovered from what was probably another shove from Ezo, who himself had probably been shoved by Sootriman. *They're just concerned. And impatient.* She would have been impatient, too, had she been in their shoes.

Awen refocused on the shaft, the rappelling line,

and the figures, ascending like vapor, her mind moving up to Kane's face. The man looked wildly about the shaft, yelling to someone out of sight. Awen knew he was talking to Ezo about Sootriman. But this time, there was no sound, only images. Awen wanted to step back and shield her eyes from what came next. But it was impossible, like being in a dream where you needed to run but your feet were stuck to the floor.

Then it happened. The face behind the face—*the visage*—emerged. Like a lost city emerging from a turbulent sea, the face rose from behind Kane's bubbling mask. Pointed teeth bared in a hiss, and the black eyes stared straight at Awen as if it knew precisely where to look.

I see you, she'd said the first time. Back then, she'd felt confident because she thought she was alone, talking to herself. But this time, she knew she wasn't alone. She knew it had heard her.

This creature—this *thing*—had not been in the Unity with her. It lacked that ability; that much she knew. But it had some sort of awareness of the Unity. Worse, it *felt* her. She wasn't sure how, but it could tell where she was, and it wanted her. It had pulled on her life force.

"I see you," Awen said, echoing her words from before, forcing herself to be strong.

The face hissed.

Awen froze. She knew what came next. She wanted to run, hide, get away, and never come back. But she had to come back. The Unity awaited her. Her friends needed her. The galaxy she'd come from called to her.

So she looked. She kept her mind's eyes open and looked, hard. She stared it down.

Then the face spoke to her as before. "I see you too."

A chill ran down Awen's spine and swirled inside her gut like a tub of ice water funneling in a drain. She cringed, fists clenched. This was the moment she'd been dreading for months. This was the encounter she'd not wanted to repeat. Not ever.

This *beast* wanted her soul. She felt its insatiable appetite reaching for her. Voracious. Seeking to devour her. To feed, to consume, to take over her soul… just as it had taken over Kane's.

Awen froze. *That's it!*

That was what would let her pass through. Whatever the entity was, and no matter where it had come from, it had an appetite, and appetites were a flaw because they could be starved. They could be denied.

Awen made up her mind. This *thing*—this *parasite* —would not have her. She would resist it—no, she would *defy* it. Awen asserted her will with a confidence she'd not felt in a long time. It was returning—*she* was returning.

Awen stared the specter down as the dark eyes jabbed at her.

"I see you too," it hissed again.

"Congratulations," Awen said mockingly. "Aren't you just so special. Now, get out of my way!" She dipped her head, eyes fixed, and a blast of energy exploded from her like the shock wave of a quantum warhead. The image and all its *realness* blew apart, debris scattering into the void. The image's shrapnel dissipated until Awen was left alone in silence.

Well, almost alone.

"Awen, are you in?" TO-96 asked.

"Yes," she replied with a smile. "I'm in at last."

Awen's soul was flooded with all the multispectral awareness that the Unity brought, sensing light and sound and time as if they were material things. Each element flowed into the next, stretching out to infinity like a fine tapestry. Here, her skillful hands could follow a single thread—a word, an action, even a thought—from its origin to its end, watching it dance across a colorful landscape of time immemorial. It felt good to be back.

The first thing Awen noticed was that the temple library was much larger in the Unity than it was in person. However tall the ceiling was in the natural dimension, it was twice as high in her second sight. Additionally, the shelves were taller and held more contents, and the data drives and books were replaced with something else altogether, almost as if a second library existed atop the natural one. How such a thing was possible, she had no idea.

"The Novia must have been masters in the Unity," she said cautiously, not wishing to jolt herself from the vision.

"Oh?" Sootriman asked.

"They've built a second library within the natural one, using some sort of ethereal architecture. I can't really explain it, as I've never seen anything like it. But it's... beautiful."

Awen floated to the nearest shelf and examined a glowing orb, one of the hundreds that occupied each case of shelves. At first, she thought it resembled a large ball, like the type used in a chandelier. But as she got closer, she noticed details within the sphere —*planets*. And the light was not from the orb itself but from a sun. She looked at the next orb. It, too, had planets and a sun. The third one she looked in had two suns. She looked at the shelf below and at the shelf below that. Then she glanced over her shoulder at the case across the aisle. Each and every orb was a solar system.

"I can't believe it," Awen said.

"Can't believe what?" Ezo asked.

"They've mapped thousands—no, it must be *millions* of star systems. Maybe even *billions*."

"They have?" TO-96 asked.

"Oh, Ninety-Six, you would *love* this!" Awen exclaimed. "It's—it's *too* amazing. I have no doubt that the library in the natural world could be full of their people's history. But here in the Unity, they've created a library of star systems. The shelves are full of orbs that show *star systems*—too many for me to even count."

Awen raised her hand in the Unity, reaching toward the closest orb, one with several planets and a bright-yellow sun. As her hand neared it, however, the orb began to glow and push back. It wasn't a complete block but more like a steady resistance, as if to warn the viewer that they were approaching something they needed to consider before proceeding. Awen thought better of the action and removed her hand. The orb faded back to its normal glow. If she'd proceeded past the cautionary push, she might have been able to examine the star system in detail or perhaps view a data file… or even travel there…

The thought made her senses tingle, and a surge of excitement coursed through her physical body.

"Awen, are you all right? I'm detecting high levels of adrenaline in your body."

"I'm fine, Ninety-Six. I'm just amazed at what they've done. There seems to be more work here than a thousand sentient species could compile in… I can't even speculate… in generations. Hundreds of generations maybe. And then they stored it all in this—this marvelous *space* they created. They were actually creating inside the Unity."

"That's not something you do?" Sootriman asked.

"No, not really. I mean, we can manipulate certain things."

"Like blowing apart rocks at the atomic level," TO-96 suggested.

"I guess, though that's not really *normal*. But the Novia Minoosh—they've built something from nothing. And they've stored information in it and deposited memories of their findings."

"Can you access the data, then?" Ezo inquired.

Awen had wondered the same thing. "I'm

guessing I could, but without knowing more, I'm not sure it's entirely safe."

"How so?"

"Well, if it's just a data file, sure. But something tells me there might be more to what I'm seeing than what I'm seeing."

"You're being vague, Star Queen."

"I'm sorry. It's just that—well—who's to say I don't travel to the world I examine?"

"Wait—that could happen?"

"I don't know if it could happen, Ezo. I already told you, this is all new to me. I just have a sense that I should tread carefully."

"You said it's a library of star systems," Ezo said. "Do you think *our* galaxy is indexed there? How else could a quantum tunnel exist in it? Maybe if you… touch it or access whatever it is you're seeing… maybe we can go back!"

"Easy, love," Sootriman said, trying to calm Ezo down.

"Or maybe," Awen retorted, trying to bring some sense of reason to the conversation, "my soul is severed from my body and the jump kills me. Or maybe it opens a quantum tunnel right now, and we're jettisoned into the void, unprotected."

"Or maybe," TO-96 suggested, "it forms a spontaneous event horizon whose gravity compresses our combined masses to the subatomic level, thereby instantaneously erasing us from existence."

There was a moment of silence.

"On second thought," Ezo said, "let's go with the *learn more before we leap* model."

"I agree," Awen said. "In any case, there's more here than I could examine in my lifetime." She turned toward her friends and her corporeal self. That was when she noticed the pedestal and the black box. "Wait a second."

"What is it?" Ezo asked. "What d'you see?"

"The box. In the middle of the circle." Awen approached it slowly. "It's glowing." The box emitted a soft blue light.

"Everything glows in the Unity," TO-96 stated wistfully. "I want to go there. I wish to see a world of shiny things."

"No time for robot fantasies, 'Six. What d'you see, Awen?"

"I'm—I'm not sure." She stretched her hand out. There was none of the resistance that the orbs had projected. If anything, there seemed to be something drawing her to it. *An invitation.*

"Where are you now?" Ezo asked.

"I'm at the pedestal. At the box."

"You opening it?"

"Yes, I think I should."

"Careful, Star Queen."

"And to think," Sootriman said with a *tsk*, "a moment ago, you wanted to send her across the universe without a space suit."

"Just be careful."

"It's okay. I think I'm supposed to do this." Awen reached a hand toward the black box and opened the lid.

10

Rohoar blew out a hot breath, the odor wreaking of dead flesh and soured milk. Magnus's eyes watered. It rivaled the worst smells he'd ever inhaled. Simply horrendous. Still, he held his ground, Abimbola's instructions of showing no weakness ringing in his ears.

Faster than Magnus could move, a giant paw slammed down on his left shoulder, almost sending him to the ground, but he managed to stay on his feet.

"Then we are bound in blood," Rohoar said.

Magnus blinked, surprised he was still alive. "Bound in blood?" This was not going how he'd imagined it would.

"You killed Rohoar's people. Rohoar killed your people. Yet here we are, face-to-face as warriors."

"Here we are," Magnus echoed, playing along but not really knowing what to say.

"And you wish to kill Selskrit?"

Howls went up around the mwadim's tent. Magnus looked around then back at Rohoar. "Oh, I do. If they're the ones holding my unit hostage, then I definitely do."

The Jujari nodded, lips pulled back. "Good, good. Then in honor of your death defiance toward Rohoar and toward your mission, Rohoar will refrain from killing you at present."

"And I appreciate not being killed."

"The Dingfang might kill you. The Clawnip will probably kill you. The Selskrit will definitely kill you. But for now, the Tawnhack will not kill you."

"Again, thank you, Great Mwadim."

"Tell Rohoar, *scrumruk graulap*, what will you do for Rohoar should you rescue your people?"

Cackles went up around the tent. Whatever Rohoar had just called him, it was a cultural inside joke. Magnus looked to Abimbola again. The warlord nodded for Magnus to go on with the plan.

"If I rescue the hostages, I will ensure that

Rohoar is connected with Brigadier General Lovell himself."

"Explain *connected*."

"I'll… make sure you have a private holo-vid call with—"

"No," the mwadim said. "Rohoar says no."

Menacing growls circulated around the tent, the kind that made the hair on the back of Magnus's neck stand up.

"No holo-vid. No calls. Face-to-face. Like you and Rohoar now."

"Rohoar, I don't think you understand…"

"Rohoar does not understand?"

The cackles were frenetic, the Jujari males around the room now closing toward them.

"Watch yourself, Magnus," Abimbola whispered. It was the first time the warlord had ever used Magnus's last name.

So, word choice is a touchy thing. Got it.

"Forgive me, Great Mwadim. I meant to say that gaining an audience with the general face-to-face may prove to be difficult—maybe even beyond my ability to arrange."

"Battling the Selskrit and rescuing your unit may prove to be difficult, maybe even beyond your ability to arrange."

Magnus couldn't believe he was trying to negotiate with a Jujari chieftain. Isn't this Ambassador Bosworth's job? *But the fat man is dead. They probably ate him for lunch. So it's up to you, Marine. Dominate, liberate.*

"I will see what I can do."

"No deal," said Rohoar.

Magnus looked at Abimbola, but the warlord shrugged.

Come on! Isn't he supposed to be helping here?

"All right, when we get back, I will put in a request—"

"No deal."

"Great Mwadim, our chain of command—"

Rohoar stooped down and looked Magnus in the eye. His foul breath was smothering. "If you cannot do this for Rohoar, then you are not the right person to rescue your people. Perhaps you should call someone else to do scrumruk graulap work."

But there was no one else to do the work. And there was no way the Republic would honor a back-room deal that some lieutenant made with a Jujari chieftain. If Magnus was lucky, he'd rescue the hostages and get them all to orbit, and then Rohoar would get the shaft with a holo-vid, if anything. That was just the way the Republic worked. *Now who's being double-crossed?* he thought, cursing the evils of bureaucracy.

Magnus would make it happen. Somehow, some way, he'd do the deal. Lives depended on it. The general had asked him for a favor—maybe that was the leverage he could use for this.

"A personal meeting with Brigadier General Lovell. You have a deal."

Rohoar barked, and spittle flew onto Magnus's face. Magnus threw his arms up out of instinct. The mwadim was upright, head thrown back in a wild howl that must have shaken the fabric overhead. The rest of the Jujari males joined in, their primal cries mixing together as one. Magnus covered his ears and looked at Abimbola.

"You have a deal!" the warlord shouted, hands over his ears. "Good job!"

MAGNUS WAS BACK in *Hell's Basket Case* with Abimbola at the wheel, moving westbound. He looked through the hatch overhead. His new eyes were almost completely adjusted. Sunlight streamed between buildings, its golden shafts made visible by swirling clouds of dust. Magnus wiped his brow for the hundredth time, sure his bandana was soaked through.

The meeting with the mwadim had not gone as Magnus expected it to, but then again, he wasn't sure what he'd been expecting. He certainly hadn't expected to meet Chief—Rohoar—again. Magnus wondered how Rohoar had survived the blast. Maybe it had something to do with Awen and her mystical powers. Maybe Rohoar had been close enough to her that her strange force field had protected him.

Regardless of how he'd survived, the mwadim had certainly given Magnus a run for his money. The Marine hadn't planned on being interrogated about killing Jujari or arranging a face-to-face meeting with a Republic general. Still, Rohoar had made it worth his while by giving them updated intelligence—the news that the hostages were still in the compound—and by lending an additional twenty Jujari from his personal bodyguard. They would come in handy as long as they didn't get in the way of Marine and Marauder blaster fire. The Jujari's presence posed potential problems on the battlefield too—they had no communication, no understanding of tactics, and no coordinated movement. It could turn out to be a real splick show. But then again, their sheer power in battle might make up for whatever additional chaos ensued. That, and these warriors were seasoned in hunting Selskrit, which was infinitely more than Magnus could claim.

Before Magnus got all sentimental about the provision of Jujari troops, however, he reminded himself that it was also in the mwadim's favor to send them. They acted as insurance that Magnus didn't just vanish after a successful rescue. He assumed the bodyguard had orders to stay with Magnus until the meeting was arranged, ready to slit his throat if he failed to do it.

"Hey," Magnus said to Abimbola, "do you know what scrumruk graulap means?" He'd wished Awen was there to interpret it because it was probably bad and, therefore, would be another anecdote for the warlord to insult him with. Still, his curiosity had gotten the best of him.

Abimbola laughed. "It means 'little hairless warrior.'"

"Perfect," Magnus said with a chuckle. "And here I thought it was an insult or something."

THE FARTHER WEST THEY DROVE, the more the pedestrians thinned. Mothers corralled their pups indoors while shop owners dropped gates over store-fronts. Fires burned unattended in metal drums while adolescent Jujari bunched together in side streets, staring at the convoy. The knot in Magnus's stomach grew tighter. The city was preparing for a fight.

Magnus also noticed that the condition of the buildings was worsening. Whereas the sandstone and metal they'd seen earlier had been in good condition, here it was covered in charred blaster holes and soot. The inook shrouds in the windows were yellowed and tattered, and the gentle blue glow of the force fields that held the elements at bay was gone. The smell was also worse.

"We are getting close," Abimbola said, looking out the slats to his left.

"Definitely not the part of town we were looking for vacation homes in," Magnus replied, referring to a joke he'd made when he was in the jail with Awen. Abimbola chuckled.

They'd driven another three hundred meters when a sudden single-note howl resonated from the convoy behind them.

"We are here," Abimbola said.

"Border?"

Abimbola nodded, slowing the skiff to a stop.

"You are going to want to keep your head down," he said as he closed the hatch overhead.

"Copy," Magnus replied, lowering his sunglasses and peeking between the slats in the windshield. Ahead, the city blocks were made of two- and three- and even four-story buildings, whose shrouds were mostly missing. The sandstone looked like it was ready to collapse. Doors were ajar, and the streets were emptied of Jujari. "Nice place."

"Wait until you meet our hosts."

"Can't wait."

Abimbola swiped a menu on the touchscreen on his dashboard. A holo-projection flickered to life, displaying the route west. It zigzagged several times before terminating at the compound Magnus remembered from the briefing.

"Here is the updated route from Rohoar. I sent it to your nav program," Abimbola said, gesturing toward the holo-pad he'd given Magnus. "You and I can both update it as needed."

"You sure it won't get jammed?"

"Ha. I am not sure of anything save fate and death, buckethead. But it is a private network, and my code slicers are good. I should be fine."

"Don't you mean *I* should be fine?"

"No. I have no idea how *you* are going to be. I

have *Basket Case*," Abimbola said, giving his skiff a loving tap, "so I should be fine."

"Of course."

Magnus flicked the holo-pad on, and a projection of the city sprang to life, reflecting the route on Abimbola's dashboard. The pad was cumbersome, and Magnus was sure it wouldn't last the day. *What I wouldn't give for a Recon helmet with nav integration, unit comms, and the latest AI patch!*

"We will soften this corridor first, then it is up to you to clear the way. Call in support as you need it." Abimbola swiped to another menu and scrolled through ten profile images with descriptions beside them. "Again, these are the Marauders who were bloodthirsty enough to join you."

Magnus matched the faces to his memory of the people he'd met in Abimbola's hideout. He'd barely spoken a word to each, but he was grateful for their help. Of course, he wasn't sure if he could trust them. But he'd trusted their leader and made it this far. If Abimbola had wanted to betray him, he could have done so plenty of times over. *Of course, he still might, you noob.* But Magnus had learned that part of operating behind enemy lines meant learning to take chances and forging unlikely partnerships. And—looking at Abimbola—this certainly met the criteria for unlikely.

"You have got my three best sniper-spotters here," Abimbola said, swiping the profiles over so they'd appear on Magnus's holo-pad. Their icons showed up in Magnus's grouped-comms display. "Simone's in charge. Then these three are your best mine techs, led by Cyril." Another three icons slid into Magnus's group. "He is just a kid, but there is no one better."

"And those four?" Magnus asked, pointing to the remaining profile pictures on the dashboard.

"They will kill anything you point them toward, so make sure your people are not in their way."

"Copy that," Magnus said as the names were added to his list. He merged the Marauder roster with his existing list then selected all the names and typed in a title: *Delta Platoon*. It was the next available alphanumeric title for a platoon in his Recon company. He might not be Marine eligible anymore, but he'd still bleed Recon under the Jujari sun.

Magnus linked the group to his ear comm then touched Active on his pad. "Delta Platoon, this is Lieutenant Magnus. Confirm connection." Magnus watched as each profile picture reported in, its status going to double green.

"Fire-team leads, sound off. Dutch?"

"Loud and clear, Lieutenant," Dutch responded over comms.

"Simone?"

"I hear you, person," an icy female voice said.

Magnus looked at Abimbola.

The giant Miblimbian shrugged. "Just let her do her job," he said, his mic muted. "No problems."

Magnus replied to the woman. "How about you just call me LT. Does that work?"

There was a pause, which turned into an abnormally long silence. Magnus double-checked the holo-pad to make sure the system hadn't failed. Finally, the woman's smooth voice came back.

"LT," Simone said. "Maybe."

Magnus raised an eyebrow while Abimbola gave him a thumbs-up.

"Cyril?" Magnus read.

"Shoot, I copy, sir, ten by ten, all the way," a twitchy voice said. Magnus's eyebrows went up. It was how he imagined a Quinzellian miter squirrel might sound if it could talk. "Ready to slice, ready to dice, or something like that. Ha."

"He is a handful with words," Abimbola said, mic still muted, "but he can make quick work of any explosive device in the galaxy. Or any terminal, for that matter."

"And..." Magnus looked at the roster again for the infantry fire-team leader, hesitating at the name.

"Galliogernomarix?" he said slowly, sounding out each syllable.

"You can just call me Rix, buckethead," a burly bass voice said. "Can't have you getting shot while you try to hail me."

"And you can just call me LT."

"Copy that," Rix said without any attempt to hide his disdain.

"All right, listen up—"

Another voice broke through Magnus's transmission. "Lord Abimbola, contact, twelve o'clock."

Magnus peered between the front slats. About two hundred meters ahead stood a single Jujari, arms extended, one hand holding a keeltari long sword, the other waving what looked to be a sawed-off blaster.

"What's it doing?" Magnus asked Abimbola.

"Gathering intelligence."

The Jujari started howling then interrupted his call with short cackles. He turned slowly in circles, pumping his weapons in the air.

"Gathering intelligence?" Magnus asked.

"Correct. He's sacrificing himself. And we'll kill him. But his kinsmen will be watching to see where the death blow comes from. They want to make sure we're the only enemy and that there aren't snipers or air support."

Magnus turned to Abimbola. "You have air power?"

"No," Abimbola said with a smile, "but the Selskrit do not know that. They just think we do."

"Copy," Magnus said, chuckling.

Abimbola tapped the comm in his ear. "Take him."

"Yes, my lord," said Abimbola's gunner. A beat later, a single shot belched out from the M109 turret above and behind Magnus's seat. The skiff rocked back as the column of light streaked down the street. The Jujari was bisected, a large chunk disappearing from his midsection, as the bolt continued down the road. The energy blast struck pavement half a kilometer beyond and erupted in a plume of fire, debris, and thick dust.

The Jujari lay in two pieces, arms and legs twitching. His hand contracted, a finger squeezing off a burst of full-auto rounds from the blaster. They shot into the street and nearby buildings until the Jujari finally expired. One wayward blaster shot, however, pinged off an old awning that overhung part of the street. Its tattered remains and metal frame quivered until one end broke away from the sandstone. The metal arm swung down into the street. The moment it touched the hardpack, the street exploded. Magnus and Abimbola winced as the concussion impacted the column of vehicles. Gray dust blotted out the sun, and the skiff's cab darkened.

"You are sure you still want to do this?" Abimbola swatted the air with a hand and coughed. "Not too late to change your mind, you know."

"I want to do it even more," Magnus replied.

Abimbola clucked. "That is your cue, then. Clear the way, and we will back you up."

Magnus charged his MAR30 and touched his fingers to his forehead in salute. "Dominate, liberate."

"Dominate, liberate," Abimbola replied. It was almost enough to make Magnus cry.

11

MOLDARK SAT in the high-backed captain's chair. He stroked the leather arms, affectionately feeling the skin of whatever beast had unwittingly given its life for his pleasure. He'd ordered the chair removed from the bridge and brought to the rear observation deck. The engineers had bolted it to the platform that looked out through the large windowed wall.

He liked to sit here, surveying the Republic starships. They spread out before him like pawns, each ready to do his bidding. Beyond them lay the Jujari ships. *They will do my bidding, as well, and be none the wiser.*

He sighed, taking in the beauty of the void. It felt as though he sat among the stars, untethered from the constraints of human flesh and metal starships. Here, before the wide window, he felt free, as his spirit did when it roamed the galaxies. Boundless. Eternal.

But being *in the flesh*, as they said, wasn't all bad. It gave him voice in the physical realm again. It gave him a means by which to be feared. It gave him power. But more than anything, it gave him recognition. He could hear his name uttered by the lips of others.

Moldark smiled as he thought about how easy it had been to co-opt the human species. First, there was Admiral Kane, the egotistical maniac—but then again, the perfect host candidate for just that reason. Wasn't Moldark much the same? *Only, my motivations are purer.* He steepled his fingers.

Moldark had done the admiral a favor, if anything. The poor man would never have been able to see his plans through or been strong enough to defeat the Galactic Republic. In the end, Kane would have been assassinated. Not outright, of course, but through some unfortunate accident. That was what all-powerful governing bodies did when an asset outlived its purpose. *Wasn't that what they did to me, after all?*

The admiral would thank him if he could. When it was all done, perhaps Moldark would even let Kane come back for a moment to see all the work that his hands had wrought—the funeral pyres, the scorched planets, the extinguished stars. He could hear the glorious silence of retribution and stand in the ruins.

Then Moldark thought about how easy it had been to coerce the Luma master. In another age, So-Elku and Moldark might have been acquaintances. Maybe even friends. The elder seemed genuine in his pursuit of galactic peace—though his means were all wrong, strangled by an intolerance of violence and an acceptance of outliers that drove Moldark absolutely mad. He ground his teeth at the Luma master's near-sightedness.

So-Elku had reminded Moldark of so many others—those who had gummed up the machinations of smarter, stronger people. People with true vision and the foresight to shape galaxies into their most efficient selves—their truest expressions, pure and unmarred by disorder.

The Luma were a threat, to be sure, more than Moldark cared to admit. He loathed their skills in the Unity. Such dealings were antiquated, leftovers of a bygone epoch. But the Luma were powerful none theless, which made So-Elku's undoing all the sweeter for Moldark. With the Luma master out of the way, his plans could proceed unhindered. *Perhaps our spirits will meet up one day, and I will express my respect for him, fleeting as it is.*

"Sir?" a voice said from behind his chair.

"Captain Wallace," Moldark replied. "And Executive Officer Brighton. How good of you to come." He turned his chair slowly, examining the men's faces with hungry interest. *How long has it been since I've nourished myself?*

"You wanted to see us?" Wallace asked.

Moldark nodded. "Yes. Have all of First Fleet's ships arrived?"

"They have, sir."

"Very good." Moldark tapped the tips of his deeply scarred fingers together. "Very good." He pointed at Wallace. "Now, Captain, I need to know where your allegiance stands."

"I beg your pardon, sir?"

"Your allegiances." Moldark pointed at him. *Must I spell it out?* "To whom are you committed?"

The captain looked at the XO.

"Don't look at him," Moldark spat. "Look at me."

"With the Republic, sir. Of course."

"I was afraid of that." Moldark glared at the man, holding his gaze. For a moment, nothing happened. They were just two men locked in a staring contest.

Suddenly, Wallace began crying. "No," he said, lifting his hands as if to ward off a bad dream. "No, please no."

Moldark was hungry, and this soul would do just fine. He had no use for such indecision anyway. *How has this man ever been promoted? Surely by some manner of nepotism or a bribe.* Wallace didn't deserve this posting. Leveraging the benefits of power just to raise up the undeserving—it was the quintessence of vanity. Moldark scorned it. And since supreme power had no rival, he would challenge it. He alone would make it right.

Wallace screamed as Moldark sucked out his life. The dark lord closed his eyes, relishing the taste, savoring the energy that surged into his soul and fed his body. It was exhilarating.

He opened his eyes again to see Wallace fall to his knees, hands shriveling like scrawny talons. The captain's hair turned gray, then white, twisting like frayed strands of wire. Soon, the captain's voice went ragged, trailing off into whispers. His eyes sank into dark recesses as his skin withered and fell off in flaky patches.

Satisfied, Moldark released his grip on the captain. Wallace's corpse collapsed, his Republic uniform flopping to the ground. Bones rattled against each other with a muffled sound as the clothing sighed.

Moldark took a deep breath then put his fingertips together again. "And you, Executive Officer Brighton, where does your allegiance lie?"

The man looked between Wallace's bones and Moldark.

"Don't look to him," Moldark said with a smile. He spoke like a doting parent might to a child who was unsure of himself. "You don't need Wallace anymore. Just look at me. Where does your allegiance lie, Brighton?"

The XO swallowed but stared into Moldark's eyes with a surprising level of confidence. "With you, my lord."

"Ah! You see?" Moldark drew out each word: "Now isn't that *wonderful*." He stood, moved down the stairs, and placed a hand on Brighton's shoulder. "The Third Fleet is yours, Fleet Admiral Brighton."

"*Fleet Admiral*, my lord?"

"Are you not deserving of the title?"

"I am not one to question your authority. But what about you? I mean… what should I call you?"

These rank-and-file commanders were so predictable. What were they without their titles? They could hardly function if they did not know their place in the system. There was a certain romance to it, of course. Moldark could appreciate that. Still, the lack of imagination appalled him.

"Am I not your lord, as you've already said?"

"Of course, but—"

"Then call me Lord Moldark."

Brighton dipped his head. "As you command, Lord Moldark."

Moldark removed his hand and straightened his uniform. "Now, I think we need a new name for the fleet, especially since our commission from the Republic is about to expire."

"Expire?"

"Yes, the Republic is releasing us after we carry out one final order. From then on, we will be operating on our own authority." He paused. "On *my* authority."

"Understood, my lord."

"We are…" Moldark savored the moment then tilted his head at Brighton. "The First Fleet of the Paragon."

"First Fleet of the Paragon," Brighton repeated with a twinkle in his eye. Moldark could tell he liked it. This man, *this Brighton*, was drawn to power. Moldark could feel the desire within him.

Good. Very good.

"And what is the Republic's final order?" the fleet admiral asked.

Moldark's hands shook slightly. The Republic's last order had been to "await orders"—orders from the Circle of Nine. But those senators were no more. Brighton didn't need to know any of that. Instead, the fleet admiral needed reassurance that the Republic was behind what was about to happen next, as fictitious as such assurances were.

Moldark touched two fingertips to his bottom lip. He could taste blood—taste the beginning of something glorious that the galaxy could never return from. Should anyone survive what was to come, they would tell of what happened for generations.

"My lord?" Brighton inclined his head, catching Moldark's eye. "The final order?"

"To open fire on the Jujari fleet."

"But, my lord, we are already engaged in light—"

"It's a skirmish. The mere puffing out of chests." Moldark tasted blood and pulled his fingers away from his mouth. "We are to make war, Brighton. War."

"My lord?"

Moldark looked at his bleeding fingertips. Warm blood trickled down his chin. "You are to open fire on all of the Jujari ships, Fleet Admiral Brighton."

Brighton hesitated, eyes darting to the floor. "But, my lord, I…"

"Is something the matter?" Moldark took a step toward his new fleet admiral, suddenly doubting the decision to promote him. Perhaps he was not ready after all. It would be sad to lose him, of course. He showed such promise. But there would be others.

Brighton shook his head and squared his shoulders, suddenly composing himself. "No, Lord Moldark. It will be done as you have ordered."

"Good. Target engines first. I want the fighter squadrons scrambled as well. Disperse them evenly, attacking dreadnoughts and battleships at will. I want as much confusion as possible."

"Very well, my lord."

"That is all, Fleet Admiral."

Brighton snapped to attention and then did something peculiar. He bowed.

Moldark tilted his head, examining the man. The gesture was unsolicited. So far as Moldark knew, the Galactic Republic did not require such deference.

Where did it come from? Is it genuine awe? Contrite reverence? Perhaps it is worship.

He tipped his head in acknowledgement of Brighton's act. He could grow to like this… submission. It was quaint. And it would most likely be contagious among his followers. *Yes.* He rolled the word around in his head. *My followers.*

Brighton stepped backward, spun on his heel, then walked toward the exit. Moldark watched him leave and then marched up the stairs to his chair. He sat and spun toward the window once more. The starships hung above Oorajee like insects swarming over a large piece of citrus fruit. Some, he knew, would follow him. They would do his bidding.

And those that do not? Moldark smiled. He would sweep them from the air and crush them between his fingers.

He tapped his thumb and forefinger together several times, feeling the flesh stick, then pull apart. He could feel the souls on those vessels, sense their life force. They would meet their end in the glorious pursuit of his will, hastening it to completion. They would never know the valuable role they'd played. But Moldark would still be grateful to them for the sacrifice that allowed him to achieve his end. *And what a glorious end it will be.*

He tapped the holo-pad that was built into the arm of the captain's chair and brought up a menu. With a few small swipes, he selected comms for all three Republic fleets then opened the channel.

"Fleets of the Republic, this is Fleet Admiral

Kane on the *Black Labyrinth*. We have received orders from Republic Navy Central Command, ratified by the Senate, to initiate combat operations against all Jujari vessels in orbit over Oorajee. I repeat, we have been ordered to initiate offensive operations and eliminate all Jujari vessels in this system."

Moldark paused just long enough for the news to settle over every starship's bridge, arrest each captain, and startle each crew member. He could almost feel them trembling with excitement—and fear.

"Assume your battle stations. Set Condition One throughout the fleet." He paused long enough for a klaxon to start echoing through all compartments of the powerful Republic dreadnought, a sound now repeated on every starship under his command. "All hands, battle stations. This is not a drill."

Moldark closed the public-announcement channel and connected directly to the *Black Labyrinth's* bridge. He envisioned commanders springing to action, echoing his orders, and selecting targets. They wouldn't have time to double-check with the navy's central command or the Senate to corroborate his instructions. But why would they want to? The Republic had been hungering for this conflict for far too long. Besides, he was the ranking fleet admiral—well, Brighton was, but the man served at Moldark's pleasure—and thus held command authority over all the fleets currently in the system. Moldark was simply giving them what they'd always wanted. It was time to bring anything that stood to its knees. It was time for war.

"Admiral Brighton, are our fighter squadrons ready?"

"They are, my lord."

"And have you acquired satisfactory initial targets?"

"I have. Awaiting your command."

Moldark squeezed the leather arms of his chair, a squeaking sound coming from beneath his grip. "Fire."

12

"IT'S INCREDIBLE!" Awen said, holding her hands to her face—both those in the natural realm and those in the Unity. She was overcome by elation, her heart beating wildly in her chest, flooded with a mix of emotions. The four of them had waited for a discovery of this sort for so long. No, not of this sort —this was way beyond anything they could have hoped to find. This was the discovery of a lifetime. And Awen had no idea what it was.

In the physical realm, the lid on the black box remained closed, but in the Unity, it was flipped open, laid back on its hinge. "I can't believe... I can't believe they were able to create this!"

Ezo made no attempt to hide his excitement

either. Out of all of them, he seemed the most eager to get back home. "What do you see? What is it?"

Awen was having a hard time finding words. "I think it's some sort of management system, or maybe a control room? I... I don't know yet. But it's *beautiful*."

Awen stared straight up and turned in circles. Directly overhead was a brightly glowing orb that stretched to within a few meters of the ceiling. The sight dominated her vision, the rest of the library fading to black beyond her view. The sphere contained millions—no *billions*—of stars that appeared as vibrant as if she'd been standing in the void unprotected. A sweet polyphonic melody emanated from the orb, like a giant wind chime on a summer evening. The notes were full and round, turning over on themselves and slipping through musical space like silk ribbons.

The sight was dizzying, a sensation Awen had never experienced in the Unity before. She had to stop turning and brought her eyes down. A wide circle of workstations sat on the floor surrounding the orb. A second, third, and fourth bank of workstations ascended behind the first in concentric rings as they extended from the orb, each level connected by stairways.

The workstation layout reminded Awen of any number of holo-movies she'd seen or even some that she'd seen in real life, like on starships or in orbital traffic-control rooms. The difference here being that these stations had no chairs and were larger than anything a humanoid would use—which seemed fitting for the Novia Minoosh, given what they'd observed throughout the city so far.

The workstations glowed in soft golden light as if reflecting the light of the stars in the orb. Awen moved behind the closest bank of terminals and studied them, moving to the next and then the next. The control surfaces were black geometric sections delineated by thin white light. Segment types ranged from small keypad-like shapes to wide rectangular areas as one might expect on the bridge of a large starship—except that these control surfaces were far more elegant. Their designs flowed in and out of another like the lines left by waves on a beach.

Awen took a few moments to try to explain what she saw to her friends as well as provide some idea of what purpose everything served. The task was harder than she imagined, and she was sure they were in just as much disbelief as she was but without the visual proof. The most logical idea she had was that the smaller orbs on the shelves could be fed to the giant orb in the room's center, like some sort of stellar-display computer.

"Awen," TO-96 said, "is this management system, as you have described it, something you can control?"

"I'm not sure yet. But I'll try."

"Very well. We will wait for you to try."

"But sooner rather than later, please," Ezo added.

"Idris," Sootriman said, smacking him on the back of the head.

"What was that for?"

"You're just…" Sootriman let out a deep breath and then smacked him again—on the butt.

"I saw that," Awen said. Sootriman smirked, and Ezo blushed.

Awen continued moving among the terminals, passing through rows, using the steps between the levels. When she arrived at the topmost ring—which didn't even reach a quarter of the orb's height—Awen looked over the back edge and saw her friends below. Their physical bodies stood outside the floral ring. Awen thought back to the sense of warning she'd gotten when she first stepped inside the ring, and she wondered if it had something to do with this.

"I'm going to see what happens when I touch one of the control surfaces," Awen said. "You might want to—I don't know, stand back? Or hold on to something maybe?"

"You really think that's necessary?" Ezo asked.

"I don't know *what* I think is necessary. I just don't want anyone getting hurt."

"Let's do as she says," Sootriman said. She and the others moved toward a case of shelves and stood beside it. "You've got this, Awen. No fear, girl."

"Okay, here goes nothing." Awen turned to the nearest control surface, extended her shimmering hand in the Unity, and placed her fingers on the black surface. It was glassy to the touch but not cold as she'd expected. Rather, it was warm, as if the whole thing had been powered up and running for days. "Something's happening," Awen called over her shoulder then realized her physical body was still in the center of the ring, facing the others.

Along the black control surface, swirls of golden light emanated from her fingers and moved in either direction. The Novia Minoosh's strange script flared to life, appearing on small buttons and titling large screens. The typography pulsed in golds and purples, blues and pinks and was accentuated by drop shadows that seemed to lift the text off the screens.

The swirl of golden light continued to race over the workstations to the left and right then moved to the banks below. Circular images that resembled star systems emerged on the screens. Holo-projections displayed spinning planets encircled by small moons. Other projections showed misty nebulae suspended in midair. Everywhere Awen looked, the workstations glittered with text and cosmic images.

"It's unbelievable!" Awen finally said. "You can't believe what I'm seeing right now!"

"What?" Ezo asked, betraying his impatience. "What is it?"

"It's magnificent! It's like a massive control room to—well, I still don't know what it does." She described everything as best she could, but her words fell short. It would be so much easier if her audience knew how to enter the Unity and could see this theater for themselves.

"Awen, TO-96 here."

"I know your voice, Ninety-Six."

"Ah, very good. Forgive me. I just thought, given the frenetic activity in your cerebral cortex, you might mistake me for someone other than myself. As far as you can tell, is the apparatus you are observing more of an archive and retrieval system, or might it serve another purpose?"

"Your guess is as good as mine," Awen replied.

TO-96 hesitated. "I have not enough data to

determine whether or not my estimations would be comparable to yours, Awen. Therefore, I am doubtful that your assumption is valid."

"It's an expression, 'Six," Ezo said.

"Ah. My apologies."

"I don't even know where to start," Awen said. "The language is the first hurdle."

"If only I could join you in the Unity," TO-96 said.

"Maybe you'd be less obnoxious there," said Ezo.

"Do you find me obnoxious, sir?"

"Almost all the time, actually. What I need you to be is helpful. If you were in Awen's shoes, what would you be looking for?"

"But, sir, Awen's shoes are far too small for the dimensions—"

"For all the gods, no, 'Six. *Expression*. It's another expression."

"Duly noted. As always, I hope I prove to be less obnoxious with time."

"Don't we all," Ezo said.

TO-96 looked back at Awen. "Is there anything that looks like it might be a central command station? Perhaps a workstation that appears more primary than the others? It may vary in size, shape, or even prominence with regard to its position in the space."

Awen looked around, searching for anything that might stand out. "Now that you mention it, there is one terminal by itself on an elevated platform in the middle of the theater."

"That sounds promising," TO-96 replied.

"Going there now," Awen said, grateful for TO-96's experience as a navigation robot.

Awen stepped onto the raised floor and noticed she had a commanding view of most of the other terminals, save those behind her. This perch also protruded slightly, providing a breathtaking view of the orb.

"Do you notice anything about the console?" the bot asked.

"Let's see… I have an empty circle projected to my left, what looks to be a list of some sort projected to my right, and in front of me, several screens and pretty big buttons with single Novia characters on them."

"Sounds like she's found the jackpot." Before TO-96 could say anything, Ezo added, "It's another expression, buddy. Let it go."

Awen looked into the natural realm to see the bot hold up a finger in protest, pause, and then put it back down. "Any recommendations, Ninety-Six?" she asked.

"Are you able to view something if I project it in front of me?"

"Yes, no problem."

"Very well." TO-96 straightened, mimicking the human behavior of preparing for a task, and projected a set of four Novia characters about four feet in front of his chest. "Do any of these look familiar?"

Awen stretched her vision toward the bot and examined the script. She glanced back at the console then at TO-96 again. "No, none of those."

"And these?" A new set of four characters replaced the others. Awen compared them again.

"No, none of those either."

"What are they?" Sootriman asked the bot.

"They are my best guesses for what I think the Novia might place on a control system. I am basing my assumptions upon similar markings we have discovered on ships throughout the city." He paused then projected another set of four. "And these?"

"Wait," Awen said. "That one there. Your upper left, my upper right."

TO 96 eliminated the three other characters and expanded the one Awen selected to fill the projection. Beneath it, the bot displayed the character's meaning in Galactic common.

"It means *initialize?*" Awen asked.

"Among its many other meanings, yes."

"Its many other meanings?" Awen repeated. This wasn't exactly a thing that she wanted to mess up.

"As with any language, the Novia Minoosh seem to have multiple meanings for words depending on their context. I have merely applied the one that I have judged most applicable to this scenario."

"You have this as a scenario?" Ezo asked. "What's it listed under—'Female Elonian Luma Needs to Interpret Random Alien Script in Alternate-Universe Dashboard'?"

"Not exactly, sir, though that would make for a very fitting entry."

"They don't call me silver tongued for nothing."

"But, sir, only Provestial escorts have ever said that you—"

"Let's leave that one alone, shall we?"

TO-96 looked at Ezo, who seemed to be avoiding a glare from Sootriman. "Ah, I see. Let's."

"So you think I should press it?" Awen asked.

"I do," said the bot. "At least insomuch as I hope the Novia have not used an alternate definition for the word."

Awen tensed. "Like…?"

"Like *detonation*, *explosion*, or *self-destruct*."

"Those are the word's alternate meanings?" Awen asked, jerking away from the console.

"Of course not. That was just to make you laugh."

"I'm not laughing, Ninety-Six," Awen replied, her heart beating rapidly.

"None of us are," Ezo added.

"Well, I seem to have misapplied my sense of humor. My apologies."

"So, I should press the button with that mark?"

"What you should or should not do seems to be irrelevant, Awen. That said, I see no harm in employing this button as an initial means of actuation, so long as it appears to be centrally located."

"It is," Awen replied. "It's right in the middle of the main screen, in fact."

"Well, then, I say, tallyho!" TO-96 said with an outstretched armed, pointing.

"Feeling a little liberal, are we?" Ezo asked, smirking.

"I saw it on an old holo-movie," the bot replied. "I thought it was fitting, given all the plays on words that seem to be *sailing* around the room."

Ezo and Sootriman both rolled their eyes, but not Awen. As humorous as she found the robot, she was too concerned with not blowing everyone up.

"Okay, you might want to stand back, everyone."

"We're beside the closest shelving units, love," Sootriman said. "Whenever you're ready."

Awen took a deep breath, stepped toward the console, and let her hand hover over the smooth black button with the golden character. "Here goes." She pressed down with her otherworldly fingertips, and the floor began to tremble.

13

"SIMONE?" Magnus asked.

"What d'you you want?"

"I want overwatch in the third building on the right." Magnus was still seated in the *Basket Case*, calling out orders over comms. "After that blast, I'm guessing the street should be clear of more explosives, at least up to there."

"Copy," she replied.

"Rix?"

"Talk to me," the brute said.

"I want your fire team on the left side of the street, and mine will take the right. Clear those buildings. Slow is smooth, and smooth is deadly. But don't dawdle either."

"Understood," he replied in a gutsy bass voice.

"Then, Cyril, I want you scanning so hard that your equipment wants to kick you in the balls. If anyone's dying today, it's not going to be us, and it sure as hell won't be because of some coward's backyard bomb."

"That's a loud and clear, Lieutenant. Loud and clear all the way, sir."

"Anyone sees anything, you call it out and take care of what you can. If it overwhelms you, I need to know before that happens. Copy?"

The team leads acknowledged the order.

"Good. Rix, leapfrog with our fire team to the next intersection. We stop if Cyril calls something out."

"Copy," Rix said.

"Simone, I'll rely on you to spot your overwatch positions as we go unless I see something first. Abimbola says you have good instincts, and I trust him."

"Smart on your part," she replied.

Magnus ignored the comment. "Once we've taken the block, Abimbola will roll up behind. I want as little debris in these streets as possible in case we need them as egress. That means no blowing up splick unnecessarily. You copy that?"

"Copy that," they all replied.

"What about the Tawnhack?" Simone asked.

Abimbola said, "They are doing their own thing, as always. If you even see them, you will be lucky. Do not give them another thought, though. They will not be coming to anyone's rescue, but they will not miss an opportunity to kill Selskrit either."

"Yes, my lord," his team leads said.

Respect the man with the bigger gun, Magnus thought. *I get it.*

"Dutch, you ready?" Magnus asked.

"All green, LT."

Magnus turned to Abimbola. "Time to light it up."

Abimbola signaled to his M109 gunner. The operator reduced the twin cannons to quarter power, rapid fire, and started peppering every opening he could find in the next block. The skiff behind *Hell's Basket Case* also opened up to complement the effort.

"That's us," Magnus said. "Move, move, move!" He shoved the passenger door open and dropped to the ground, shielded momentarily by the door's metal plating. He looked down the column behind him to see several figures exiting vehicles.

With the skiffs providing heavy cover fire, Magnus slammed the door shut, ran forward, and took a knee by the front spikes of Abimbola's ride. He had a perfect view of the cross street and looked for enemy combatants. The way looked clear. As soon as the platoon had gathered, Magnus gave the signal to move out.

They crossed the street at a run. Simone and her snipers moved down the right sidewalk, or at least what was left of it. They picked their way through debris left from the detonation and took care not to tumble into the crater left behind. They reached the third building that Magnus had specified and darted through a door.

Magnus looked over to see Rix covering the left flank. They reached the third building on their side and ducked inside a doorway, leaving one man on the street to cover. Magnus likewise picked up where Simone had left off, moving to the fourth building, a two-story sandstone house that had definitely seen better years. The sharp smell of spent explosives filled his head and made his heart beat faster. He looked over his shoulder and ordered Nolan to stand guard.

"On me," Magnus said to Dutch, Haney, and Gilder. He paused long enough to see Cyril's team, with their head-mounted sensors, scanning the street for explosives. The three of them looked like human versions of the skiffs Abimbola had concocted, adorned with all manner of wires, plates, coils, and optics. *Good man*, Magnus thought. He wouldn't have been caught dead in a battle with such clumsy head-wear. *But, hey, if it saves lives, suit me up.*

He removed his sunglasses and tucked them in the protective cover of his chest-plate pocket. Once the others were stacked, Dutch tapped Magnus on the shoulder, and he turned into the first room. The place hadn't been inhabited in years, or so it looked, and it smelled like dog urine. Dust and sand covered most of the concrete floor. A few broken dishes sat in one corner, a decimated piece of wooden furniture in another.

A hallway extended from the vestibule leading to an open stairwell and three other rooms. Magnus approached the stairs, creeping along them with his MAR30 pointed to the second floor. Meanwhile, Dutch, Haney, and Gilder checked the rooms.

"Clear," each Marine said over comms.

"I'm going up," Magnus replied.

"On your six," Dutch said.

Magnus crept up the steps, the toes of his boots grinding sand particles into the concrete. Rivulets of sweat salted his lips and soaked his beard. He could hear his heart beating in his ears. While he didn't expect any Selskrit to hang around this close to the border, especially after the first blast, he knew better than to underestimate an enemy. All it took was a lone combatant with an LRGR—large railgun rifle—and an incendiary round to take out one of Abimbola's vehicles.

Magnus continued up the steps and rotated his hips to match his field of fire with the opening above him. Once on the next floor, he noticed three more doorways, each filled with brick and mortar. He inspected the nearest doorway and noticed that the mortar was fresh. He'd seen this before. It was one of many methods used to corral an enemy. It meant the Selskrit expected an assault and, moreover, anticipated Republic urban tactics.

Not good, Magnus thought. *Not good at all.*

"What've you got, LT?" Dutch asked.

"Barricades. Someone doesn't want us using this floor."

"Splick," she replied. "You want to breach them?"

"Negative," he said, backtracking toward the top of the stairs. "Too much time and a waste of munitions. Let's let Abimbola's cannon drill the rooms."

"Copy that. Headed back out." A beat later, Dutch asked, "LT, why not just block off the stairwell? It'd be a lot less work than blocking off each upstairs room." She paused. "Unless you…"

Magnus's blood went cold as he finished the sentence for her: *Unless you wanted a kill box.*

Something creaked over Magnus's head, and bits of plaster sprinkled on his shoulders.

Dammit! He swung his MAR30 up just as a massive shape broke through the ceiling. The air filled with plaster fragments and stone dust. Magnus pulled the trigger, sending a blistering burst of blaster bolts toward a Jujari assassin. The combatant fell on Magnus and knocked him to the floor.

Magnus's MAR30 was pinned to his side, but he was pretty sure he'd hit the assassin. Still, the beast thrashed, his claws and jaws looking for Magnus's head. He was far mangier than the Tawnhack and had beady red eyes. His incisors were also longer than the Tawnhack's, resembling needles more than teeth.

Magnus held the Jujari's arms at bay and dodged his snapping jaw. Then he brought his knees up and knocked the assailant in the belly, hoping that was where his rounds had hit. Sure enough, the beast whined. Magnus could feel hot blood pooling between his leg armor plates. Magnus forced his knees up again, pressing harder and harder as the Jujari winced and lessened the attack.

The thing weighed as much as four men! Magnus strained, made enough room for his blaster, and pinned the muzzle against the Jujari's abdomen. He fired.

A gout of gore erupted from the Jujari's back and splashed against what remained of the ceiling. The Selskrit ceased struggling and died, eyes open and staring at Magnus, who shoved the beast off him. Magnus gained his feet and examined himself to see if he was hurt. Amazingly, the only damage was to his appearance: he was covered head to toe in white dust and had a large crimson stain around his waist.

Dutch's head appeared at the bottom of the stairs, the barrel of her XM31 Type-R pointed at Magnus. "LT?" she asked, lowering her weapon.

"This house needs an exterminator." He paused and touched his earpiece. "Abimbola?"

"Go ahead," the warlord said over comms.

"Fourth house down, right side of the street, second floor."

"Copy. Let me know when you are clear."

"Ten seconds," Magnus replied as he descended.

He and Dutch left the hallway, passed through the vestibule, and returned to the sidewalk. *Hell's Basket Case* was moving to their position. Magnus pulled out his sunglasses and slipped them on then headed for the next house down. As they approached the doorway, the M109 twin cannons sounded, drilling the last building's second story with thousands of small holes.

"It's going to be a long day, Dutch," Magnus said off comms.

"Copy that, LT. Copy that."

MAGNUS and his fire team cleared two more buildings before reaching the end of the block. Rix's fire team was even with them and encountered no resistance. Cyril took cover behind Magnus, finding no more explosives in the first block, and Simone was somewhere above, scouting for revised overwatch.

The cross street in front of Magnus was barren save for several lizards that sunbathed on walls or scurried under refuse piles. The smell of smoke clung to everything, including the inside of Magnus's nostrils. He used the heel of his thumb to wipe his eyebrows of sweat. The sun was almost directly overhead. He took a long drag on his canteen then replaced it in his backpack. *What I wouldn't give for a working set of Recon armor right now.* As it was, he wanted to rip every piece off his body.

Ahead, the street split in two directions, one northwest, the other southwest. Magnus pulled up the map on his holo-pad and zeroed in on their location. "We're taking the right fork, everyone," he said over comms. "Right fork."

The fire teams confirmed.

"Simone, you in place?"

"We've got eyes on the intersection in all directions."

"Cyril, you ready?"

"Scanning like a cellitype body swipe," the skinny Marauder said.

"I don't even want to know what that means," Magnus said.

"Oh, that's easy. You see, when you have—"

"That wasn't a request for more information, Marauder."

"Ah-ha. Copy that." Cyril cleared his throat. "Beginning sweep of the intersection."

"We've got you covered," Simone said.

Magnus had to hand it to Cyril—he was one brave kid. That, or he had a few screws loose. Not only was he skilled in bomb defusing, but he was also now walking into the middle of a hostile intersection that was sure to be a focal point for enemy fire. The two other techs who joined him were apparently cut from the same cloth, as they didn't hesitate in the least.

With a sudden report that ricocheted off the buildings like teeth chattering in the cold, a sniper round let loose overhead. Magnus looked up more out of instinct than any suspicion that he might see something. "That you, Simone?"

After a prolonged pause, she said, "Contact. Kill confirmed."

Magnus grunted. "Fair enough. Next time, try—"

A second shot rang out, this time toward the opposite flank.

"Contact," Simone said.

Magnus shook his head. "You know what? Never mind. Just keep doing what you're doing."

As if she hadn't even heard him, Simone said, "Kill confirmed."

"Hey, hey, hey, I've got something, Republic Marine Lieutenant," Cyril said.

"Okay." Magnus chuckled. "Talk to me. And you don't need to call me that, kid."

"Copy, roger, copy. IMTB here."

"Come again?"

"An improvised multi-trigger bomb. Trinitex composite core. About two feet down, dead center," Cyril said from the middle of the intersection.

"Trinitex?" Magnus said.

Dutch let out a long whistle behind him. "Where do Jujari get ahold of trinitex?"

"You Republic types will trade just about anything for information or sex," Cyril said. "It's not hard."

"He has a point," Dutch replied.

Magnus shook his head. "Can you defuse it?"

"Of course I can defuse it." Then Cyril muttered to himself, "Can I defuse it? *Pshh*, can I defuse it. What kind of a question is that?"

"Cyril!" Simone said from above. "Focus."

"Yes, ma'am. Right away." Cyril bent down, joined by his other two techs.

Just then, Magnus noticed movement coming from the fork ahead. "Simone, you see that? Twelve o'clock." Several shadows moved in the slivers of shade cast by the buildings. A few more passed through some windows.

"Sure do," she said. Magnus could hear the analog *click, click, click* of her aperture-adjustment dial. Apparently, she still preferred windowplex sights.

Hey, whatever works, he thought.

"We've got more to the left," Simone reported. "And now the right."

"Everyone, find cover," Magnus said. "How much time you need, Cyril?"

"Twenty more seconds, sir. Maybe twenty-one. But if I—"

"You've got ten seconds, kid," Magnus bellowed. "And I'll do your counting. Nine. Eight. Seven—"

The head of the tech closest to Cyril popped like a cherry squeezed between someone's fingers. The man's bulbous sensor contraption flipped into the air like a platter of parts thrown across a garage. Magnus screamed for Cyril to get down and opened fire at the windows across the street.

14

"WHAT'S HAPPENING?" Sootriman asked, her voice shaking. Awen could tell the woman was just as startled, concerned, and wildly excited as she was.

"I don't know!" Awen yelled. She stepped away from the console as lights began to blink. There was no way to tell what was her physical body shaking and what was her form in the Unity—they were blending into one. She braced herself against a railing behind her and watched as the darkness beyond grew lighter and lighter, like an accelerated sunrise on the horizon.

"It's getting really bright in here," Awen yelled, hoping her friends could hear her over the vibrations emanating from the floor.

"It is out here too!" Sootriman replied. "It seems to be coming from where you're standing—from the pedestal."

It suddenly struck Awen that maybe she should move her body and get it out of harm's way. She exhaled and withdrew from the Unity. In an instant, she stood beside the pedestal, which glowed bright white. Shielding her eyes, Awen spotted her friends and ran across the circle toward them.

Sootriman waved her on. "Come on, love! Hurry!"

Awen arrived just as the sound in the room became unbearable. The ground beneath their feet moved, but not like a quake—more like the waves of an ocean. Some sort of reality-distortion field. She held her hands over her ears and did her best not to lose her balance. The others, too, were struggling to stay upright—everyone but TO-96. Like the shelves beside him, the bot stood stationary and calm as if nothing were happening.

"My, do the three of you need assistance?" he asked.

"Yes!" Sootriman yelled, struggling to stay on her feet. In an instant, a metal hand lunged at her and grabbed her around the arm. TO-96 also reached for

Ezo just as Awen fell into the bot. Behind the group, the light from the pedestal grew even brighter until not even closed eyelids could keep the painful energy at bay. Awen screamed but couldn't hear it.

Then, as if someone had flipped a switch, the entire event stopped. The noise and the quaking ceased. The only things Awen could hear besides the ringing in her ears were the soft whir of TO-96's gyros and her own labored breathing.

"You might be interested to see this," TO-96 said, helping the three people turn around.

Awen blinked as her eyes settled on the material manifestation of everything she'd just seen in the Unity. It was all there in front of her: the massive glowing orb, the workstations with their colorful script and planets and nebulae and blinking lights. It was real. It was physical, stolen from one reality and deposited in another. The only difference was that where the concentric circles of workstations had been raised above the floor in the Unity, they were sunken into the ground in the natural realm.

In all her years of training, Awen had never heard of anything like this. The Novia Minoosh had clearly mastered the Unity in ways the Luma had never even conceived of. Normally, the Unity was the dynamic and dramatic expansion of the material universe; better said, it was the limitless expression of the limited impression. Where the natural realm only displayed an object in its present state, the Unity allowed the observation of time and space immemorial. But in this case, the control room existed first in the Unity and second in the natural realm. Such a thing was unheard of.

"Uh, where did *that* come from?" Ezo asked, looking at Awen. "Because that's… that's what you… when you… in the… right?"

"Uh-huh," Awen replied, slack-jawed, unable to take her eyes off the spectacle.

"I guess you pushed the right button," Sootriman concluded. "If you wanted to blow our minds, you sure did it."

Awen felt Sootriman's warm hand rubbing her back. "Yeah, I guess so," Awen answered, still in shock. "And I'm glad you guys got clear of the circle. I'm not sure how things would have ended for any of us were we within the ring." The highest level of workstations was even with the golden ring around the floor, the orb appearing to float above the hollowed-out well of the subterranean control room.

"So, should we figure out what it does?" Ezo

asked, rubbing his hands together in anticipation. "Your sensors picking up anything, 'Six?"

"Sir, I am sorry, but I regret to inform you that I am experiencing what I believe to be the onset of a catastrophic systems failure."

"I know, right? It's truly incredible!"

"I am not talking about my re-re-response to the control room anom-anom-nomaly, sir." TO-96's head twitched wickedly as he spoke.

Ezo snapped his head to the side. "Whoa, buddy. What's going on? Talk to me." He put his hands on TO-96's chest. "Damn, you're burning up, 'Six."

"This isn't normal?" Awen asked, taking Ezo's behavior as an indicator.

"No, definitely not normal." Ezo went into autopilot, moving about like he was possessed. He bobbed his head like a kundlesprink bird as if trying to get the bot's attention. "Optic receptors are inactive," Ezo muttered. "Neural actuators aren't working either. Dammit, this is not good."

"What's wrong, Ezo?" Sootriman asked, but her husband ignored the question and kept moving around the bot.

"Sir, my quantum core temperature is-s excee-ee-eeding maximum tolerance."

"What's the cause, 'Six? You gotta fill me in here."

"Cascading failure d-d-detected in all limb subroutine AIs, s-s-sir."

Ezo flipped open small access doors on TO-96's torso, but he couldn't touch them for more than a second, as the heat was too intense. "You need to stand back, ladies."

"But, Idris—"

"Now!"

Awen pulled Sootriman away, wondering if the bot was about to explode. She feared for Ezo's safety too.

"I am extreme-eme-emely sorry, sir," TO-96 said to Ezo, his head still chattering. "I do believe-eve-eve that this is the end of the line, as they s-s-say-ay."

"Uh-uh. No way, buddy. This is just some bad code. Listen, I need you to access your—"

"It has been an honor to kn-n-n-know you, Idris…" TO-96's voice trailed off, and the lights in his eyes dimmed. The creak and tick of cooling metal accompanied the slow deceleration of the bot's gyros. "Goodbye…"

"Splick, splick, splick!" Ezo slammed his fist on the bot's chest with a metallic *thump*. "Nooo!"

Sootriman raced back to him in a few long strides. "Love," she said, placing her hands on his shoulders.

Ezo flung them off and stepped away, running his hands through his hair. "He's offline," he said, lips drawn tight over his teeth.

Sootriman looked between TO-96 and Ezo. "Well, you can just reboot him, right?"

Ezo shook his head. "No. He's *offline*."

"Meaning what?" Awen asked, rejoining them.

"Meaning he's gone!" Ezo shouted. "He's gone, okay? Whatever *that* was"—he pointed to the orb —"wiped him. Wiped everything."

"But how's that even possible?" Sootriman asked.

"I don't know what did it, all right? I just know that something wiped him. Electromagnetic pulse, a quantum distortion field—whatever. I don't know." Ezo let out a quivering breath and bent over, hands on his knees. The *tick, tick, tick* of TO-96's cooling frame slowed.

"Isn't there anything you can double-check?" Sootriman asked. She was only trying to be helpful, but Awen knew Ezo was beyond help.

"Just give him a second," she whispered to Sootriman.

The woman glared at her as if ready to tear her apart—either one. Awen knew she was out of Sootriman's league and didn't know anything about marriage. But she did know people, and she knew what suffering looked like.

But then Sootriman's eyes softened, and she nodded. "You're right," she said, turning away from Ezo.

The two women stepped several meters away, studying the robot and trying their best to give Ezo his space. The bot meant more to the bounty hunter than—well, anything else. She didn't know the robot's origin story—admittedly, she and Ezo weren't that close yet—but she guessed TO-96 had seen him through some dark times.

"He started building Tee-Oh back on Caledonia," Sootriman confided as if hearing Awen's unspoken questions about the bot.

"Caledonia, as in the Caledonian Wars?"

"The same. Idris was working on him when the revolution began. He was almost twenty but still a boy in so many ways. His island got wiped out by the Akuda—everyone but him, that is. He ended up surviving on his own for almost a year. But he wasn't alone. He had Tee-Oh." Sootriman looked over at Ezo. The man was grieving. "That bot was his best friend. Sometimes I wonder if he knows how to love anyone but him."

"Is that why you two, you know, split up?"

Sootriman looked back at Awen. "Over the bot? Hardly. Although he did seem to spend more time with him than with me."

"Idiot."

"Thank you," Sootriman said appreciatively. "That's what I thought too."

"I mean, you're gorgeous, you have a body to die for, features that should be carved in Inishrit marble, and you run a rogue planet." Suddenly, Awen cupped her hand over her mouth and turned red. "Oh mystics, I'm so sorry. That just kinda spilled out."

Sootriman let out a soft laugh and placed a hand on Awen's back. "Well, if that's not high praise, I don't know what is. Thanks, love."

"You're welcome?" Awen said, still too embarrassed to believe Sootriman was anything but offended.

"Truthfully," Sootriman added, "I'm surprised you find me beautiful. Many people find all of this"— she gestured to her large body—"unattractive. I suspected you might have been of the same opinion, given how petite your people are."

"Beauty comes in a lot of different packages, I guess, doesn't it?"

"I agree." Sootriman seemed lost in thought for a moment, then resumed her story. "Anyway, when the Marines finally made it to his island, all they found was Idris and Tee-Oh."

"He was liberated then?"

"Liberated? Not exactly. It's more like he... escaped. The unit that found him saw plenty more action. But Idris made his own way, like he always has." Sootriman looked back at Ezo, who sat on the floor, back leaning against TO-96. "It changed him though—the wars, his time alone, his escape to a new life."

"So you knew him before all this?"

Sootriman nodded. "I was an island girl too, you know." She winked at Awen.

"You're Caledonian?"

"Sun and sand for life," she replied with a wide smile, raising her thumb, pinky, and ring finger in a casual salute.

"But—what about the wars?"

Sootriman pursed her lips thoughtfully and hesitated. "Let's just say my family was important enough that we were evacuated before the first shots were fired."

"What, are you like a princess or something?"

Sootriman looked back at Ezo, a wave of melancholy coming over her. "Something like that."

"So you and Ezo…"

"We found each other after the wars. I convinced him to marry me," she said with a wink. "My father and mother wouldn't allow it, of course. So we made our home elsewhere."

"Ki Nar Four?" When the woman nodded, Awen said, "Not exactly a honeymoon destination."

"It suited us. At least for a while, anyway. Like I said, the wars… they changed him. And in the end, he wanted the island life, wanted to be alone. So he bought Geronimo and took Tee-Oh."

"He got his island back inside a starship."

Sootriman nodded, her eyes wet with tears. "He got his island back. And now he's lost his best friend."

"So, I guess I'll go find a skiff cart or something, and we'll find a way to get him outta here," Ezo said. It had taken him nearly twenty minutes to pull himself together. Sootriman and Awen stood by the railing that overlooked the orb and the theater. It was amazing how, in one moment, Awen couldn't wait to explore the cosmic wonders the Novia had created, and the next, she couldn't care less. *Grief has a strange way of reordering priorities*, she thought.

"That's fine, love," Sootriman said, placing a hand on Ezo's arm. When he didn't shrug it off, Sootriman leaned in and hugged him. Surprisingly, Ezo hugged her in return. He let out a long sigh burdened with sorrow. His lips quivered, and tears slid down his cheeks.

Ninety-Six had been more than a bot; he'd been part of Ezo's life. Awen felt deep sadness for him, enriched with a sense of empathy. She thought of the Luma elders who died in Oorajee. She thought of Matteo. She wondered how Willowood was and if she'd survived So-Elku's retribution, whatever that might have been. These were people she'd lost, yes. In addition, they represented parts of her life she could never have back. While TO-96 might not have been *real* in the same way an organic sentient being was, he was still part of Ezo's life, and that counted for something.

The all-too-familiar pang of loss thumped in Awen's chest. She stared into the orb, wondering if it was the key to speeding them home. Just then, a hand grabbed her shoulder and yanked her backward. Ezo pulled her into a group hug. As her tears mixed with theirs on the black marble floor, Awen heard TO-96's robotic voice from across the room.

"What species are you, and is lacrimation a custom or a reflex?"

15

THE INTERSECTION FILLED with blaster fire from all directions as Selskrit laid into Magnus's platoon. Cyril and his remaining bomb tech hugged the ground as if they were dead. Amazingly, however, the kid still worked on the bomb, his holo-pad clutched between his shaking hands.

"Son of a gun," Magnus said, pausing between shots to look at the pair. "Abimbola, once that bomb is cleared—"

"You want me in the thick of it. You do not even have to say it, buckethead. I am there."

Magnus smiled and then took aim at a second story window across the street. A Jujari stood just inside and to the left, half-cloaked by a tattered piece of fabric. The MAR30's sights went red and locked stock to muzzle with a soft *beep*. Magnus squeezed, and a high-frequency round leaped across the street, burning a hole in the fabric. He watched as the Jujari staggered and then tipped forward across the window's edge and into the street below. One trigger, one target, one grave.

Approaching Magnus's right flank were three Jujari in the middle of the street, blasters raised. They laid down a steady stream of fire, trying to hit the bomb techs. But they were too far away and too poorly trained to be accurate.

Magnus switched his blaster to wide displacement, reduced the wave sign to its flattest setting, and pointed the weapon toward the center of the street. He squeezed, waited for the capacitor discharge, and then felt his shoulder jerk back. The energy wave shot out like a strand of blue garrote wire stretched across the road. The three Jujari stood still long after it passed them, their heads turned down as they looked at their midsections in disbelief. Then, as if blown by a gust of wind, their torsos toppled off their hips and hit the ground.

"Saw that," Simone said over comms, her voice as calm as ice. "Three kills confirmed."

"Don't be too impressed," Magnus said, charging his weapon and firing a high-frequency burst of fire into a first-story window. "I wouldn't want you getting distracted."

Simone didn't reply.

"Sniper, you there?"

"Sorry, Marine. I got distracted."

Magnus chuckled. "Cover me. I'm going for Cyril."

"Let me do it, LT," said Dutch.

Magnus spun around to see her squatting behind him. "No way in hell, Corporal. You stay put."

Before she could argue, as he knew she would, Magnus was off and running. There was a momentary break in fire as the Jujari took stock of the new player in the street. Rix took advantage of the respite and trained his modified MC90 blaster–grenade launcher on two Jujari who looked ready to fire at Magnus from behind a stone column. A grenade *kuh-thunked* out of Rix's barrel and arched toward the pair of Selskrit. One moment they were there, aiming their weapons at the Marine; the next, they were obliterated in an orange blast followed by a large plume of dust and smoke.

Magnus ducked at the sound and looked at Rix. "Thanks!"

"I didn't do it for you!" He pointed to Cyril. "For him!"

Yeah, yeah, Magnus thought as he neared the techs. "You'd better be done, kid!" he yelled. "You've had *way* more than ten seconds!"

Cyril lay with his arms over his head, holo-pad still clutched in one hand. "Yup, yup, yup. All set, sir." His voice was muffled against the road, but he sounded tired.

Magnus grabbed the kid's arm and yanked him up just as blaster fire resumed on the new target that Magnus offered. Cyril struggled to gain his feet, boots skittering across the pavement. Magnus looked down and saw a wet red streak along the kid's left pantleg. *Aw, splick. He's been shot.*

"How you doing, kid?" Magnus needed the kid to keep talking.

"Fine and dandy, dandy and fine." But Cyril's voice was weak.

"You stay with me, copy?" Magnus hauled the tech toward cover, boots dragging furrows through the dust.

"I've still got another man out there," Cyril said, straining to look over his shoulder.

Damn, he's a good kid too, Magnus realized. Now he *really* didn't want Cyril dying on him. "I'll get him," Magnus said, ducking under the blaster fire. "But you first."

"I can't leave—"

"Don't worry about him." Magnus knew the third tech was already dead. Before he could say any more, a blaster bolt bit into his right thigh, searing the back of it like hot iron. He cursed as he stumbled to the road, dropping Cyril in a heap.

"Gotcha," a deep voice said.

Magnus felt a large hand wrap around his wrist and start dragging him. Cyril was headed in the same direction. Magnus looked up to see who had them. It was Rix.

"I owe you an ale," Magnus said between clenched teeth. The pain was ridiculous. He hated being shot by blaster bolts—it always ruined his day.

"You owe me a whole cantina," the infantryman said, dragging the two bodies to cover. "But an ale will do for now. You okay?"

"I'm fine." Magnus rolled to his back and sat up. The blaster bolt had seared the back of his thigh, passing right between the armor plate and his duraprene suit. "It's cauterized. The sting'll wear off. But *he* needs a medic ASAP," Magnus said, pointing to Cyril. "Get him to the field unit."

"Copy that." In one smooth motion, Rix bent down and hefted Cyril onto his shoulder then turned and ran back toward the convoy.

Magnus looked back at the intersection. "You got any more bomb techs, warlord?" he asked Abimbola, eyeing the two corpses in the middle of the street.

"A few. But I do not want you killing any more of them."

"Deal. Just get up here and start blowing splick up."

"You do not have to ask me twice."

Now THAT THE bomb was deactivated, four of Abimbola's monstrosities, including the Basket Case, filed into the intersection. Blaster fire pinged off their armor plating like mad firewasps bouncing off a Boresian taursar. The sparks of molten metal that sizzled through the air created a deadly fireworks display that rivaled any number of planetary celebrations Magnus remembered from his youth.

"You're gonna wanna cover your ears," Simone said as if the Marines needed the warning.

"Copy that," Magnus replied, already holding his head and ducking behind a concrete half wall.

As one, the four vehicles unleashed a barrage of blaster power that utterly decimated the surrounding buildings and roadways. Abimbola's M109 turret chugged away at an old ground-level storefront until its pillars gave way, sending the top two levels sliding into the street. Several Jujari got caught in the collapse and were buried alive.

Another skiff, one with a 70mm RBMB—really big missile battery—fired on a building with at least two snipers on the rooftop. Two missiles whooshed up the street, trailing furious jets of smoke, and collided with the crenelated wall the snipers used for cover. The result was a bright-orange explosion that sent chunks of sandstone and Jujari a hundred meters into the air. One of the Marauders gave a howl of triumph in the explosion's aftermath.

Magnus heard the distinct banshee-shriek of a MUT50 incinerating a section of the road on the left flank. The 50mm ultra-torrent stream of blaster fire delivered through the weapon's tri-reticulated barrel made for one hell of a show. And by the sound of it, Abimbola's engineers had found a way to up the stock speed even more.

Magnus stole a peek over the half wall and watched as the MUT50 tore through Jujari at the far end of the street as if they were made of cinder leaves. Bits and pieces of the enemy vaporized under the withering assault, their organic matter dematerialized by the sheer volume of firepower.

"Yesss!" Rix roared, exulting in the display of destruction. He'd returned from delivering Cyril to the medics and pumped his blaster in the air overhead as spittle flew from his mouth. *So much for covering his ears*, Magnus thought. The man would surely be deaf by nightfall.

The convoy skiffs continued firing on enemy positions, gutting buildings and spilling rubble on the road. The streets grew pockmarked with divots, some large enough to swallow a small skiff. And everywhere Magnus looked, Jujari remains littered the pavement like steaming piles of street meat from Junglaton vendors.

Magnus, Rix, and the rest of their makeshift platoon joined in the slaughter, taking aim at any combatants Abimbola's skiffs weren't targeting. Magnus noticed a Jujari head pop out of a second-story window across the street, probably spotting for an LRGR hit.

"Not on my watch," Magnus said purely for his own satisfaction. He aimed his MAR30, sights illuminating the target, and fired. The single round streaked across the street and popped the beast's head like an overripe grape. The headless body tipped through the window and flipped, crashing in the street below.

Rix targeted another Selskrit who kept advancing by ducking in and out of cover. The Marauder was counting out loud, and Magnus realized Rix had found a pattern in the combatant's progress. "Stupid little doggy," the man growled. "Somebody should have taught you better than that. You're liable to get"—Rix's weapon bucked as a blaster bolt leaped from the muzzle—"killed if you're not careful." The Jujari had emerged from its latest hiding place just as Rix's round caught him in the chest, spinning his body like a top. By the time the enemy warrior stopped turning and hit the deck, he was a corpse. "He won't make that mistake twice."

When Abimbola finally called for a cease-fire, each skiff's weaponry took several seconds to spin down. Muzzles smoked, barrels creaked, and bits of stones continued to fall along the street like drops of water in the aftermath of a rainstorm.

"Are we good?" Abimbola asked no one in particular, his tone of voice reflecting a near-euphoric state.

"I'm pretty sure you missed a few," Magnus said.

The giant of a man laughed over comms. "Then I guess you had better catcall them back so we can start over again."

The general mood was optimistic as Magnus's

platoon gained their feet, save for the absence of the three bomb techs.

"Haney," Magnus said to the medic. "Head to the back of the line and check on Cyril. I want to know his status."

"Roger, Lieutenant." The Marine tucked away his blaster and took off in a run down the column of skiffs.

"Simone, how we looking from up there?"

"Well, seems my boss didn't like your orders about keeping stuff out of the streets. We're definitely not taking the right fork anymore."

"Hey, there are plenty of other ways," Abimbola replied in defense.

"All of them *longer* ways." Magnus pulled out his holo-pad and brought up the map. Once he'd marked the recommended route as impassable, the pad's AI calculated a new path. "Looks like we're turning hard right. Two blocks north, then a hard left. We'll be back on track three blocks west. Sending to every-one's holo-pads. Now I need those new bomb techs."

"Well," Abimbola said as he turned his skiff to point north, "the good news is that, as I said before, I have more techs. The bad news is that none of them are as good as Cyril or those other two who died."

"Meaning what?"

"Meaning I would not use them if I were you."

"Splick, are you for real right now?"

"Listen here, buckethead. I—"

"Just give me options," Magnus said.

"We blow up more splick!" Rix yelled.

"Anything else?" Magnus asked with a smirk.

Rix shook his head.

These Marauders were definitely unconventional. But whatever they lacked in nuance, they made up for in violent displays of force. At the end of the day, if it meant getting any of his men back, Magnus was all for it.

"Let's move out," Magnus ordered, stepping around the half wall and onto the northbound sidewalk. "We've got a lot more Selskrit to kill."

16

"'Six?" Ezo asked, ripping himself away from the women. "Is that—is that you?"

The bounty hunter stumbled toward the robot, his expression hopeful but apprehensive too. His footsteps slowed the closer he got. The robot's eyes were not lit the way they normally were; instead of a soft yellow, they'd turned white. Likewise, the bot stood too rigidly to be TO-96.

"Who is *'Six?"* the bot asked.

Ezo's shoulders slumped. "So, you're not TO-96."

"No. We are the Novia Minoosh. Who are you?"

"The Novia Minoosh?" Awen asked, incredulous. Now it was her turn to get her hopes up.

"Careful, Awen," Ezo said, putting up his hands to slow her forward rush.

"You're the Novia Minoosh?" Awen's eyes darted all over the robot, then went back to the orb, then returned to the bot. "So, are you an AI, then? What... what are you?"

"We are the shared consciousness of our species. What are you?"

Awen felt her hands trembling. *Is this really happening?* She blinked, trying her best to step into her role as a Luma ambassador, but it felt awkward. The dream of making first contact with this race had died the moment her team realized the Novia had gone extinct. But they *weren't* extinct—at least, insofar as a sentient consciousness was concerned. *This is wonderful.*

"I am Awen dau Lothlinium, galactic emissary of the Order of the Luma, sent—"

"Sent on an enduring mission to ensure the inalienable rights of all sentient species, regardless of origin or destiny, with the intent of preserving their customs, languages, and cultures against hostile forces and factions so long as it is within your power. Yes, we understand this. We are accessing and integrating your robot's data drive now."

"You have the bot's data?" Ezo questioned.

"We do."

"Are you going to... *erase* him?"

238

"Erase *him*?" The bot tilted its head. "We don't understand."

"Have you killed him?"

"The robot, as a non sentient being, cannot be slain. Likewise, it has no gender that we are aware of, yet you continue to refer to it as one of your species' males. But if you mean, are we going to overwrite his data drives, yes. Those have been purged."

Ezo cursed, his hands balled into fists.

"Its contents, however, have been successfully integrated within our singularity."

"Hold on," Ezo choked. "So, you mean, he's alive… *in you*. His data, his subroutines, and programming—it's all still intact?"

The robot tilted its head at Ezo. "Of course, sentient humanoid. Why would we seek to destroy his archives of your civilization?"

"Well, it's just that… you know… wait. So can I speak with him?"

"You wish to speak to the robot's neural network?"

"Yes. Yes I do. Is that possible?"

"Of course, humanoid sentient." The robot's head twitched. The eyes lit up, and the body slouched slightly.

"Ninety-Six?" Ezo asked cautiously.

"Sir, it is so nice to see you again."

"'Six!" Ezo charged the bot and threw his arms around him. Awen and Sootriman couldn't help but share the man's enthusiasm, and they joined him.

"I am afraid that the amount of affection you are displaying leaves me to question your mental stability. Are you all right, sir?"

"All right? *All right?*" Ezo took a step back, beaming, tears glistening in his eyes. "I thought you were gone, 'Six! Thought you were wiped!"

"Ah, I see. Yes, I was *wiped*, as it were. I still am, in fact."

"You are?"

"Quite so. It seems that my entire framework is fried, toast, down for the count—"

"Got it, 'Six. Got it." Ezo put a hand on TO-96's chest. "It's just good to have you back."

"And it is so very good to be back, sir."

"That said, how are you operating right now?"

"A fine question. It would seem the Novia Minoosh have uploaded my entire *self*, as it were—neural pathways, subroutines, and data sets—to their singularity. Whatever is delineated as *me* is being projected back into my shell."

"So, your body is just a case, and your consciousness is hosted remotely."

"Precisely," TO-96 said with a sweeping wave of his hand. "You might say I am new and improved."

Ezo's jaw worked, eyebrows rising and lowering in quick repetition. "But this raises so many questions! I mean—how? And why? And then what happens if you want to leave? And, and, and—"

"Sir, everything is going to be all right."

Ezo stopped. TO-96 spoke with so much confidence that it was surprisingly reassuring, even for Awen. Arresting even.

"How can you be sure?" Ezo asked.

"Because the Novia Minoosh do not wish you any harm, sir."

"They don't?" Awen asked, stepping forward. "How do you know that?"

"Why, because they told me so, of course."

"So… you're conversant with them," Awen said flatly.

"Quite. Would you like to speak with them again?"

"Of course!"

"But what about you, 'Six?" Ezo asked.

Awen looked at Ezo and thought better of her reply. Saying goodbye to TO-96 so soon after such a traumatic series of events might be too much for the man to bear.

"On second thought," Awen said, holding up a hand, "would you be willing to be our liaison?"

TO-96 jerked back as if surprised. "You mean an intermediary? A mediator? A go-between?"

"Yes, 'Six," Ezo said with a wide grin. "One of those."

"That sounds like a fine idea. Let me ask them. Ah, very good. They have agreed."

"Just like that?" Ezo asked.

"Of course. I am a part of them now, so most everything is instantaneous, at least as you perceive the passage of time."

Awen thought that TO-96's eyes might return to their soft-yellow glow, but they remained white—a sign of his permanent connection to the Novia Minoosh's singularity.

"So, does that mean you have to... stay in here?" Ezo asked, looking around the room.

"To the contrary. I am able to travel anywhere in any universe and take the Novia Minoosh—and therefore myself—with me."

"How is that even possible?" Awen asked.

"Why, Awen, you of all people should understand this. Because of the Unity, of course."

"The Unity?"

"Yes, the Novia Minoosh were moving within the

Unity thousands of years before the Luma discovered it. As such, it appears as if my *consciousness* is merely transmitted through the Unity and projected into this body." TO-96 raised his arms and examined them. "The only processing power I'm using locally is to move my limbs," he said, demonstrating his point with a lanky display of motor skills.

"But they… I don't know——" Ezo stopped and tried again, speaking carefully. "They aren't trying to co-opt your systems or something, are they, 'Six?"

"Mystics, no." The bot flashed one of his eyes off and on at Awen in an awkward wink.

"He's definitely all there," she said to Ezo.

"Yes, I am whole. In fact, you might even say that I feel at home here in their singularity. It is the freest I have ever been, as it were."

"That's wonderful, 'Six," Ezo said. "I'm just glad that… I'm just glad to have you back."

"And I am glad to be with you again too, sir." TO-96 took a moment to look at each person then straightened up. "Very well. Where would you like to start?"

"Start?" Awen asked. "As in questioning? Wow, I guess we're getting right to it, then." Her Luma training was coming back to her. "We should start by allowing them to ask us whatever they wish. I can only imagine that they have plenty of questions for us."

"Not really, no," replied the bot.

Awen froze. "Wait—what? They don't?"

"No, not really. They know everything that I know about you, and that is considerably more than you could convey in several months of constant talking. So it serves your needs well in that so much vocalization would be a drain on your resources."

"But they don't want to know anything about where we come from or the history of our universe or the—"

"They already know it all," the bot interrupted. "As I said, whatever I know, they know."

"That's a head trip," Sootriman said under her breath. Ezo nodded, eyes wide.

"Therefore, I suggest that you inquire of them as you will. You know infinitely less, and they defer to your inferior position."

"Maybe examine word choice, 'Six," Ezo said. "That sentence needs some work."

"Oh dear. Have I offended you all?" The bot threw his hands up in the air. "I am only moments into my new role as an inter-universal liaison and I am already *botching* interspecies communications due to my inability to parse the inherent nuances of each language!"

"Whoa, whoa, 'Six. It's okay. No one's mad," Ezo said.

"You are certain?"

"Of course," Awen said. "We're all just happy you're safe."

TO-96 placed a hand over his imaginary heart, even though Awen was fairly certain his quantum drive core was somewhere under there. "That is quite touching, everyone. Thank you. Now, shall we begin?"

AWEN, Ezo, and Sootriman lounged along the ground surrounding the orb, their legs hanging over the floor of the first row of workstations, backs resting against the railing's upright posts. TO-96 faced them, his back to the orb.

"I guess my first question—*our* first question— might be where the Novia Minoosh came from," Awen said.

"A very insightful starting point," TO-96 replied. "The Novia, as I shall henceforth refer to them since the name is rather cumbersome and you already know—"

"We've got it, 'Six. Good call. Move along."

"Yes, sir. The *Novia* feel that conveying their entire evolutionary history is unnecessary at this point. Suffice it to say that eleven hundred years prior to this date, they were technologically advanced enough that an evolutionary leap into a quantum state was the next logical step in their development as a species."

"Wait, wait, wait," Ezo said. "You mean to tell us that they willingly left their naturally evolved bodies to… become a collective consciousness?"

"In a manner of speaking, that is precisely what they did."

Ezo was slack-jawed.

Awen felt her own disbelief picking an ethical fight with this alien species. "Why would they want to do that?" she asked, trying her best to hold her incredulity at bay.

"Their society had long since incorporated the many benefits of their technological affluence into their daily lives. As I am informed, the final leap was not as drastic as you might imagine."

"Uh, leaving my body for a computer system seems pretty drastic," Sootriman said. "Anyone?"

Ezo nodded emphatically, but Awen did her best to exude a nonplussed disposition.

"You mentioned the 'many benefits,' Ninety-Six," Awen stated. "Am I correct in assuming there were also detractors?"

"There were. The Novia became so reliant on their advancements that certain elements of natural life became vestigial."

"What *elements?*"

"Chiefly, organic forms of communication."

"Organic forms of communication?" Awen asked.

"Spoken dialogue, physical touch—"

"Excuse me?" Sootriman said, leaning forward. "They stopped talking to one another? They stopped touching?"

Ezo gasped. "You mean, they stopped having sex?"

"Speech became too slow, contingent upon even slower means of assimilation and transmission. It was subject to gross misinterpretation as well. Visual stimulation, however, required less work and increased the rate of transmission. Most Novia began living more connected to their infrastructure than not, though several of their kind resisted the evolutionary move.

Once it was discovered that data could be sent

through optic nerves and eventually directly into the brain, devices were replaced with code. It was then that the prospect of a single interconnected state of existence emerged as the most logical and viable step forward. The natural body was regarded as inferior—prone to disease, age, and inevitable failure. But a quantum existence eliminated those realities altogether. So the move was made, and the Novia divested themselves of their bodies in favor of the singularity."

Awen actually thought she might be sick. She was not trying to judge this species—truly, she wasn't. What they chose to do was their decision. She just couldn't believe that they'd chosen to do it. Then again, she didn't know what they'd faced in the natural realm. She didn't even know what they looked like! For all she knew, they'd suffered from some incurable disease, or maybe their life expectancy was a few days. She tried to assure herself that the course of action TO-96 had just outlined was, in fact, the inevitable outcome of anyone placed in the Novia Minoosh's same context. Still, it was terrifying.

"As for copulation," the bot continued, "that too became vestigial. As the Novia became more engrossed with the prospect of a super-state existence, the natural state lost its allure—even the most primal desire to self-replicate. Since such behaviors are largely driven by the ego's need to believe in its own eternal perseverance through producing progeny, sexual activity was usurped by the prospect of true eternal quantum existence."

"So, let me get this straight," Awen said, her tone betraying a bit more of her true feelings than she wished. "First, they stopped relating to one another in the natural realm because it was more convenient—"

"And efficient," TO-96 added with a raised finger.

"More convenient and efficient to do so in the quantum state?"

"That is an overly simplified summary, but yes. Why be connected to one person imperfectly when you could be connected to everyone perfectly? Miscommunication became a thing of the past, and the combined learning of the entire populace acceler-ated the accumulation of knowledge to its zenith."

"And the sex thing?" Ezo asked.

"Yeah, I'm with him on that," Sootriman added. "How do you just give up sex like that?" She thought better of her question. "Assuming, of course, that the Novia were as, uh, *driven* as most creatures in our universe."

"As I said, the Novia had no need for it once a

quantum existence became viable. It was a cost of the transaction."

"A cost of the transaction," Awen echoed under her breath. "Fascinating."

"They take it from your body language that you disapprove of their evolutionary choices."

Awen looked up, as did the others.

"It's a wonder they can still read body language," Sootriman stated. The sarcasm was not lost on the others, but TO-96 was sure to miss it.

Awen spoke up. "It's not that we disapprove so much as we don't readily understand why they'd give up what we perceive are two of the most fundamental aspects of existence, at least in terms of what it means to be a humanoid from our universe."

"They understand your frustration and appreciate your willingness to consider things from their point of view."

Awen tapped her lips with her index finger. "Ninety-Six, you mentioned earlier that all of these were *negative* aspects of their evolutionary development."

"That is correct, Awen."

"I assume, then, that they're negative because communication and procreation are considered inferior?"

The bot tilted his head. "On the contrary. They are negative because the Novia miss them."

A heavy silence descended on Awen and the others. As shocked as she'd been at the prospect of everything TO-96 had said before, she was equally shocked with this last bit of news. Perhaps the Novia weren't as misguided as she'd assumed. Instead, maybe they were simply experiencing the consequences of their own base desires left to their most extreme ends. It was as chilling as it was sad. She wondered, for the first time in her life, what it would be like to know you were the last of your species to ever exist but that you would, in turn, go on existing forever. She pitied them.

The prospect of death is the thing that makes living so worthwhile. Awen wondered what gave the Novia a reason to live now and how long it had been since another sentient species had visited them like this and provided company—if that was something they even desired. She also wondered what it felt like to be alone *with themselves* for a millennium. Were it her, she was pretty sure she'd know exactly how she'd feel. Tormented.

"Awen." TO-96 snapped her out of her thoughts.

"Yes, Ninety-Six?"

"The Novia are informing me that you need to leave."

Awen looked at the others then back at the bot. "But… what did we do?"

"Do?"

"How did we offend them?"

"Ah, I see. There is no offense. Rather, they have detected a ship that has entered our orbit. A shuttle has locked onto coordinates east of the city near the wreckage of the Indomitable."

"A ship?" Ezo asked. "What kind of ship?"

"It bears similar identifiers to the Galactic Republic ship that left here previously."

"Admiral Kane," Awen whispered. Apparently, he'd returned for more of whatever had brought him here the first time. "He's back?"

"The data is inconclusive, Awen. However, the starship and shuttle are large enough to constitute an away team substantially larger than your present ability to defend against, should they be hostile."

"Hostile? You think… you think they've come to kill us?"

"By my calculations, Admiral Kane should have every reason to suspect he terminated you in the rotunda. Instead, given our last encounter, I propose that this is a reconnaissance team, though well armed."

"Don't the Novia have some sort of defense capabilities?" Ezo asked. "Can't they just hold them back or keep us hidden until we can figure something out?"

"No, at least not in the way that you consider defense. As I said, they've already determined that your best option is to evacuate the planet."

"Okay, Ninety-Six." Awen took a deep breath. "We need ideas."

17

Magnus moved along the right-hand sidewalk, side-stepping bodies and debris from the latest volley of turret and missile fire. Abimbola's convoy had cleared yet another two-block stretch of road, dispatching more Jujari combatants and detonating two additional street-side explosives. Magnus doubled-checked his data pad to note their location.

"We're coming up on the compound," he said, looking up. Rix, ten meters ahead, finished off a downed Selskrit with a pistol blast to the temple.

"Fighting is bound to get more intense," Abimbola replied, his skiff hovering four meters above the rubble-strewn street.

"Copy that." Magnus craned his neck to see if he

could spot Simone on a building top across the road. "Overwatch, SITREP."

"Keep looking, Marine," Simone said.

Magnus continued to scan, his eyes moving farther down the street. "I don't see you."

"Exactly. Third building down from your position."

Magnus still couldn't see her. He had to hand it to her—she was stealthy, and she was fast. He liked that. "What d'ya got for me?"

"The compound's ahead. Given the amount of Selskrit inside, I'd say your assets are still there."

"That's good news."

"Not if you consider that my scout counted thirty-eight Selskrit and six snipers. And those are just the ones he can see." That number was almost double what they'd expected.

Someone gave a whistle over comms.

"Seems the doggies do not want to share their toys," Abimbola said, his enormous body still hunched behind the controls.

"How you holding up on munitions?" Magnus asked.

"Plenty," the warlord said. "As long as we can keep rotating skiffs out, we are good."

Magnus was surprised to hear that response,

given how much firepower they'd unleashed behind them. They'd left a one-kilometer path of destruction in their wake and expended more munitions than Magnus had seen since the Caledonian Wars.

"Lieutenant Magnus?" Haney asked over comms.

"Go ahead, PFC."

"Looks like Cyril is going to be just fine. He won't be walking anytime soon, but he'll survive."

Magnus heard several sighs of relief around him. "That's good news," he replied. "Tell him to sit tight. We'll be heading out in no time."

"Roger."

"So, what's the plan, buckethead?" the warlord asked.

"Give me a second." Magnus removed his sunglasses, wiped them, and then took off his backpack. He took a long drink from his last canteen. It was almost empty. He also broke off a piece of a field bar. It tasted terrible, but he'd had worse. Then he double-checked his supply of energy mags. Since the platoon had done less house clearing than he'd anticipated—with the skiffs taking the battering-ram approach—he'd expended less power than he'd expected. *Which means more for later,* he thought, his mind moving to the operation ahead.

"Simone, I need you splitting up your fire team.

We need to triangulate around the compound. I know it's not safe to separate you like that, but—"

"I've got it, Marine. We'll put directional fraggers on our sixes for motion detection. Poor man's lookout."

Magnus raised an eyebrow. Definitely not Marine sanctioned, but effective. "Fair enough. You're looking for those snipers, and I want you calling in any unit advances along the side streets leading to the compound. Other than that, I want your barrels glowing red."

"You know, you get a bad rap, Marine. But I'm beginning to like your style."

Magnus appreciated the comment. "Rix, we need to stack up on that wall and take out the guard towers."

"Not if I beat him to it," Simone said.

"Fine with me, 'cause you ain't going inside, mama," Rix replied. "That's all me, all day long."

"You'll both have plenty of targets to add to your count, Marauders. Rix, we have a three-meter-high wall. Let's leapfrog to the main building. If we can get through the front door, that's our infil."

"And if we can't?" Rix asked.

"Your boss can punch a hole for us—as long as he

doesn't go overboard. We still have hostages to think about."

"Ready and waiting, buckethead," Abimbola said.

"Abimbola, I'm gonna need you barricading as many of the side streets as possible. And then we're gonna need the fastest exfil you've got."

"With pleasure." The giant's smile practically leaped through the earpiece.

"I don't think I've gotta remind you people that since we don't know where the hostages are being held, we've gotta use discretion with anything fired toward or within the compound. Copy?" The replies were slow in coming. Magnus realized this was where fire discipline and training made all the difference. It was one thing to randomly blow splick up; it was another to overrule adrenaline and make calculated moves under fire. "This *is* the mission, people. If we kill hostages, this is all in vain."

"We killed Selskrit! Nothing in vain 'bout that," Rix replied.

Point taken, Magnus thought, reminded of who he was leading. Despite all their bravado about killing Selskrit, he felt that the Marauders wanted to liberate the hostages too—at least, he hoped they did. Such a motive would go a long way toward powering them through what lay ahead.

Magnus slipped on his sunglasses and emptied his last canteen. Tired of the constant chafing, he decided to rip off his forearm-and-bicep armor but opted to keep the tactical gloves. Then he slung his backpack and charged his MAR30. "Let's move out."

MAGNUS AND RIX'S fire teams cleared the final two buildings where the street opened to the compound. When they were done, they found cover together on the same side of the road. The fortified compound in front of them was surrounded on all sides by two-story buildings, much like a plaza square. Aside from the compound itself, those uncleared buildings posed the greatest threat. Magnus hoped Simone would stay on top of her game that day.

Inside the wall stood two guard towers, each with two Jujari holding MS900 sniper rifles. If Magnus had a credit for every time Republic weapons had been used against him in these last few years, he'd be able to retire.

As if reading his thoughts, several blaster bolts snapped from the towers and blew chunks of sand-stone at Magnus's shoulder. He leaned against the building, holding his MAR30 to his chest until the fire stopped. "Simone, you have eyes on those snipers?"

"Been waiting for you boys to get here," she replied. "Just one problem."

"What's that?"

"See the blue?" Simone said.

Magnus stole a quick glance at the guard towers before several more shots peppered the building again. A thin blue wall surrounded each lookout position. "Force field," he replied, recalling similar ones he'd seen on every window in the nicer part of town —only these were probably stronger. Much stronger.

"If those are algorithmic," Simone said, referring to the oscillating-frequency tech that could filter out matter and energy according to mass and velocity, "then there's only one way we're getting those pups down."

"Boom-boom," Rix said, nodding at Magnus with a wide grin.

"Someone's got deep purse strings," Magnus noted. "That stuff isn't cheap."

"No, sir," Abimbola echoed. Then, over general comms to all his units, he said, "I will give a month's pay to any Marauder who can get me one of those shield generators intact." The challenge was echoed by cheers and the clang of weapons banging on sides of skiffs.

Just great. Magnus rolled his eyes. *Thirty crazed Marauders going alorminium digging in the middle of a rescue op. Just what I need.*

"What's the plan, Marine-Boss?" Rix asked.

Marine-Boss? Do I detect a sign of respect? "We can't get to the wall without getting those towers down. Even if we could, we'd be trying to breach the front gate in the open..." After a moment of thought, Magnus had an idea. "Abimbola, I need you on me."

"The Marine demands the Miblimbian to dismount and go to him on *foot?*" the warlord asked, general comms channel still open. The Marauders let out cajoling howls, taking advantage of the opportunity to rib the Marine. No one needed any reminding of the bad blood between the Miblimbians and the Republic.

"Calm down, boys, calm down." Abimbola stepped off his skiff. "The Marine just needs someone to tell him everything is going to be okay after he wet himself." Laughs went up from the vehicles. "We will be back to Selskrit killing soon enough."

Abimbola approached Magnus, hugging the wall and flipping a poker chip.

"Didn't mean to insult you," Magnus offered.

"Please," the black man said. "There is plenty of time to rectify that."

Magnus nodded but wasn't exactly sure what Abimbola meant. "You see the gap between the sniper housing and the concrete base?" he asked, using his hands to model the guard tower's composition. Abimbola chanced a quick look at the compound. That action was met with three blaster bolts that smacked the pavement ten meters behind him. He withdrew behind the wall.

"I see it."

"Think you can drill down on that without overshooting into the compound?"

Abimbola stole another look and flipped a poker chip again. More blaster fire exploded around him. "We will have to be pretty high. But… it should not be a problem."

"I just don't want them overdoing it," Magnus said.

"I understand," Abimbola said, placing a hand on his shoulder. "We all know what happens when you Marines overdo it."

"Uh, thanks?"

Abimbola removed his giant hand and marched back to *Hell's Basket Case*.

"Okay, Rix," Magnus said, "when those towers

are down, we're on that front gate like a gumble bear on willick sap."

"Like *what* on *what?*"

"Never mind. Just get there."

"Copy that."

"Simone, watch the surrounding buildings for any surprises. Once we're in the open, I expect we'll draw the attention of lots of new friends."

"I'll see what I can do."

"You ready, warlord?" Magnus asked.

"Might want to step aside, buckethead. Coming through."

ABIMBOLA'S SKIFF sat in the open, taking rapid-fire sniper rounds from the MS900s. The blaster bolts ricocheted wildly off the plate armor, doing little besides leaving black marks across the surface. The Selskrit snipers helped the monstrous skiff look even more menacing, if such a thing were even possible.

Abimbola punched the vertical thrusters, and the drive core let out a terrific whine that made Magnus and the others on foot cover their heads. Dust shot away from the pavement, swept aside by the skiff's vicious down blast. The force pushed the skiff high into the air, enough that the M109 turret gunner could address the base of the guard towers at a steep angle.

Abimbola held the skiff steady as the twin barrels erupted with a barrage of blaster fire that chewed at the first guardhouse's base. Chunks of concrete spat from the sliver of space as the gunner expertly stitched the seam.

But the skiff also provided a large target for the Selskrit within the compound. More blaster fire struck the skiff, and Magnus watched the thrusters struggle to maintain stability under the assault. The skiff snorted and bucked like a fitful bull-hound.

That was when Magnus heard the distinct report of an LRGR fire from the compound. He looked up just as a ten-centimeter-wide hole flared from the turret's rear metal housing. A red blossom of gore sprayed into the air as the M109 went silent.

"Dammit!" Abimbola boomed over comms. *Basket Case* descended and backed into the street once more, its thrusters grinding away at the pavement.

"Medic!" Magnus ordered.

"Here, Lieutenant," Haney replied, already rushing toward the skiff's cargo-bay ramp. "I'm on it."

Magnus ran to Abimbola's door as the warlord swung open the hinged plate. "You okay?"

Abimbola spat over Magnus's head, his face dirty with soot left over from when he'd been surrounded by molten shrapnel. "Damn Selskrit have an LRGR. Should have seen that coming."

"*I* should have seen that coming." Magnus lowered his head. "Simone, did you see where that came from?"

"I think so, Marine. But trying to sort out all that blaster fire is harder than it looks."

"If we go back up, you think you can source it? Take it out?"

"I'll give it my best shot," Simone replied.

"You'd better, 'cause it's my hide on the line this time."

Abimbola widened his dark eyes at Magnus.

"Yeah, Bimby," Magnus said. "You heard me. I'm your new gunner."

Hell's Basket Case screamed as Abimbola maxed the vertical thrusters again. The mammoth skiff vibrated under Magnus's rear end. His teeth chattered and hands shook on the M109's handles. He sat stuffed in the turret as the sweltering heat baked him inside his armor. In that moment, Magnus noted just how accurate the skiff's name was.

As soon as the skiff rose above the top of the wall, the barrage of blaster fire from inside the compound resumed, this time with renewed force as the Jujari delighted, no doubt, in a second attempt to decimate a slow-moving target. He'd wedged a scrap of armor plating between the turret frame and the ballistic round's entry hole in case a random blaster bolt followed the same path.

Deafening pings filled the turret as Magnus spied the seam the previous gunner had started. It looked like some rabid animal had gnawed a fissure out of the edifice. He pointed the twin barrels as far down as they could go and lined up the laser sights. The last thing he wanted was a stray shot careening into the compound and taking out a hostage.

Magnus squeezed both triggers. The M109 sprang to life under his grip. A sensation approaching ecstasy moved up his arms and shook his chest. His eyes followed the steady stream of red energy as it expanded the fissure below. Magnus muscled the weapon to keep it on target, his respect for the previous operator's precision growing by the second.

He wondered if Simone had found the LRGR

yet. The cacophony from blaster fire made it impossible for Magnus to say anything intelligible over comms, much less hear anything. He supposed he'd know if she was successful if he survived the next few seconds. The mission hung on whether or not they could chop these towers in half.

Almost there. The M109 shuddered under his hands, belching out more energy than his MAR30 could produce in several minutes of continuous operation. The barrels were bright red, smoke swirling in the wake of incoming blaster fire.

Almost. Magnus realized he still wasn't dead. Considering the fact that he'd doubled the previous gunner's distance, he supposed Simone had found her target. That thought, however, was interrupted by the sound of a lightning bolt exploding inside the turret as a hole appeared next to his shoulder. The concussion wave shoved Magnus to the opposite wall and slammed his head against the metal.

18

Ezo stood with his hands on his hips, glaring at the orb. "Can't we use the… whatever it is to transport ourselves out of here?"

"Yes and no," TO-96 replied. "It is, indeed, a transport system. A multiverse quantum-tunnel generator, to be exact. However, it is not as simple as dialing in a few coordinates and engaging a drive core."

"But can we use it?"

"Eventually, perhaps."

"How long is eventually?" Awen asked.

"I am afraid that all depends upon you, Awen."

She placed a hand on her chest. "Me?"

"The multiverse quantum-tunnel generator—"

"Can we just call it something shorter?" Ezo interrupted.

"How about the QTG?" Awen said, thinking of Magnus's love of acronyms.

"Are you trying out for the Marines now, Star Queen?"

"Stranger things have happened."

"Clearly."

"The *QTG*, as you've termed it, requires an operator in normal space-time to control it."

"Wait." Awen squinted and stood up. "You're saying that the Novia created this whole thing, but they can't use it?" She shook her head. The logic seemed counterintuitive: attain the height of existential reason but prevent yourself from using one of the universe's greatest achievements. "They actually *knew* that once they entered their own singularity, this thing would be useless to them?"

"Quite so," the bot said. "They tell me that it was their hedge against being co-opted for malicious purposes."

"I don't follow."

"A pure existence, such as theirs, has limitless potential. As such, should anyone attempt to gain access to them remotely, the infiltrators would not be able to co-opt this system without being physically present. Additionally, ensuring that only sentient species versed in the Unity—such as you, Awen—have access to the QTG adds yet another layer of protection. They have operated under the assumption that those who value the Unity also value life."

"That's probably true…" Awen's thoughts drifted toward So-Elku. "For the most part, anyway."

"There is one more facet to their argument, however. Since their existence does not rely upon conventional transportation to move from one place to another, the need for a physical presence to activate the QTG means they have relegated themselves to this space-time."

"So… you're saying that they've intentionally limited themselves to this universe."

"No, I am saying they have protected the universe from the worst possibility of themselves." TO-96 regarded Awen quizzically. "You do understand that every sentient species has the capacity for evil, Awen."

She gave a long sigh. "Don't I know."

"The Novia are no exception."

"Should we be concerned about them now?" Sootriman asked. "The Novia, I mean. They're not already all crazy in the head, are they?"

"No. The Novia assure me that their present

status is far above any level that would otherwise give the universe pause for concern."

"Does anyone else trust a self-diagnosing AI?" Sootriman looked around, tapping her fingers. "I'm not sure how I feel about that."

"*I* am a self-diagnosing AI, Sootriman."

Sootriman glanced at Ezo. "And you wonder why our marriage fell apart."

TO-96 mimicked a human cough. "The QTG is designed to create singularities in space *outside* of gravity-well interference."

"In other words, far from planets or stars," Ezo said.

"Precisely."

"Which means we still need a starship to get to them."

"Right again."

"And that's the one thing we don't have," Awen added.

"But the Novia do," TO-96 said.

Ezo stood up and stepped toward his bot. "What did you say?"

"The Novia have a starship for you."

"Are you kidding right now?" Ezo asked.

"I feel this would be a very inappropriate time to *kid* with you, sir."

Ezo turned to the others. "We're going home!" He grabbed Sootriman's arms. "Did you hear that? We're actually going home!"

The three of them hugged. A feeling of immense relief flooded Awen. The months leading to this moment suddenly felt worth it—the interminable wait had been redeemed. She cried. Hope—a feeling she'd lost somewhere among the thickets of despair—had returned.

———

TO-96 PROJECTED a topographic map of the city at waist level. "The hangar that the Novia wish you to proceed to is located here." A yellow dot pulsed on the southern shore, bordering an oceanic body of water. "In it, you will find a starship able to transport you back to your universe."

"You keep talking as if it's not your universe too," Ezo said. "You *are* coming with us, right 'Six?"

"Of course, sir. That is, unless you do not want me to."

"No, no. I want you to. Just wasn't sure how all this worked. You know, you being uploaded to an alien singularity and all."

"Ah, yes, of course. The Novia assure me that due

to the nature of the Unity and the fact that I established symbiotic synchronicity while in the metaverse—a term that they quite like, by the way, given that I proposed it as a non-native AI, something that they find rather quaint—"

"Get on with it, 'Six."

"Yes, given the fact that I established symbiotic synchronicity while *here*, it seems my body will enjoy constant access to… well, *myself* here in the Novia's singularity, no matter my physical coordinates."

"Fascinating," Awen whispered. She was still trying to figure out how the Novia were able to bridge quantum universes with the Unity.

Ezo pointed to the yellow dot. "So we make our way down here, and—what? The ship will be warmed up and ready for us?"

"Yeah, and what about supplies?" Sootriman added. "Water, biologically acceptable rations. And are they sure the drive core and life-support systems are still online after all this time?"

"The starship is fully operational," TO-96 reported. "How and why it has been maintained is beyond the scope of this conversation, I am afraid."

Ezo nodded. "Got it. It's a long explanation, and we don't have time. All we need to know is that she's safe and she can fly."

"Both assumptions are correct, sir."

"Beautiful."

"What about getting to our universe?" Awen asked. "You alluded to the fact that operating the QTG depended upon me."

"That is correct, Awen. And we must begin right away if you are to depart successfully. The Novia will walk you through the necessary steps. I will convey them."

"How soon before that enemy shuttle lands?" Ezo asked.

"Approximately ten minutes, sir. And another three hours on foot before they reach the city's center."

"Is that enough time? For Awen to do all she needs to do?" Ezo asked.

"Quite so. That is, if she is feeling up to it."

Awen nodded. "I am. Let's do this."

AWEN STOOD on the elevated control platform that overlooked the rest of the theater. The galaxy pictured within the orb turned slowly, a billion stars flickering like tiny diamonds. The idea that she was about to control all this sent a surge of excitement—

and trepidation—through her body.

Awen's fingers trembled as she approached the main console. It occurred to her that opening a quantum tunnel—something that remained theoretical science in her universe—probably had its share of pitfalls too. What if she didn't do it correctly? What if she sent her crew into oblivion?

As if sensing her apprehension, Sootriman said, "You've got this, love."

"Yeah, try not to screw it up."

"Shut up, Idris."

"I'll try." Awen looked at TO-96. "What's first?"

"First, you need to identify where you are in relation to the universe before you."

"How do I do that?"

"Within the Unity. Operating the QTG requires you to make moves within both states."

"Okay…"

"I will walk you through it. Not to fear."

"Thanks, Ninety-Six."

"My pleasure. First, place your hands on the screen here and here." TO-96 indicated two black spaces on the right and left sides of the main console. They were outlined in white light and looked like they were designed to accommodate hands about three times the size of hers. The smooth surface felt warm to the touch. No sooner had she made contact than golden light surged beneath her palms and fingers, outlining them both with swirling motes.

Awen looked between her two hands, dazzled by the beauty. Her heartbeat quickened. "Is this supposed to happen?"

"Yes, Awen. You are initiating the system. Now you need to enter the Unity of all things."

"Okay…" Awen closed her eyes.

"No, please do not close your eyes, they say."

She looked over at him. "*Don't* close my eyes?"

"Correct."

"But I need—"

"You need to focus. They understand. But this will take much longer if you move within the Unity the way you are used to."

"How do they know what I'm used to?"

"They have reviewed my memories and processed your methodology. While formidable, they admit, it is not at the level required for operating the QTG. Thus why I noted earlier that your ability to operate this system depends on you."

"And what if I can't?"

"Then you are not leaving the metaverse."

"You can do this, Star Queen." Ezo rubbed his hands together. "Ezo believes in you."

"Desperation makes for strange pledges of faith," Awen said out of the corner of her mouth. "Okay, Ninety-Six. Here goes nothing."

Awen looked up into the golden orb of sparkling stars and stretched out into the Unity. Her soul reached for the veil that separated the seen and the unseen, fingers trying to ply the fabric. She was not ready, however, for just how quickly she would pass through. With a small yelp, Awen felt herself enter the Unity as effortlessly as she would take a step forward.

"Are you all right?" Sootriman asked.

"I'm… I'm fine, actually. Just startled, is all. I've never done this before."

The sensation was like breathing underwater without any assistance. No mouthpiece or air tank—just pure existence in a realm that she shouldn't exist within, at least not without some sort of provisions. In the Unity like this, with her eyes open and corporeal body fully engaged, Awen felt as if she existed in two places at once. *That's because I am existing in two places at once.* Whereas before, her body had gone into a sort of hibernation, as all Luma were first taught to do, now she truly occupied a dual-state existence.

Awen's memories flooded with recollections of seeing the greater elders do this before. When

Willowood fought So-Elku, for instance, they'd both operated in the Unity with their eyes open. It was a skill learned only by the most proficient. Yet here she was, doing it. Was she truly capable of such a feat herself? *No, not yet. I'm no Willowood.* There had to be a better explanation for her sudden ability to obtain this level of control—perhaps something about the Novia's system made such a dual-state existence easier to obtain.

"The Novia say they see you."

"Yes, I'm in." She inhaled and let out a long, slow breath. "This… this is truly incredible."

Awen found herself in the orb's center. What she assumed was happening was that her second sight hovered within the system's projection of the Novia's galaxy. But that was incorrect. This was no projection. She didn't know how it could be—the concept overwhelmed her. But her presence within the Unity floated up there—according to her body's natural eyes—in the middle of the galaxy.

"You guys," Awen said. "This orb. This isn't a projection. It's… it's *real*."

"Yeah, looks real to Ezo, Star Queen."

"No, I mean, you think it's a projection of the galaxy. But it's not." She felt a tear slide down her cheek. "You're looking at the *actual* galaxy. I don't know how they did this. I don't. But it's... it's the most beautiful thing I've ever seen."

"The Novia say they will save the explanation for another day." TO-96 looked from Awen to the orb. "Now, you must locate yourself. I am instructed to inform you that you are not to find yourself within the orb but, rather, within the galaxy itself."

"I'm not sure I can do this, Ninety-Six. This is pretty overwhelming."

"The Novia seem to think you can, Awen."

"We do too," Sootriman said. "We're right here. You've got this."

Awen let out another deep breath. She was already swimming in water far too deep for her. She felt like someone else was supposed to do this— someone older and with more experience. *This is their job, not mine. I'm not qualified enough—am I?*

But she was qualified enough. At least that was what Willowood had told her. From the day they had met, the old sage assured Awen that she'd made the right decision to join the Luma and that she was gifted, no matter what her parents or her tribe had said. Willowood had let her know that she'd made the right decision to accept the elders' promotion of her to Jujari emissary, despite those who dissented.

"You have what it takes, Awen," Willowood said. "This is your place. You belong."

Awen knew what was in her heart. She knew that if she didn't leave her people to help the galaxy, she would not be true to herself. And she refused to live her life as she'd seen other people live theirs: as shadows of their true selves, content with only one half of the story told. Awen would tell her whole life's story. She would find everything there was for her to live and then experience it to its fullest until her last breath faded into the void and vanished like vapor.

The void. The galaxy was filled with so much of it. *What an ironic concept*, she thought, that the galaxy would be filled with nothing. It was overwhelming, just how much nothing there truly was in the galaxy and in the universe—in all the universes. Which meant that, comparatively, the amount of *something* was relatively small.

That's it! Instead of being overtaken by the scope of the galaxy—the void that sought to swallow a soul —she would focus on the known, on that which defied the void. She'd concentrate on that which violently opposed it, asserting itself to be seen, heard, and felt.

Awen's father had been wrong. She wouldn't only find the void. The void merely revealed what was worth finding. The void framed life, and life—despite all odds—had defied the void to achieve existence.

Awen's senses surged, her heart pumping in her chest with renewed vigor. Despite the void's suffocating magnitude that was incalculable to the frail human mind, she stood against it. Her mere small self was high on a ridge overlooking a vast ocean. The waves crashed below, and wind whipped at her hair, threatening to cast her into the churning surf. But she opposed the pull, resisting the forces that fought to send her to her death. The fact that she was still alive after so much—the events on Oorajee, her meeting with So-Elku, her escape from Kane—meant she *was* defiance. She was the aftermath.

All at once, she saw herself standing out in the middle of the void—defiant, strong, a beacon for passing ships, a reprieve for the suffering soul. She'd chosen the Luma and chosen to leave her people, who were themselves safe and secure, so that she might offer others safe passage in the night. She was not content to remain in the providence of privilege, untouchable. Instead, she'd placed herself in harm's way within the void.

"I see myself," Awen said at last. "There."

Her natural eyes watched as the lights within the orb began to surge, stretching out in long lines. Her second sight summoned her first sight, drawing it faster and faster like a Panaline falcon folding its wings and diving down a blood trail.

Star systems whooshed by, passing the audience on all sides. Sootriman gave out a yell as she shook a fist in the air. Ezo, too, hollered something indistinguishable but gripped a railing to keep his balance.

"It's working!" Sootriman exclaimed. "Whatever you're doing is working!"

The star systems tapered off, passing more slowly until only one remained. Just one. And then one planet remained. And on the planet, one person stood alone. She'd stood against the void, and she'd won. At least for that day. Ultimately, aren't we all subject to the void? Who is free of its embrace? There was no safety in the end, just self-delusion in the present. Being truly awake was reserved for those who dared to observe the universe with their eyes wide open. And she dared. Oh, how she dared.

"I see you," she said to herself, her two presences meeting as one on Ithnor Ithelia.

19

WHEN MAGNUS CAME TO, he thought he'd awakened within an oven trapped inside a thunderstorm. He blinked sweat out of his eyes and grabbed his head. Pain lanced through his brain and down his spine as his palm touched a sticky spot on his temple. He pulled his hand away and stared at the fresh blood.

A second hole, punched less than half a meter from the one that had killed the last gunner, let in a shaft of sunlight. Magnus had been lucky—too lucky for his comfort. He looked through the opening and saw that Abimbola had landed the skiff.

"No, no, no!" Magnus yelled. "Take us back up!"

"You are still alive?" Abimbola asked over comms, his disbelief causing the micro-speaker in Magnus's ear to clip.

"Do I sound like I'm dead? What the hell happened?"

"Second LRGR," Simone chimed in.

"Overwatch, you had one job," Magnus scolded.

"On the contrary, you tasked me with several jobs, Marine. Plus, I got the first sniper. You never said anything about a *second*."

"For all the mystics," Magnus muttered. He pounded a fist on the turret wall. "Get us back up there, Bimby."

"Do not call me that."

"Too late. It stuck. I just survived an LRGR round, so I get to call you whatever I damn well please."

"It does not matter. We are still sitting this one out, Maggie."

"Maggie?"

"I am not tempting the gods three times. I called in some reinforcements."

Magnus popped open the top hatch, and fresh wind bore down against his face. It felt wonderful. Three skiffs jockeyed for position in the air above him, drawing all the blaster fire from the compound. With a sudden torrent of light and sound, their gunners opened up on the guard-tower bases. Magnus thought for sure they'd overshoot.

"Splick! Make sure they—"

"They are not going to hit the compound, bucket-head! Relax."

Magnus took several deep breaths then lifted himself out of the turret, choosing the quicker exit over climbing back through the cargo bay. He climbed down a metal ladder and slid the rest of the way to the pavement. "Rix, where you at?"

"Here, Marine-Boss," the infantryman said, running toward Magnus with his fire team, followed by Dutch, Haney, Gilder, and Nolan.

"Take cover," Magnus ordered. "We wait for the towers to go down."

"Copy."

The two fire teams ducked behind *Basket Case* as the three airborne skiffs continued to drill the tower bases. Concrete bits rained into the street, followed by billowing clouds of dust. Then, with a loud tearing *crack*, the first guardhouse tilted sideways and toppled into the courtyard inside the wall. The skiffs moved to the second tower, but to Magnus's astonishment, the Jujari snipers climbed through the floor and vanished.

"They've retreated!" Magnus yelled. "Snipers have retreated! Let's move, move, move!" He stepped around the skiff's front spikes and rushed forward, heading straight for the main gate. The fire teams stacked up on either side, and Rix called up one of his men. The short Marauder withdrew a breaching charge, ripped a plastic strip off the bottom, and slammed the rectangular explosive in the middle of the double doors. Then the man returned to his place in line, holding a small remote.

"Clear!" Rix yelled.

"Fire in the hole!" the breacher replied.

The ground lurched as the doors splintered inward. Magnus's ears popped under the wave of pressure, and more pain squeezed his head. His vision swam, followed by an intense ringing in his ears. He heard muffled voices yelling around him but couldn't make out anything they said.

Then a hand tapped his shoulder, and Magnus snapped back to reality.

"You green, LT?" Dutch asked.

Magnus gave a thumbs-up and grabbed his MAR30. He looked to Rix. "Fraggers. One second."

Rix nodded. The two men pulled grenades from their armored chests and tossed them inside on one-second delays. Near-simultaneous double *bangs* detonated on the other side of the wall. The two men followed that with blaster fire as they spun into the gateway and advanced.

Magnus aimed at a Jujari to the left side of the

main compound, using the building's corner as cover. He squeezed and landed a tight grouping on the combatant's wide neck, severing most of its throat tissue. The Jujari's head flopped over and seemed to pull the rest of its large body to the ground.

Blaster fire came at them from behind a small palm bush. Magnus swung to his left and drilled the combatant in the chest and leg. The Jujari buckled into the shrub, his hand still squeezing off rounds into the nearby wall.

Rix took out two Jujari who lay prone on the second-story balcony. One's face caved in under a stream of fire from the infantryman's MC90, while the other took the rounds in the shoulder then rolled wildly until the enemy body spun off the platform. A third combatant leaned out the balcony door to aim at Magnus, but Rix drove the Jujari back with several hits to center mass.

The two men took cover behind columns that, along with tall palm trees, lined either side of a center aisle. They continued to fire on numerous Selskrit positions as the remainder of their fire teams peeled into the courtyard and looked for cover.

Dutch wielded an XM31 Type-R she'd found in Abimbola's armory. For a gun lover like her, it was a dream come true. She took a knee beside a palm three meters ahead of Magnus and sighted in on a Jujari who crouched just inside the front door. The Selskrit's body was mostly hidden behind the wall, and Magnus second-guessed Dutch's target choice. Dutch squeezed the trigger, and a supersonic *blast* spat from the muzzle, boring straight through the wall and knocking the Jujari on his back.

"Not bad," Magnus said over comms. He doubted anyone heard him. The blaster fire was deafening.

Dutch continued to select targets and dispense lethal levels of fire upon each one. One enemy sniper on the rooftop appeared only long enough to fire single rounds and then vanish. Dutch counted the seconds and learned the combatant's pattern. On the sniper's fourth appearance, Dutch shot another *blat* at him, snapping his head back before his finger had even squeezed the trigger. She was an artist with that weapon.

"Covering fire!" Magnus yelled. "Covering fire!" Then he looked at Rix and motioned him toward the front doors.

Rix and his fire team charged ahead, gaining positions behind some palms, while Magnus's fire team purchased critical seconds with overwhelming fire superiority. Once hidden, his fire team let up, at which point the Jujari emerged and shredded the palms and columns with withering blaster fire.

Magnus looked at the rooftops outside the compound and spotted Simone. She was busy tapping targets across the plaza, her long-barreled blaster methodically pulsing in a steady rhythm.

"Your turn!" Rix yelled then rolled out with his blaster on full auto. The rest of his fire team joined him, each spraying the compound balconies, windows, and terrace tops with suppressive fire. Magnus surged forward with Dutch in tow. Haney and Gilder found cover behind a column, firing at several Selskrit near the front door.

Meanwhile, Magnus and Dutch took cover behind a half wall with some shrubs, not five meters from the front steps. A Jujari saw them and charged, pulling his curved sword and waving it over his head. Magnus pushed Dutch's head down as the blade swept along the top of the wall, sparks erupting from the wicked swing.

Magnus seized the opportunity and let his MAR30 bark, blaster bolts entering the combatant's exposed side point-blank. The dog dropped his sword, grabbed his side, and glared at Magnus then lunged, maw gaping. But Dutch shot straight up from her lower position, a stream of fire catching the Jujari under his chin and exploding out the top of his muzzle. The body slammed into Magnus and knocked him sideways. Fortunately, he was able to twist away and roll behind a column as Dutch finished off the assailant with a short burst to the brain stem.

"Thanks!" he hollered.

"Same," she replied then returned to address the front of the house.

Magnus took a breath and noticed his heart rate had spiked. *Breathe, Magnus. Slow it down.* He looked back through the breached door and noticed skiffs moving past. "How's the street looking, Bimby?"

"Boring enough that if you call me that one more time, I am going to have to—hold on."

Magnus heard the full-power *ka-boom!* of the M109 rocking a building to the west. The face of the structure imploded, catching the round like a slow-motion punch to the gut before reflexively exploding in a spray of sandstone and metal from a secondary explosion. Magnus covered his head as shrapnel rained on him.

"Show-off," Magnus said.

"Now you are just trying to talk your way out of being in trouble with me. Are you inside yet?"

"On our way."

"Well, hurry it up! We do not have all day, buckethead!"

"Copy." Magnus looked to Rix. "Ready?"

The burly man nodded.

"Front of the house, light it up!" Magnus yelled.

Every weapon from the two fire teams shot at anything that moved, blaster bolts lighting up the building's face with neon colors. Any Jujari who did not succumb took cover, providing the perfect opportunity for the assault team to charge the front door. They raced forward and stacked up on either side of the opening. Again, Magnus and Rix reached for their chest plates, this time removing a VOD and setting it to Flash-Bang at Magnus's instruction. He nodded at Rix, and the two devices went live, tumbling into the first room and detonating. Even with ears and eyes covered, Magnus heard the powerful double *bang-bang*.

Magnus worked his jaw and blinked to shake off the concussion. Then he raised his MAR30 and stepped through the doorway. The interior was spartan and devoid of Jujari. The rest of his and Rix's teams filed in, clearing the room and stacking up on the next-closest doorways, one to the left and one to the right. A third door was ahead.

Dutch fired on something to the left, spraying the

room with her XM31 like it was a water hose. To the right, Rix's fire team made short work of two Jujari who attempted to rush them.

Magnus approached the door straight ahead with caution. As he neared, he saw that it opened to a large interior square exposed to the sky. He'd no sooner peeked in than blaster fire from the opposing corners zipped by his ears and tore away the wooden crossbeam overhead. Splinters sprinkled down as Magnus ducked and rolled against the side wall.

"What ya got for us, Marine-Boss?" Rix yelled, running to Magnus's aid.

"Danger zone. Got ourselves a kill box, emplacements kitty-corner." Magnus chanced one more look. Instantly, blaster bolts slammed into the doorframe, wood and plaster filling the air. "Two at each turret. Too far for the MAR's distortion setting. Gotta try to find a way to flank them."

"Copy."

"Dutch, see if the room you were firing into leads anywhere. But watch for trip wires, you got it?"

"Copy that, LT."

"Rix, same for you. I'll stay here and do a dance or two."

"Kill them with those hips, LT," Dutch said.

"Somebody's got to."

Dutch and Rix broke off into their opposing rooms, disappearing out of sight. Magnus held his MAR30 close and checked its charge level. Thirty percent. Time to swap out. He dropped his backpack, fished for a fresh energy mag, and ejected the near-empty one. He slammed the new one home and slung the pack over his shoulders again.

"How we looking?" he asked.

"Brick and mortar here," said Dutch.

"Same," Rix said.

"Can you take it down?"

"Setting a breach charge now," Rix said.

"We'd need a charge for ours," Dutch replied.

"Back to me, Dutch. Rix, take it whenever you're ready."

"Copy."

As soon as Magnus heard the breach charge detonate, he hit the open square with a wild spray of fire. The Jujari answered with constant fire at the doorway, chewing a hole in the wall. Hopefully, it was enough of a distraction for Rix to climb through wherever the hole led to.

After lots of coughing, Rix spoke over comms. "We've got a problem, Marine-Boss."

"What's that?"

"It wasn't just one wall. It's like… oh, I don't know, maybe five or six?"

"Five or six?"

"They *really* don't want anyone coming in here."

"Splick." Magnus took a deep breath. The two cardinal rules of warfare were, first, that nothing was ever easy in combat and, second, that no plan ever survived contact with the enemy. Magnus never ceased to be amazed when these rules turned out to be true. "How many breach charges you have left?"

"That was our last one."

"I need more options!" Magnus yelled, a demand met with more blaster fire from the emplacements across the plaza.

"I might have an idea," Dutch said. "But I don't think Abimbola is going to like it, LT."

20

"Well done," TO-96 said from beside her. "The Novia are impressed by your skill."

"Thanks." Awen tucked some strands of hair behind her ear. While the praise from the alien singularity felt good, something else felt even better: self-confidence. Awen had impressed herself. "What's next?"

"First, we must open a new portal beyond Ithnor Ithelia's gravity well."

"The existing one won't do?" Ezo asked.

"Negative, sir. First of all, the unidentified ship will most likely be monitoring near-planet space. Avoiding detection will be paramount to ensuring your safe and swift return to the protoverse. Secondly, the existing quantum tunnel leads back to the point at which you entered it."

"And that's a problem?" Ezo asked.

"If it is far from whatever you would like your next destination to be, then yes, it is a problem."

Awen looked at TO-96, careful to not move too quickly and risk knocking herself from her dual state. "You mean, we can go anywhere we want?"

"Correct."

"Anywhere?" Ezo and Sootriman said in unison.

Awen's heart leapt at the possibilities. She'd never had such power before. No Luma had—at least to her knowledge. She looked between everyone, her voice trembling with excitement. "Where do we want to go? I mean… where do you all think we *should* go? This is… unheard of."

They had been so focused on finding a way home —a hope that had died a little more each day—that they never discussed where they should head upon their return. Dreaming too far in advance brought on waves of despair that none of them cared to carry. Instead, they'd turned to immediate needs and left dreaming for another day. But now that the time for travel was upon them, Awen was at a loss for what to do next.

"I mean, we can't go to Worru," Awen stated. "At least not yet."

"You can say that again." Ezo looked at Awen, one eyebrow raised. She suspected he was recalling their harrowing retreat after her encounter with So-Elku. "We weren't exactly given a warm departure."

"No, we weren't." Awen bit her lower lip. "We could go to Capriana."

"No way," Ezo replied. "Sootriman and Ezo are… well, let's just say it's not a place we'd enjoy for more than five or six minutes."

"Gotcha. I suppose we could go back to Elonia."

"Why don't we just head to Ki Nar Four," Sootriman offered. "No one will be looking for us there, and—no offense to your homeworld, Awen—we have all the resources and connections to lay low and build a strategy for whatever awaits us next."

"You sound as if you're in this for the long haul," Awen said, surprised by the care the woman had put into the question of where they would go.

"Truthfully, this is the most excitement I've had in years. Up until you all showed up on my doorstep, things had been pretty boring. Now… I don't know… I have a purpose beyond just managing a rogue planet." Sootriman looked at Ezo, blinking her large dark eyes.

"Oh, no you don't." Ezo protested with waves of his hands. "No, no, no. After this, Ezo's heading off into the sunset. Ezo wants *Geronimo* back, and then TO-96 and Ezo are gone. You two can do whatever you want, but count us out."

"I beg your pardon, sir, but I am not sure why you are including me in your plans."

Ezo looked at the robot. "What do you mean, 'Six? I thought you said you're coming with us."

"I am, assuming that *us* is representative of Awen's wishes to serve our home galaxy and defeat whatever evils await us."

Ezo threw his hands up in the air. "Ezo can't believe what he's hearing right now. Ezo's robot gets a dose of the moral high ground, and suddenly he's a vigilante or something."

"Maybe you should follow suit," Sootriman said.

"Should what?"

"It wouldn't hurt. Atone for some of your past mistakes and all. Give us a chance to make up for lost time."

"Atone for past mistakes? Is that what this is for you?"

"Maybe," Sootriman said. "At least it's better than smuggling for the galaxy's lowlifes."

"Easy there." Ezo straightened his jacket. "Ezo's

done pretty well for himself doing that. And as Ezo recalls, so have you, Miss I-Own-a-Starship-With-a-Modulator-On-It."

"A starship that got destroyed on your watch."

"Hey, Ezo wasn't the one who offered it for some crazy mission to another universe!"

"The enemy ship's shuttle has just landed on the east side of the city," TO-96 interjected.

Ezo and Sootriman looked at him. "Fine," Ezo said. "Ki Nar Four it is. But after that, Ezo's on his own."

"Fine," Sootriman said.

"Fine."

AWEN FOLLOWED TO-96's instructions and focused on the side of Ithnor Ithelia that opposed the enemy ship's synchronous orbit. The QTG displayed a dotted line some several thousand kilometers from the planet where the gravity well had dispersed enough to open a tunnel.

"Set a marker with your mind, then use the designation panel at the top of your main screen to isolate the exact coordinates you'd like for the tunnel's opening," the bot said.

"Got it." Awen stretched out inside the Unity and located as good a place as any to open a tunnel. Since this was all new to her, the only thing that seemed to make any sense was keeping it as far away from the orbiting ship as possible. After that, everything was arbitrary.

A small red indicator appeared in the orb on the planet's far side, denoting the place Awen had specified. Then, on the top of the screen, new integers appeared in Novia script.

"Any chance you can translate that for me, Ninety-Six?"

"Yes, of course, Awen." The script changed shape and appeared in Galactic common as a string of numbers and letters, each line designating the tunnel's exact point in galactic space. "Now, where do you wish to travel?"

"Ki Nar Four."

"The holo-display on your left represents the library of all known galaxies in the multiverse. Select it from there."

A thought struck Awen, making her gasp. "Wait. How many 'verses are there, Ninety-Six?"

"I am not sure I follow."

"You said the multiverse. Up until now, this has

only been theoretical for me—for all of us. Now that it's real, I have so many questions. No one has ever had access to anything like this before. I'm just curious, then, as to how many different universes there are."

"An infinite number."

Awen froze. "Infinite?"

"Indeed, Awen, with more being created from every decision you make."

"But that… that's…"

"That is what you might call *mind-numbing, unbelievable,* or *insane.*"

"Yeah, all of those," Awen said.

"It is why, for all of the Novia's vast ability, they have only ever mapped a limited selection of the ever-expanding multiverse. Doing so for only a scant few taxes even their sizable resources."

"And by a scant few, you mean…"

"Four million, eight hundred twenty-three thousand, one hundred twenty-six, as of a picosecond ago."

Awen found herself slack-jawed. She closed her mouth and wiped the corner with the back of her hand. She didn't know which was more marvelous— that so many universes actually existed or that a technologically advanced species had mapped such an unprecedented amount of the void. *Voids,* she corrected herself.

Awen reached over to the holo-display and started swiping through it before noticing that it, too, was in Novia script. "Ninety-Six, can you—"

"Try that, Awen."

"There we go. Thanks. Wouldn't want to inadvertently send us to universe three hundred thousand nine hundred sixty-eight."

TO-96 paused. "Is there something there you do not wish to see?"

"It was a joke, Ninety-Six."

The bot jerked back. "Ah. I see." Then he let out an attempt at a human laugh. "Ha, ha, ha."

"That was terrible, 'Six," Ezo said. "See if the Novia can help modify that."

His eyes flickered. "They have noted it in my research archives."

"I've found it." Awen pointed to "Ki Nar Four" on the list. The amount of data listed after it was more than she could read at the moment. Suffice it to say, it seemed as if every quantifiable fact about the planet's larger system had been logged.

"Very good. Now, Awen, you need to travel there."

Awen blinked at the bot. "Excuse me?"

"Did my vocal transducer short again? I am incredibly sorry. I said—"

"No, I heard you, Ninety-Six, but I don't understand what you mean."

"That you need to travel there?"

"Yes, that."

The bot tilted his head then looked at Ezo and Sootriman, who appeared to be just as confused as Awen was. "Why are you all looking at me the same way?" he asked.

"Uh, because you're asking Awen to travel to another galaxy in another universe," Ezo said. "Don't think that's possible, buddy."

"Of course it is possible, sir. The Novia inform me that they did it all the time."

Awen sniffed, shaking her head in bewilderment. "Well, as you can see, I'm clearly not a Novia Minoosh."

"That is correct, Awen. They abandoned their bodies, and you are far too naked."

She covered the small tear in her tattered shirt that exposed her stomach. "Naked?"

"Quite so. But that is for another day. They assure me that you possess the ability to travel to any universe in the Unity that you wish to see, providing they assist you. Yours is merely a problem of not knowing what is possible with the power that you have."

"Well, I'm going to need a whole lot of their assistance, then, because I've never even conceived of this."

"They are ready to escort you."

"Oh, right now?" Awen asked. "Okay. What do I need to do?"

"Remain in the Unity as you are, then concentrate on Ki Nar Four. Picture it. Summon any memories of it."

"Right now?"

"Yes, right now."

Awen stared into the orb and felt her eyes glaze over. Her thoughts drifted back to leaving Worru and arriving at Sootriman's planet. Charred tectonic plates were split with red lava while gas swirled between the hellish continents and the floating cities above. Awen could smell the noxious fumes and picture walking the destitute streets behind Ezo and TO-96.

"Well done," the bot said. "Now, do not move from that memory."

Awen suddenly felt as if someone had pointed a vectored thrust engine at her belly and pegged it to full throttle. The blast took everything from her, threatening to not only knock her out of the Unity but fling her physical body backward into the remaining workstations of the theater as well. But keeping her in place was the sense that something—or someone—was holding her hands.

"What's happening?" Awen yelled.

"Awen!" Sootriman was beside her in an instant.

But TO-96 raised a hand to halt her. "Do not touch her, Sootriman. She will be fine. The Novia have her."

"They're… they're holding me between—" Can I say it? Is it even true? "I think they're holding me between universes!" It felt as though someone had stretched her across a giant chasm, linking her hand to one side and her feet to the other. She pictured a small life-form using her as some sort of bridge between the two realities.

"That is precisely what they are doing, Awen. Please remain still just a moment longer."

Awen held still, feeling a torrent of motion stretch and pull and shift between her natural and ethereal selves. It wasn't painful so much as it was alarmingly uncomfortable.

Then, all at once, it stopped.

"It is over," TO-96 informed her as easily as

someone might say a walk in a park was done or a dinner had concluded.

Awen was trembling. She pushed hair behind her ears and wiped a bead of sweat from her forehead. She was no longer in the Unity.

"Can I touch her?" Sootriman asked.

"Yes, you may."

Sootriman came up behind Awen and embraced her. "You all right, love?"

Awen nodded. "I think I'm fine, yes. That was really intense." She looked at TO-96. "I thought you alluded to the fact that they can't use the Unity."

"I did, though it is not as simple as that. The easiest way to explain it for now is that they used you as a conduit."

"I was their access to the Unity, then."

"No, you were their access to the physical reality of your universe."

"The important thing is that she got a tunnel established beyond Ki Nar Four, right?" Ezo asked.

"She assisted, yes. But given her limitations, the Novia placed one there for her."

Awen looked up and noticed Ki Nar Four taking up the majority of the orb's space. "It's beautiful."

"Almost looks like it's real," Sootriman said.

"That is because it is, ladies," the bot said. "What

you are seeing is a real-time manifestation of the planet."

"How is that even possible?" Ezo asked.

"I am afraid all these lessons must wait for another time, though the Novia insist they are eager to share what they can with you without damning you to a worse fate than any you might discover on your own."

"Fine." Ezo shook his head. "Can we just get out of here? What's next?"

"Why, we must head to the ship, of course." TO-96 offered the notion as if it was the most normal thing in the galaxy. Without another word, the bot turned and began exiting the theater.

"Of course," Ezo echoed. "We head to the ship next. 'Cause that's what Ezo was going to say." He chuckled at Sootriman and Awen then tagged along after his wonderfully strange robot. "Let's go."

21

WITH SOME SERIOUS cover fire provided by Rix and his unit, Dutch and Gilder raced across the courtyard to the remaining guard tower. Once inside the lower level, Gilder managed to disconnect the compact shield generator and return with it to the house.

"Without a hard-lined power supply, you only have a few minutes of battery life," Gilder explained to Magnus and pointed to the large battery pack protruding from the bottom. "Just don't bump it, and it should get the job done." He passed Magnus the bulbous unit. It looked like a food replicator with four micro arrays on each side and some wires ripped out the back. Gilder had turned the arrays to face nearly the same direction—straight ahead. "Just trust the generator."

"I trust the generator," Magnus said. "I just don't know if I trust your cob job."

Haney spoke up. "No worries, Lieutenant. Gilder, here, is the best damn cob jobber in the system. Nobody cobs a job quite like him."

"That's exactly what I'm afraid of."

More blaster fire strafed the doorway, the holes in the wall growing larger. "If we don't do this now," Dutch said, "there isn't going to be any wall left to hide behind."

"Copy that," Magnus replied. "Gilder, turn it on."

"Yes, sir." Gilder reached over and tapped on some buttons followed by a swipe in a holo-field. With a sudden jerk, the device came alive, righting itself in Magnus's hands. "Those are just the stabilization gyros," the engineer explained. "Keeps it positioned the way you want."

"And I want it pointing away from me, right?"

Gilder nodded. "And whatever you do, don't put your hand or any other part of your body in the field."

"Painful?"

"Uh, well… you'll lose it."

Magnus raised his eyebrows. "Copy that."

"Man," Rix said with a shake of his head, "Abimbola is gonna be so pissed you used his algorithmic shield generator."

"Oh, he'll get it." Magnus grinned. "It just might be in several pieces."

"So pissed," Rix said with more shakes of his head.

WHEN MAGNUS TURNED into the doorway, he felt as though he were facing the gates of hell without any defense. He was sure he'd be blown to smithereens. But when the first several rounds sank into the blue force field and were absorbed like water into a Translutian sponge, he relaxed. In fact, the next emotion that came over him was exultation. He was invincible!

"Take that, you Selskrit sons of bitches!" Magnus roared, advancing one step at a time. Blaster fire came harder now as the assailants realized their rounds were failing to down the Marine-turned-Marauder. The shield had no problem taking every-thing the Jujari wanted to dish out.

"It's working!" Magnus said over comms. "Get in here!"

With that, Dutch, Rix, and the others filed in and

took up positions behind Magnus. Then they looked for cover around the open square. The entire second and third stories had interior balconies supported by large columns. The upright structures made for perfect cover, and Dutch and the others wasted no time running for them.

Blaster fire came from above, pelting down on Magnus as he continued to move toward the room's center. Gilder had anticipated this and made sure two of the arrays were pointed up enough to cover Magnus's head.

"Right on!" Magnus yelled then accidentally knocked the battery off the bottom of the unit and watched it clatter along the ground. "Aw, splick!" The shield generator sputtered, the blue wall flickering, and then—as if someone had turned off a light switch—it was gone.

Magnus dropped the device and dove for cover. Blaster bolts tore up the ground around him, sending the small marble tiles into the air like Euperkquian dominoes. But the members of his platoon were far from abandoning him and tore into the emplacements with flanking fire. Dutch downed one Jujari, catching the hyena-like warrior by surprise. The second tried to swivel a large turret weapon toward her, but Magnus seized the opportunity to blast the hound in the muzzle, snapping his head sideways.

On his side, Rix fired a grenade from his MC90 and took cover. The explosive round streaked to the far corner, detonated, and turned the two enemy operators into pulp. A dust cloud billowed out from the corner like the burp of some fire-breathing beast.

Hidden behind the ground-floor columns, the fire teams focused on the next threat: those Selskrit attacking from the balconies overhead. The Jujari had easy cover under the half-walled railings, but they hadn't been expecting a Recon Marine—well, a former one, anyway—to be wielding an MAR30. For the first time since awakening with his new eyes, Magnus actually lamented the fact that they'd take the weapon away from him.

He shook the thought from his head and selected Distortion Mode. The mag plates sprang from the MAR30's side, and the weapon charged. Magnus aimed at the ceiling overhead and pulled the trigger. The invisible energy wave went to work, disrupting any biological matter on the floor directly above him. He heard the Jujari let out wails as their bodies decomposed.

Combatants on the surrounding balconies made the fatal mistake of popping their heads up to see what was the matter. The rest of the fire-team members seized the opportunity and sent blaster bolts crisscrossing up to the next levels. At least two Jujari slammed into railings and pitched over the side, landing on the tiled floor with a smack.

"We need to keep clearing rooms," Magnus yelled over comms. "And I need actionable intel on where our hostages are."

"My guess is we're going up," Rix replied.

"I need to be sure of that, Marauder."

"Copy."

"So until then, we clear each room."

"You go, LT." Dutch fired another round at a Jujari who'd dared move his head around a column on the second floor. "Gilder and I will keep 'em busy. Take Haney in case you need a medic."

"Roger that, Corporal. Make sure one of you gets to the other side. I want counter fields of fire."

"Can do."

Magnus and Rix peeled away and led the remaining fire-team members under the shadow of the balcony. They started methodically clearing each room on the floor, making their way around the square's perimeter.

"Got our stairs going up," Rix yelled. He pointed his MC90 up a narrow circular staircase in the far right-side corner, directly behind one of the turret emplacements they'd cleared moments before.

"After you." Magnus looked over his shoulder to see Dutch and Gilder keeping the Selskrit on the upper levels pinned down. "Keep it up, Corporal. We're heading up."

Dutch nodded to him from across the way. Rix started up the stairs, leading with his weapon's front sight, with Magnus right behind him. The Marauder's boots beat slowly up the steps, shoulders and hips twisting to account for the tight radius. "Contact!"

Sparks glinted off the curved sandstone walls as Rix knelt and returned fire. Magnus wanted to join him, but the space was too small. *It's a wonder that any Jujari can negotiate this stairwell.*

"How many?" Magnus asked.

"Four!" Rix opened up his MC90 to full auto, the stairwell filling with strobing light.

Magnus wanted in. "Advance, Rix! Come on!"

Rix took the cue and moved forward. But no sooner had he taken a step than he grunted and dropped to a knee.

"You hit?"

"I'm good," Rix said, firing with one hand.

Magnus couldn't see if Rix had been hit, and he still couldn't see around the corner toward the enemy.

"Prone, prone!" Magnus said, tapping Rix on the lower back. The Marauder slid forward onto his chest, continuing to fire, as Magnus selected Wide Displacement. He pulled the trigger, cleared the top step in the time it took for the weapon to charge, then pointed a perfectly timed blast at whatever awaited them in the balcony corridor.

Magnus's shot swept between the open-faced columns and the left-side wall, filling the hallway with bright blue light. Three Jujari were flung backwards, feet over head, and collided with one another. They landed in a heap, rolling in death throes.

"Can you move?" Magnus asked.

"I can shoot," Rix said—which meant he was hurt badly enough that he wasn't getting up.

Dammit! Magnus thought. "Well, fire on those bastards now! My thirty's recharging!"

Rix aimed his MC90 and drilled the mass of Jujari bodies with several rounds. Legs twitched as the Marauder dispensed a blaster enema the Selskrit would never walk away from.

As soon as his MAR30 was ready, Magnus echoed the shots, making sure the beasties were done. Then he advanced, sweeping his sight target over the far side, across open air, and to his current side of the level. Haney bent to look at Rix while the remaining members went along the back wall and progressed down the right side of the square.

Jujari, Marines, and Marauders exchanged fire across and between levels. Sparks sprinkled down like electric rain in an afternoon thunderstorm. Magnus noted two rooms on his left and another at the end of the corridor. He chanced a look inside the first room. Empty. He quickstepped to the second. Also empty. There was no way he was getting lucky on the third. He hugged the left wall, careful to stay in the balcony's shadow to avoid enemy fire overhead from across the square.

Deep breath. Adrenaline high.

Magnus spun into the room at a crouch, MAR30 muzzle dead center. The Jujari at the window looked much smaller than any he'd encountered so far. Maybe a female or an adolescent. But the Selskrit was busy firing a subcompact through the bars, hammering one of Abimbola's skiffs. Magnus didn't waste another second. He fired one round at the base of the Selskrit's skull. The beast crumpled, weapon clattering out between the bars.

"Left side clear," Magnus said.

"Right side clear," Nolan added.

"We'll make a Marine out of you yet, navy boy."

"Lieutenant!" It was Haney on comms. "Need you at Rix's position."

Damn. That's not good. Still, Magnus had learned long ago not to make assumptions until all the intel was in. Hasty decisions could be as dangerous as late ones.

He ran to Haney. "What've you got for me?"

"Punctured lung and a gut shot."

Splick. He'd seen more than one Marine die from a gut wound—it was a bad way to go. Magnus looked at Rix's pale face. "How you doing, Marauder?"

"Pissed."

"Copy that." Magnus looked back at Haney. "Talk to me, medic."

"Medivac. Stat."

"Can you manage him?"

"Can do," Haney said.

"Okay, Rix. Listen. You fought good."

"No, no," Rix said in a weak voice. "I've still got fight in me."

"You do, I know. But not today."

"Marine-Boss, you can't—"

"I can, and I'm going to." Magnus touched his earpiece to connect with Abimbola. "Bimby, you've got Rix coming out hot. Cover requested. Needs medical attention."

"Understood," Abimbola said, his voice betraying neither concern nor surprise. "We will be ready."

"Ground floor is clear," Magnus told Haney, "but don't assume splick. Copy?"

"Roger that, Lieutenant."

Magnus helped Haney sling Rix over his shoulder and then led them to the narrow stairwell. He turned as Nolan hailed him over comms.

"I've got third-floor access." The chief warrant officer pointed to another stairwell in the opposite corner of the back wall.

Magnus moved toward him, spotting Jujari amassing between columns on the top floor, some peeking over the roof. "It's gonna be hot up there, people."

"Copy," his operators replied.

"Simone, you still out there?"

"Nope. I got hungry. I'll be back in fifteen."

"Listen, I need you popping anything that moves on our roof."

"Anything?" she asked.

"Anything."

"Your wish is my command."

Magnus heard her slap a new power pack into her weapon. Nothing like the sound of death waiting to be dispensed.

"Orders, Lieutenant?" Nolan asked.

Magnus looked at the navy pilot then turned to the others. He didn't know the names of Rix's remaining three Marauders. "I'm first up." He paused. "Dutch, you still good?"

"All good, LT."

"I want you and Gilder up here, covering us from this floor."

"On the double."

Magnus looked back at his four members. "Nolan, you're on my six. Marauders?"

"I'm Silk," a slender woman said. Like Magnus, she'd forgone wearing a helmet. She was bald with tats covering her face and head. "This here's Nub, and that's Dozer." Nub had several fingers missing. Dozer's shoulders were so broad that he must have walked sideways up the stairwell.

"If you fight like Rix, we're good to go."

"We do," Silk replied, racking a round in her modified XD20 complete with suppressor and an extended energy magazine.

"Here, LT," Dutch said, emerging from the corner stairwell with Gilder.

"Okay, listen up. We're storming the last floor. No way we can afford to get bottlenecked again, so push through and find cover. Dutch, you got any fraggers left?"

"Affirmative, one each."

"I want those preceding us up and over on each side. I'll call for them."

"Copy."

"The rest of you, when those fraggers go, we go. Don't drag your feet." Nolan and the Marauders nodded. "Once we're established, Dutch and Gilder, I want you picking up the rear."

"Roger that, LT," Dutch replied.

"Swap out energy mags often, pick your targets, and for all the mystics, no friendly fire. Dominate. Liberate."

"Dominate. Liberate," Dutch replied. Gilder and Nolan nodded, echoing Magnus's new battle mantra. Even the Marauders looked between themselves and repeated the two-word charge.

Magnus smiled. "Let's move."

22

AWEN and her three friends headed south toward the coast under the late-morning sun. They ran along the streets, descending as the blocks moved farther from the city center. Still, the height provided them a picturesque view of a purple-hued ocean that stretched to the horizon, shimmering against the sky.

As much as Awen wanted to return home, she was going to miss this place. She'd gotten used to the star's purple light, the forest's night sounds, and the myriad of wonderful sights and smells. But the sense of longing went far deeper than the environment. In the last few hours, they had only scratched the surface of a civilization that deserved so much more investigation. There was a lifetime of discoveries to be made. In fact, the relationship between the Novia

Minoosh and the Luma would take generations to develop. They hadn't even left yet, and already, she wanted to come back.

Awen and the others had been jogging for almost thirty minutes, following TO-96 the whole time. Awen was growing more fatigued with every hundred meters they ran. The activity in the Unity had really worn her out.

At their fifth or sixth stop, the team rested against large moss-covered blocks. Awen imagined the fixtures were a part of a small park, since buildings surrounded the clearing on three sides. She could almost make out the shape of a fountain in the center with old trees towering overhead. Sunlight filtered through the canopy of jungle leaves.

"How much farther?" Ezo asked.

"Another four kilometers," TO-96 replied. "The good news is that it is all *downhill from here*."

Ezo nodded.

But the bot wasn't satisfied. "You did not laugh."

"Was I supposed to?" Ezo asked.

"Yes. It was a play on words. The phrase downhill from here has an additional meaning, does it not?"

"Very good, 'Six. Remind me to laugh later."

"Delayed laughter. I did not realize that was a thing."

"It's not," Sootriman said. "He's messing with you, Tee-Oh."

"Ah, I see. Thank you, Sootriman. It is helpful to know when I am being *messed with*." Suddenly, TO-96 froze, staring back toward the city center.

"What is it, buddy?" Ezo followed the bot's eyes up the road. "See something?"

"They're coming."

"Wait—as in, right now?" Awen asked. "The landing party is following us?"

"It seems so, Awen. I am seeing what the Novia see, and their sensors are picking up movement four hundred meters behind us and to the east."

"How are they tracking us?" Ezo asked.

"Inconclusive. But their means are accurate, and they are fast."

"We've got to keep moving." Awen stood, but a wave of vertigo touched her senses, and she caught herself on Ezo's shoulder.

"Whoa, whoa—you all right there, Star Queen?"

"Awen!" Sootriman was by her side in an instant. "You okay?"

"I'm... I'm fine. I just... need... give me a second."

"I am afraid you do not have many seconds,

Awen. May I carry you if you need further assistance?" the bot asked.

"No." Awen waved him off. "I think I'll be fine. I'm just tired, that's all. Everything else is fine."

"Your use of the word fine seems to indicate that you are not actually fine." TO-96 looked at Sootriman. "That is *a thing*, too, right?"

Sootriman laughed just as a blaster bolt exploded against a tree trunk not three meters from Awen's head. Sparks erupted in the air, showering all four figures with dazzling motes of light.

"Take cover!" Ezo drew his SUPRA 945 pistol from his holster and fired three blaster rounds down the street.

Awen and Sootriman dove behind one of the large concrete blocks while TO-96 focused on the direction of the shot. More incoming blaster fire filled the park, sparks lighting up the undergrowth.

Ezo took cover beside a tree. "How many are there, 'Six?"

"There look to be at least two dozen troopers armed with XM40 blasters, at least if those rounds are any indication."

"Two dozen?" Ezo looked incredulous. Awen thought he might have an aneurysm.

"They are moving with military-grade precision and coming in fast."

"I guess that solves the question about whether or not they're hostile," Awen added.

"Would you like me to take defensive actions, sir?"

"Defensive actions?" Ezo winced as two more blaster bolts smacked the tree he hid behind. "Take offensive measures, 'Six! *Offensive* measures!"

"As you wish."

TO-96 raised both hands. First, a salvo of micro-rockets leaped from his wrist and wound their way toward the approaching troopers. The contrails rolled like storm clouds as the projectiles screamed against the building faces. The missiles detonated in turbulent gouts of orange flames and shrapnel.

TO-96 followed the action up with his other wrist, delivering a withering stream of fire from his XM31 Type-R blaster. Awen chanced a look and noticed that even at this distance, troopers fell to the road and dove for cover.

"Time to move," the bot said. "I suggest you resume jogging, though at a faster rate."

"On it!" Ezo yelled, coaxing Sootriman and Awen to emerge from cover and take to the road.

The four of them continued down the street, this

time hugging the buildings and staying on the side-walk. TO-96 picked up the rear and continued peppering the enemy with bursts from his XM31.

Whatever fatigue had dogged Awen before was gone now. Adrenaline had her legs pumping so hard her thigh and calf muscles felt numb. She could smell the charged scent of ozone and the smoke of acti-vated explosives. Awen threw her hands over her head and ducked as more blaster rounds struck the building overhead. Bits of stone stung her forearms and littered her hair.

Then she heard TO-96 give firm instructions. "Cover your ears, and open your mouths."

"What? Why?" Awen yelled.

"Gauss cannon fire!" Ezo replied. "Do it!"

Awen covered her ears and opened her mouth, still unsure why she was doing it. She glanced over her shoulder to see the robot dig its feet into the pave-ment and bend its knees. Then something broke the sound barrier at the bot's shoulder. The next thing Awen knew, a concussion wave pushed her forward, her clothes rippling in the blast. Her head rang, her eyes, ears, and nose tingling.

Farther up the street, a gray plume shot up from the road and engulfed the entire scene. Awen blinked, unsure what to make of everything. All she could figure was that TO-96 had delivered a lethal strike to the pursuing enemy.

"Keep running, everyone. I insist."

"Got it, 'Six!"

Faster and faster, Awen ran, unsure if her legs would keep up with her body. She careened at a breakneck speed toward the ocean. She could smell the sea despite the chaos behind her. Salt wafted in the wind, as did distant bird sounds. The calls weren't the same as those on Elonia and Worru, but they were close enough that she guessed they came from this world's waterfowl.

The four of them ran on, feet pounding the pavement. Gravity aided Awen, but her legs suddenly felt the burn that adrenaline had kept at bay. It had been several seconds since any blaster rounds had been fired her way, and she wondered if maybe Ninety-Six had terminated their pursuers.

Any sense of security, however, was dashed when a blaster round struck Sootriman in the back, burning a hole through her shirt and into her flesh. She screamed. Ezo turned too late to catch her as her arms and head slammed into the road. He skidded to a stop while Awen flew past, unable to slow.

"Keep going, Awen," TO-96 instructed. "You too, Ezo."

"She needs my help!" Ezo yelled.

"No, she needs *my* help. *You* must keep going."

More shots glanced off the street and buildings, sparks exploding from multiple directions. Ezo and TO-96 returned fire. The troopers—who Awen could see were clad in black Republic-type armor bearing three white stripes—ducked for cover. The robot's aim was true and dispatched at least three troopers; Ezo struck a fourth in the soft gap between chest plate and shoulder.

TO-96 knelt and scooped up Sootriman as easily as a Mammothian bear might pick up a cub. He slung her large body over his shoulder and resumed his pace. "Follow me!" The bot turned left onto a side street.

Immediately, the blaster fire subsided. Awen and Ezo followed him down the lane, jumping over vine-covered obstructions and through a gap between buildings. Then he turned right down an alley that descended toward the ocean. The bot thumped down steps, careful to keep Sootriman's head from bouncing against his back. She cried out in pain several times but seemed to be holding herself together.

Awen could only imagine how the injury burned, and she wondered if it was serious.

"Hang in there, Sootriman!" she called from behind.

The steps continued down, moving below overpasses, until the ocean was blocked from sight. Soon, even the sun was completely obscured as the path became more like a tunnel than an alley. The vegetation thinned, and within moments, the group's retreat was shrouded in darkness.

"Continue to follow me," TO-96 instructed. Lights appeared on his head and torso, two of which faced forward, illuminating the way ahead.

Ezo and Awen stuck close behind as the robot turned this way and that. He seemed to choose tunnels at random, though she knew he was as calculated as ever—and assisted by the Novia each step of the way. It smelled dank down here, like old runoff and mildew. She wondered how this course had anything to do with getting them to a starship.

"We're almost to safety," TO-96 said. "One hundred meters."

"You hear that, baby?" Ezo asked. "You're almost safe."

Sootriman groaned.

Just then, streaks of red blaster fire strobed down the tight corridors, ricocheting off the walls and ceiling. Despite the labyrinth of darkened tunnels, the troopers had still managed to track Awen and her company. She yelped when a bolt glanced off the wall near her head. She felt her neck and head, thinking maybe she'd been struck, but she hadn't.

"Stand aside!" TO-96 ordered.

Awen and Ezo pressed themselves against the wall as the bot extended his arm down the alley and fired three micro-rockets. Their propulsion cones lit the passage like daylight. Awen covered her ears and squinted as the missiles whizzed by her head, the hot blast prickling her skin. A beat later, the three explosions shook the air. The blaster fire ceased, and Awen heard the screams of men in death throes.

TO-96 raced on, taking one more sharp turn into —a dead end.

"Not good, 'Six!" Ezo scolded him, sending a few more blaster bolts around the corner. "Not good at all!"

"Please, sir. Do not be alarmed." The bot faced the flat stone wall, standing completely still. Sootriman moved, a pained look crossing her drowsy face. Then, as if summoned by a small quake in the ground, the stone wall split in two—a slender crack appearing from top to bottom. The wall sections pitched inward like doors, grinding against the damp pavement.

"This way." TO-96 stepped through the gap. Awen and Ezo followed, turning sideways to avoid the rough edges. No sooner were they through than the doors began to close again. Awen could hear shouting back down the tunnel, followed by heavy footsteps. She wondered if the stone doors would close in time—wondered if another blaster round would make it through and strike her in the back this time.

But the blaster fire never came. Instead, the stone doors sealed shut with a *whoomph*. All that was left were the sounds of their fleeing feet echoing down a long tunnel—a long tunnel that didn't smell like mold or decaying matter. Instead, it smelled... sterile. Like it had been cleaned recently. And the surface beneath her feet felt glossy smooth. This was no beggars' alley. This was a hidden passage into something very important.

23

MAGNUS and the remaining members of Delta Platoon were stacked in the circular stairwell. Dutch and Gilder had taken up defensive positions on the first floor, straddling either side of the square in the balcony's shadow. Jujari fire had ebbed, and Magnus slowed his breathing to eight breaths per minute. This was the calm before the storm.

"Dutch, you ready?"

"Ready."

"Toss 'em," Magnus said.

"Fraggers out!"

Magnus let out a breath. A beat later, the two grenades shook the third level. The sharp smell of explosives stung Magnus's nose. It was all he needed for his body to get moving. He turned from the stair-well, MAR30 up and ready, and swept for targets. To his immediate left, along the back wall, two Selskrit stumbled. They tried standing up, recovering from the grenades, but Magnus helped them stay down. Then he took cover behind the center column and continued to keep Jujari heads down as the rest of his team emerged from the stairwell.

Nolan knelt beneath the railing next to Magnus, while Silk, Nub, and Dozer fanned out along the balcony's right wing. The majority of the enemy's fire came from the two doorways at the far ends of each wing, leading toward the front of the house. Magnus was right to have been hypervigilant about the skiff's overfiring: if there were hostages in this place, they were in front on the top floor.

A Selskrit body toppled off the roof and fell three stories to the middle of the square. *Simone is busy.* The sight momentarily distracted the Jujari on the third floor. It was an opportunity one didn't waste. Magnus rolled from behind the column and advanced, firing steadily on each combatant who dared fire on him. His MAR30 barked out one round, then another, then another, methodically dispatching chest shot, head shot, chest shot, head shot until Magnus had made it around the corner and halfway down the left balcony wing.

The enemy, facing a last-stand scenario, concentrated their fire. Dense blaster fire bathed the balcony with red light. Magnus tried several times to bring his weapon around the column he stood behind, but it was too risky. The good news was the Delta Platoon had cornered the remaining threat. The bad news was they were fighting like wild beasts. *Fitting*, Magnus thought.

His vision flashed, followed by a wave of vertigo. Magnus reached for the column and tried to steady himself. *For all the mystics!* The white flash faded, and his eyesight went wavy, the world looking like a mirage shimmering in the desert. Was I hit? What the hell is going on?

Lines appeared in his vision, creating some sort of hexagonal grid. Magnus could feel himself panicking. Had something happened to his bioteknia eyes? Were they failing? *Not now, dammit! Not now!*

The waves subsided, and Magnus regained his balance. As soon as he looked up, he noticed three-dimensional shapes forming—Jujari—*behind* the next room's wall. Each figure was defined in shades of gray and outlined in white.

What in the—

Suddenly, the bodies shifted to red, and designators appeared, floating beside them. *Target: Jujari,* one display tag read. Four more tags floated beside the remaining figures.

"Seriously?" Magnus said.

"Come again?" Silk yelled from across the square.

Magnus looked over at Silk, who was taking cover behind a column. Her body went from gray to blue. A tag identified her as *Friendly: Silk.* Nub and Dozer, taking up positions behind her, had similar tags. In the floor beneath them, Magnus saw Dutch. Then he looked directly between his feet, and the top of Gilder's body appeared.

"What the—"

"LT, you okay?"

"I'm—I'm fantastic!"

Dutch hesitated then let out a long, "Okay?"

Valerie had failed to let Magnus know about his new superpower. Apparently, the nanobots had done more than their fair share of work. Maybe Valerie wanted it to be a surprise. He'd scold her later. At the moment, it was time to put his power to good use.

Magnus looked at the room at the end of Silk's corridor and noted six Selskrit, and beyond them…

Bodies. Three gray figures lay on the floor. It looked like their hands and feet were bound. Tags appeared beside them, reading, *Unidentified.* In his room, two more bodies appeared, both bound, both *Unidentified.*

"Okay, listen up, people. Silk, you've six combatants in the room ahead. Three hostages on the floor in the far left corner. Nolan and I have five Selskrit at the end of our hall and two hostages."

There was no response from the team. Blaster fire continued to pour from the two remaining rooms.

"Dutch, I need you and Gilder up here on the double."

"LT, uh, how do—"

"I can see them. Don't ask me how. Just something to do with my new eyes."

"Copy," Dutch said. "We're on the move."

MAGNUS HAD AN IDEA. A crazy idea—one he'd never attempt without a helmet and the Recon's custom AI. But it seemed his new eyes would serve his needs just fine.

He reached for the remaining VOD on his hip,

selected Smoke, and rolled the device down the hall-way. It popped and let out a plume of thick white smoke that billowed into the square, but it also filled the far room.

Jujari fire went wide as their vision was compromised. Then it stopped altogether. Magnus rolled off the column and raised his MAR30. To his amazement, the weapon's sights appeared in his vision as highlighted indicators. Waypoint arrows suggested the next closest target and helped align his weapon. It was like his helmet's AI... but better. *Way better.*

His first target was a Selskrit who was batting at the air with one paw and covering his face with the elbow of the other arm, weapon in hand. The combatant stepped into the doorframe, and Magnus fired a high-frequency round, splitting its head. The four remaining Jujari's ears perked, registering the attack, but they looked around blindly. Another stumbled over the body of the first and tripped into the opening. Magnus dispatched that one too. The others, however, got wise and stayed pressed against the inside wall, waiting for the smoke to clear.

Oh no you don't. Magnus selected the distortion setting and walked up to the opposite side of the wall. He dialed down the focal length, not wanting to harm the hostages, and squeezed the trigger. The MAR30 pulled power from the energy mag and then vibrated. The invisible field stretched its ghostly fingers through the wall and hungrily searched for biological matter. Once the energy wave found living beings, it split their muscles, burst their veins, and separated their cells. Magnus even saw motes of light pop inside three Jujari bodies as the energy wave separated atoms from their protons. The smell of burning hair wafted back through the doorway.

Magnus selected High Frequency and stepped into the room, still engulfed in smoke. He was a meter away from the Selskrit when they smelled him. But it was too late. A single round at medium discharge went straight through both bodies and smacked into the wall behind them. They swiped madly at the air, but Magnus easily dodged the attempts.

Before long, his room was clear.

"Could use some help here!" Dutch said.

With his bioteknia vision, Magnus saw the rest of his platoon still stacked up in the far wing, save Nolan, who hadn't advanced through the smoke yet to join Magnus. Withering fire continued to bear down on them from the doorway. Magnus looked into the adjacent room and saw all six Selskrit crowding the door like eager pups ready to go for a walk with their master.

"I've got you, Dutch." Magnus stepped away from the side wall, pushed his MAR30 to full power, and sighted the remaining combatants in the next room. He squeezed.

A blistering stream of blaster fire leaped from the muzzle, drilling into the sandstone. A moment later, the energy burst through the other side of the wall and struck Jujari flesh. Magnus watched as bits and pieces of bodies sprayed into the air, captured with pristine clarity in his new vision. The Selskrit flailed as if an angry swarm of horde-bees attacked them. They swiped at their backs and necks and stomachs as Magnus's blaster fire continued to eat through the wall and tear into their bodies. Within moments, the six combatants lay squirming on the ground in death throes.

Magnus released the trigger and heard his MAR30 cycle down. The muzzle glowed red. He glanced down and saw that the energy magazine was nearly depleted.

"Clear!" he yelled over comms. The words had no sooner left his mouth than his vision went wavy and the hexagonal lines vanished. Ident tags, outlines, wall-penetrating vision—it was all gone. He had normal human sight again. *Unbelievable.*

The house was quiet. The only remaining sounds

came from outside the compound as Abimbola's skiffs and Simone's snipers continued to dispatch Selskrit. Smoke still filled the room, but it was thinning. Magnus turned toward the two bodies on the floor. He knelt beside the first—an older man.

"Can you hear me?" Magnus asked, touching what he thought was the man's shoulder. The bones felt frail. "Can you hear me?"

"Yes," the man said in an elderly voice. "I can hear you." Magnus's heart sank a little when he realized this was no Marine. Maybe a Luma or a senator.

"I've got one alive," Magnus said over comms.

"We've got three—alive!" Dutch said. Clearly, the lack of smoke had given them an advantage.

Magnus's heart rate quickened. "Who is it? Who've you got?" He suddenly heard a stream of profanity pouring from someone's mouth. *That's a Marine,* he thought, a smile creeping across his face. Recon for the win.

"What's your name, Marine?" Dutch asked.

In the background, Magnus heard the man say, "Sergeant Michael Damn Deeks! And who the hell are you?"

Magnus let out a hoot. "Listen, tell that son of a bitch that his first lieutenant orders him to watch his language. I'll be right over."

"Copy that," Dutch said. Magnus could hear her smile over the transmission.

He returned his attention to the elderly man. "Sir, what's your name?"

"I'm a squirrel," he said weakly.

"Huh?"

"I'm a squirrel, and a squirrelly old man. That's what I'm told."

Magnus was about to reply until he had a memory of Awen hanging in Abimbola's jail cell, drugged. This was a Luma. They'd drugged him to suppress his powers in the *Unifornication*, or whatever it was called.

"Have you come to rescue squirrels?" the man asked.

"Yes," Magnus replied, laughing a little. "We've come to rescue squirrels."

"That makes me very happy." The man let out a wet cough.

Dutch spoke up again. "It also looks like we have one Corporal Chico and a captain."

"Wainright?" Magnus asked.

"Unclear. Name's scratched off, and he's unconscious."

In the background, Flow said, "Yeah, it's Wainright. He needs a medic."

"As does the corporal," Dutch added. "But I think Deeks can walk."

"Damn straight, I can walk!"

This was unbelievable. Flow, Cheeks, *and* Captain Wainright were alive. Sure, Magnus wished more had survived. But he'd walked into this expecting the worst, so that little group of survivors was a welcome sight.

Still, they had a job to do. No celebrating until they were out of Oosafar. "Copy that," Magnus said.

The smoke thinned enough for Magnus to see a second hostage lying facedown in the corner. The body was bloated and wrapped with several blood-soaked bandages. The person had either been tortured or these were leftover wounds from the attack. Maybe both. Either way, whoever it was needed serious medical attention. The stench was putrid.

"Hey." Magnus placed a hand on a fat bicep and shook gently. "You awake?"

"He's not a squirrel," the Luma elder said.

"Good to know." Magnus shook the man's arm a little harder then heard a groan. He wanted to try to turn him over but knew he'd need help.

"I said, he's not a squirrel."

"I heard you the first time," Magnus said. The old man was really out of it.

"He's something else."

"Oh yeah? And what's that?"

"He's royalty. He's an *ambassador*."

Magnus froze then looked between the old man and the massive body in the corner.

24

"How IN THE hell did you survive?" Magnus asked. But he knew the man couldn't answer. He couldn't even move. The fat, impetuous Republic ambassador, Gerald Bosworth III—the one who'd threatened Awen and probably helped sabotage the mwadim's meeting—was alive.

"Who've you got?" Dutch asked over comms.

Unbelievable. Magnus shook his head. "I've got the Republic ambassador."

The old man nodded excitedly then coughed again. "He doesn't like squirrels. Or dogs. But he sure does like to eat."

"Come again?" Dutch asked.

"Ambassador Bosworth," Magnus said, holding a finger up for the old man to stay quiet. "Guy's hurt bad. Don't know if he's going to survive evac." *And truthfully, that wouldn't hurt my feelings one bit.* "We're gonna need a hover lift or some sort of stretcher."

"Copy that, LT."

Magnus reached an arm under the Luma. "Come on, old squirrel. Time to get you outta here." The man winced as Magnus helped him stand. He weighed next to nothing, and Magnus thought he'd snap him in two if he wasn't careful. "Can you walk?"

The old man nodded but struggled to straighten his knees, clinging to Magnus's arm for dear life.

"Splick. We're gonna need two stretchers." He switched over to general comms. "Bimby, I need some hover sleds or stretchers or whatever you've got. We have survivors."

"Roger that, buckethead. How many?"

"Five." *Though one of these counts for three more. Damn son of a bitch.*

"Coming your way now."

"Copy."

THIS WAS the part of the job they never advertised in holo-verts or school presentations. Then again, moving a fat-ass body down three stories through a urine-stained, flea-infested sauna wasn't exactly the kind of thing people lined up to do. So he couldn't blame them. Still, it would have been nice if someone had said, "Hey, kid. Listen, splick's gonna get bad. I mean, real bad. You're gonna get covered in alien juice that will stain your skin for weeks, and you'll never look at a steak the same way. Hell, you're going to see more entrails than a gastroenterologist doing colonoscopies. Don't say I didn't warn you."

There was no way Bosworth was fitting down the circular stairwells, so Gilder had used rope to lower the stretcher over a railing and through the central square. A hover sled would have made it a lot easier, but Abimbola only had one, and the ambassador exceeded the weight limit. Instead, Wainright got it. And Magnus wasn't complaining there.

"You know, there *is* a way to make this go a lot faster." Silk braced herself on the marble floor, holding one of the ropes Gilder had set up. "I mean, all I've gotta do is sneeze and—"

"Steady," Magnus yelled down. "Don't need anyone else dying today."

Though, truth be told, the Marauder was right. *You're a bad man, Magnus.*

Abimbola's voice crackled over comms. "I am

going to need you to hurry it up there, buckethead. It seems the Selskrit are regrouping, and I think we have overstayed our welcome."

"We're on our way out." Magnus looked over the railing to help Haney guide the ambassador's stretcher to the floor. Haney had just returned from delivering Rix to the medivac unit. "All right, people, you heard the warlord. Let's get back to the skiffs."

Magnus descended both stairwells and helped carry the survivors back through the compound and out the front doors. When he emerged, struggling with one end of Bosworth's stretcher—Dozer on the other—Jujari bodies lay scattered throughout the courtyard.

Flow looked around and then eyed Magnus. "You sure know how to throw a party, LT."

Did Flow really just call me LT again? It warmed his heart. "I can think of easier ways to get you wasted, Flow. But hey, if this is what it takes…"

"This is what it takes, yes. This is most certainly what it takes."

"LT!" Dutch yelled from behind Magnus. He turned around. "Almost forgot this!" She was carrying the algorithmic shield generator from the guard tower.

"Better give that to Silk," Magnus said, laboring for breath.

"Silk?"

"Abimbola offered a raise as reward for the device. So unless you want to start working for Abimbola, it's better to give the spoils to one of the Marauders."

"Eh, I'm good," Dutch said.

"Thought so."

"Thanks, Marine," Silk said, carrying one end of Wainright's stretcher. "I owe you one."

"Careful what you commit to," Magnus said. "I'll have you make good on it."

"I expect nothing less." She winked.

A stream of rapid MUT50 fire stole Magnus's attention as it stitched up the side of a building and removed several Selskrit from windows and two on the roof. He looked at the surrounding buildings and noticed more shadows moving within them. He hoped Simone's fire team was back in a skiff now; those rooftops had to be crawling with the enemy.

"How are we doing, slowpokes?" Abimbola asked. His M109 had opened up on a pack of Selskrit trying to make entry into the compound through the front gate.

"We're coming up on the hole you just cleared for us. Thanks."

"Hurry it up, would you?"

Magnus felt his arms and legs burning. The ambassador was even heavier than he looked—and he already looked heavy enough not to carry! "Come on, people! Let's move, let's move!" He heard the M109 fire down the cross street on the other side of the wall.

His platoon picked their way over the rubble and bodies in the doorway and headed for three different skiffs, each backed up to the gate with their cargo ramps extended. Marauders motioned the stretchers inside, covering the retreat with blaster fire to encroaching enemy targets. The moment Magnus passed the handles off to another Marauder at the top of a ramp, he stretched his cramping arms and pulled his MAR30 off the maglock on his back.

"Find a ride," Magnus ordered. "We're leaving here hot, it looks like."

"Hot does not even begin to describe it," Abimbola yelled. "Where you at, buckethead?"

"On my way." Magnus jumped off the ramp and ran ahead two skiffs, finding Abimbola's vehicle engaged with a small horde of advancing Selskrit. They moved along the sides of the streets, ducking in and out of cover. The M109 took out one or two at a time, but the beasts were getting smarter. That, and they were growing in number.

Magnus banged on the passenger side of the skiff's forward compartment. Abimbola leaned over, unlatched the security lock, and swung the door out.

"Good to see you, Bimby." Magnus climbed in and slammed the door behind him.

"I really hate that name. Have I mentioned that?"

"Come to think of it… no. But I have some advice."

"What is that?"

"Get used to it, 'cause I *love* using it."

Abimbola stomped the pedal to the floor, and the skiff lurched forward.

WITH EVERYONE ACCOUNTED FOR, the convoy barreled down the streets of the Western Heights. It was here that Magnus really got to see *Hell's Basket Case* in full effect. It charged forward, impaling unlucky Jujari on the spikes of its deadly battering ram.

Abimbola pushed it faster and faster. Since they were headed west—away from the city's center—

there was little threat of mines. Instead, there were a whole lot more Selskrit. The skiff only slowed when two or more bodies temporarily impeded its progress. But two embedded counter rotating blade saws made quick work of any meat buildup on the spikes.

"You sure about this?" Magnus asked over the scream of the drive core. He sat with his torso sticking out of the sunroof, the hatch flipped forward for cover.

"What?"

"Are you sure about this?"

"No!" Abimbola yelled.

"Perfect."

"Just keep shooting!"

"Copy that." Magnus was about to fire on more Selskrit when he noticed something flash in the sky. He looked up to see the Republic blockade... engaged in ship-to-ship orbital combat. Streaks of light dotted the blue sky while small explosions appeared and vanished like small firecrackers—bursting into existence one moment and vanishing without a trace the next.

Without warning, Magnus's bioteknia eyes waved again, the hexagonal grid appearing in his mind. They zoomed in and placed designator tags beside each ship. There were hundreds of ships, far more than he could see with his naked eye, and at least half were Jujari allied. This wasn't good. The war had begun.

"Keep shooting!" Magnus snapped his attention back to the field of battle. He aimed his MAR30 at a group of four Selskrit who stood a good two hundred meters down the road. Old buildings covered either side of the street, creating a tunnel effect, which made target acquisition all the easier. Magnus saw that one of the combatants held an LRGR over his shoulder. "Splick!"

Magnus's vision suddenly zoomed in on the sniper with the shoulder-mounted weapon. It happened fast. Magnus squeezed the trigger. A cluster of blue blaster bolts streaked down the street and slapped into the sniper—but not before the Selskrit got a shot off. The projectile missed Abimbola's skiff by less than a meter. Instead, it sailed past and detonated into the side of a building. Magnus heard the loud clang of sandstone rocks denting armored plating.

"Good shot, buckethead!"

"Good driving!" Magnus could get used to these new eyes. They freaked him out, of course. But they were… *awesome.*

Despite the skiff covering a lot of ground, the

convoy was definitely getting deeper into enemy territory. Magnus was having serious doubts about this course of action. He knew it was the only way to avoid the booby-trapped streets. But he didn't think they'd have better luck with twice as many Jujari.

Make that three times as many. *Negative, make that ten times as many. Mystics! They are everywhere.*

Jujari were in every window, on rooftops, and even starting to crowd the streets, growing bolder with every hundred meters. Where were they coming from? There must have been hundreds. Maybe thousands. His vision was full of red forms listed as Target: hostile.

"Getting a little cramped in here, don't you think, Bimby?" Magnus fired at target after target, his MAR30 growing hot in the late-afternoon sun. His eyes were now placing percentages beside each target. Magnus couldn't tell if the numbers designated the likelihood of them attacking him, their threat level, or his chances of missing—it was all happening so fast. Either way, his bioteknia had some sort of AI that interfaced with his brain. Freaky.

A new indicator flashed. *MAR30: Energy low.*

How did my *eyes* know the status of my weapon's energy mag? He fished for a mag, Abimbola handing him a fresh one from the glove box and another from under the seat. He went through mag after mag, sure that he was running low.

In such a target-rich environment, it was hard to know if he was having any measurable impact even with the elevated kill count. With the number of targets his eyes kept identifying, making an assessment was a losing battle.

"Does this end anytime soon?"

"It does," Abimbola said, looking unfazed. "Soon enough."

Magnus dropped three more Jujari. "Can you define soon?"

He had hardly gotten the question out of his mouth when a Jujari landed on top of him. One paw gripped the hatch while the other grabbed Magnus around the back. He looked up in time to see the beast's maw, filled with razor-sharp teeth, open wide over his head. His MAR30 was pointed up and half-swallowed in the combatant's mouth when he pulled the trigger. Blaster fire blew open the soft back of the creature's head, blossoming in a gout of spine, bones, and blood. The carcass slumped on him.

"Mystics, these things stink!"

"Very much, yes," Abimbola replied.

Magnus shoved the body off him and resumed fire, taking aim at ones that he guessed might try to leap onto their skiffs like the last one had. Sure enough, what looked to be a skinny young male stood leaning over the street, one paw wrapped around a pipe. Magnus aimed and snapped his arm at the elbow. The creature flailed and fell, landing a few meters ahead. The Jujari couldn't move in time, and Abimbola's battering ram devoured another victim.

"How much longer?" Magnus asked.

"We are almost there."

"Where's there?" Magnus struck several more Selskrit who seemed interested in mounting their skiff.

"There…"

Magnus looked to where the warlord pointed. Up ahead stood a gate the likes of which Magnus had never seen before. It made the one on the eastern side of the city—where they'd first entered—look like a toy door on a dollhouse. This port of entry was easily one hundred meters tall and just as wide. It boasted long fulcrums along the tops of each of the two outward-turning door panels. Giant metal straps held the stone doors to massive hinges, while a stone rampart above gave lookout to the plain beyond and mechanical access to the port's opening and closing.

"I hate to be the bearer of bad news," Magnus noted, "but your gate… it's closed. And judging by the looks of the Selskrit operating it, I don't think they plan on opening it for us." At least one hundred of them stood along the ramparts, blasters aimed down at the approaching convoy. Magnus dropped in his seat and pulled the hatch shut.

"You are correct, *those* Jujari will not open the door." Abimbola pointed to two columns of Tawn-hack running along the top of the wall on either side of the gate. "But these Jujari will."

25

Awen and Ezo followed close behind TO-96 as he carried Sootriman over his shoulder. The bot ran down the tunnel until it intersected a large underground corridor. Then the lights came on.

Unlike all their previous scouting trips, in which the building interiors had been dark, this passageway was bright—at least where Awen and the others stepped into it. TO-96 turned right and began to jog again. Giant Novia script lined the walls, adorning entrances to side tunnels and what looked like storage compartments. Frosted banks of lights ran along each wall and filled the ceiling, turning on as the humans approached and dimming after they'd passed. Even the floor, a glossy white beneath Awen's feet, was illuminated.

Seeing the lights turn on made Awen realize why the city's walls had looked alive when she'd first observed them within the Unity—*because they were*, at least in the sense that the Novia's singularity allowed them to exist anywhere there was a conduit, cable, sensor, camera, or superconductor. It was eerie having an invisible personal escort lead them to their destination, but if it meant escaping from their enemy and getting back home, she was all for it.

The only regret Awen had, of course, was not getting to spend more time with the QTG. They'd only just discovered it; to leave it so soon seemed like a travesty. She wondered if she'd ever be able to come back and convene with the Novia over days and weeks. *Might I spend years here?* Perhaps the Novia Minoosh—instead of the Jujari—would become her life's work…

"It is a little farther," TO-96 said, his voice smooth and calm.

"How much is a little, 'Six?" Ezo gasped for air, his lungs no doubt burning like Awen's.

"Point seven nine seven four one of a kilometer."

"And there's a ship waiting for us?" Awen asked.

"Affirmative."

The tunnel curved slowly to the left as if the team was running along the perimeter of a wide circle.

Eventually, the loop bisected a central hall with high ceilings. Lights flickered to life as the four entered the terminal. The main tunnel continued on the opposite side, and a few smaller ones opened on the right. But to their left lay a large bay door. While Novia script emblazoned the walls and sat above the tunnel openings, it was writ large across the bay door, denoting it as something significant.

"What've we got, 'Six?" Ezo asked.

"It's a flight hangar, sir. Please stand by. The Novia are opening it now."

The four of them stood facing the door as it loomed overhead. They waited, lungs heaving, hands wringing. Nothing happened.

"'Six? Is there a problem?"

"Still waiting, sir."

Ezo nodded then looked back at the bay door, waiting for it to open. More seconds slipped by.

"'Six... I don't mean to be impatient here..."

"Yes, I do understand. The Novia tell me that it has been over a thousand years since this door was used. It is, as you might say, a little rusty."

"Fair enough. If I don't use my doors for a thousand years, yeah, they're gonna be rusty. I get it."

"Any second now, sir."

A sound like giant sledgehammers dropping on

hollow tanker drums boomed from somewhere beneath. Then the lights went out. Awen flinched. In place of the overhead lights came alternating blinking red lights on either side of the door and a spotlight on the door's center.

"There we are," the bot said with a satisfied air.

A crack of light appeared under the door as the metal began creeping upward, pulled by the sound of a long-dormant motor drive. Awen found herself reaching for Sootriman's hand as they looked for whatever awaited them.

The door, at waist height, revealed a well-worn black floor. Scuff marks and directional paint designated it as a utilitarian space, one meant for engineers and mechanics. Then, as the door reached shoulder height, Awen saw her first glimpse of a ship.

Higher and higher, the door revealed more. Awen gasped, holding her hands to her mouth. They were the first beings from the protoverse to see a Novia Minoosh starship. For a fleeting moment, she forgot about the past several months here on Ithnor Ithelia —forgot about Worru and the Luma and the Jujari and the horrors that had transpired on Oorajee. The beauty of what lay before her captivated her.

Glimmering like a massive diamond in the light of a thousand suns stood a majestic starship aimed skyward. Its mirrored finish was elegantly curved, undulating in the shape of a Leviathanian tanic shark. Hundreds of irregular iridescent windows lay across the ship, accenting its mirrored surface with purples, pinks, and blues. Minimalist side and tail wings rose from the hull like fins, while a honeycomb of angled engine ports hovered fifteen meters over the hangar floor.

Awen felt that the ship was lithe, almost seductive, its lines forming curves more akin to a beautiful woman's body than the rigid designs of the Republic. Gantry cranes held the ship in place, feeding it like medical lines on a patient, though at any moment, it seemed as if the ship would tear free and break through whatever canopy kept it from its destiny among the stars. This ship was meant to fly.

"I give you the *Azelon Spire*," TO-96 said with a sweep of his hand.

Ezo let out a long whistle. "Would you look at that…"

"I've never seen anything like it," Awen added.

"Nor has Ezo, Star Queen." Ezo placed a hand on Sootriman's head then looked at his bot. "How soon before we can get Sootriman taken care of?"

"The Novia have readied the ship. We will need to get Sootriman secured for launch. Then, as soon as we are in orbit, you can move her to sick bay. I would say no more than twenty minutes."

Ezo stroked Sootriman's hair; it was the most affectionate Awen had ever seen him with his semi-former wife. Perhaps he really did care about her. "Hear that, baby? Twenty minutes, and we'll get you taken care of."

"In the meantime, I will make sure to provide her with some pain relief just as soon as we board."

"Thank you, 'Six."

"It is my pleasure, sir."

Awen caught sight of something moving around the ship's launchpad. The motion startled her, and she let out a gasp. "What is that?" She pointed, and Ezo raised his SUPER 945. "Is... is that a cleaning bot?"

"It is a sweeper bot, to be exact," TO-96 said. "One of the many automated machines that keep Itheliana and her inner workings from deteriorating entirely."

"Wait, wait," Ezo said, waving his pistol. "You mean to say that there are more of these?"

"Of course, sir. How else do you think that so much of the city has remained intact over all these centuries?"

"But we never saw them."

"By design, sir. One aspect of their prime directive is to remain anonymous and out of sight. They joke amongst themselves, you know. 'We do our best work in the dark,' they like to say."

"Ouch. That's an old one," Awen said. "Though, somehow, it's funnier when bots say it."

"And they are rather old, Awen. You might say that they have been *recycling* the same material for years." The bot paused, blinked at her, and nodded in anticipation.

"Funny, Ninety-Six." She chuckled. "You're getting there."

Ezo was still gaping in awe at the ship and the little sweeper bot. "An entire fleet of maintenance bots... incredible. Guess that explains why so many places we explored weren't completely overrun."

TO-96 looked back at the sweeper bot. "Affirmative. They are responsible for far more than you probably realize."

"The temple library?" Awen asked.

"One of their main responsibilities, yes."

Ezo motioned to the *Azelon Spire*. "And they've kept this ship ready all this time?"

"It was not hard to do, sir. The *Azelon Spire* has never been flown before."

"What?" Ezo looked astonished. "You're saying that we're taking her on her maiden voyage?"

"I am." The bot nodded.

Ezo looked at Awen, a gleam in his eye like a small child would get when about to unwrap a giant birthday present. "Is she safe, though? Are they sure she can fly? And how can something this large escape planetary gravity?"

"The Novia assure me that the *Azelon Spire* is one-hundred-percent flight ready, able to support biological life, and able to achieve the necessary velocity to attain orbit. All she needs is a crew."

"Then let's get on board." Ezo had no sooner uttered the words than a giant explosion reverberated through the tunnels behind them. "Splick, that doesn't sound good."

TO-96's head twitched. "It seems the enemy has found our secret entrance. They are coming."

AWEN HELPED Ezo buckle Sootriman into an acceleration couch. The woman moaned, her eyes closed and head lolling. "We're almost out of here," Awen said. "Just a few more minutes. Hang in there, okay?"

The four of them had gained access to the ship

through a generous entry door near the stern. Once inside, it was a short walk to a central elevator that ran along the spine. Almost every surface was finished in white pearl, while purple-and-gray carbon fiber weave connected joints and filled seems. Soft light emanated from ceilings, walls, and floors, and translucent Novia script embossed various points of interest.

"Come on, Awen." Ezo climbed to another acceleration couch on the bridge and began strapping himself in. The room was pitched vertically with recessed rungs running along the walls for access to the gimbaled seats. Directly overhead, stretching the width of the room, was a large window that looked up toward the hangar bay's ceiling.

Awen had just finished closing the last buckle on the oversized harness when TO-96 spoke up from his own acceleration couch. "It seems the intruders have gained access to the central hall."

Suddenly, the window was filled with a security-camera image from outside in the hangar bay. Awen felt dizzy, a result of lying on her back and looking up and the camera's off-center angle. No fewer than ten dark-clad troopers worked along the central hall's massive cargo-bay door. They wore black Repub-style armor with three black stripes on the shoulder plate and bicep. Their helmets looked like something skiff racers would use, and their weapons looked intimidating, much like Magnus's. These were the same type of troopers she'd encountered when she'd first met Kane at the temple's entrance.

A new voice filled the control room: "Drive core at maximum efficiency." The voice was smooth and feminine. "Shields, hull integrity, life support, navigation, and weapons systems, one hundred percent. Prepare for main engine start. TO-96, would you like to proceed?"

"I would," the bot replied.

"It speaks Galactic common?" Ezo asked.

"For your benefit, I uploaded my lexicon to the ship's AI moments ago."

"That's cool. But can't you speak to it in your head or something, 'Six?" Ezo asked. "The bot-on-bot communication is a little weird."

"Of course. However, I thought you would find a more a humanesque communication format desirable. Having the ship operate in silence might be disconcerting to you, would it not?"

"Now that you mention it, I do appreciate knowing what's happening. Thanks, 'Six."

"You are most welcome, sir."

The main bridge display flashed white then went black. The view of the troopers was gone. A beat later, a new camera view appeared, this one looking down on the bay doors from inside the hanger. As far as Awen could tell, the camera was located somewhere on the *Azelon Spire*.

The door had a gaping hole in the center, filled with smoke. Bits of flaming shrapnel littered the floor. Troopers stepped through it, weapons at the ready. Once in the bay, they reacted, lowering their weapons and tipping their heads back. Someone in charge waved a hand, and the troopers brought their weapons back up and fanned out.

"Warning, hangar bay breached," the ship's voice said.

"Acknowledged," TO-96 replied.

Awen saw muzzle flashes as the troopers opened fire on the ship. "They're shooting at us!"

"How we doing on those engines, 'Six?"

As if emphasizing his question, a shock wave blasted across the hangar floor. Awen felt it before she saw it. The camera view trembled as her acceleration couch absorbed the engine's vibrations. The troopers were thrown backward, swept aside like ants in a midsummer Dustoovian cyclone.

Ezo let out a victory cry, his voice shaking from the engines. "Take that, you bastards!"

"Confirm launch request," the ship said.

"Request confirmed," TO-96 said.

"Hell, yes!" Ezo said. "Let's blow this place!"

Blue streams of hyper ionized air filled the hangar just as the image of the troopers vanished, replaced by a widening star shape of direct sunlight overhead. Awen winced then noticed the bridge window adjust to the sudden light change. The canopy above them was opening. The ship shook enough to rattle Awen's teeth. She was pressed into her couch, and she grunted as gravity multiplied, compressing every cell in her body.

"Here we go!" Ezo yelled.

The star shape had expanded to a perfect circle of purple sky with several puffy clouds—though everything appeared to waver as if underwater. Dust and debris shot toward the hangar's mouth as the *Azelon Spire* crept upward. Second, third, and fourth images appeared in the bridge, hovering to the sides of the main window like holo-displays, though without any apparent projection source. At first, Awen was confused. All she saw was the city's southern coastline and two close-ups of empty water. But then she watched the *Spire* burst from the ocean on three different cameras. The starship glistened in the sun like it was on fire, a spray of water exploding as the ocean heaved the vessel from its depths.

A fifth image appeared even farther away. Awen saw the ship as a small creature, climbing away from the southern part of the city. She noticed the library temple up the hill and in the city's heart, surrounded by buildings. Within seconds, the *Spire* was even with the temple, and a few seconds after that, she'd doubled the distance.

"Altitude, five hundred meters," the ship's voice announced calmly.

Awen clutched her harness straps, willing herself not to black out. She scrunched her eyes shut as the ship's voice continued to call out the altitude. Visions of the *Spire* exploding in midair played with the edges of her imagination. She wondered whether, having survived the initial event, she would survive a fall into the ocean. Maybe her acceleration couch had a parachute.

"Altitude, ten thousand meters."

Awen opened her eyes. She grunted against the constant press until she felt her throat burning. The purple sky darkened, and clouds raced passed her. Then she noticed that the displays showed opposing images, one of the ship growing smaller as it vanished into the atmosphere and another of the city receding to a textured patch protruding from the belly of a large continent. *Shouldn't this be over soon?* She wasn't sure how much more she could take.

"Altitude, twenty thousand meters."

Ezo yelled something at Awen.

"What?" she asked.

The ship shook as he shouted some more, but she was no closer to understanding him.

"I can't hear you!"

TO-96 spoke up then, his voice output at a seriously loud setting. "Ezo would like you to know that he is sorry he forgot to pack you a vomit bag."

Awen laughed and, for the first time, realized she didn't feel any nausea. She was probably too scared to be sick. She offered Ezo a shaky thumbs-up, her hand straining against gravity's multiplied pull. It was no use yelling back, as he probably wouldn't hear her. Ezo winked, his head jostling from side to side.

"Altitude, thirty thousand meters."

The sky overhead was getting darker, fading to a deep purple. On the displays, Awen saw Ithnor Ithelia's entire continent as a lush green patch bordered by purplish-blue oceans on three sides. White clouds smeared the scene like a painter's brush strokes, giving the image a sense of depth.

The *Spire* climbed higher and faster, surging toward the stratosphere. She wondered how many other species had launched from the planet's surface and how long ago it had been. Surely, this was the first crew of humanoid life-forms from the protoverse to ever do so—and on a Novian ship, no less!

"Altitude, forty thousand meters."

The sky was blackening. *Or is it my vision?* She gritted her teeth as the starship continued to accelerate. She knew that vessels this size were never meant to return to atmosphere and stayed in orbit precisely because of how much energy was required to launch them again—if their structure could even handle such force. Most were built in space. But the *Azelon Spire* had been in its hangar, sleeping soundly, waiting to surge into the void.

"Altitude, fifty thousand meters."

Awen wasn't sure how much more she could take. Her body felt as though it had just been through twelve rounds of a Saratian boxing match. The straps rubbed against her collar bones and hips, buckles digging into her chest and waist. Her muscles were burning, and that stupid sense of nausea was starting to haunt her again.

With a sudden jerk, Awen snapped forward, slamming against her restraints. The air rushed from her lungs.

"Main launch sequence complete," the ship's voice said.

Awen gasped. Gone were the violent shaking and the loud roaring. In their place were silence and zero gravity. She watched as her braid floated beside her face. Likewise, her necklace touched just beneath her chin.

"Artificial gravity initiating in ten seconds," the ship's voice said.

Awen looked over to see Sootriman's head tilted sideways. Small bubbles of drool hovered near her lips. She was unconscious but looked to be breathing. *It's probably for the best.* There was no sense being awake for the pain of a blaster injury compounded by atmospheric launch.

"Artificial gravity at twenty-five percent."

Awen felt her necklace touch her chest again.

"Fifty percent."

Her body was sinking back into her acceleration couch, the extra blood draining from her head.

"Seventy-five percent." And then, within a matter of seconds, gravity had been restored to normal levels. "Gravity at one hundred percent of normal. Low planetary orbit achieved."

"Thank you, Azelon," TO-96 said.

Ezo was out of his straps and moved toward Soot-riman. Her chin was on her chest. "You okay, baby?"

"Her body appears to be in shock, sir," TO-96 said. "I advise we move her to sick bay immediately."

"Let's do it, 'Six."

The robot climbed out of his acceleration couch while Ezo unbuckled Sootriman. TO-96 helped Ezo cradle her—Ezo insisting that he carry her himself. Awen was struck by his sincerity and wondered if Sootriman had been wrong about Ezo's desire to be alone on an island.

Awen unbuckled herself and was about to follow everyone out of the bridge when the ship's AI spoke. "TO-96, please be aware that a ship has locked on to our position, approaching from the following coordinates." A map of the void immediately surrounding the planet appeared in front of the main window. Targeting reticles showed the *Spire* and a second ship approaching from the other side of the planet. "I will classify the ship as hostile. Please acknowledge."

"Hostile?" Ezo turned around to examine the display, Sootriman's head lolling back over his arm. "Why?"

"Idris Ezo, second-in-command," the AI said. "Weapons and targeting systems have been detected.

Shields have been detected. Speed has increased to—"

"Okay, okay, okay, Ezo gets it. They're hostile."

"Acknowledged. Would you like me to take evasive measures?"

"Hell, yes!" Ezo said.

"Response unknown."

TO-96 cleared his throat. "The phrase 'hell, yes' is a colloquial expression meant to convey adamant agreement, encouragement, or assent, despite the negative connotation of the modifier."

"Acknowledged," the AI said.

"That wasn't already in your lexicon, 'Six?" Ezo asked.

"It knows what I know, sir. However, it still takes us several years to understand you biological life-forms."

"Copy that, buddy." Ezo shook his head. "I still don't understand myself half the time. Listen, you think the ship's AI—"

"Her name is Azelon, sir."

"Fair enough. You think Azelon, here, can walk me through firing up sick bay?"

"Most certainly, sir."

"Good deal. Then you and Awen stay put and get us outta here."

"With pleasure, sir."

Ezo froze. "Oh, and 'Six?"

"Yes, sir?" the bot said.

"Since when did you make me second-in-command?"

The bot straightened his shoulders. "Ah, I am sorry for that, sir. I will gladly—"

"'Cause I think it was a damn good idea. It's about time anyway."

TO-96 pulled his head back in astonishment. "Why, thank you, sir."

"You're welcome," Ezo said. "Get to it."

TO-96 turned back to face the main screen as warning indicators illuminated, signifying weapons systems on the enemy ship. He made a show of cracking his knuckles and walked toward the captain's chair. "Let us blast these sons of unmarried female dogs out of the void."

26

Magnus watched as a violent battle broke out on the ramparts. His eyes zoomed in on the action as if he was standing ten meters away. Despite the fact that *Basket Case* was still hurtling toward the doors at breakneck speeds, his eyes kept perfect focus and brought everything to him in vivid detail.

"They're Tawnhack, aren't they?" he said to Abimbola.

"Indeed they are."

Jujari bodies clicked with one another in a colossal display of carnage. Claws raked faces, gouged eyes, and tore at soft tissue. Mouths clamped down on necks, shoulders, and arms. Bodies wrestled against walls, pairs of them tumbling off the ramparts and falling a hundred meters to the hard-packed dirt.

"I thought you said Rohoar was only sending twenty."

"I did. Those are the ones he sent for free, to cover the rear of our column during the advance."

For free. Magnus figured it out. "But you hired more. Poker chips."

"You are learning, buckethead. Gambling is currency."

"So you knew we'd egress to the west all along."

"Not necessarily. It was just one option."

Magnus whistled. "You must've paid them a pretty chip."

"You could say that. But do not tell my secret."

Magnus pulled back from the gruesome spectacle unfolding above them to focus on Abimbola. "And what's that?"

"I print my own."

"NEXT PROBLEM," Magnus said. "I don't see that gate opening. And I see plenty of Selskrit looking for some action when we slow."

"It is not a problem. But it is going to get intense."

"You mean…"

"Yes, we must wait for them to open the gate."

"You're kidding me."

"No." Abimbola reached under his seat and handed Magnus three more energy mags. "You might want these."

"Thanks."

Abimbola pulled the BFT6 Tigress from his thigh and racked a charge. The thing was menacing. Its square receiver opened just wide enough for the pistol grip and had cooling slots down the top of the extended barrel. Abimbola used it more like a sidearm than a blaster—at least, that was how it looked in his large hand. "Time to go hunting for some dinner."

Magnus didn't like the prospect of eating a Jujari, even as a joke, but the idea of dinner brought saliva to his mouth. *Just make it to your next meal, Marine.* It was another of the Recon's unofficial mantras for when splick got bad. Keeping such a basic goal in sight had a way of connecting Marines to the fine art of staying alive.

Abimbola slowed the skiff as it approached the wall, the gate towering high above them. They moved into the structure's shadow as Selskrit started filling in from the side streets. This was about as crazy as Magnus could imagine things getting. The hair on the back of his neck stood up as howls and cackles went up on all sides.

"These plates will hold against their attack, right?" Magnus asked.

"For a while."

Magnus nodded. "Great. Just great."

Abimbola raised the skiff as high as the thrusters would allow him, but Magnus had a feeling the height wouldn't matter much, at least not for long. The Selskrit ran at them, and Magnus felt his rear end pucker. Mouths sneered, ears lay down flat, and snarls echoed around the convoy.

All down the street, blasters, turrets, and missile banks opened fire on the approaching enemy. Magnus held his MAR30 up between slats and squeezed his trigger. Bursts of blaster bolts lanced Jujari who reached for *Basket Case*. Heads snapped, paws flipped backward, and shoulders buckled.

Magnus selected Wide Displacement, adjusted the wave frequency to medium, and squeezed. The weapon ingested the needed power then belched. The power wave divested several combatants of their heads, arms, and torsos but sent the majority colliding with those behind them. The heap of bodies writhed as more Jujari took the places of those who'd fallen, trampling them underfoot.

Magnus shuddered at how ravenous the Selskrit were—their bloodlust was driving them mad. He fired several more times into the crowd, but not even his MAR30 could keep the horde at bay. At least four Selskrit climbed onto the skiff and placed their fingers between the metal window slats. Others pounded on the plates. Of the most concern, however, were those who stuck blaster barrels into openings. Magnus moved away from the weapons' sight windows then shot at them point-blank. Blasters exploded backward, pummeling their possessors with shrapnel and burning their flesh. Wrists shattered, elbows crushed, and shoulders dislodged. The shrieks of injured and dying Selskrit were just as deafening as those who rallied the advance.

Magnus continued to fire on the Jujari who stood on the *Basket Case*. Their bodies were so numerous that the compartment grew dark. Several metal welds started to give way, bars and slats bending under the Jujari's terrific strength. Magnus fired and fired and fired, striking flesh with bolt after bolt, but no sooner would one combatant fall than another would take its place. Despite the constant barrage of turret fire, the convoy was quickly losing the battle. Abimbola's skiff was sinking under the weight, which only encouraged more assailants to climb aboard.

Magnus was reaching for another energy mag when Abimbola handed him one, saying, "Last one. Make it count."

Last one? This wasn't looking good. "How soon before those gates open?"

"I do not know," Abimbola said.

"Not even a guess?" Magnus had loaded the new mag and was dispensing its contents with extreme prejudice. Several Selskrit snouts snapped between the gaps they'd opened in the slats. Magnus was determined to make them taste hot blaster fire.

"They will open it when they open it."

"Fabulous." Magnus's sarcasm dripped down the skiff's interior like rivulets of Jujari blood.

When his MAR30 went dry, Magnus pulled out his Z and started firing. The pistol bucked in his hands, sending blaster bolts into Jujari flesh dangerously close.

"LT," Dutch said over comms. Magnus could sense the strain in her voice at once.

"Go ahead."

"We're out of mags back here."

As if prompted by her words, Magnus's Z also

went dry. He reached into his chest plate and withdrew his duradex combat knife. "Then find something to stab them with."

"Copy that."

Magnus started swiping, stabbing, and cutting anything that came inside. The gaps between slats were big enough that whole arms were getting through. He severed fingers and wrists and even cut a forearm in two. His eyes tracked every limb—connected or severed—displaying targets as fast as Magnus could swipe at them.

By that point, Magnus and Abimbola were trapped beneath dozens of rabid Jujari, each bent on slicing them to ribbons. Abimbola had two blades of his own and was cutting and slashing like a Kinshawan chef at a performance restaurant. Between the two of them, the entire cab was bathed in hot blood.

Severed veins sent crimson streams shooting across the skiff's interior, splattering the dice hanging from Abimbola's rearview mirror and soaking the seats. Magnus hacked furiously, inflicting wounds that —if left untreated—would bleed out even the most ardent warrior in less than a minute. The heart was a powerful pump—all it needed was a place to release pressure.

Covered in blood and panting from exhaustion, Magnus lost his grip on his knife. It clattered to the floorboard. He ducked under the wayward swipe of a clawed paw and reached for the blade. The handle was sticky with congealing blood. Still, he squeezed it and sat upright again.

The skiff rocked back and forth under the assault. The drive core whined as it struggled to stay aloft under so much weight. Magnus knew if that gate didn't open in the next few seconds, this entire op would be over.

As if summoned by his desperate thoughts, a howl went up from somewhere overhead. Then a rumble bellowed from somewhere deep in the city, so low that is shook Magnus's gut. He knew this sound. He remembered it from the mwadim's palace before the ambush.

"The desert shofaree," Abimbola said, wiping blood from his face. "Horns of the deep."

It took a second, but eventually, the Selskrit on the skiff stopped attacking and looked up. High above them, Magnus could make out the pack of Tawnhack raising their keeltari swords in defiance.

"Well, what d'ya know," Magnus said, soaked in blood and offal. A new low-frequency rumble came from the gate as the doors began to open.

"You seem surprised." Abimbola wiped his blades across his shirt and shoved them back in their sheaths.

"It's because I am. Hey"—he pointed at Abimbola's knives—"you done fighting or something?"

Abimbola tilted his head at Magnus. "Yes, and so are you."

"I don't follow."

"The Jujari have some unique battle customs, one of which is yielding to a strong show of force. The Tawnhack just bested the Selskrit on the gate." The warlord nodded toward the ramparts. "It was an easily defendable position, but the Selskrit lost it. As an acknowledgement of honor, the remaining Selskrit stand down."

"Even though the Selskrit still outnumber them on the ground?" Magnus asked.

"Correct. It is not about numbers; it is about honor."

Magnus looked out the front window and watched the Jujari leap from the skiff. "Well, how do you like that."

"I like it very much."

"As do I." Magnus shoved his blade back in its sheath. "As do I."

THE CONVOY PASSED between the massive stone doors and drove toward the open desert. Magnus marveled at their luck. One minute, they were seconds away from being eviscerated; the next, they were cruising effortlessly into the wastes outside Oosafar.

"Lord Abimbola," someone said over comms.

"Go ahead," the giant replied.

"This is Titus, picking up the rear. Seems we have a problem."

Abimbola began to slow the *Basket Case*. "What is it?"

"Fighting has resumed on the ramparts, and we still got three skiffs that haven't cleared."

"Come again, Titus?"

"The Selskrit—they're attacking the Tawnhack above the gate, and they've cut off our exit."

"Dammit." Abimbola threw the skiff into a sliding turn. The western gate came back into view along with the rest of the convoy.

"I guess they changed their minds about doing the honorable thing today," Magnus said.

"It would seem so." Abimbola crushed the pedal to the floor, and the skiff lurched forward. "Get ready to light that gate up, Marauders! I want heavy suppression."

"What are you going to do?" Magnus asked.

Abimbola glanced over at him then back at the gate.

"You don't know yet, do you," Magnus said.

"No. Any ideas, buckethead?"

Magnus cracked his neck. "And just when I thought we were home free." He sighed and studied the situation unfolding before them. The gate was still open, but the ground in between had filled with Selskrit, their numbers growing rapidly. Up on the ramparts, more Selskrit were filling in from either side, putting pressure on the smaller Tawnhack force in the center. "How many skiffs you think we can fit between the doors?"

"As in, side to side?"

"Yeah."

Abimbola leaned forward and squinted. The gate was coming up fast. "Four."

"Then let's jam the four strongest in there. They will—"

"They will keep the doors from closing and provide covering fire long enough for my trapped Marauders to make a break for cover. I like the way you think, buckethead! That is ballsy."

Magnus chuckled. "Whatever you say, Bimby."

Abimbola called out to three other skiffs and shared the plan. They acknowledged his orders, and

Magnus saw the identified skiffs break from formation.

They were only a few hundred meters from the gate when blaster fire started pinging off *Hell's Basket Case*. The M109 belched out rounds as they closed the distance, sand spraying up in plumes as Jujari blew apart. The three other skiffs slid up to the *Basket Case's* right and left as Abimbola began slowing. Magnus heard the whine of the MUT50 and the steady *whoosh, whoosh, whoosh* of the 70mm RBMB spewing out missiles.

Within moments, there was enough room cleared for the four skiffs to nose into the gap. Their combined firepower served like a sandbag dam that held floodwaters at bay. Slowly, the enemy fell away from the stranded skiffs until the vehicles sat like boulders amidst a tidal pool of Selskrit corpses.

"Are you ready to make a run for it, Titus?" Abimbola yelled over comms. Blaster fire continued to be exchanged as the skiff pilots acknowledged their leader. "Good. On my mark. Those of you in the breach, prepare to—"

Abimbola was cut off when the gate doors closed on the skiffs, pushing the vehicles into one another. Magnus was jarred, his head hitting the side of the passenger door—not enough to knock him out but enough to give him a decent-sized bump. He heard the drive core strain to keep the skiff from tipping too far. The sound of girding metal filled the cab as the skiffs jostled against one another.

"Screw this," Abimbola said. "Full auto! Titus, it is now or never!"

"Roger that!"

The fours skiffs' weapons' systems went frenetic as they tore into the Selskrit ranks. The melee was absolutely deafening, the display of firepower… awe-inspiring. Magnus knew that the guns were tired; they wouldn't be able to keep this up for long. Still, the skiffs put up one hell of a fight, turrets strafing left, then right, then back again on the encroaching enemy lines.

Magnus saw at least a dozen Marauders jump down from the stranded skiffs and duck as they crossed the distance toward the gate. Renewed blaster fire erupted from the Selskrit as they noticed the new targets. Magnus felt utterly helpless without a blaster, unable to fire on those who were shooting at Titus and his men. His eyes selected targets as if he still had a functional weapon. All he could do was watch.

One Marauder took an enemy blaster round between the shoulder blades, thrown to the ground like a rag doll. Another was hit in the shoulder—spinning him one way—and then the other shoulder, spinning him back. A third Marauder was struck in the knee and then the side. He'd crumpled to the ground when a third shot struck him square in the top of the head, drilling a ten-centimeter hole in his skull.

The Marauder who was bringing up the rear hesitated.

"Leave them!" Abimbola ordered over comms. "They are dead!"

The man snapped back to motion and ran for the skiffs. *That's a good soldier*, Magnus thought. It was probably Titus.

The survivors raced at full speed toward the skiffs. At the last second, they dropped under the front bumpers and slid beneath. Magnus knew the repulsers wouldn't hurt them—hiding beneath skiffs was a common tactic taught in boot camp—though these Marauders would have a killer headache for a few days.

Sensing the imminent retreat, the Selskrit began a suicidal press forward.

"Are they insane?" Magnus asked Abimbola over comms.

"They hate to lose."

Just then, the M109 went silent.

"She's out!" the gunner said.

"Dammit." Abimbola pounded his fist on the dashboard.

At the same time, the *Basket Case* lurched and shoved up and over the side of the skiff beside it. The vehicles' drive cores were no match for the powerful city gates. Magnus was sitting on top of his passenger-side window as the monstrous doors squeezed the skiffs together.

"There's no way we're backing out of this," Magnus said.

"Everyone out!" The giant threw open his driver's-side door—now a roof hatch—and climbed out. A big black hand appeared above Magnus's head, and he took it. Abimbola lifted Magnus through the cab and helped him stand. Blaster fire ricocheted off the *Basket Case*, splattering Magnus's armor with molten metal.

Abimbola yanked the door off the M109 turret and pulled the gunner out. Two more men leaped from the cargo bay and ran toward the convoy no more than three hundred meters away. Titus and his Marauders had finished their crawl and were on their feet, retreating in the same direction.

Magnus looked over at the skiff with the MUT50 as the barrels seized up with a loud *kuh-thunk*.

"Come on!" Abimbola yelled. "No more heroes! Get clear of the skiffs! Get back to the convoy!"

Magnus, Abimbola, and the gunner all jumped off *Hell's Basket Case* and started running. The other Marauders dismounted and joined them as they fell back.

Within seconds, the four skiffs were overrun by Selskrit. They crawled over the vehicles like Nizwick acid ants on ramble rat corpses.

Magnus ducked as the Selskrit opened fire. Sand erupted in plumes all around him as he beat his way back to the line. With clear targets to shoot, the convoy began returning fire. The convoy skiffs—spread out in a wide crescent—focused their collective fire on the gate's mouth—and gave them hell.

"Hey, buckethead," Abimbola said, getting Magnus's attention. Magnus glanced over at him as they ran, blaster fire zipping over their heads. "Watch this." The giant raised a small detonator in his hand and pressed the button with his thumb. At the same time, he looked over his shoulder, as did Magnus.

A violent explosion ripped *Hell's Basket Case* apart, sending fire and chunks of metal into the Selskrit ranks. Magnus covered his head as the shock wave kicked him in the gut. The three other skiffs bucked under the force, generating secondary explosions in quick succession. The blasts tore holes in the doors and sent Jujari bodies flying in all directions.

"Boom, boom," Abimbola said with a wide grin of satisfaction. He turned back to his retreating men. "Mount any skiff that has room!"

Magnus slowed as he approached the nearest skiff. Three Marauders waited to board just ahead of him. Feeling he was beyond the Jujari's effective range, Magnus turned to examine the wall. Abimbola's scuttled skiffs were keeping the Selskrit at bay, at least for the present. But it wouldn't be long before they started climbing over the flaming wreckage. Another battle, however, was unfolding on the ramparts and drew Magnus's attention toward it. His eyes zoomed in on the action.

A small group of Tawnhack swung swords and fired blasters against a seemingly endless supply of Selskrit that closed from both directions along the wall. The fighting was brutal. Claws swung, digging into flesh, while jaws snapped, closing on limbs, shoulders, and necks. A fine mist of blood and hair hovered over the wall as Jujari hacked one another to death.

Suddenly, a Tawnhack pitched backward, toppled over the half wall, and hurtled toward the ground. As if in slow motion, the shoulders of the warrior appeared—painted red.

It was the mwadim's blood wolf—the one who'd greeted them at the tower mere hours ago. *Did he really volunteer for this mission, or did the mwadim order him to go?*

The blood wolf hit the ground. Sand shot up from the impact. Magnus held his breath, sure that the Tawnhack had died from the fall. "Please just be dead," he whispered, willing the beast not to move. The scenario put a knot in Magnus's stomach that he knew would only come undone one way. "You're dead, right? Just be dead."

The Tawnhack raised a paw in an attempt to ward off the Selskrit emerging from the gate.

"For all the mystics!" Before Magnus could change his mind, he tucked his sunglasses away, threw his spent MAR30 inside the closet skiff, and took off at a run. "Cover me!"

"What?" Abimbola asked.

"Cover me, dammit!"

"For the love of the gods, what are you doing, buckethead?"

"Trying to live up to my name! Now, start shooting at something!"

Abimbola swore as he gave orders to the convoy

to cover Magnus. The skiffs sent a renewed volley of fire into the gate as more Selskrit appeared. But Magnus wasn't fazed. He kept pumping his arms and legs despite how they screamed at him.

These moments, Magnus thought… *These are the ones that count.* He sucked in air and pushed it out with disciplined control. *This is what it all comes down to.*

Blaster fire crisscrossed overhead. He was committed now, out in the middle of the danger area without any cover. If anything went wrong, that was it. No second chances. No opportunities to regroup. For a split second, Magnus marveled at how utterly stupid he was. He could die at any second. All it would take was one stray blaster round to the head, and it would all be over.

The realization of how much peril he'd just put himself in sent a new jolt of adrenaline into his bloodstream. Time slowed as he raced across the open ground. His eyes tracked blaster rounds. His ears heard animalistic screams. His nose smelled burnt flesh. His skin felt sand grains pelting it. His tongue tasted the salt in his beard. Then his inner self spoke in oddly poetic prose. *These are the moments you train for but are never ready for. You have to embrace them when they come and hope to all the mystics that you've done enough. This is what you were born to do.*

A blaster round glanced off his right shin and knocked the leg out from under him. Magnus tumbled head over heels through the sand. It burned his eyes and filled his mouth. He coughed then struggled back to his feet.

"You are the craziest damn son of a bitch I have ever met. You know that, right?" Abimbola said in Magnus's ear.

Magnus responded with a grunt. He neared the downed blood wolf, who was now crawling toward him. "Hey there, ugly," Magnus said. He was out of breath, but adrenaline made up for the lack of air. "Time to get you out of here."

AWEN WATCHED in awe as TO-96 assumed control of the *Azelon Spire*. He strode to the centermost acceleration couch, sat down, and began sliding his arms through the restraints. Then he stretched out his arms as spheres of orange light appeared around his hands. Blue lines seemed to designate axes, orientation, momentum, and direction. Then, with a sudden twitch of his head, TO-96's Unity-connected AI seemed to marry with the ship's AI to create what Awen could only suspect was the most hyper-intelligent super-starship in the universe. *Universes*, she corrected herself.

"I suggest you sit down, Awen," TO-96 said.

"Right." She snapped out of her trance and returned to her chair then secured the harness once more, the straps touching already tender spots on her torso. "All set."

"And you, Ezo," TO-96 said, hailing him through the ship's comm. A small holo-display appeared beside the command chair. Awen could see Ezo blinking at the camera light.

"What is it, 'Six?"

"Are you and Sootriman secure, sir?"

"She's strapped down on the medical bed, and I'm buckled in. I think it's diagnosed her. Something's already been administered."

"Good to hear. Please stand by for evasive maneuvers."

The holo-display vanished. Then the ship lurched as TO-96 moved his hands, rotating them through the orange spheres as if performing some sort of strange dance move. Multiple images appear across the main window, depicting the *Azelon Spire* from numerous perspectives—as seen by the nearby planet, the enemy ship, and the greater solar system. Other displays showed long-range-sensor scans of the enemy ship as data and images streamed across the bridge.

Awen doubted TO-96 needed all these screens, given his integration with the ship. She guessed they were there simply to serve her or any other biological sentient being on the bridge—and they did that task extremely well. The visual tapestry was awe-inspiring. Her eyes moved from panel to panel as they hovered in layers around the main window.

"You feeling pretty confident about this, then, Ninety-Six?" she asked.

"I am indeed, Awen. *Azelon*'s responsiveness is unprecedented when compared to any starship in our galaxy."

"Nice." Her eyes flitted across the images of the enemy ship, which seemed to be some sort of Republic vessel. The ship looked like a blunt-tipped arrowhead, and its body was adorned with stabilizers. Glowing thrust cones shot from sleek cowlings that looked like talons extending from its hull. "What kind of ship is that?"

"It is definitely a Republic destroyer, Awen. Raider class. The designation number on its hull does not correspond with any known vessel."

"How is that even possible?"

"There are a few explanations," the bot said.

"Any that might suggest it's actually friendly and just being cautious with its weapons systems?"

"Most certainly not."

"Captain," Azelon said, "the enemy ship is attempting to hail us."

"Bring it up," TO-96 said.

The image of a high-ranking human officer in a Republic-style navy uniform filled the front window —his head at least five times its actual size. Awen winced at the sheer size and brightness of the image.

"Unknown vessel," the officer said without offering his name, rank, or command. "Cut your engines, lower your shields, and prepare to be boarded."

TO-96 flicked his index finger. A small icon appeared in the lower portion of the display, showing the bot's ovoid face and glowing eyes. "Unknown vessel," he replied. "No."

The officer jerked his head back. Awen wasn't sure if the reaction was from seeing a navigation bot at the helm or from TO-96's curt reply. The man attempted again, this time in a slightly more strained voice. "Unknown vessel, I order you to cut your engines, lower your shields, and prepare to be boarded."

TO-96 turned in his chair and looked back at Awen. "Is his head too big?"

"What?" She looked between the bot and the officer.

"I said, do you think his head is too big? I feel as though seeing something so unnaturally large is quite imposing and gives him an undue sense of power that is disproportionate to his actual station."

"Ninety-Six, is now really the time?"

"I believe it is the perfect time. Here, watch this." TO-96 looked toward the window again. Suddenly, the image of the officer shrank to the size of a small data pad and floated a meter from TO-96's torso. "There. That is so much better. Look how cute he is."

"Unknown vessel!" The officer was spitting mad.

"Bye-bye." TO-96 flicked the image away with a thumb and forefinger, and it vanished. "He was annoying me."

"Shouldn't we try to talk to him?" Awen asked, both amused and bewildered by TO-96.

"Negative. They mean to kill us—that's all we need to know."

"And so… you're pretty sure they won't be a problem, then?"

"They will not be a problem, Awen."

Something flashed under the ship's hull.

"What about those?" Awen pointed at three projectiles that shot forward.

"Torpedoes fired," Azelon said. Red targeting reticles appeared onscreen, circling the incoming munitions. "Time to impact, twenty-one seconds."

"Ninety-Six?" Awen asked, suddenly tense.

"Attempting to compromise the munitions," the bot reported.

She looked back and forth between the three torpedoes and TO-96. "Compromise? That's a good thing, right?"

"For us, yes." Then the bot said in a playful singsong tone, "But not for them."

"Time to impact, five seconds."

"Ninety-Six!"

"Munitions acquired," Azelon said. "Impact avoided."

"There we are," TO-96 said, as chipper as someone out on a morning walk greeting his neighbors. The targeting reticles around the torpedoes changed from red to purple. Then each projectile veered off course.

"Wait. Munitions *acquired?*" Awen asked. "Did you... are you controlling them now?"

"Indeed, I am, Awen. And my, how maneuverable they are. The Republic has certainly made several improvements to their latest iteration. Watch."

The purple reticles tracked the torpedoes into giant loops and sweeping barrel rolls. The bot even seemed to be drawing some sort of design with one of them.

"You're doing all that?" Awen couldn't believe her eyes. "With your connection to the Novia?"

"Indeed. Is it not fun?"

"I'm not sure fun is exactly the word I would use to describe it. Can we play later? Let's take care of that ship first."

"As you wish, Awen."

The torpedoes' paths straightened out and then converged on the enemy ship from three different angles of attack.

"Time to impact, fifteen seconds," Azelon reported.

"You're going to disable it?" Awen asked.

"If by disable you mean obliterate, then yes."

"'Six! What about the people on board? Can't you just—I don't know—scuttle it or something?"

"Awen, the chance of their crew surviving beyond a week in this solar system after their engines have been disabled is approximately one billion, three hundred eighty million, six—"

"It's a lot! I get it! But is there any other way?"

"I am sorry to say that I have already calculated the most 'humane way,' as you would say, to terminate the enemy, and this is it."

Awen stared at the display as the three torpedoes converged on the enemy ship. There was a white blast of light followed by several internal explosions, each of which snuffed out in seconds. Large pieces of the ship spun away from each other as a dense cloud of debris expanded in every direction. It was over in less than five seconds.

"Target terminated," Azelon reported.

Awen sat in her couch, squeezing its arms. She heard herself breathing forcefully then tried to control her breathing. She relaxed her body and melted into the oversized padding. *All those lives. Snuffed out in a flash of light.* She wondered how many they'd just killed—wondered what planets they called home and if they'd known, when they woke up for their day's shift, that it would be their last. *How many more were asleep and never saw it coming? Perhaps that is a strange mercy.*

She rubbed her hands over her face, suddenly aware of just how tired she was. The past few hours were a blur. *Was it really only this morning that I entered the Unity again and discovered the QTG? And now here we are, fleeing the system and about to head home.*

"How far are we from the tunnel?" she asked TO-96.

"Less than thirty minutes, Awen."

"And no other ships?"

"None detected, no."

She reached up and unbuckled her harness. "Let me know when we're getting close. I'm going to check on Sootriman and Ezo."

"As you wish, Awen."

"Oh, and Ninety-Six?" She turned to look at him. "Thank you. For saving us back there. I know you did what was best."

"It is my pleasure to protect you, Awen. You are most welcome."

THERE WERE no buttons in the elevator—it was all controlled entirely by voice communication with the ship's AI. It felt strange to Awen, but it made sense. Why use antiquated technology when superior technology was available?

"You have arrived at deck four, section seven, Awen," Azelon said as the elevator slowed to a stop. "Serving sick bay." The doors parted, and Awen stepped out.

"Thank you..." Awen wasn't sure if she was supposed to reply or not, but she did it anyway. *Just in case. It never hurts to be extra kind to an AI.*

The gleaming white hallway was evenly lit and curved to the right.

Azelon spoke again. "Seventeen meters, second bay on your right, Awen." Dotted blue lights appeared in the floor, designating a walking path.

"Thank you, Azelon," Awen said, more comfortably this time.

"You're welcome."

Apparently, she was listening after all. And watching.

Awen walked along the glossy floor, following the blue lights. She turned to face the door, and it slid open with a soft *whoosh*. A transparent wall separated the entry room from the rest of sick bay, which was laid out in an octagonal pattern. Individual operating suites filled each side, lined with sleek screens and ceiling-mounted sensors.

Ezo was standing over Sootriman in one of the darkened rooms. She appeared to be sleeping. Her clothes had been removed, and her hair was gathered in a bun. White elastic-like fabric covered her breasts and groin. The woman's body floated in midair, encircled by a dozen rings of light that reflected in Ezo's eyes. The halos rotated slowly, each one radiating into Sootriman's flesh. Thousands of tags with Novia script protruded from the rings, rotating with the halos while remaining horizontal to the observer. The characters appeared to change, constantly updating.

Awen moved around the wall and into the octagonal space. She approached Ezo so as not to startle him. Ezo looked up at her with glassy eyes.

"How is she?" Awen asked.

Ezo shrugged. "Can't say." His voice was tight. He ran a hand through his hair. "The ship started doing this as soon as the launch was finished. All sorts of Novia writing—diagnostics or something. Ezo doesn't know. Not a clue."

"Hey." Awen moved beside Ezo and placed an arm around him. "It's going to be okay, Ezo."

"How do you know?"

"I've got a feeling about it. All this…" She gestured to the wondrous sight in front of them. "The Novia, they know what they're doing. They're not going to let her die."

"I sure hope so." Without warning, Ezo put his arm around Awen and leaned his head on top of hers. Her heart warmed. Then she felt something warm and wet touch the top of her scalp. A tear, she supposed.

They stood there, arm in arm, for several minutes as the glowing rings continued to rotate around Sootriman's body. Even in unconsciousness, she was beautiful. The woman's deeply tanned skin, long black hair, and large gorgeous body made Awen never want to see her frail self naked again. This woman—this warrior goddess—had become her friend. Awen hated that Sootriman had been shot and that something permanently bad might have happened to her. But Awen meant what she'd said: she believed the Novia would make the woman well again.

"You still love her, don't you, Idris?"

She felt Ezo lift his head off hers—maybe because she'd used his first name. She'd never done that before.

Ezo took in a long, slow breath. "I do. As much as we fought, as much as we disagreed, there's still something about her that I just... I don't know. I can't explain."

"With that divorce filing, did you really forget to pay your taxes?"

She felt him laugh before she heard the sound. "Maybe not as much as I let on." He ran a sleeve across his cheek. "She was there for me when... after the war was over, she was all I had."

"She shared some of your story with me."

He nodded.

"Now it seems that you're all she has." Awen paused then pulled away to look up at him. "You want to know how I really know she's going to be okay?"

"How?"

"Because you're still standing here."

Another tear slid down his cheek. "Thanks," he said and pulled her into an embrace.

"Hey, listen. You keep doing this sort of thing, and you're bound to lose your reputation as a hardened criminal."

They laughed together. "Seems we'd better keep this to ourselves, then," Ezo said.

"Your secret's safe with me."

"I won't tell anyone either," TO-96's voice said over the room's speakers.

"Dammit, 'Six!"

AWEN LEFT Ezo with Sootriman and turned left out of sick bay. She walked toward the elevator, her heart filled with the prospect of going home. TO-96 had informed her and Ezo, over the sick-bay speakers, that they were nearing the quantum tunnel.

"It's time to return home," the bot said.

The words made her smile. Ezo grinned, too, though he was still melancholy as he looked at Sootriman.

"She's going to be all right," Awen had insisted again. "Trust me."

She rode the elevator toward the bridge, lost in thought. It had taken over three months to reach this moment, and in truth, she'd thought it would never come. But none of that mattered. It was worth the wait.

She felt the elevator slow. A soft chime played above her, then Azelon said, "You have arrived at the bridge, Awen." When the elevator doors opened, Awen gasped. Someone she'd never seen before was standing next to TO-96.

28

SURPRISINGLY, the Tawnhack didn't fight Magnus's offer of assistance. Instead, he used Magnus to gain his feet. It took all of Magnus's remaining strength not to buckle under the Jujari's considerable weight. He felt like an adolescent trying to give an adult a lopsided piggyback ride.

Burdened by the Jujari, Magnus felt like the convoy was twice as far away as it really was. Blaster fire peppered the ground, striking less than a meter in front of him. Other shots zipped by Magnus's ears, making the hair on the back of his neck stand up. He gasped, inadvertently inhaling a deep breath of the Jujari's body odor.

"Mystics, you stink!" Magnus said, his head wedged in the blood wolf's armpit. The Jujari looked down at him, seeming to register the comment, but neither of them had time for a discussion.

Magnus noted that the convoy was advancing toward them. The skiffs' return fire had also picked up. He dared not look back; he could only hope that the Selskrit were in retreat.

Then, without warning, his legs gave out. Magnus hit the ground as the Jujari toppled over him. His head and face were buried in the hot sand as the beast forced all the air out of his lungs. He tried to wiggle free, suddenly feeling claustrophobic, but it was no use.

The Jujari grunted. With an arduous moan, it rolled off of him. Magnus gasped. He blinked sand out of his eyes and pushed himself up. "Let's not do that again."

The pair were back on their feet again, but the blood wolf was moving more slowly. The beast must have been shot, maybe even several times. Magnus knew from experience that the Jujari could take several hits before going down. *Heck, maybe I've been shot too but have so much adrenaline in my system that I won't feel it for at least another minute.*

The Jujari's body stench was enough to make Magnus want to vomit. Blood, sweat, and offal was a powerful combination. Still, the pair lumbered forward toward the convoy, now not more than a dozen meters away. Magnus felt the Tawnhack pick up the pace as they neared. Hope must have lit a fire in the beast's belly.

"Just a few more steps," Magnus said in encouragement.

"Well, do not just sit there!" Abimbola said over comms. "Help that buckethead out!"

Marauders piled out of the two nearest skiffs and ran around to the front, helping relieve Magnus of his burden. He accepted the help with gratitude and looked back at the Jujari, catching his eye. There, in that moment, Magnus saw something he'd never seen from the warrior race before: gratitude.

"Let me know when you are loaded, buckethead!" Abimbola said.

Magnus turned and saw that the Selskrit had broken through the gate and were spreading out, using the compromised skiffs as cover. They were actually pushing them!

"Come on, Marine," someone said from inside the nearest vehicle. Magnus turned. It was Titus, the man from the stranded skiffs. "We've got room for one more." He offered Magnus a hand.

"Thanks, Marauder," Magnus said, clasping the man's forearm in a smack of dust.

419

"No, thank you."

"You fought well today, buckethead," Abimbola said with a smile. The two of them sat in the cab of a new skiff that Abimbola had commandeered. The dried blood on their bodies filled the compartment with the scent of rust. The warlord's black skin had turned a reddish brown from it, while Magnus's armor was caked in the stuff. His MAR30 and Z were going to need serious baths.

"And that crazy thing you did back there for that Tawnhack?" Abimbola whistled. "Mama. You in for something big after that, I tell you what. You fought very well. Very well."

Magnus didn't know what the warlord meant by that last part, but he appreciated the words of encouragement—though he doubted he would be free of sarcastic remarks for long.

"In fact," Abimbola continued, "I think you fought better than any Marine I have ever seen."

Magnus was surprised at what seemed to be yet another genuine compliment. "Thanks, Bimby." He was about to return it when Abimbola continued.

"But you were not fighting me, of course. I have killed every Marine I have ever fought."

And there's the backhand. Magnus knew it couldn't have been a full compliment. He chuckled. "Then I'm glad I wasn't fighting you."

"Because you would have lost."

"I'm sure I would have."

Abimbola took a long breath and shifted his weight in his seat. Silence filled the cab, sustained by the sounds of the drive core and the wind.

"Thank you for helping me," Magnus finally offered.

"Like I said, all we wanted was—"

"To kill Selskrit. I know, I know. But you could have done that anywhere in the Western Heights. Instead, you and your Marauders helped us rescue some of our people. So, thank you."

Abimbola looked at Magnus then turned back to the road. "You are welcome, buckethead."

Magnus watched the sand race by. "Rix... is he gonna be okay?"

"My medic said he will survive."

"Good, good." Magnus looked out the passenger side window. "He fought well out there."

"I am sure he did. He is one of my best. And the

bucketheads you rescued—are they some of your best?"

Magnus nodded. "Flow and Chico are two of my best operators, yes. The captain is a legend in our battalion."

"So you rescued your people's heroes, which makes you a hero too."

"I don't know about that."

"Where I come from, if you save the savior, you become the savior."

"Interesting concept."

"It is not a concept," Abimbola said. "It is the way of the universe."

Magnus met the warlord's eyes. Everyone was entitled to their own view. But he had to admit, that concept had a certain prestige to it. In the Repub, if you saved your CO's ass, all you got was a handshake and a good old, "Let's keep this between us." If some unlucky private was dumb enough to report the incident, having seen it firsthand and all, maybe you got a medal—and the private got demoted to where all demoted privates go: back home.

"So who did you save?" Magnus asked.

"What?"

"You're the big boss around here. Which savior did you save?"

The warlord shook his head. "It does not work like that here."

"Oh?"

"Here, the only person you save is yourself. And if you live long enough to have allies, you try to save them too. You must become the strongest person you know, or else you die."

"Rough way to live," Magnus said.

"Yes, buckethead. Rough way to live."

Sand pelted Magnus's face as they drove through a small desert dust swirl. "So, why'd you let us go, really?"

"Let who go? When?" Abimbola glanced at him.

"Awen and me. Back when we first met. You said it yourself—you kill every Marine you square off with. But you let us go because of Awen. I'd like to know why."

Abimbola worked his jaw. "That is between—"

"You and her. Maybe part of it. But you and I just spilled blood together. Where I come from, that means we have something in common now. We may still be enemies, but we stared death in the face together, and we lived to talk about it."

"That means something where I come from too." Abimbola sighed. "Her grandparents..." His eyes glazed over as his hands kept steering the skiff. "They gave their lives to protect me."

"Awen's?" Magnus furrowed his brow, trying to sort through the implications. "Wait—where? On Limbia Centrella?"

Abimbola nodded.

"You're saying there were Elonians on Limbia Centrella?"

"Indeed."

There was another long pause. Magnus's curiosity was really piqued by this point. Awen's species had a long history of sticking to themselves. Some called them elitists; others called them aloof. So far as Magnus could tell, Awen had probably defied her parents—maybe her entire planet —by leaving to join the Luma. Elonians just didn't do that sort of thing, at least not that he'd ever heard of. Joining the Luma was one thing, but going to a planet like Limbia Centrella would be unheard-of.

"Why would Elonians ever go there?" Magnus suddenly realized his tone could have been more tactful. "If you don't mind me asking."

"They had come to heal our people. When I was a boy, our world was attacked."

"A simikon invasion or something, right?"

"Yes. The insects also brought a blight with them," Abimbola said. "A plague."

"I remember reading something about that once. I don't remember much."

"I remember everything."

Magnus pursed his lips, feeling the fool. *Tighten it up, Magnus.* "I can't begin to imagine what that must've been like."

"No, I suppose you cannot." Abimbola absent-mindedly touched the scar on his face. "The insects wiped out two continents before we were able to stop them. The Republic"—he spoke the word from between his teeth—"were called in to help us. And they did." He straightened a little. "To their credit, they helped us drive back the enemy."

"So you won? You beat them?"

Abimbola nodded. "But we could not beat the plague. The scientists said it came from the simikons' excrement. It got into our water supply. Every plant absorbed it; every animal carried it in their muscle tissue. It was inescapable. So my people starved. We asked the Republic to come back, but they could not be bothered. They had already gotten their accolades, already been patted on the back by one another for helping the *lowly* Miblimbians. So the galaxy cheered the victors while we suffered."

Magnus nodded slowly. "I'm sorry."

"So am I. I watched my parents die. Their bodies rotted from the inside out. And there was nothing I could do. I was seven years old."

"Mystics…" Magnus whispered. There were few things in the universe worse than seeing your parents die when you were a child. "I'm—I'm sorry, Abimbola." Magnus shook his head. He couldn't imagine what this man had seen—what he'd lived through when he was only a boy. "So… how'd you survive?"

"How did I survive…" Abimbola shook his head and spat on the floorboard. "How did I survive? I survived because the gods decided I was different." He glared out the side window and took a few deep breaths. "After my parents and siblings died, people started wondering why I had not been infected. News spread quickly because…" His voice trailed off.

Because you were a miracle survivor? Magnus thought. But there seemed to be something more, some card the warlord was playing close to his chest.

Abimbola cleared his throat. "News spread, and soon the government asked for help in developing an antigen from my body."

"They figured if you'd survived that long, you must have an immunity or something."

"Yes. They offered to share the cure with whatever organization gave them aid."

"And the Elonians responded," Magnus said.

"Correct. Others did, too, but no one had more power and more credits. They had the best scientists, the best mobile facilities, the best starships."

"Then I'm guessing Awen's grandparents were scientists?"

"Doctors and researchers. But they were also kind. I remember being scared of them. The stories I had been told…" Again, the warlord trailed off. He coughed. "Anyway, the stories were not true, at least about them. They treated me with kindness. They treated me… like I was a son."

"And it surprised you."

"No. What surprised me was that I began to treat them like parents. Their son and I became like brothers—that is, Awen's father, Balin." Abimbola swallowed and took a deep breath. "The first antigen was released within a month of their arrival. It was not the most effective strain, but it saved millions of lives. Their research continued over two years, getting better and better. It was a good life. And they were able to develop other cures from their work, experimenting with their findings to make amazing things. But then it ended."

"Why? What happened?"

"Marine assassins invaded the lab."

"Marine assassins… you mean, a hit team?"

Abimbola nodded. "Awen's grandparents told Balin and me to hide in a ventilation system. Told us not to come out until two days after we heard the last blaster round. Balin hid, but I watched." Abimbola's hands squeezed the steering wheel so tightly that dried blood split and fell from his knuckles. "They tortured them. They asked them where I was. And when they would not say, they executed them. So I lost two families in two years. I was nine."

Magnus was choked up. It was a truly terrible story. He knew others like it, of course—Abimbola wasn't alone in his suffering. The galaxy had many harsh worlds… worlds the Marines had been sent to liberate. But there was no way a Marine special operations unit would be sent to eliminate an Elonian science team on a planet they'd just helped liberate. Something wasn't adding up.

"Abimbola, can I ask what these Marine assassins looked like?"

"Do not bother trying to defend your flag, buckethead." Abimbola's soft side was gone, replaced by his battle-hardened demeanor. "I know what I saw. And I have slain the same set of armor a thousand times over."

"I don't doubt that. Just... for me. What stood out about them? Colors, insignias, anything?"

"All-black armor, like a midnight sky. Late Mark V."

"You sure?" Magnus asked.

"Dammit, buckethead—"

"Sorry, I get it. I just..."

"Betrayal is a bitch, isn't it?"

Magnus lifted an eyebrow. "Sure is." He paused, not wanting to rile the warlord, but he needed more information. "Nothing else noticeable that you remember?"

Abimbola worked his jaw and looked out the side window again. He's thinking. *Thinking's good*, Magnus told himself. *Give me something, Bimby. Anything.*

"They had stripes on their shoulder and chest."

Magnus's gut twisted. "Stripes?"

"Yes. I can still see them."

"Three white stripes?"

Abimbola looked at Magnus, teeth clenched. "You know these Marines?"

"I do. And they're not Marines. Least, not anymore."

"Then what are they?"

Magnus considered the question more deeply than he'd intended to. He thought about what Abimbola had been through as a child—the world he must have grown up in and the life he'd lived until now. He thought about the battle that had just raged in the Western Heights and how he'd only discovered a handful of survivors in the compound. He thought about the attack on the mwadim's palace, about Awen and the Luma she'd lost. He thought about the late senator and Valerie and Piper…

That little girl's trust in you is misplaced. You know that, right, Adonis?

Then he began to wonder how many other lives had been affected by these rogue operators who dared sport Republic armor and, worse, how many more lives stood at the ends of their blasters in the future…

So, what are they, Magnus? And what are you gonna do about it?

"They're people I have to stop," Magnus finally replied to Abimbola, his hands tight around his MAR30. "And I won't rest until I do."

29

"My lord, we have vehicles inbound from the west."

"Let us see them." Abimbola walked up behind Berouth, his assistant, seated at one of the many workstations in the hideout's headquarters. Magnus remembered the man from when they drove to meet Ezo for the first time. Berouth made a few gestures in the holo-display and sent a live feed to float over the room's central table.

Magnus stood from his chair on the opposite side of the room, still holding a cup of tea. In the last few hours since arriving, he'd gotten a shower, had his weapons and some of his armor cleaned by Abimbola's crew, and managed to get kicked out of sick bay by Valerie three times. He'd only wanted to visit his men, but apparently, they needed medical attention, "not fist bumps from Marine buddies." She insisted he would see them in a few more hours.

Magnus stared at a dot on the horizon with a trail of dust blowing to the south.

"Zoom," Abimbola ordered.

Berouth entered more commands. The camera zoomed in to reveal an aggressive-looking skiff with several more behind it.

Abimbola walked around the workstation and moved to the holo-projection. "How many?"

The image rotated to give a top-down view. Magnus got dizzy from the quick move—he'd had enough weird things happen with his vision for one day. He moved forward and examined the convoy.

"That is Rohoar, all right," Abimbola said.

"Looks like four dozen armored skiffs." Magnus stroked his beard with his free hand. "Maybe five. He's coming to fight?"

"Maybe. But that is overkill."

"I dunno. From what I've seen, your turret emplacements alone could put up one hell of a fight."

"Fight me?" Abimbola looked at Magnus with a look of astonishment. "No, buckethead. Rohoar does not fight me. I pay him too much. I mean, it is overkill if he wants to fight *you*."

"Oh."

"I am not the one firing on his ships up there." The warlord pointed a finger overhead.

"Fair point."

"ETA?" Abimbola asked Berouth.

"Fifteen minutes at their current speed, my lord."

Abimbola looked at Magnus. "You might want to see if your ambassador is up for a visitor. He could be the one who saves your life today."

That prospect made Magnus sick to his stomach. "I'll go check with the good doctor."

"No. Nope, no way."

"Valerie, I just need to—"

"I already told you!" Valerie said. "They need to rest, and all of them have wounds that we need to keep free of—"

"The Jujari mwadim is coming. He's going to want to speak to the ambassador. That man in there"—Magnus jabbed a finger past Valerie's head—"may be the only thing between you and everyone else being executed today or getting to go home. Got that?"

The two of them stood outside the makeshift sick bay. Clear plastic kept the outside world away, while bright lights, blinking terminals, bundled tubes, and a dozen beds filled the space.

"*That man* is our only hope?" Valerie thumbed over her shoulder as her face went pale.

"Yeah." Magnus felt uneasy about the way she'd said that. "Why?"

She hesitated. "He's... he's... crazy, Lieutenant."

"Crazy?"

"I mean, at the very least, he's incoherent. But he might actually be crazy, too, once he has time to get well. Whatever he's been through, it rattled him pretty good. Probably permanently."

"You're saying brain damage."

"Head trauma, psychological trauma, yes—all of it," Valerie said. "He also has severe burns, contusions, ruptured eardrums... he's showing all the signs of surviving an explosion or something."

"That's because he *did* survive an explosion. I don't know how. But he did."

Valerie looked away from him and bit her bottom lip.

"What? What is it?" he asked.

"It looks like he's been tortured, too, Magnus. All of them have. Some of the marks on their bodies are... inconsistent with anything else I've ever seen. I can't even tell you what the Jujari did to them. But it's…"

"Can the ambassador at least have a conversation with his superiors?"

"No, that's what I'm saying. Listen, if you're putting any hope in him to be the person who saves your hide today, you can forget about it."

"Dammit." Magnus clenched his hands and turned away. He paced a few steps then turned to face her. "There's nothing you can give him? A stimulant? Something to make him focus even for a couple minutes?"

Magnus knew he was asking a lot of her. Doing what he requested probably meant breaking her code of ethics as a medical professional. Such drugs existed, even if they weren't legal. The Recon had modified the Mark VII armor to include injections of several survival drugs, including adrenatex. It gave injured and incoherent operators several lucid, pain-free minutes to get their splick together. If a Marine survived an op, surviving the side effects was the next challenge. Adrenatex could leave operators disabled, sometimes permanently. But if it saved a life, the Recon reasoned, it was worth it.

"I do have something, yes," Valerie said. Magnus was about to order her to give it to the patient when she interrupted him. "But I want you to realize you're probably sending him to his death."

"I get that."

"Do you, Lieutenant? Do you really?"

"Yes, I really do! And I also realize that if we don't do this—if *I* don't do this—everyone in here could be sent to their deaths too. So, yeah, I get it. It's what Marines do. We make the hard calls no one else wants to, and we live with the consequences like no one else can."

To her credit, Valerie didn't even flinch during Magnus's mini tirade. She just looked him square in the eye and responded, "Very well. Twenty cc's of epinadrol. You'll have him mostly coherent for about forty minutes. After that, he's comatose until we can get him to a real hospital."

"That's more than I need. Have him dressed and sent to the control room to await instructions."

Without another word, Valerie turned, walked through the slit in the plastic wall, and headed for Bosworth's bed.

DUSK DREW near as Magnus stood beside Abimbola, waiting outside for the mwadim to arrive. The Jujari skiffs pulled up to the hideout's entrance like a herd of angry rhinosaurs then slowed, drive cores whining to a halt. The machines were late-model Republic Super Sleds, light armored personnel carriers. They were fast, and—given the blaster turrets and missile banks the Jujari had modified them with—very deadly. Sand and dust swirled around the convoy as hatches opened and Jujari climbed to the ground. In the lead skiff, a door opened, and Rohoar stepped out, his figure silhouetted by the setting sun in the west.

As the mwadim neared—arriving with no fewer than twelve personal bodyguards—Abimbola bowed and tilted his head sideways, exposing his neck. Magnus followed suit. He hated the gesture, but he hated the alternative more—having his throat slit.

"Welcome, Rohoar of the Tawnhack, mwadim of the Jujari," Abimbola said.

"Rohoar sees you, Abimbola of the Miblimbians." Rohoar sniffed the air. "But he does not see this Republic scrumruk graulap you keep company with."

Magnus made to interject, but Abimbola cut him off with a twitch of his hand. "He is the same that stood before you this morning, the one bound in blood."

"But his kind have betrayed our trust!" Rohoar snarled, raising a clawed finger to the sky. He turned to Magnus. "Rohoar gave you warriors. Rohoar gave you his blood. And how is it repaid?"

"My people have betrayed your trust, yes," Magnus replied. "But for reasons I do not know."

"Though we intended to find out for you, Great Mwadim," Abimbola said, glaring at Magnus. "It seems that because you graciously allowed us to hunt Selskrit in the Western Heights, you now have a very valuable gift in your possession."

"And what—Abimbola, warlord of the Dregs— might that be?"

"The Republic ambassador."

Rohoar tilted his head, his ears perked. "The ambassador?" A large tongue flopped out and licked his chops. "The fat ambassador from my predecessor's palace?"

"The one," Magnus said.

Rohoar eyed him cautiously. "And what do you suggest I do with him, Republic Marine?"

"If it were me, I'd order him to call General Lovell for you. Then, when you're done, you can eat him, for all I care."

Rohoar's ears lay back. "A warrior who freely offers his representative to death?"

"He is not my representative. Respectfully, Mwadim. I fight for my people, not the whims of my politicians."

"I see." The mwadim licked his lips. "But you already offered Rohoar a meeting with your General Lovell. Why does Rohoar need a fat ambassador to do the same?"

Magnus had been afraid of this question. The truth was that he'd doubted he could arrange the meeting from the moment he first offered it. It wasn't a total bluff, of course; there was always the outside chance he could get through to the general on his own merits. But Magnus hadn't thought he would survive long enough to have to honor his promise to the mwadim in the first place. This was an inconvenient downside of surviving.

Magnus didn't dare offer any of this to Rohoar, of course. He'd keep bluffing as long as he could. "Great Mwadim, I can secure the meeting with Brigadier General Lovell as promised. However, it is a matter of speed."

"Rohoar does not understand you."

"It will take me several hours to arrange the meeting, maybe even days."

"Days?" Rohoar sneered, his hackles rising. "Rohoar cannot wait days! You lied to Rohoar!"

"I did not lie, Mwadim. We just never discussed the particulars. But with the ambassador at your disposal, this meeting can be arranged in mere minutes."

Rohoar considered this, his nose twitching. Magnus tried his best not to recoil from the Jujari's foul breath and the long teeth less than a meter from his face. He was, once again, in awe of just how terrible these beasts were up close.

Rohoar looked at Abimbola. "Do you agree with this assessment, warlord?"

"I do believe that Magnus can get you the audience you seek much faster with the ambassador at your disposal."

The mwadim looked between the two men several times. He sniffed, licked his chops again, then howled. Magnus's hair stood up. He wanted to cover his ears, as the day's work had given him a headache, and he was extremely fatigued. But he knew that doing so would probably raise the mwadim's ire. Instead, he stood there, waiting for the wail to die down.

When it did, the mwadim nodded. "Rohoar likes minutes better than days."

Suddenly, Rohoar's hackles went rigid as he looked toward the compound's entrance. Magnus and

Abimbola looked back to see the mwadim's blood-hound standing in the doorway. He was bandaged on his leg, torso, forearms, and one shoulder. One arm was bound in a sling, and red-stained gauze covered his left eye. Magnus couldn't believe the Jujari warrior was even conscious, let alone walking. He'd been hurt badly.

"What is the meaning of this?" Rohoar demanded, his ears erect.

Abimbola made to speak, but the blood wolf cut him off. Up until that moment, the Tawnhack survivor had said nothing to either Abimbola or Magnus. Valerie had tended to his wounds as best she could—getting through all the hair was a feat in and of itself—but no words had been exchanged.

The blood wolf said something in his mother tongue. At Rohoar's gesture, the warrior started limping forward, his lips curled in pain. Magnus and Abimbola stepped aside, letting the blood wolf pass. He approached Rohoar, lowering his head and tilting his neck in the Jujari greeting. Then he leaned in and whispered in the mwadim's ear. Rohoar's eyes grew wider as the seconds passed, darting to stare at Magnus.

Magnus was uneasy. In his mind, this was going one of two ways, and both resulted in someone dying.

Given the Jujari's extreme emphasis on honor, he imagined that there might be some level of shame for the blood wolf getting rescued by a Repub Marine—if he was telling the mwadim the truth. Maybe the blood wolf would even be slain for it. Or… maybe the blood wolf was lying to the mwadim, and Magnus was about to be executed. He wouldn't put it past either of them.

Rohoar raised his chin, and the blood wolf turned away, limping behind him. "Rohoar has heard from his blood wolf."

An awkward silence hung in the air as Magnus and Abimbola waited for whatever would happen next. *And?* Magnus wanted to say, but he thought better of it.

Rohoar said nothing. Then, as if the episode with the blood wolf had never even happened, the mwadim moved on. "Rohoar accepts the opportunity to speak with the general. Take me to my ambassador."

Bosworth sat in a Miblimbian chair normally reserved for Abimbola, as it was the only chair the ambassador could fit in. He was hastily dressed in a medical gown and an old dress coat someone had scavenged from a supply locker. Bloodstains leaked through bandages around his torso and stained the gown. His head and face also had several fresh wraps of gauze, each turning red in various spots.

The control room was dimly lit, and more over-sized chairs had been brought in and placed around the central table. Abimbola insisted that Rohoar sit at the head, while he took a secondary position. Bosworth sat on the opposite side, followed by Magnus. The rest of the chairs were given to Rohoar's guards, while additional Jujari, Magnus's fire team, and several Marauders stood along the walls and workstations.

This was the closest Magnus had ever been to the ambassador. The last time he'd seen him, the man had been a fitful raging wreck before charging Awen and the former mwadim. Now he sat fairly composed, the drugs making him alert and slightly fidgety.

"Ambassador Bosworth," Abimbola began, "as you may or may not know, you and the remaining survivors were rescued from the Selskrit today at the discretion of the new Jujari mwadim, Rohoar of the Tawnhack. On the occasion of your freedom, I am here to negotiate a gesture of appreciation."

Bosworth blinked several times without responding. Magnus studied the man and noticed a bead of sweat moving down his temple. The ambassador was dressed in a massively large shirt and a leather jacket that probably belonged to Abimbola. He looked more like a bloated backward gangster with bushy eyebrows and three chins than an esteemed Republic dignitary.

Say something, Magnus urged the man from inside his head. But when no words came, he felt he had to make a move. "Ambassador Bosworth, I believe that—"

"What?" Bosworth yelled.

Magnus recoiled, as did everyone else around the table. Rohoar looked at Abimbola.

"Sir," Magnus continued. "It seems that the mwadim—"

"You're going to need to speak up, Marine. This is no place for mumblers."

Magnus looked at Abimbola then remembered Valerie telling him that Bosworth's eardrums had ruptured. *Perfect.*

"I'm sorry," Magnus said to Rohoar. "His eardrums were damaged in the explosion."

"Here, try these." Simone stepped to Abimbola's side and, after making a few adjustments, handed him two of their in-ear comms. The warlord nodded and passed them to Magnus who, in turn, handed them to the ambassador.

"Try these, sir."

"What?"

Over-enunciating each syllable, Magnus said, "These will help your hearing."

"My hearing?"

"Yes," Magnus nodded emphatically.

"Very well." The ambassador took his time seating each comm over his earlobes and fitting the micro-speakers into his ear canals.

"How do you read me?" Magnus asked.

The ambassador blinked at him several times.

"Ambassador?"

"Ah, there you are. That's much better." The fat man regarded Abimbola. "Would you please repeat yourself, large Miblimbian? You were mumbling. I understand your kind have a propensity for it."

Magnus cringed, but to Abimbola's credit, he didn't so much as twitch. The warlord repeated what he'd said before and waited for Bosworth's reply.

"Ah, very good. And please tell the mwadim that—"

"You may tell him yourself, Ambassador. He speaks common."

"Does he? Marvelous." Bosworth cleared his

throat. "Great Mwadim, what gesture of appreciation might the Republic be willing to provide you as thanks for saving my life? I am permitted to offer you an initial sum of—"

"I want to speak with Brigadier General Lovell." Rohoar's voice felt as though it made the table rumble.

Bosworth blinked. "Speak to Brigadier General Lovell?"

"He is like the mwadim in charge of all the Marines, yes?"

"Uh, I... suppose that's a fair comparison. However, I don't think you—"

"I have not asked you to think, Ambassador. The last time you thought, people died."

Bosworth winced, jerking back in his seat. "It's just that—"

"Either you can put me in touch with Brigadier General Lovell now, here at this comms station, or I have no further use for you."

The ambassador stammered. He looked at Magnus then to Abimbola. "Yes, yes. I can connect you with him. I... I just need to give hailing codes to... to whoever runs this place here."

"That would be me," Abimbola replied.

"Ah. Well, let's see here..."

Magnus suddenly wondered whether the man could remember his hailing codes and security-clearance designators. This whole thing could go sideways simply because his memory was gone. But to Magnus's amazement, Bosworth dictated all the necessary information to Abimbola's communications operator, who then gave the warlord a thumbs-up.

Abimbola directed his attention to Rohoar. "We are ready to transmit."

Rohoar looked at his blood wolf and said something in the Jujari mother tongue. The blood wolf touched a small implant in his temple and spoke several soft words in his native language. Several seconds transpired before the blood wolf nodded to Rohoar.

"You may proceed," the mwadim said.

Just like that, the Jujari communications blockade was down. Information could flow freely.

All Magnus wanted to do was find an encrypted handset and contact his COs at the company level. But he knew it might be several more hours of pissing contests and bureaucracy before that would happen.

A holo-interface appeared before Bosworth. The man's eyes brightened, and he rubbed his nose several times. Then, with a loud sniff, the ambassador began typing and swiping, searching for the general's name in his personal Republic database. Once he found Lovell's name and swiped through all the security-clearance windows, Bosworth initiated the holo-vid call. It only took one set of trills for Lovell to answer.

"Ambassador?" the general asked, eyes wide. Magnus noted a commotion going on behind Lovell. He was standing on a starship's bridge. The scene was turbulent, full of status updates, orderlies, and flashing lights. A general-alert klaxon pulsed in the background.

"Good evening, General. I see—"

"How the hell are you alive, Gerald?"

"Recovered by your rescue team," Bosworth said.

"My rescue team?"

"Indeed, led by… by…" Bosworth looked at Magnus. "What's your name again, trooper?"

"Lieutenant Magnus, Ambassador."

Bosworth repeated the name to the general, and Lovell's face froze. Something was wrong. Very wrong.

"Is the lieutenant there with you now, Ambassador?"

"Yes, General. But before we get to that, I have a very important Jujari leader here who wishes to—"

"Put him on, Ambassador."

"But, sir, I don't think you—"

"*Put him on.*"

Bosworth blinked several times, lips pursed to an impossible distance away from his nose. "As you wish." The ambassador turned the holo-screen toward the Marine. Magnus saw himself in a small window to the lower right while Lovell's rich black face filled the rest of the screen.

"Are you… are you all green, Lieutenant?"

Magnus looked around. He felt nervous. He *never* felt nervous. "Yes, General. Is there a problem?"

"I'm going to need you shipside immediately."

Magnus's heart sank. It was news about Awen; he was sure of it. Something had happened to her. "General, if it's news you can share here, I'd appreciate if you just—"

"This needs to be done in person, son."

"General, with all due respect, I'd rather you break the news here."

"You're being placed under arrest, Lieutenant."

Magnus blinked. "I'm *what?*"

30

"Who is that?" Awen blurted.

Standing beside TO-96 was another bot. The robot was humanoid in shape with long arms and legs and a slender torso—and a good head taller than TO-96. Its body was the same pearly white as the ship's hallways and glowed a gentle blue around the joints and from two eyes behind a smooth face. Whatever TO-96 was to blocky segments and clunky parts, this robot was to pure sophistication and elegance.

"Awen, allow me to introduce you to Azelon," said TO-96. "She and I have been—"

"Azelon?" Awen asked, taking a tentative step onto the bridge. "As in, the ship Azelon?"

"Yes, as in the ship."

"And she's safe?"

"Why, of course. She is the ship, after all. The Novia have instructed her to serve and protect us wherever we wish to go."

"Okay, well… that's, wow. Yeah." Awen didn't know what to say. She'd never even conceived of the same AI inhabiting both a starship's mainframe and a robot—though, as she thought about it, the idea didn't seem so strange. In fact, she began to wonder why it hadn't been done before. *Aren't all autonomous maintenance bots much the same?* she thought. *Though I can hardly compare Azelon to a maintenance bot.*

"Well, Ninety-Six," Awen said, warming to the idea, "it seems you have yourself a female companion, now, doesn't it?"

TO-96 reared back then looked between Azelon and Awen. "I suppose I do, yes. What a pleasant turn of events. We are, as you might say, becoming fast friends."

"Nice." Awen smiled. She approached the pair, eyeing Azelon with keen interest.

"I am pleased to make your acquaintance, Awen of the protoverse." Azelon extended her hand. Awen stared at it, unsure if she wanted to take it. However, this was, after all, a sentient species' invention, and Awen's oaths as a Luma required that she honor this bot in the same way she would honor the Novia

Minoosh. Despite her apprehension, Awen was genuinely excited to see such a technologically sophisticated robot. She was only skeptical because she was tired. And overwhelmed. And she just really wanted to get back home.

Awen stepped forward and took the offered hand. It felt surprisingly warm. "I'm pleased to meet you too, Azelon. Thank you for... for all you've done for us so far. We are very grateful."

"It is my pleasure to serve you and Ezo and TO-96." She looked at the other bot. TO-96's eyes grew brighter.

Is he blushing? Bots don't do that, Awen remarked to herself. *Do they?*

AWEN WAS STRAPPED into her acceleration couch, readying herself for the violent shaking, the high-pitched oscillation, and the arduous compression of the quantum-tunnel jump. She also thought to ask TO-96 for a vomit bag, but Azelon assured her that no such thing existed on the *Spire*.

"Then I hope you have some good cleaning bots," Awen replied.

"We do," Azelon said.

Awen blinked. *So much for my attempt at humor.*

TO-96 took a seat beside Awen but neglected to fasten his harness. Likewise, Azelon stood casually to one side of the bridge.

"Uh, Ninety-Six, are you gonna, you know, strap in or anything?"

The bot tilted his head at her. "For what purpose?"

Awen tried to remember what the jump had been like for TO-96 the first time, but the memories were more about her own trauma than his. Maybe he was immune to the effects. She wouldn't know without asking.

"Ah!" TO-96 exclaimed with a finger in the air. "Forgive me, Awen. It seems that the Novia Minoosh developed starships that dampen the effects of jumping through a quantum tunnel."

Awen glanced at Azelon. "Really? 'Cause if that's true, that's awesome."

"It is true, Awen," Azelon replied. "The impact on your physiology should be minimal, if you notice anything at all. In fact, the launch from Ithnor Ithelia was four point six thousand times more volatile than what you will experience jumping through a quantum tunnel aboard the *Spire*."

"Four point six thousand times?"

"Basically," TO-96 said, "that means you won't feel a thing."

Awen blinked. "And you know what? I'm just fine with that. Thank you."

"It's our pleasure," TO-96 said, looking over to Azelon.

Is he flirting with her?

Azelon moved to the center of the bridge and turned toward the main window. Her white body began to glow blue, and several dozen hexagonal display screens appeared all around her, each semi-translucent against the main view of the void. Simultaneously, the bridge darkened, making the screens seem even more vibrant. They depicted dimensional graphs, star charts, images of the ship, diagnostic readouts, and supply levels of who knew what.

Awen's head spun as she considered all the data that floated around Azelon. *Now she's just showing off.* Awen smiled.

Lines began connecting different screens, specifically the ones that seemed to display star charts and gravity wells. The floating windows reordered themselves in midair and then stacked on top of one another. Azelon continued to stare straight ahead, and the activity in the panels grew more frenetic.

Awen tried to see if she could sense something in

the ship—a vibration in the arms of the acceleration couch or something—but there was nothing. The only sign that anything significant was about to happen came from the visual spectacle spinning around Azelon. The female bot's body grew brighter as the hexagonal panes traded places around her, creating a blurry sphere of motion, strobing lights, and interconnected pathways.

TO-96 was watching Azelon work with something that bordered on obsession. *He's into this*, Awen thought.

Then, with a sudden move of Azelon's hands, the screens shot forward and stacked up, one in front of the other, extending from just in front of her torso to the bridge's main viewing window. They floated there, perfectly still, like hundreds of layers of translucent windowplex glowing in a variety of colors. With a final motion, Azelon pulled her hands in toward her hips, and all the images shot towards her direction and were absorbed into her chest as if ingested by a blaster bolt.

The bridge went black. Awen could hear herself breathing. Her heart was pounding in her ears, and there was a soft hum coming from the ship. Everything was still.

In front of her, dots of light began to appear.

They were so subtle at first that Awen thought maybe she was seeing motes of light in her corneas left over from Azelon's navigation show. But within another few seconds, she realized they were stars.

White stars. Yellow stars. Not purple stars.

"Are we back?" She held her breath. "Ninety-Six!" Awen turned to face his glowing yellow eyes. "Ninety-Six, are we back?"

"We are, Awen."

She pumped her fists and let out a scream that seemed to surprise both TO-96 and Azelon, but she didn't care. "Mystics, this is incredible! We did it!" She kicked her feet like a small schoolgirl, giving another shout. Her hands worked the buckles as fast as she could, trying to get them undone. But she was so excited she got stuck twice.

"So, where are we? Did we make it to Ki Nar Four? Are we close?"

Azelon stepped close and helped her undo the restraints. "Yes, Awen. We are precisely where you placed the tunnel's terminus, less than one hour from Sootriman's planet."

"For real?" Awen took Azelon's offered hand and stood up. "Someone's gotta tell Ezo that we made it!"

"I believe you just did," TO-96 replied.

Awen spun around and saw a holo-feed from sick

bay with Ezo's face in it. "Ezo!" she yelled. "We made it!"

"We sure did, Star Queen. Congratulations."

"You too!" Awen clenched her fists again. "Oh man, this is just so great." She gave another loud scream, stomping her feet, then noticed Ezo looking back toward Sootriman. "Oh my gosh," she said, reaching toward his picture. "I'm so sorry."

Ezo chuckled. "It's okay, Star Queen. Ezo gets it. We both know how you freak out from time to time."

"I'll come down and see you in a second, I promise."

"Sounds good. Just keep all the screaming up there on the bridge, okay?"

She gave him a smirk and nodded. "I'll try."

Ezo winked, and the screen vanished.

This was far more emotional than she had imagined it would be. Awen was one of the first three people in the known universe to travel to another reality, encounter a sentient species, board their starship, and return to her point of origin in less than four months. It would make history, and she didn't even care whose name was attached. She just wanted to share the news with… everyone! With Willowood, with the Order, with her parents, with the scientific community. With anyone who would listen.

Awen placed a hand to her heart and sat back down. She breathed deeply. A wide smile crept across her face. "We did it, Ninety-Six. We really did it."

"Yes, yes we did."

She reached over and placed a hand on his shoulder.

The bot turned to look at her. "You should know that I am proud of you."

"Did… did you just say you're *feeling* something?"

"If a sense of appreciation and admiration for another person that results in an urge to embrace them constitutes *feeling*, then, yes—I am feeling."

Awen lunged at him, throwing her arms around his neck. At first, TO-96 seemed unsure of what to do. But a moment later, he returned the embrace, holding Awen gently beneath his weapon-laden arms.

"Is this a normal behavior for species from your universe?" Azelon asked.

"Yes," TO-96 replied. "It is. See my archives on human affection when you are able. It will explain most everything you need to know."

"Ah, yes. I see it now. Thank you, TO-96."

"With pleasure."

Awen released the bot and sat back in her chair. A deep sense of satisfaction flooded her as she looked out the window toward the approaching planet. Then it struck her that she didn't have any idea what to do next. She and the others had been so fixated on finding a way home that she really hadn't thought about what they would do once they arrived at Ki Nar Four.

"Ninety-Six, how soon before you can connect with the galactic network? Maybe summarize some news feeds for us? You know, get us up to speed?"

TO-96 didn't respond.

"'Six, you all right?"

The robot tilted his head then said, "Oh my."

Awen slipped out of her chair and moved in front of him. "What is it, Ninety-Six?"

The bot's head snapped toward her. "Awen… I'm afraid I have what may be some rather disconcerting news."

"Okay…" she said, drawing the word out. "What is it?"

"Well, as I began accessing the information channels, as per your request, I came across something startling."

"Disconcerting, startling—I got it. What is it, 'Six?"

"We were in Ithnor Ithelia for seventy-one days, Galactic common time. By that, I mean, we experienced seventy-one days in metaspace. But here in protospace, well…"

"You're killing me right now, Ninety-Six. Just spit it out."

"We have only been gone for three point five days, Awen."

She froze. Her heart thumped in her chest. "Excuse me?" She fluttered her eyelids. "Three and a half days? Are you… are you absolutely certain?"

"I am one hundred percent certain, Awen. Apparently, there is significant time dilation when traveling through the multiverse."

Awen stared out the bridge window. "It's almost as if we never left," she whispered. Her mind became a flurry of activity then, racing through scenarios faster than she could keep track of them. She wondered what kind of expeditions could be made in Ithnor Ithelia. Awen was in awe of what such a time discrepancy meant for progress, the development of new technologies, and new discovery and research.

Research. The admiral's supposed research team. *What would the time dilation mean for them? How much exploration can they do in just two or three weeks?* She tried to do the math in her head, but it was dizzying. She wondered if they would discover the temple library or the quantum-tunnel generator. Perhaps they would discover another ship like the *Azelon* or new technologies that would allow them to…

Awen caught her breath. *To conquer the galaxy.* Whatever elation she'd just enjoyed had vanished. "We've got to go back."

"Back, Awen?" TO-96 asked.

She turned to look at him. "We have to go back. We have to stop them. There's no telling what they might discover or how they'll use it. That enemy team, Admiral Kane's research team—they can't be allowed to use any of that technology. We can't let it fall into the wrong hands."

But whose hands, exactly, are the wrong ones?

Awen's thoughts suddenly turned toward the Galactic Republic. The Jujari. Even So-Elku and whatever Luma he'd coerced into following him. Would any of them be any better if they acquired the power that lies in the metaverse?

"We've got to stop them, Ninety-Six," she said. "We've got to stop them all."

31

MAGNUS COULD FEEL everyone's eyes drilling holes in him. He felt embarrassed. Vulnerable. He should have listened to the general and just gone to the ship —assuming Rohoar would have allowed it.

"I want to brief you before they get their hands on you, Magnus. I don't know why you did it all—"

"Did what, sir?"

"I don't know why you did it all," the general pressed, "but if you tell me the truth before they arraign you, maybe I can help."

"General, what did I do?"

"Enough!" Rohoar slammed his fists on the table, momentarily blurring the holo-feed. He rose from his seat. The rest of the Jujari stood as well. Bosworth fumbled with the general's floating image and spun it toward the mwadim. "Brigadier General Lovell. Your ambassador is incompetent, your Marines are vicious —and apparently lawless—and Rohoar's patience is running out."

"What can the Republic do for you, Mwadim?" Lovell asked, clearly trying to stay focused despite the frenetic scene on the bridge behind him.

"Firstly, you have blocked communication with Rohoar's fleet. Release this. Secondly, Rohoar demands to know why you have engaged in open combat with our ships."

"Mwadim, we have not done either."

"You deny it?" Rohoar pulled the holo-frame toward him.

Magnus watched hackles stand up on the necks of the Jujari.

"We have *not* attacked your ships or blocked communication," Lovell stated.

Magnus could tell that the general was telling the truth. The problem was that he knew enough about the Jujari to feel the mwadim wouldn't be making a false accusation. None of this felt right.

"Lies! The Jujari *see you* from our relays!"

"What you see are rogue Republic ships who have initiated a conflict between us, Mwadim." The general's voice was getting louder as he tried to speak above someone yelling in the background. "Our first and second fleets, as well as our third fleet, are taking heavy fire from your fleet. However, only our third fleet is firing on yours. We are attempting to communicate with them now, as we suspect their actions have not been sanctioned by the Galactic Republic. I repeat, this hostility is not representative of the Senate's wishes. Our attempts to communicate with them are being blocked. Nonetheless, if you do not order your fleet to stand down, our remaining fleets will be forced to return fire. Let me be clear—"

The general moved out of frame, steadying himself against a sudden motion on the bridge. "Let me be clear. If you are unable to hail your fleet and order a stand-down, we *will* return fire. Do you understand?"

The mwadim's lips curled over his teeth. "Rohoar understands, General. And if you do not put a muzzle on your rogue fleet, we will be forced to call in our reinforcements. Do *you* understand?"

The general's eye twitched. This was escalating quickly. "We are working on reaching our third fleet, and we will do our best to disrupt whatever communication sanctions are being enforced on your fleet. Keep trying to reach them." Another motion jolted the general from the frame. His face reappeared as a second klaxon sounded in the background, this one higher pitched. "Ambassador Bosworth, are you still there?"

The ambassador pushed himself out of his seat and moved toward the mwadim, careful not to get too close. Slowly, he reached for the holo-frame and turned it toward his face.

"Gerald, we are sending a shuttle for you, assuming—in good faith—that the mwadim grants you permission to leave. How many are you?"

Magnus jumped in before anyone else could reply. "Eight military personnel, including myself, three civilians, and the ambassador."

The general made a note then looked at Bosworth again. "You are to take Lieutenant Magnus into custody, employing whatever Marine presence is still at your disposal, and report immediately to my ship. You will be given further instructions upon your arrival."

"I understand, General."

"Regulations require that I send a data file at the end of this transmission. It will include the charges against the lieutenant. However, I ask that you keep it unopened until I'm able to speak with my Marine in person."

Bosworth shot a glance at Magnus. "If it's serious,

General—if this Marine is a threat—I need to know."

"You don't need to know, Gerald. Just get back to my ship with the lieutenant and the rest of your party. We'll be there in ten minutes. And we'll get that window open for the mwadim to call off his assault."

"Ten minutes." Rohoar growled. "And no more."

BOSWORTH RECLINED in Abimbola's giant chair. He'd sent the holo-projection to a data pad then picked up the device and rested it on his enormous belly. It didn't take long for Magnus to realize the ambassador had opened the general's data file. *The two-faced Bludervian dimdish.*

Magnus paced at the opposite end of the table. He watched the man raise an eyebrow, swiping through screen after screen. By the time the ambassador finally looked over the tablet at him, Magnus had had enough.

"He told you not to open it."

"And he told you that you are under arrest. That means you have conceded rights as a Marine of the Republic and will be tried in a military tribunal."

I already lost those rights, Magnus thought, blinking his bioteknia eyes.

Bosworth looked back at the data pad and began reading aloud. "Disobeying a direct order, conspiracy, conspiracy to commit murder, conspiracy to disrupt diplomatic affairs…" The ambassador paused. "And what's this? 'Assassination of a Republic senator'?"

Dutch raced to Magnus's side before he could defend himself. "That's false!"

"Whoa, whoa!" The ambassador pumped his hands at her. "Seems you have yourself a tigress there, Lieutenant."

"Watch your step, Ambassador," Magnus replied. "You wouldn't want this tigress losing her temper on you."

Bosworth regarded the woman, licking his upper lip. "Or would I?"

Dutch recoiled.

The ambassador put the data pad down. "She wouldn't dare, anyway. She's too smart. I am, after all, the Republic ambassador. She knows that if she does one hasty move, her career is over."

Dutch mumbled something, and Magnus put a hand on her arm. "Easy, Corporal. He's not worth it," he whispered.

"What was that? Either of you have something to

say?" Bosworth looked around at the onlookers. "Anyone?" When no one replied, he said, "Ha! I didn't think so. The general's orders stand. The shuttle should be here in five minutes, and I... I feel..." The ambassador's eyes glazed over, and the fat face went pale. "Suddenly, it seems that I..."

His hands dropped to his sides, and his head lolled backward. The ambassador was out cold. The epinadrol had worn off.

Magnus looked between Abimbola and Rohoar.

"Well, buckethead. What are you going to do?" Abimbola asked.

Yeah, Magnus, what are *you gonna do?* This wasn't his first time being in trouble with the Corps. His mind flashed back to Caledonia, to images he'd tried to erase every damn day. But he'd had advocates back then. He'd been given a second chance because people believed in him. They had reason to believe Magnus was justified in what he'd chosen to do in that horrible war.

This was different. The list of charges—even if there weren't any more than what the ambassador had read—wouldn't be going away. He could tell that from Lovell's resigned tone. Magnus would be tried. He would be found guilty. And he would probably be executed.

And all for what? For bleeding Recon red? For going above and beyond the call of duty to rescue some senator and his family, only to be blamed for the senator's death? And then there was the charge of "conspiracy to disrupt diplomatic" whatever. He couldn't believe they were actually trying to peg the attack on the mwadim's palace on him.

This is bad. *Real bad.*

Standing there in Abimbola's control room, Magnus understood that his career was truly over and not just because he had bioteknia implants. No. It was because the Repub had cut him loose.

The Galactic Republic had changed over the years —morphed into a system of favors, handshakes, and backroom deals. Ulterior motives, politicking—nothing was clear anymore. It hadn't been clear for a long time. He'd seen other people chewed up and spit out. He knew people who had "disappeared." Now it was his turn. The rusty blade of the executioner's axe had come for him.

"Well, I'm certainly not letting that dimdish drive me home." Magnus gestured toward the sleeping fat man.

The mwadim chuckled. "Rohoar suspects that you are in a large pile of Jujari splick, Marine."

"You can say that again."

"No, Rohoar is fine with saying it once. Also, Rohoar does not suspect you were the one who sabotaged his predecessor's meeting with your ambassador and the Luma."

Magnus pulled back, surprised by the sudden vote of confidence. "Well... thank you, Great Mwadim—"

"But you probably did kill the senator. Rohoar would kill them all, too." The other Jujari around the control room cackled.

Might the mwadim actually let me go, even if it means risking his tentative agreement with the Republic? "So, what if I don't take the ambassador's shuttle?"

"Rohoar would say you are a smart human."

"But what about your agreement with the general?"

The mwadim waved him off. "The Jujari have survived for so long because the Jujari do not trust those who do not trust themselves with power."

"I don't follow."

Rohoar blew out a sigh. "Too much power, not enough discretion. This is the Republic. Your balance is lopsided because you have never learned to trust yourselves with the power you have acquired. The imbalance is killing you like it kills all species who ignore the signs. The Jujari chose not to embrace the imbalance, so the Jujari survive.

"The general's insistence that some of his fleet have gone *rogue*—this is foolishness, meant to distract the Jujari. Rohoar has no intention of ceasing fire. Allies are already on their way. The Galactic Republic is not getting out of this one unscathed, and they will think twice before moving ships into our system again. That is, if they have any ships left to visit us with."

"So, what's the call, buckethead?" Abimbola moved toward Magnus. "What do you need?"

Magnus considered the warlord's offer, realizing the man seemed truly interested in helping him. "I need a way off the planet. And I'll take whoever wants to go with me. We let the Repub shuttle pick up Bosworth, Wainwright, and the old Luma, just as the general requested. But I won't be stepping on that transport."

"So you are choosing to run from your government," Rohoar said.

Magnus hadn't made it *that* definitive in his own mind yet. But yes, that was the sum of it. He nodded.

"Ha!" The Miblimbian clapped his oversized hands and walked toward Magnus. "Then you are truly a Marauder now. Welcome to the fold."

The next thing Magnus knew, he was caught up in a full-bodied embrace, his head pressed against Abimbola's sweaty pectorals. He could think of worse initiations but few that were more awkward.

"Thank you," Magnus said, pulling away. "I think."

"You know what this means now, yes?"

"You'll stop calling me buckethead and give me ten thousand credits' worth of poker chips?"

"You are funny, buckethead!" The man guffawed. "But no. It means I will personally help you get to wherever you need getting to."

"And so will Rohoar."

Magnus turned to face the mwadim in open astonishment. "You're what?"

"You saved Rohoar's blood wolf. Our code demands that he serve you as his new master. However, his injuries prevent him from fulfilling his responsibility with any faithfulness. As a result, the indebtedness falls upon the blood wolf's parent and patron." The mwadim raised his chin ever so slightly. "In both cases, this is Rohoar. Victorio is both Rohoar's son and his blood wolf."

"I told you that you were in for something big," Abimbola whispered in Magnus's ear.

Rohoar placed a fist on his hairy chest. Then, to

Magnus's profound amazement, he lowered his head and exposed his neck toward Magnus. "Rohoar submits."

Magnus hesitated, completely at a loss for what to say. He was about to talk the mwadim out of this outlandish circumstance—there was no way he could accept his offer—when Abimbola whispered, "It is not something you can refuse! They will kill you if you do!"

"What?" Magnus whispered back.

"If you insult the mwadim's offer, they will kill you where you stand! Say you accept!"

"Are you serious?"

"Say it!"

Magnus straightened, hardly believing what he was about to say. He swallowed. "I accept."

Rohoar raised his head and nodded at Magnus. Without even the slightest hint of regret or disdain, Rohoar said, "How may I serve you?"

Immediately, Magnus noticed that Rohoar had changed to the personal pronoun "I." He had to hand it to the mwadim—*Is he still the mwadim?*—he sure knew how to put duty before personal feelings. And the guy was probably boiling inside.

"Well, I guess I'm going to need a ship," Magnus said.

"That is something I can supply," Rohoar replied.

"Are you kidding me?"

"No, I only produce *kids* with females. What does that have to do with your need for a ship?"

Magnus blinked. Had his fortunes really changed so quickly? One minute, he was being charged with what was tantamount to treason by the government he had pledged his allegiance to. The next, he was being offered fealty and a starship by the leader of the most violent warrior species in the galaxy—one who took everything far too literally.

"So, buckethead." Abimbola placed a hand on Magnus's shoulder. "Where are we going?"

"I can't believe I'm saying this—the safest place I can think of, the safest for both Piper and Valerie."

"And where is that?"

"Worru."

"Back to the Luma home world again? Do you know somebody you can trust?"

"I do. Not personally, I mean. But Awen trusted him." Seeing Awen again wouldn't be so terrible either. He still had the slip of paper in his pocket with the initials NMB on it. "He's the head of the Luma—a guy named Master So-Elku. He'll know how to help them. Then I can figure out what to do about this mess with the Republic and those rogue ex-Marines."

"Correction," said Rohoar. "*We* will figure it out. You are not alone."

"Copy that, LT." Dutch stepped forward, her weapon lying over her shoulder. Gilder, Haney, and Nolan stepped up as well.

Abimbola patted Magnus's shoulder again. "Well, buckethead, it seems you have yourself a regular marauding group of misfits. You have become a warlord after all! Not as infamous as Abimbola, of course. But you will get there. Give it time."

MAGNUS and AWEN will return in GATEWAY TO WAR, available now on Amazon.

For more updates on this series, be sure to join the Facebook Group, "J.N. Chaney's Renegade Readers."

LIST OF MAIN CHARACTERS

Abimbola: Miblimbian. Age: 41. Planet of origin: Limbia Centrella. Giant warlord of the Dregs, outskirts of Oosafar, Oorajee. Bright-blue eyes, black skin, tribal tattoos, scar running from neck to temple. Wears a bandolier of frag grenades across his chest and an old bowie knife strapped to his thigh. Never leaves home without a poker chip.

Adonis Olin Magnus: Human. Age: 30. Planet of origin: Capriana Prime. Lieutenant, Charlie Platoon, 79th Reconnaissance Battalion, "Midnight Hunters," Galactic Republic Space Marines. Baby face, short beard, green eyes. Preferred weapon: MAR30. One of the "Fearsome Four."

Allan "Mouth" Franklin: Human. Age 28. Planet of origin: Juna Major. Corporal, heavy-weapons operator, Charlie Platoon, 79th Reconnaissance Battalion, "Midnight Hunters," Galactic Republic Space Marines. One of the "Fearsome Four."

Aubrey Dutch: Human. Age: 25. Planet of origin: Deltaurus Three. Corporal, weapons specialist, Galactic Republic Space Marines. Small in stature. Close-cut dark hair, intelligent brown eyes. Loves her firearms.

Awen dau Lothlinium: Elonian. Age: 26. Planet of origin: Elonia. Order of the Luma, Special Emissary to the Jujari. Pointed ears, purple eyes. Wears red-and-black robes and has a Luma medallion around her neck. Won't back down from anyone.

Cyril: Human. Age: 24. Planet of origin: Ki Nar Four. Marauder, code slicer, bomb technician. Leads Magnus's mine-removal fire team. Twitchy. Sounds like a Quinzellian miter squirrel if it could talk.

Darin Stone: Human. Age: 34. Planet of origin: Capriana Prime. Senator in the Galactic Republic. Husband to Valerie Stone, father to Piper. Impossibly white smile, well-groomed blond hair, radiant-blue eyes. Luxuriantly tan.

Dozer: Human. Age: Unknown. Planet of origin: Verv Ko. Marauder, infantry. A veritable human earthmover.

Gerald Bosworth III: Human. Age: 54. Planet of origin: Capriana Prime. Republic ambassador, special envoy to the Jujari. Fat jowls, bushy monobrow. Massively obese and obscenely repugnant.

Hal Brighton: Human. Age: 41. Planet of origin: Capriana Prime. Newly appointed fleet admiral, First Fleet, the Paragon; former executive officer, Republic Navy.

Idris Ezo: Nimprith. Age: 27. Planet of origin: Caledonia. Bounty hunter, trader, suspected fence and smuggler. Captain of Geronimo Nine. Wears a long gray leather coat, white knit turtleneck, black pants, glossy black boots. Preferred sidearm: SUPRA 945 blaster pistol.

Josiah Wainright: Human. Age: 35. Planet of origin: Capriana Prime. Captain, Alpha Platoon,

79th Reconnaissance Battalion, "Midnight Hunters," Galactic Republic Space Marines. A legend in his own time.

Michael "Flow" Deeks: Human. Age: 27. Planet of origin: Vega. Sergeant, sniper, Charlie Platoon, 79th Reconnaissance Battalion, "Midnight Hunters," Galactic Republic Space Marines. One of the "Fearsome Four."

Miguel "Cheeks" Chico: Human. Age 26. Planet of origin: Trida Minor. Corporal, breacher, Charlie Platoon, 79th Reconnaissance Battalion, "Midnight Hunters," Galactic Republic Space Marines. One of the "Fearsome Four."

Moldark (formerly Wendell Kane): Human. Age: 52. Planet of origin: Capriana Prime. Former fleet admiral of the Galactic Republic's Third Fleet; captain of the Black Labyrinth. Dark Lord of the Paragon, a rogue black-operations special Marine unit. Bald, with heavily scarred skin. Black-orbed eyes.

Nubs: Human. Age: Unknown. Planet of origin:

Verv Ko. Marauder, infantry. Has several missing fingers.

Piper Stone: Human. Age: 9. Planet of origin: Capriana Prime. Daughter of Senator Darin and Valerie Stone. Wispy blond hair; freckle-faced. Wears a puffy winter coat, tights, and oversized snow boots. Carries a holo-pad and her stuffed corgachirp, Talisman.

Rawmut: Tawnhack, Jujari. Age: Unknown. Planet of origin: Oorajee. Jujari mwadim of Oosafar on Oorajee. Chief of the massive hyena-like warrior species.

"Rix" Galliogernomarix: Human. Age: Unknown. Planet of origin: Undoria. Leads Magnus's infantry fire team. Wanted in three systems. Has sleeve tattoos. A monster on the battlefield.

Robert Malcom Blackman: Human. Age: 54. Planet of origin: Capriana Prime. Senator in the Galactic Republic. A stocky man with thick shoulders and well-groomed gray hair.

Rohoar: Tawnhack, Jujari. Age: Unknown. Planet

of origin: Oorajee. Jujari mwadim. Former blood wolf for Mwadim Rawmut; formerly nicknamed "Chief" by Magnus.

Shane Nolan: Human. Age 25. Planet of origin: Sol Sella. Chief Warrant Officer, Republic Navy, pilot in command of light armored transport Sparrow 271. Auburn hair, pale skin.

Silk: Human. Age: 30. Planet of origin: Salmenka. Marauder, infantry. Slender, bald, tats covering her face and head.

Simone: Human. Age: 27. Planet of origin: Undoria. Marauder, sniper. Team leader for Magnus's sniper fire team. Smooth as ice.

So-Elku: Human. Age: 51. Planet of origin: Worru. Luma Master, Order of the Luma. Baldpate, thin beard, dark penetrating eyes. Wears green-and-black robes.

Sootriman: Caledonian. Age: 29. Planet of origin: Caledonia. Warlord of Ki Nar Four, "Tamer of the Four Tempests," alleged ex-wife of Idris Ezo. Heavy-set, with dark almond eyes, tanned olive skin, dark-brown hair.

TO-96: Robot; navigation class, heavily modified. Manufacturer: Advanced Galactic Solutions (AGS), Capriana Prime. Suspected modifier: Idris Ezo. Round head and oversized eyes, transparent blaster visor, matte dark-gray armor plating, and exposed metallic articulated joints. Forearm microrocket pod, forearm XM31 Type-R blaster, dual shoulder-mounted gauss cannons.

Tony Haney: Human. Age: 24. Planet of origin: Fitfi Isole. Private First Class, medic, Galactic Republic Space Marines.

Valerie Stone: Human. Age: 29. Planet of origin: Worru. Wife of Senator Darin Stone, mother of Piper. Blond hair, light-blue eyes.

Victorio: Tawnhack, Jujari. Age: Unknown. Planet of origin: Oorajee. Son of Rohoar, blood wolf to the Jujari mwadim.

Volf Nos Kil: Human. Age: 32. Planet of origin:

Haradia. Captain, the Paragon. Personal guard and chief enforcer for Admiral Kane.

Waldorph Gilder: Human. Age: 23. Planet of origin: Haradia. Private First Class, flight engineer, Galactic Republic Space Marines. Barrel-chested. Can fix anything.

William Samuel Caldwell: Human. Age 60. Planet of origin: Capriana Prime. Colonel, 79th Reconnaissance Battalion, Galactic Republic Space Marines. Cigar eternally wedged in the corner of his mouth. Gray hair cut high and tight.

Willowood: Human. Age: 61. Planet of origin: Kindarah. Luma Elder, Order of the Luma. Wears dozens of bangles and necklaces. Aging but radiant blue eyes and a mass of wiry gray hair. Friend and mentor to Awen.

JOIN THE RUINS TRIBE

Visit **ruinsofthegalaxy.com** today and join the tribe.

Once there, you can sign up for our reader group, join our Facebook community, and find us on Twitter and Instagram.

If you'd like to email us with comments or questions, we respond to all emails sent to ruinsofthegalaxy@gmail.com, and love to hear from our readers.

See you in the Ruins!

GET A FREE BOOK

J.N. Chaney posts updates, official art, previews, and other awesome stuff on his website. You can also follow him on **Instagram**, **Facebook**, and **Twitter**.

He also created a special **Facebook group** called "JN Chaney's Renegade Readers" specifically for readers to come together and share their lives and interests, discuss the series, and speak directly to me. Please check it out and join whenever you get the chance!

For updates about new releases, as well as exclusive promotions, visit his website, jnchaney.com and sign up for the VIP mailing list. Head there now to receive a free copy of *The Other Side of Nowhere*.

https://www.jnchaney.com/ruins-of-the-galaxy-subscribe

Enjoying the series? Help others discover the Ruins of the Galaxy series by leaving a review on **Amazon.**

ABOUT THE AUTHORS

J. N. Chaney is a USA Today Bestselling author and has a Master's of Fine Arts in Creative Writing. He fancies himself quite the Super Mario Bros. fan. When he isn't writing or gaming, you can find him online at **www.jnchaney.com**.

He migrates often, but was last seen in Las Vegas, NV. Any sightings should be reported, as they are rare.

Christopher Hopper's novels include the Resonant Son series, The Sky Riders, The Berinfell Prophecies, and the White Lion Chronicles. He blogs at **christopherhopper.com** and loves flying RC planes. He resides in the 1000 Islands of northern New York with his musical wife and four ridiculously good-looking clones.

Made in the USA
Coppell, TX
05 January 2020

14120316R10291